Sun Up

Sun Up

Tales of the Cow Camps

BY

WILL JAMES

MOUNTAIN PRESS PUBLISHING COMPANY
Missoula, Montana
1997

Third Printing, August 2004

Tumbleweed Series is a registered trademark
of Mountain Press Publishing Company.

Library of Congress Cataloging-in-Publication Data

James, Will, 1892–1942.
    Sun up : tales of the cow camps / by Will James.
        p.   cm. — (Tumbleweed series)

    ISBN: 978-0-87842-365-1

    1. West (U.S.)—Social life and customs—Fiction. 2. Cowboys—West
(U.S.)—Fiction. 3. Western stories. I. Title. II. Series: James, Will,
1892–1942. Tumbleweed series.
PS3519.A5298S86   1997
813'.52–dc21   97-29561
                                                                      CIP

PRINTED IN THE UNITED STATES OF AMERICA

Mountain Press Publishing Company
P. O. Box 2399
Missoula, Montana 59806

PUBLISHER'S NOTE

WILL JAMES'S BOOKS are an American treasure. His writing and drawings captivated generations of readers with the lifestyle and spirit of the American cowboy and the West. Following James's death in 1942, the reputation of this remarkable writer and artist languished, and nearly all of his twenty-four books went out of print. But in recent years, publication of several biographies and film documentaries on James, public exhibitions of his art, and the formation of the Will James Society have renewed interest in his work.

Now, in conjunction with the Will James Art Company, Mountain Press is reprinting all Will James's books as the Tumbleweed Series, taking special care to keep each volume faithful to the original. Books in the Tumbleweed Series contain all the original artwork and text, feature an attractive new design, and are printed on acid-free paper.

The republication of Will James's books would not have been possible without the help and support of the many fans of Will James. Because all James's books and artwork remain under copyright protection, the Will James Art Company has been instrumental in providing the necessary permissions and furnishing artwork.

The Will James Society was formed in 1992 as a nonprofit organization dedicated to preserving the memory and works of Will James. The society is one of the primary catalysts behind a growing interest not only in Will James and his work, but also in the life and heritage of the working cowboy. For more information on the society, contact:

Will James Society • c/o Will James Art Company
2237 Rosewyn Lane • Billings, Montana 59102

Mountain Press is pleased to make Will James's books available again. Read and enjoy!

JOHN RIMEL

BOOKS BY WILL JAMES

Cowboys North and South, 1924

The Drifting Cowboy, 1925

Smoky, the Cowhorse, 1926

Cow Country, 1927

Sand, 1929

Lone Cowboy, 1930

Sun Up, 1931

Big Enough, 1931

Uncle Bill, 1932

All in the Day's Riding, 1933

The Three Mustangeers, 1933

Home Ranch, 1935

Young Cowboy, 1935

In the Saddle with Uncle Bill, 1935

Scorpion, 1936

Cowboy in the Making, 1937

Flint Spears, 1938

Look-See with Uncle Bill, 1938

The Will James Cowboy Book, 1938

The Dark Horse, 1939

Horses I Have Known, 1940

My First Horse, 1940

The American Cowboy, 1942

Will James Book of Cowboy Stories, 1951

Pryor, Montana
1931—

GET ON —

It seems to one like, with all the airplanes, sporty cars and all the machinery there is today that folks would hanker to get in touch with what is left.

I was in the town of New York for a spell and, going along one day, I heard a boy ask—"Mother, will you get me one of those?"—he was pointing at a horse hooked onto a hack—Tin and bolts is about all that most folks get to see now—

The "rigging", as we call our saddles, is made of good cow leather, they're put on many different kinds of range and wild horse flesh, and on top of that rigging sets a cowboy who goes thru many cowboy happenings, as is told in this book—

Writers who write of the West but never rode the range have got folks thinking that the cowboy and open country is all gone—To make folks happy, and go against that, I'd like to say that the open West still holds a third of the U.S.A—

On my own little country in Southern Montana there's an outfit running 45.000 head of cattle, and many horses—I can ride out from my ranch house and, in an hour's time, find antelope and many bunches of wild horses—and keep on riding for 75 miles without striking a fence—There's many parts of the West still more open—

It took two generations to make the cowboy and it will take many more to lose him—

WILL JAMES

CONTENTS

"His Spurs"

S ANDY BORDEL of Ocate, New Mexico, coming out on Broken Box, chute number ten. . . . Watch chute number ten."

Them words was announced thru the radio magaphone and echoed over the big arena at Soldier Field Stadium. . . . The annual Chicago Rodeo was on at full swing, and Sandy Bordel, one of the top-hands from the Cimarrons, was easing himself in chute number ten and feeling with his toe for the stirrups that hung down on both sides of eleven hundred pounds of T N T which all was wrapped up in brown quivering horse hide.

"Ready, judges."

The wide gate of chute number ten was pulled open, and Broken Box, also from the ranges of the cow country, blinked at the bare sod of the arena, where in a few seconds he figgered on being free from the rider who was now setting on him. Broken Box was a true bucking horse, and a mighty hard one to set, specially so when going by the rules the Rodeo boss, Tex Austin, had marked down for every cowboy to follow in order to qualify for the prizes and trophies.

Them prizes and trophies is what had brought Sandy Bordel and the many other riders there. He'd come to *ride* for them, and it was a contest all the way thru, not only between man and horse but between rider and rider, where the least little slip meant being disqualified, and going back home broke.

None realized that more than Sandy Bordel did, and that's why, while Broken Box blinked at the space before him, Sandy took that second's chance to test his grip on the bucking rein once more, and feel out his saddle. He was there to win, not to play or show off.

His face was set and hard, as with a choking beller Broken Box tore out clear of the chute, went up in the air, spun around up there, and

"Watch chute number ten."

got into a twisted shape that sure disguised him to looking like anything but a horse. The saddle strings popped, Sandy's teeth rattled, and when that horse hit the ground it shook as if a ten ton truck had fell out of the sky. A cloud of dust came up, Broken Box and his rider soared above it, to light again and stir another, and another, and another.

Thru the short lasting, but long seeming, commotion, there was "Oh's" and "Ah's" from the grandstand, all mixed with hard jarring sounds, and bellers from the man-fighting horse. . . . Was that rider going to stick?

Then, all at once, thousands stood up in the grandstand, a few cowboys was running acrost the arena, and all eyes was on the huddled figgure of Sandy Bordel a setting on the earth and as if he was in a trance. Broken Box, head and tail up and proud of another victory, was loping away, packing only an empty saddle.

"Hurt?" asked a "pick-up" who'd got off his horse close to Sandy.

But Sandy didn't seem to hear him, he was staring at his boots and the spurs that was on 'em. Finally he spoke.

"Just look at them daggone spurs, will you? They sure put me out of the money."

The pick-up man glanced at 'em, but seeing that the rider wasn't hurt he didn't waste no more time. He waved both hands at the crowd the same as to let 'em know that all was o.k. and rode on towards the chutes. The crowd settled back to watch another rider who, as was being announced, was coming out of chute number nine on another bucking horse.

The contest went on, not at all checked by Sandy's hard fall to earth. He was disqualified, of course, and his name was scratched off the list of riders who'd entered in the bucking horse contest. But that made it all the better for the other contestants, because he was one less to compete against. Then again, Sandy was getting to be such a bronc rider that the average contestant was finding it hard to keep up with him on points. Many of 'em drawed a long breath after seeing him "buck off."

But if Sandy drawed a long breath as he stared at his spurs it sure wasn't one of relief as it was with the other boys. He'd come from a long ways, put out a lot of money on railroad fare, a lot more on entrance fees to the contest, all hard money to scrape too, and that to back the confidence he'd felt that he could outride every other contestant and win the big purse that was offered.

But the other riders had done the same, they'd also come a long ways to back *their* confidence, with the understanding that all was at their own risk, wether they went back to their home range loaded down with prize money, or broke, or on a stretcher.

3

Sandy didn't care about the other riders, this contesting was every man for himself, each to outdo the other, and all at once he was disqualified, out of the contest, and the blame for that could be layed to nothing only to what he was now staring at, his spurs.

Here he'd rode all his broncs in fine style. If he'd rode Broken box as he did the others he'd been good for the finals, but just as he was getting by with that both of them spurs of his begin to twist and crawl up his ankles, then as he went to "reef" that bronc up the shoulders one of the spurs' taped rowels worked between his boot and the stirrup, like working against him and pushed the stirrup off his foot. That was enough to disqualify him right there, but that wasn't all. As he went to feeling for the stirrup he kind of neglected watching Broken Box's action, and being that pony couldn't be trifled with that way, it wasn't long when Sandy seen himself spread out over the arena.

So, after getting so far in the game only to be barred out, it was no wonder that Sandy just set there and stargazed at his spurs. They'd been the cause of his sudden loss of the good chance he figgered he'd had at the prize money. As it was now he just had enough money to pay for his hotel bill, and no more, and then, how was he going to get back home?

But Sandy wasn't thinking about that last as he stood up and started walking towards the chutes. His mind was still on spurs, not them ill-fitting things which he put back in place at his heels, but on some others, his own spurs. These was just borrowed.

If he'd had his own spurs, he thought, he'd have qualified and made the finals. He was sure of that because them old spurs had never failed him, they'd always set where they belonged and had a balance about 'em and weight that made him rely on them as no other spur had.

It was good for Sandy that he could lay the blame of his downfall to earth to the borrowed spurs, because, being sure of that, his confidence

4

wasn't shook up any, and he still felt that he could of made the f
and qualified for a big prize if he'd had his own reliable spurs.

The Chicago Rodeo was the first big contest that Sandy had ever
entered in. The other little rodeos he'd contested at had only been
play, but Sandy hadn't realized that as yet, and being lucky in the first
few horses he'd drawed, he didn't notice much difference. The hard set
rules and slick saddles, which gave the horse all the advantage, hadn't
bothered him, and he was getting into the hard part of it when Broken
box took him out for a roll.

He didn't know that, even if he'd had his own pet spurs, Broken Box
would of throwed him anyway, because, as hard as that pony bucked from
the start, he was only feeling out his rider, and Sandy had fell off before the
horse found his stride. Sandy would of found the little saddle mighty slick
and hard to keep track of before he got thru, spurs or no spurs.

So, as it was, Sandy went on blaming his bad luck to the borrowed
spurs, but as hard as that bad luck hit him at first he didn't grieve about
it long. The only thing was, them old spurs of his which he'd left back
home had sure loomed up sudden in his estimation. He got to missing
'em and thinking of 'em often, and picturing them in his mind.

And what a picture they made there, now that he needed 'em, and
how priceless they got to be.

He remembered the old ranch blacksmith who'd made 'em for him.
That old boy had made many pairs of spurs for the cowboys around
and he'd needed very little coaching when he shaped out Sandy's pair
out of spring steel. Just plain steel they was, one inch and a quarter heel
band, two inch quarter drop shank, and a small round-pointed five
point star rowel. There was a mighty reliable feel to the weight of the
spurs, and the swinging buttons was set on 'em so that no time did
they ever need being tied down. They stayed put.

5

Sandy was just a kid when he started wearing them spurs, not much over fifteen, and like most range kids of that age, craving to be a real bronc rider, there was nothing much could of took the place of 'em. His dad had a few good hands working for him always, and it was with them that he started in. Rodeos was getting popular around his home country by then and whenever the riders saddled up to go to one of the doings Sandy was sure to tag along, his home-made bronc spurs jingling at his boot heels.

There'd come a day when Sandy entered for steer riding. He'd practiced that home on the range, and even tho he got bucked off at the rodeo grounds he'd got a lot of fun out of it, and it made him feel like a real contestant.

At another rodeo later on he entered for steer riding again, and in a few other events, like the potato race, stake race, and wild horse race. He didn't do so good in the wild horse race, but he was encouraged some in the other events, and after the doings was over he came home with a little money in his pocket, the first money he'd made at a contest.

The plain home made spurs jingled at his heels and jingled on thru many events after that, from the rough hide of a wild steer to the smoother one of a wild horse. They never got a chance to get rusty. Instead they'd developed a polish that only steady wear can give. Sandy nearly slept with them on.

One day, at a little bigger rodeo than Sandy had ever contested in before, he surprised the boys and himself by paying down his entrance fee on "Bronc Riding." He felt mighty proud to see his name on the list amongst the contestants for that event, and prouder yet when that name was called the first day, but luck was sort of against him, he drew too hard a horse for the tryouts, and that's as far as he got, for as he went to hook his bronc in the neck with his taped spur he missed connections and he hooked a lot of ground instead.

Sandy just grinned at that because he'd just entered in that event more or less for fun, and he didn't expect to win anything anyway, so he said, but the older hands around shook their heads at that and predicted that he sure had it in him, and that before long he'd make 'em all ride for their money.

And sure enough, it wasn't more than two years later when Sandy rode back to the home ranch one day with two hundred dollars, first prize for bronc riding, in his pocket. Besides that he was awarded a full flower-stamped silver-mounted saddle, and a solid sterling silver cup with his name engraved on it. In his vest pocket was a clipping out of the newspaper, and on his face was a smile a mile long.

Sandy went on practicing at home the rest of that year. He straddled everything that could be corralled which would give him a rough ride, and every few days, whenever his dad happened to be gone, he'd run in a bunch of stock horses off the range, put 'em thru a chute at the corral and saddle and ride the spookiest. Some of them he rode bareback and with just a mane holt.

He got many a fall and many a bruise, but he was young and wiry and it was all in the training to his ambitions, which was to be a champion bronc rider. His hand-made spurs was with him thru all that training and they got to be part of him, just like the thumbs of his hands, and in the months and years Sandy wore the spurs he'd developed a way of using them which very few riders get the hang of. He'd growed and rode his first bronc with them on his heels, he'd never used no other, and his ability on riding got to be near as dependant on 'em as the fiddler is dependant on his own particular fiddle for a tune.

But he never hooked or hung with 'em, because that wasn't his style of riding, and he knowed that such a stunt would never go in a contest. Instead he used them as feelers and the blunt rowels, most always covered with tape while contesting, would only sort of play along the horse's shoulders and sides. That was his way of keeping track of the side-winding bronc under him, and if in a pinch, when he felt himself slipping, he did grab a holt he done that in a way that very few judges would notice. It would be for less than a second, and by all appearances he was in the motion of "Scratching," which is only a motion that stacks up the points for the rider but leaves no scratches.

When winter set in on the Cimarrons that year Sandy had felt a whole lot like he had the world by the tail, far as bronc riding was concerned, and one day while a storm howled and snow filled up the arroyos, a whistling sound could be heard coming from the little blacksmith shop on the ranch. A pitch pine smoke was pouring out of the chimney of the little out of the way building which told some of the comfort inside, and there, setting on a stool and close to the light of the only window, sat Sandy. On the work bench was what had been the silver cup he'd won at the rodeo the summer before, but it was hard to recognize any more because big strips had been cut off of it with steel saw and chisel. Whistling away, Sandy was busy engraving all kinds of designs on one of the silver strips which once had been the cup, and a glance at the work went to show that as a silversmith he ranked near as high as he did in bronc riding. Somewhere, maybe at some jeweler's shop, he'd got some engraving tools, a few he'd made himself, but the design he worked in the silver was all his own.

Month after month thru the winter, when he wasn't busy on the range or keeping up his practice on some bronc, Sandy was in the little blacksmith shop and busy with his silver work, sometimes till away into the night, and then one day in early spring he gave the riders at the ranch the surprise of their lives by strutting out to the bunk house with a pair of spurs on his heels which, far as the boys knowed, was the prettiest spurs a man could get to see.

There's where the silver strips from the cup had gone, also the time he'd put in the blacksmith shop that winter, Sandy had been decorating his spurs, and wether it was thru his love for them or just for the sake of decorating, he'd sure done a mighty fine job at it, and the work was a piece of art that'd make many an artist stutter.

The whole spur was covered up with the silver and all engraved in sort of Aztec design, then somewhere Sandy had got a hold of an old watch of solid gold, and out of that he'd cut pieces which he shaped up into flowers and inlayed in the silver. There was stems of gold running thru the silver work, and in the center of each flower — there was many of 'em — was imbedded stones, either rubies or California diamonds.

Even the small rowels was inlaid with gold and silver and engraved, but with all that work on the spurs, Sandy hadn't stopped at that, for much of it was on the spur straps. There was two-inch silver conchas on each of them which he'd also made himself, all engraved to match the spurs and inlayed the same, then bordering them conchas and on the leather was a binding of silver and gold flowers which went all around the strap to stop at the gold buckle.

"Them spurs ought to be worth a good string of horses," says one of the admiring riders.

"And I wouldn't do this work for a string of horses," answered Sandy, "not as much as I like 'em."

"But you ain't going to ride with them spurs, are you, Sandy?" asked a rider. He seemed worried. "They won't stand the gaff, and they're too pretty to knock around."

"Don't you worry, old boy, I put that work on 'em to stay and when I come out on a bronc this summer these spurs are going to be something that'll be worth watching by the judges, the way I'll use 'em."

So that's the way it was with Sandy, Them spurs was his pride, he had a feeling for them, and in decorating 'em the way he had he'd only given them a dress that fitted 'em as to their worth *to him*, and now he was going to flash 'em around the arena so folks could admire 'em and watch how well they worked while he's astraddle some long-geared limber-backed bronc.

The first initiation of his flashy dressed spurs came as the spring round-up was near over. A Cowboy's Reunion and Rodeo was being pulled off at a shipping point a hundred miles away, and the day before the contest was to start, Sandy was right there at the grounds, sizing up the mean-eyed bucking string.

As he strutted along from corral to corral the cowboy kept a grinning his confidence. The stock was well picked and wild and spooky but none of them had any effect on that grin of Sandy's, and every once in a while he, natural like, felt the weight and balance of his spurs, in about the same way that Babe Ruth might feel the weight and balance of his bat before tossing a homer.

Sandy went thru the tryout, semi finals, and finals of that rodeo like a roaring prairie fire licks up dry grass. He copped first money without having to worry about a close second, and all the judges remembered of that rodeo a month later was a pair of slashing silver mounted spurs a shining to the sun. Them spurs had scratched further up and both ways than any spur they'd ever seen, and watching the harmony of them with the movements of the horse, near made the judges and riders forget that there was a man's boot heel inside of 'em.

Sandy and his spurs was seen again at another Rodeo, and with the same results. Everybody, even them in the grandstand, remembered the spurs, for it seemed, the way they played from rump to shoulder of every sky-tickling, earth-jarring bronc and critter, that they was alive.

Every stone on 'em as they flashed to the sun was like the spark of an eye that twinkled with every motion, as if with enjoyment.

As Sandy went on to compete at the different rodeos from one neighboring town to another, them spurs got to be as well known as he did. When the newspaper spoke of him as the winner it also spoke of his spurs, and come a time when the sight of him with them spurs at his heels went as much as to spell "first money."

Only a couple of times did he slip and fail to win that summer, but luck sometimes works against a man and that's to be expected, but as it was, Sandy Bordel and his famous spurs got to be known by every bronc rider, also many spectators, and from Texas to Arizona.

Them spurs had scratched further up and
both ways than any spur they'd ever seen.

Many contestants failed to come to Rodeos when they learned Sandy would be there, and when they'd hear of his coming to one they'd go to some other. So, when winter set in that year, Sandy had many trophies and belts to his credit, also a good wad of prize money, and when he went to look at his spurs to see what the summer's work had done to 'em he found that only one of the rubies was missing. He grinned and run a hand over 'em in a way that showed his feeling for them. The ruby would be easy to replace, and next year he'd make the judges watch 'em some more.

Sandy broke many horses for his dad that winter, big strong wild geldings. He done that for practice and for the buck that was in 'em, and when each horse was inclined to quit bucking he'd turn him over to some other hand to ride and keep going while he took a fresh one and rode the rough off of him. He didn't *make* any of 'em buck, and he didn't fool with them that didn't care to, but there was very few that didn't, and as he rode on an average of six or seven horses a day during the winter, he was in mighty fine shape to compete at Rodeos when spring come. Besides, he'd lined out a mighty fine string for his dad's remuda, for there was no buck left with any of 'em after he got thru.

His old silver-mounted spurs done the work there the same as they did everywhere else, he wouldn't of used any other, and they flashed as well in the corral of the home ranch as they did in the contesting grounds of the arenas, only there was no one watching them work there at home, but Sandy didn't care just so they was at his heels.

It was early summer when Sandy got to flashing 'em at the Rodeo grounds again. He got first money there without hardly having to contest for it. The same thing happened at a second rodeo, and then Sandy got the feeling for higher ambitions, he got a hankering to go to some big contest, and where a world's championship could be rode for.

He'd heard of the Chicago Rodeo where such a championship is decided on every year, then one day he received a prize list from that association, and the sight of the figgers that went with the first prize for bronc riding near took Sandy's breath away. He couldn't see nothing else on the list, and that's what decided him right there.

He'd take on a couple more little rodeos for the practice and the money he'd need and then he'd be all set, but man proposes to do things sometimes which don't work out so well, and it was at the very next rodeo that a jug-headed bucking horse daggone near queered him from following out his high ambitions.

That horse was what's called a blind bucker, he had two good eyes, but he never used 'em when a rider was on him. He'd just lose his head and buck into or thru anything, and when Sandy came out on him, that bronc went right over the railing into the race track, onto the higher railing in front of the grandstand, and hung up there and turned a somerset, landing on most every part of Sandy.

From that time on, instead of entrance fees, it was hospital fees for that cowboy. He layed between white sheets for the first time in his life, but he didn't appreciate 'em none at all. His plans seemed to be all shot, and he worried if he'd be up in time to enter for the world's contest at Chicago.

That maybe was the cause of his recuperating so fast, and two months after he'd been packed in the hospital he staggered out, with only two weeks to go before the date set for the big Rodeo. He was weak and broke, and when he went to his dad for the money to take him to the big city, that old-timer put up an excuse and told the boy he couldn't spare it. There was threats of a long drought, he said, and if so, he'd need every cent he had to ship his cattle out and carry 'em thru till next year. Besides, as Sandy got the hint, his dad didn't agree with rodeos much on account that them goings-on took the riders from the range when they was needed most, that it was about time he should stay home anyway, and take interest in the outfit.

But Sandy was only twenty, and maybe his dad was a little early in expecting his son to take a holt much. Anyway, nothing mattered as much to Sandy right then as to be present at the big doings in Chicago, and he wouldn't be satisfied till he had a try at that world's championship.

He figgered and figgered on ways and means to gather up the money he'd need to get him there. The railroad fare was a plenty, the entrance fee to the rodeo would be plenty more, and then there was the expenses. If he went easy he'd need at least three or four hundred dollars, and he wasn't only broke but in debt. The hospital had took all the wages his dad allowed him. He'd also overdrawed considerable, and the money he'd won at the two little rodeos had also vanished along with the rest.

He begin tallying up on what he owned which he might get some money out of. There was his saddle, eight head of saddle horses, and his silver-mounted spurs. That was all he had that was of any value. Of course there was a few head of cattle which his dad let him have a few years before, they'd accumulated to a nice little herd, but he didn't dare think of selling them because, if he did, he knowed he'd sure hear about it.

He'd need his saddle if he went to Chicago, and as for his horses, he knowed that to sell 'em on such a short notice he'd sure have to sacrifice 'em. His dad had no say about them because Sandy had gathered 'em up himself in many different ways and dealings of his own, but he hated to part with 'em, and anyway, he knowed they wouldn't bring enough money for him to make the trip.

So there was only one safe way left for him to get the money, and that was thru his spurs. His old home-made, silver-mounted spurs.

There's no saying of how he hated to think of parting with 'em, but there was no other way. He knowed he could get the money out of them easy enough, because it was just a few months ago, at a rodeo, when a man came to him and offered him a thousand dollars cold cash, and on the spot, for them. Sandy had smiled his surprise at the offer, and he'd only shook his head and refused, for it seemed like them spurs couldn't be connected with cold cash that way, not even with a thousand dollars.

The man had left, after handing his card to Sandy and telling him that the offer stood for whenever he decided to take it up, and as the fever to compete at the Chicago Rodeo, where the stakes was higher and the horses harder, took a real holt on the cowboy, there come a time when he begin running his fingers over his spurs, like he'd never felt 'em before, and there was a queer look on his face.

It took him days to decide, and finally one day he seemed to brighten up some, for he'd thought of a way he could get the money without losing his spurs. He'd just borrow on them, and if he could do that he could pay the money back soon as he returned from Chicago. He was sure of winning there.

Sandy hunted up the card the man had left with him, he found it in the bottom of his war bag, and getting a few dollars from the boys on the ranch, he took the branch line the next day and headed for Raton, where the man lived.

There, for four hundred dollars, Sandy parted with his spurs. Both parties was satisfied, Sandy figgered that in another month, and soon as he came back from Chicago with the prize money, the spurs would be his again, and the man was pleased to think that maybe Sandy would never be able to gather up enough money to get his spurs back. As it was, he'd got 'em cheap.

Sandy took the next train to Chicago, all happy to think that at last he was going to contest in a real big Rodeo, and where the World Championship was decided on. He knowed he'd sure have to ride to get in the money there, but that didn't bother him none. Nobody had been able to touch him in his territory, he'd been used to winning, and he'd took it for granted that he'd win there too.

He thought about his spurs a few times while the train took him to the big city, but he didn't miss 'em much, not till he got to Soldier Field and rode his first bronc. He begin to miss 'em there, for the spurs he borrowed felt like a mighty poor excuse as compared to his own reliable hooks. He missed 'em more on the second bronc the next day, but the real worth of them didn't come to him till he came out on top of that Broken Box bucking horse.

Growing up as he had with his home-made spurs and depending on 'em always to feel the bronc under him, all in prize winning scratching motion, had got to be a great advantage to him, both in riding and winning, and now that strange spurs took the place of 'em all at once he felt worse off than if he didn't have any. He'd miscalculated by half an inch at every side-swipe. That put him out of balance some, and hindered him considerable in his old style of reefing.

If Sandy ever did need his spurs he sure needed 'em there, for there was where bronc riding was not only an art but a science, and where every rider, being at a disadvantage by the hard set rules, had nothing to back him but his skill, and as much as Sandy's spurs had been part of him in his riding ability that way, he was at a bigger disadvantage than the other riders who'd never gave much thought to such and used any spur they happened to have.

But, even at that, Sandy had got along pretty fair on Broken Box, up till the time when the borrowed spurs twisted around his ankles and started crawling up his leg. If he'd tied 'em down he'd still had better luck maybe, but he never thought of that as his old spurs never needed to be tied down, they'd always stayed put.

Anyway, that's how come, when Sandy "bucked off," that he put all the blame on the borrowed spurs, he never thought that the horse might of been too hard for him, and with the blow of his downfall, the loss of the purse money, and the title of World's Champion bronc rider, which all he'd been so sure of winning, also came the sudden realization that he'd lost his chance of getting his pet spurs back, for that time anyhow.

That hurt him worse than losing first money or the championship, and now he was in a fix where he hardly dared go back home. Everybody

When Sandy bucked off.

there knowed his spurs, and they'd all wonder and ask about 'em. Then again he needed 'em, needed 'em more than he ever realized before. He was going to work to get them spurs back, and right there he decided that the money to get 'em back with was to come from nowheres else than thru the winnings from some big Rodeo.

Sandy stuck around during the remaining days of the Chicago contest, and in a half-hearted way, went on to try and make the most out of "day money" in steer riding and bare-back bronc riding. His intentions was to rake up enough money, not to get back home, but to get to some other Rodeo and where there was chances of big winnings. Many of the boys was talking of taking on the Round Up at Pendleton, Oregon, as the next place, and when the opening day of that contest came along a month later, Sandy was right there, paid his entrance fees, and entered his name as a contestant in bronc riding. He also entered in other events but them was only to fall back on in case he bucked off as he did in Chicago.

He wasn't going to buck off this time tho, he was sure of that, but somehow or other, and for no reason, unless he could blame it on another pair of borrowed spurs, Sandy's left ear collected a big amount of arena dirt there at Pendleton and was throwed as hard as in Chicago. It sure was all a puzzle to the cowboy, and when the "pick up" rode close to see if he was hurt he seen the same expression on his face as the Chicago pick-up man had seen a month before. Sandy was gazing at his spurs.

He had to fall back on other events to carry him thru there, the same as he did in Chicago. He was broke, Pendleton was the last big contest for that year, and as it was, when the contest was over, he'd hardly made enough out of "day money" to get back home on.

But he didn't want to get back home, not till he'd won the money to pay for his spurs. One big reason for that was his pride, he'd never be able to live down the fact that he'd turned out to be a pretty small potato when it come for him to compete in the big contests. The folks back home would kid the life out of him, and they'd all make it a point to ask about them spurs of his. Then again, he'd lost them spurs to go to a contest and it would be thru a contest that he'd get 'em back. After that, he'd have the pride of flashing 'em some more at many such doings, and to maybe getting such notice for them in the big contests as he did in the small ones at home.

When the Pendleton Round Up was over, Sandy, knowing that his chances of winning big money was past for that year, went to looking for a winter job. It was lucky he was in the heart of a good range country, where thousands of fine horses was raised and run wild. So, it wasn't long when he landed a job breaking a string of 'em, and as luck would have it, these horses he'd hired out to break was the meanest bunch he'd ever run acrost. He wondered why they didn't just leave 'em be and keep 'em for rodeo purposes, but the job suited him fine, and if practice makes perfect he'd sure be in shape for the big contests next year.

He wrote his dad that he wouldn't be home, not for quite a spell, that he had a winter job and figgered on contesting during the next summer. Then thru the winter he went to laying out the dates of every big Rodeo so he could get to be at the most of 'em.

When spring opened up, Sandy felt sure enough like "first money." The hard string of ponies he'd broke that winter had shook up many a winning point in him, and when the first little rodeos begin to sprout up there, Sandy et 'em up like hot cakes and stored the winnings from them to follow up on the trail of the big contests.

If he only had his spurs now he'd sure give the judges something to blink at, but he wasn't entitled to 'em yet. He felt that nothing short of a world Championship would do, he'd have to win that before he could go home, or claim them spurs of his.

But, as Sandy went to compete at one world championship contest and then another, it gradually came to him that he was a whole lot like a county sheriff trying to run for president. His goal was a high one, and he hadn't as yet realized that it took more than good riding to get to it. He didn't consider the rules much and figgered that good hard reckless riding and plenty of reefing was all that'd be necessary, and he was surprised how one day, at the Calgary Stampede, he got disqualified when he thought he'd put up a pretty ride, and on a mighty hard bronc too.

He found out the next day that the cause of that was how he kept his left hand too close to the saddle horn and like to steady himself there against the jerk on the bucking rein.

Sandy managed to lay a little blame to his spurs for that, saying that they'd slipped down, and when he went to find his horse with 'em, he'd slipped up, but excuses don't stop a rider from being disqualified, and that instance showed him how, if he was to win a world championship, he'd better read up on the rules.

He did read up on 'em, and as he went to another contest, he found that they was sure mighty hard to follow up on such broncs as was rode there. He was bucked off, and for no reason only that he tried to ride according to them rules.

The same thing happened at the next contest, but he done better, because by then he knowed all the rules and he'd sort of worked up so he could go by 'em and still be able to ride pretty fair. He was wishing he had his old spurs to help him now, and more than ever. . . .

Sandy took on another contest, and being he had a month to practice up on the rules while a setting on some mighty hard broncs, he managed to get as far as the finals there, but he was outpointed so that he didn't make the grand finals, and there's where the money layed.

But that cowboy was encouraged a whole lot by getting so close to his goal, and when he entered at the next contest a few weeks later, he felt pretty sure that outside of some bad luck he'd give the other contestants considerable to worry about.

And luck seemed to be with him from the start. He reached the finals as second high man, and that luck stayed with him some more when the high man, the only one in his way, was bucked off, just as the big purse was about to be handed him.

Now it was all up to Sandy, and his heart beat fit to bust as he climbed the chute to settle down in the little association rig. This was to be the kind of a ride that made the others all seem as plum foolishness, and he sure felt it as, grim faced, he nodded for the gate man to "open 'er up."

It was a pretty ride, sort of hard to believe that such could be done on that sunken-eyed outlaw which looked more like something blowed up from hell than a horse, and Sandy met him at every turn and jolt with the taped rowels of his spurs. That cowboy rode on and reefed like he'd never reefed before. A couple of times he looked at the judges and laughed, like as to show them that he could ride broncs like this in his sleep, and then, all at once, and when the judges had just about decided him as first, Sandy's right spur caught in the bronc's mane. There was no loosening it, and when that pony fought his head back and forth was when the rider of a sudden found himself handicapped in keeping his balance on the limber twisting back — he was sent a sailing in the air a half a second later, to sort of snap there, then the spur gave way and Sandy landed in a heap on the hard packed earth.

There is no telling of how Sandy felt about spurs in general after that happening, all spurs but his own, which, far as he knowed, was at the time resting on the mantel of a fireplace in Raton, and looked at as an odd ornament.

They was a heap more than an ornament to him as he thought of 'em just then, and he'd made up his mind to get 'em back if it was the last thing he ever done.

But his chances was slim for that year as there was only one more world championship Rodeo to be pulled off. Sandy thought of that mighty strong, and it made him all the more determined and anxious to be at it and riding. He'd worked himself up to the point where setting on a hard bronc would be a great relief, and when the opening

It was a pretty ride.

day of that year's last big Rodeo came that cowboy was like a coil of live wire only waiting for the connection of saddle leather and horse flesh to set off the fire works.

He strutted amongst the cowboys looking for the likeliest pair of spurs which he might borrow, and it was while strutting around that way that an idea struck him. He went to one of the judges with it and asked.

"What would be the matter with me riding without spurs, any objection?"

"No."

"Well," Sandy went on, "would I be allowed any points on that?"

"Yeh, some, but I'm thinking you'd have to go some to keep them points, if you rode without spurs."

"You can allow me them points right now then, because I'm going to ride without no spurs."

The way Sandy was feeling right then, spurs was the least of his worries. Of course if he could have his own spurs that'd be different, but the borrowed spurs had only been a hindrance to him, and he felt that he could do a heap better without 'em.

And he did. Sandy's bare boot heel went in the tall motion of scratching and kept on that way straight on to the finals, but there he drawed a wampus cat as a final horse which daggone near made the cowboy swallow his Adam's apple. He lost many points on that horse, and he found out the next day, that all what saved him in getting in the grand finals was the points that was to his credit for riding without spurs.

He was the lowest man in that event which would decide on the world's championship, but he was thankful for that, for he still had a chance and maybe luck would come his way a little. But his hopes sort of shrunk as he drawed his horse for that last ride. He knowed the horse, he was bucked off of him once already a few months before, — one of the kind most every rider was mighty pleased not to get.

It was then that Sandy's confidence was shook up a little. He got to wondering if he hadn't better hunt up a good pair of spurs, but the more he thought of that the more his jaw muscles stuck out, and when that cowboy's name was called as the next contestant he was some considerable different in spirit. His confidence had come back, and not only that, but a fighting inspiration, which, with the scowl that hinted of it on his face, matched well with the fighting lantern-jawed head of the bronc he was to ride, and without spurs.

The name of the rider and bronc was no more than announced, when there was a scattering of cowboys near the chutes. A long-bodied black horse was making a noise there and raising a dust. Bellers was heard and the sound of crashing timbers, and pretty soon, out of the wreck, that long black horse, with Sandy a setting straight up and on top, made a crooked lunge out of the whole conglomeration and to where there was more room for action.

The horse landed out there in a heap, but every muscle stood out to carry him up again and in a speed that'd make folks wonder how come he didn't leave his hide behind. The rider was out of the question because it'd long ago been a miracle how he'd stayed at all, on top of that twisting hard-hitting kicking-bucker. But as much as it seemed a miracle for Sandy to stick, he done better than that, he laughed and scratched and rhymed mighty well with all the action that pony brought out.

And it was a good thing he rhymed too, for one little flaw out of tune with that action would of started him in a nonstop flight to earth with no doubt as to his getting there. But Sandy kept on a rhyming, and knowing that he had to do more than just set there and ride in order to make up on points and win, he was sure letting none of his skill in bronc riding go to sleep. He brought 'em all to the front, and even surprised himself at his own ability.

There was cheers from the grandstand, even the contestants he was riding against was cheering, for that boy was putting up a ride that would long be remembered. Then the whistle blowed, Sandy throwed up his hat, and a pick-up man rode alongside of him.

That same day, Sandy, setting on a horse that kept his head up, was introduced to the crowd as The Championship Bronc Rider Of The World. There was some howdedo and congratulations as trophies and belts was handed him, and Sandy, sort of backward about it, was smiling. Then all sounds of cheers and congratulations begin to grow faint, for Sandy was thinking of some other than the honor and winning of the Championship. He'd worked hard to get that, but when it come right down to it, the honor of title, and winnings, had only been to give him the right to claim his spurs, and Sandy had won them now, in two ways.

WILL JAMES

I hear somebody holler so close I had no choice when I was told to hold 'em up.

ON THE DODGE

I 'D HEARD A FEW SHOTS the night before, and I had a hunch they was being *exchanged*; but as the deer season was open and the town dudes was out for 'em, I just figgered maybe a couple of bucks had made their last jump, and I let it go at that.

The next morning when I went to run in the ponies for a fresh horse to do the day's riding on, I finds that my big buckskin was missing, my own horse, and one of the best I ever rode. I makes another circle of the pasture and comes to a gate at one corner and stops. On the ground, plain as you wanted to see, was boot-marks where some *hombre* had got off to open the gate and lead my buckskin through.

I sure knowed my horse's tracks when I saw 'em, 'cause in shoeing him I'd always take care to round the shoe aplenty so it'd protect the frog when running through the rocks. I'd recognize that round hoof-print anywhere, and I wasn't apt to forget the spike-heel boot-mark, either.

I remembers the shots I'd heard, and I wonders if my horse missing that way wasn't on account of somebody being after somebody else and one of 'em needing a fresh horse right bad, just "borrowed" mine.

Well, I thinks he must of needed him worse than I did, and I sure give him credit for knowing a good horse when he sees one, but I wasn't going to part with my buckskin that easy.

I runs the other horses in the corral and snares me the best one the company had, opens the gate and straddles him on the jump. Out we go, him a-bucking and a-bawling and tearing down the brush. I didn't get no fun out of his actions that morning — I was in too big a hurry; and when I started to get rough, he lined out like the good horse he was.

I picks up the tracks of the horse-thief out of the fence a ways, gets the lay of where he'd headed, and rides on like I was trying to head a bunch of mustangs. About a mile on his trail, I comes across a brown saddle-horse looking like he'd been sat on fast and steady, and says to my own brown as we ride by like a comet: "Looks like that *hombre* sure did need a fresh horse."

I'm heading down a draw on a high lope, wondering why that feller in the lead never tried to cover his tracks, when I hear somebody holler, and so close that I figgered they must of heard me coming and laid for me. I had no choice when I was told to hold 'em up, and that I done.

My thirty-thirty was took away from me; then the whole bunch that I reckoned to be a posse, circled around and a couple searched me for a six-gun without luck. "Do you recognize that horse, any of you?" asked the one I took to be the sheriff. "Sure looks like the same one," answers a few, and one goes further to remark that my build and clothes sure tallies up with the description.

"Where do you come from and where was you headed in such a hurry?" asks the sheriff.

"I'm from the cow-camp on Arrow Springs," I says, "and I'm headed on the trail of somebody who stole my horse last night." And riding ahead with half a dozen carbines pointed my way, I shows 'em the trail I was following. "Most likely one of our men," one of 'em says; and the sheriff backs him with, "Yes, we just let a man go awhile back."

"The hell you say!" I busts in, getting peeved at being held back that way. "Do you think you house-plants can tell me anything about this track or any other tracks? What's more," I goes on, getting red in the face, "I can show you where I started following it, and where whoever stole my horse left his wore-out pony in the place of mine."

"Now, don't get rambunctious, young feller. Tracks is no evidence in court nohow, and if I'm lucky enough to get you there without you decorating a limb on the way, that's all I care. Where was you night before last?" he asks sudden.

"At the camp, cooking a pot of frijoles; and bedded there afterwards," I answers just as sudden.

"Fine for you so far, but is there anybody up at the camp who can prove you *was* there?"

"No, I'm there alone and keeping tab on a herd of dry stuff; but if you'll go to the home ranch, the foreman'll tell you how he hired me some two weeks back, if that'll do any good."

"I'm afraid it won't," he says. "That wouldn't prove anything on your whereabouts the time of the hold-up. Your appearance and your horse are against you; you're a stranger in these parts, and the evidence points your way; and till your innocence is proved, I'll have to hold you on the charge of murder along with the robbery of the Torreon County Bank."

That jarred my thoughts a considerable, and it's quite a spell before I can round 'em to behave once more. The whole crowd is watching the effect of what the sheriff just said, and I don't aim to let 'em think I was rattled any. I showed about as much expression as a gambling Chink and finally remarks:

"I reckon you ginks has got to get *somebody* for whatever's been pulled off, and it sure wouldn't look right to go back empty-handed, would it?" I says as I sized up the bunch.

A couple of the men are sent toward my camp to look for evidence, and two others start on the trail I was following, which leaves the sheriff and three men to escort me to town some sixty miles away.

I'm handcuffed; my reins are took away from me and one of the men is leading my horse. We travel along at a good gait, and I'm glad nobody's saying much; it gives me a chance to think, and right at that time I was making more use out of that think-tank of mine than I thought I'd ever need to. I knowed I couldn't prove that I was at my camp the night of the hold-up, and me being just a drifting cowboy happening to drop in the country at the wrong time, looked kinda bad for suspicious folks.

After sundown when we strike a fence and finally come to a ranch-house, I was noticing a couple of the men was slopping all over their saddles and getting mighty tired; but I only had feelings for the tired horses that had to pack 'em. One of 'em suggests that they'd better call it a day and stop at the ranch for the night, and we rides in, me feeling worse than a trapped coyote.

I'm gawked at by all hands as we ride up; and I'm not at all pleased when I see one *hombre* in the family crowd that I do know, 'cause the last time I seen him, I'd caught him blotting the brand on a critter belonging to the company I was riding for and putting his own iron in the place of it. I was always kind of peaceable and kept it to myself, but between him and me, I offered to bet him that if he'd like to try it again I could puncture him and stand off five hundred yards while I was doing it. I'd never seen him since till now.

He gives me a kind of a mean look and I sees he's pleased to notice that I'm being took in for something. They hadn't heard of the hold-up as yet, but it wasn't long till the news was spread.

Between bites of the bait that was laid before us, the sheriff took it onto hisself to tell all about it. I was interested to hear what was said, 'cause the details of the hold-up was news to me too, and what was most serious was that the two masked bandits killed one man, and another wasn't expected to live; they'd got away with about ten thousand dollars. The women-folks sure kept a long ways from me after that.

The conversation was just about at its worst, for me, when the door opened and in walked a young lady, the prettiest young lady I remember ever seeing. All hands turned their heads her direction as she walked in, and the talk was checked for a spell.

"One of the family," I figgers as she makes her way to the other lady folks. I hears some low talk and feels accusing fingers pointing my way. In the meantime the sheriff and his men had cleared most everything that was fit to eat off the table; one of the ladies inquires if they'd like more, but none seemed to worry if *I* had my fill.

I glances where I figger the young lady to be, and instead of getting a scornful glance, as I'd expected, I finds a look in her eyes that's not at all convinced that I could of done all that was said; and a few minutes later there's more warm spuds and roast beef hazed over *my* shoulder, and I knowed the hand that done the hazing was none other than that same young lady's.

From then on the rest of the talk that was soaring to the rafters about me being so desperate was just like so much wind whistling through the pines. I could see nothing and feel nothing but two brown eyes, pretty and understanding brown eyes.

Arrangements was made for a room upstairs, and as the sheriff took the lead, me and the deputies following, I glanced at the girl once more, and as I went up the stairs I carried with me visions of a pretty face with a hint of a smile.

The three deputies unrolled a round-up bed that was furnished, and jumped in together; the sheriff and me took possession of a fancier bed with iron bedsteads. My wrist was handcuffed to his and we made ourselves comfortable as much as we could under the circumstances.

A lot of trouble was made, before the lamp was blowed out, to show there was no use me trying to get away.

In turning over, my fingers come acrost a little mohair rope I used for belt and emergency "piggin' string" (rope to tie down cattle). It was about six feet long, and soft.

The three deputies, after being in the cold all day and coming in a warm house tired and getting away with all that was on the table, was plumb helpless, and they soon slept and near raised the roof with the snoring they done.

The sheriff, having more responsibility, was kind of restless, but after what seemed a couple of hours he was also breathing like he never was going to wake up, leaving me a-thinking, and a-thinking.

The girl's face was in my mind through all what I thought; and the hint of her smile was like a spur a-driving me to prove that she was right in the stand she'd took. There was three reasons why I should get away and try to get the guilty parties; one was to get my good old buckskin back; another was to clear myself; but the main one, even though I didn't realize it sudden, was the girl.

If the guilty parties wasn't found, I knowed I'd most likely take the place of one of 'em. I just had to clear myself somehow, and the only way was to break loose to do it.

I was still fingering the piggin' string at my belt. I couldn't see the window and concludes it must be pitch-dark outside. A coyote howled, and the dogs barked an answer.

"Wonder if I can make it?" And something inside tells me that I'd *better* make it, and now, or I'd never have another chance.

The sheriff acts kinda fidgety as I try to ease my piggin' string under his neck. I lays quiet awhile and tries it again, and about that time he turns over just right and lays over that string as though I'd asked him to. His turning over that way scared me, so that I didn't dare move for a spell; but finally I reach over and grab the end of the string that was sticking out on the other side, makes a slip knot and puts the other end of the string around a steel rod of the bedstead; and still hanging on to that end, I'm ready for action.

From then on, I don't keep things waiting. With my handcuffed arm, I gets a short hold on the string; and with my free arm, I gets a lock on the sheriff's other arm all at once. That sure wakes him up, but he can't holler or budge, and the more he pulls with the arm that's handcuffed to mine, the more that string around his neck is choking him. I whispers in his ear to tell me where I can get the keys for the handcuffs before I hang him to dry, and by listening close I hears: "In my money belt."

I had to let go of his arm to get that key, but before he had time to do anything, my fist connected with the point of his chin in a way that sure left him limp. I takes the handcuffs off my wrist, turns the sheriff over on his stomach and relocks the handcuffs with his arms back of him, stuffs a piece of blanket in his mouth, and cutting the piggin' string in two, ties the muffler in place and uses the other piece to anchor his feet together.

The three deputies on the floor was still snoring away and plumb innocent of what was going on. I sneaks over to where I'd seen 'em lay my rifle, picks out an extra six-shooter out of the holster of one of the sleeping men, and heads to where I thought the window to be.

It was locked from the inside with a stick, and removing that, I raised it easy; and still easier I starts sliding out of the window and down as far as my arms lets me, and lets go.

I picks myself up in a bunch of dry weeds and heads for the corrals for anything I could find to ride. I'm making record time on the way and pretty near bumps into — somebody.

My borrowed six-shooter is pointed right at that somebody sort of natural, and before I can think —

"Don't shoot, cowboy," says a soft voice. "I knowed you'd come, and I been waiting for you. I got the best horse in the country saddled and ready, and if you can ride him, nothing can catch you."

I recognized the young lady; she came closer as she spoke and touched my arm.

"Follow me," she says, pulling on my shirt-sleeve, and the tinkle of her spurs and the swish of her riding-skirt sounded like so much mighty fine music as I trotted along.

But there was sounds of a commotion at the house. Either the weeds had give me away or the sheriff come out of it. Anyway, a couple of lights was running through the house, doors was slamming, and pretty soon somebody fires a shot.

"Them folks sure have learnt to miss me quick," I remarks as we push open the corral gate. Then I'm up to the snorting pony in two jumps. I see he's hobbled and tied ready to fork; and sticking my rifle through the rosadero, I takes the hobbles off of him, lets him break away with me a-hanging to his side and I mounts him flat-footed as he goes through the gate.

I was making a double get-away, one from the sheriff and the other from the girl. I knowed, the way I felt, it would have seemed mighty insulting for me to try and thank her with little words. I wanted to let her know somehow that *if* she ever wished to see me break my neck, I'd do it *for her*, and with a smile.

"I sure thank you," I says as I passes her (which goes to prove that there's times when a feller often says things he wants to say least), but I had to say something.

The whole outfit was coming from the house. There was a couple more shots fired, and with the noise of the shots, my old pony forgot to take time to buck and lined out like a scared rabbit, me a-helping him all I could. We hit a barb-wire fence and went through it like them wires was threads, and went down the draw, over washouts and across creeks like it was all level country.

The old pony was stampeding, and it was the first time in my life that I wanted a ride of that kind to last, and being that we was going the direction I wanted to go, I couldn't get there any too fast to suit me.

I'm quite a few miles away from the ranch when I decides I'd better pull up my horse if I wanted to keep him under me after daybreak, and that I did, but I managed to keep him at a stiff trot till a good twenty-five miles was between us and where we'd left.

Daybreak catches up with us a few miles farther on, and I figgers I'd better stop awhile to let the pony feed and water. I takes a look over the way I just come, and being that I'm halfways up a mountain, I gets a good view of the valley, and if anybody is on my trail, I'd sure get to see 'em first and at a good ten miles away.

The little old pony buckles up and tries to kick me as I gets off, and not satisfied with that, takes a run on the hackamore rope and tries to jerk away, but his kind of horseflesh was nothing new to me, and in a short while he was behaving and eating as though he knowed it was the best thing for him to do.

A good horse always did interest me, and as I'm off a ways studying his eleven hundred pounds' worth of good points, I notices a sackful of something tied on the back of the saddle. "Wonder what it can be," I thinks out loud as I eases up to the horse and unties it. I opens the sack, and finds all that's necessary to the staff of life when traveling light and fast the way I was. There was "jerky" and rice, salt and coffee, with a big tin plate and cup throwed in to cook and eat it out of.

"Daggone her little hide!" I says, grinning and a-trying to appreciate the girl's thoughtfulness. "Who'd ever thought it?"

I cooked me a bait in no time, and getting around on the outside of it, am able to appreciate life, freedom and a good horse once again. And wanting to keep all that, I don't forget that these hills are full of posse-men, and that the other bunch at the ranch would soon be showing themselves on my trail. There was what I took to be a small whirlwind down on the flat. If it was a dust made by the posse they'd sure made good time considering the short stretch of daylight they'd had to do any tracking by.

I takes another peek out on the flat before cinching up, and sure enough there was little dark objects bobbing up and down under that dust.

I had the lead on 'em by ten miles, and I knowed if I could get on my horse and was able to stick him, that I'd soon lose 'em; but doing that away from the corral sure struck me as a two-man's job. What I was afraid of most was him getting away from me; his neck was as hard to bend as a pine tree, and his jaw was like iron, but I had to get action, and mighty quick, 'cause the distance between me and them was getting shorter every minute.

It helped a lot that I'd hobbled him before he was rested up from the ride I'd give him that night, and taking the rope off the saddle, I passes one end of it through the hobble and tied it. About then the old pony lets out a snort and he passes me like a blue streak. I just has time to straighten up, give a flip to the rope that was running through my hands, follow it a couple of jumps and get set.

My heels was buried out of sight when the stampeding pony hits the end and the rope tightens up; he made a big jump in the air and as his front feet are jerked out from under him, he lands in a heap and makes the old saddle pop. I follows the rope up to him, keeping it tight so's he can't get his feet back under him, and before he knows it I've got him tied down solid.

I takes a needed long breath and looks out on the flat once more; there's no time to waste, that I can see; them little dark objects of awhile ago had growed a heap bigger and was a-bobbing up and down faster than ever. I straightens up my stirrups, gets as much of the saddle under me as I can, and twists the pony's head so's to hold him down till I'm ready to let him up, and starts to take the rope off his feet.

He knows it the minute he's free, and is up like a shot; he keeps on getting up till I can near see the angels, and when he hit the earth again he lit a-running — and straight toward the posse and the ranch.

I tries to haze and turn him with my hat, but he'd just duck out from under it and go on the same way. So far he didn't act as though he wanted to take the time to buck with me, and I'd been glad of it, but now, we just had to come to a turning-point and the only way I seen was to scratch it out of him.

Screwing down on my saddle as tight as I could, I brings one of my ten-point "hooks" right up along his neck far as I could reach and drags it back. That sure stirred up the dynamite in him of a sudden, and I had a feeling that the cantle of my saddle was a fast mail-train and I was on the track; but he turned, and as luck would have it I was still with him. He kept on a-turning and all mixed in with his sunfishing and side-winding sure made it a puzzle to tell which was heads or tails.

What worried me most was the fear of being set afoot, and I'd been putting up a *safe* ride on that account, but that old pony wasn't giving me a fair deal. He fought his head too much, and I was getting tired of his fooling. I reaches down, gets a shorter holt on the hackamore rope and lets him have it, both rowels a-working steady — and two wildcats tied by the tail and throwed across the saddle couldn't of done any more harm.

We sure made a dust of our own out there on the side of that mountain, and I'd enjoyed the fight more if things had of been normal, but they wasn't, and I had the most to lose. The little horse finally realized that, the way I went at him, 'cause pretty soon his bucking got down to crow-hopping and gradually settled down to a long run up the slope of the mountain. That young lady was sure right when she said that if I could ride him, nothing could catch me.

He was pretty well winded when we got to the top, but I could see he was a long ways from tired, and letting him jog along easy we started down into a deep cañon.

My mind is set on tracking down the feller what stole my buckskin horse, and I figgers the way I'm heading I'll sometime come across his trail, but I'd like mighty well to shake loose from that bunch chasing me before I get much farther; and thinking strong on that, I spots a bunch of mustangs a mile or so to my left, and there was my chance to leave a mighty confusing trail for them that was following.

I sneaks up out of sight and above the "fuzztails," and when I am a few hundred yards off, I shows up sudden over a ridge and heads their way. I lets out a full-grown war-whoop as I rides down on 'em, and it sure don't take the wild ones long to make distance from that spot.

My horse being barefooted and his hoofs wore smooth, his tracks blend in natural with that of the mustangs, and I keeps him right in the thick of 'em. The wild ones make a half-circle which takes me out of my way some, but I'm satisfied to follow, seeing that it also takes me on the outskirts of where I figgered some of the posse outfit might be.

My horse was ganting up and getting tired, but them wild ponies ahead kept him wanting to catch up; and me holding him down to a steady long lope made him all the more anxious to get there with 'em. I was wishing I could stop to let him feed and rest awhile, but I didn't dare to just yet; my trail wasn't covered up well enough.

The sun is still an hour high when the wild ones I was following came out of the junipers and lined out across a little valley. I figgers I'm a good seventy-five miles from where I made my get-away, and even though my horse hates to have the mustangs leave him behind, he's finally willing to slow down to a walk. I rubs his sweaty neck and tells him what a good horse he is, and for the first time I notice his ears are in a slant that don't show meanness.

The wild ones run ahead and plumb out of sight; the sun had gone over the hill, and it was getting dark, and on the back trail I don't see no sign of any posse. Still following the trail the mustangs had left, I begins to look for a place where I can branch off, and coming across a good-sized creek I turns my horse up it into the mountains.

"Old pony," I says to my horse as we're going along in the middle of the stream, "if that posse is within twenty miles of us, they're sure well mounted; and what's more," I goes on, "if they can tell our tracks from all the fresh tracks we've left scattered through the country behind, in front and all directions, why, they can do a heap more than any human I know of."

I'm a couple of miles up the mountain and still following the stream, when a good grassy spot decides me to make camp. The little horse only flinches as I get off this time, and he don't offer to jerk away. I pulls the saddle off, washes his back with cool water and hobbles him on the tall grass, where he acts plumb contented to stay and feed.

Clouds are piling up over the mountain; it's getting cold and feels like winter coming on. I builds me a small Injun fire, cooks me up a bait, and rolling a smoke, stretches out.

"Some girl," I caught myself saying as I threw my dead cigarette away. . . . The little horse rolled out a snort the same as to say, "All is well," and pretty soon I'm not of the world no more.

It's daylight when a daggone magpie hollers out and makes me set up, and I wonders as I stirs up the coffee what's on the program for today. My horse acts real docile as I saddles him up; he remembers when I gives his neck a rub that it pays to be good.

I crosses on one side of a mountain pass and on over a couple of ridges and down into another valley of white sage and hardpan. I don't feel it safe to come out in the open and cross that valley, so I keeps to the edge close to the foothills and junipers.

My horse, picking his way on the rocky trail, jars a boulder loose and starts it down to another bigger boulder that's just waiting for that much of an excuse to start rolling down to the bottom of the cañon; a good many more joins in, and a noise echoes up that can be heard a long ways.

As the noise of the slide dies down, I hears a horse nicker, and it sounds not over five hundred yards away. I didn't give my horse a chance to answer, and a hunch makes me spur up out of the cañon and over the ridge. I was afraid of the dust I'd made in getting over the ridge.

I'm splitting the breeze down a draw; and looking back over my shoulder, I'm just in time to get the surprise of my life. A whole string of riders are topping the ridge I'd just went over, and here they come heading down on me hell-bent for election. I know it's them, and I know they seen my dust; and worse yet, I know they're on fresh horses.

"Now," I asks the scenery, "how in Sam Hill do you reckon for them to be in this perticular country, and so quick?" And the only answer I could make out was that when I struck the mustangs and put too many tracks in front of 'em for 'em to follow, they just trusted to luck and cut acrost to where they thought I'd be heading.

My only way out is speed, and my pony is giving me all he can of that; but it's beginning to tell on him, and I don't like the way he hits the other side of the washouts we come across.

A bullet creases the bark off a piñon not far to my right; another raises the dust closer, and even though I sure hated to, I had to start using the spurs. The little horse does his final best, and I begin to notice that the bullets are falling short, and it ain't long when I'm out of range of 'em.

"Old-timer," I says to my tired horse as we're drifting along, "if you only had a few hours' rest, we'd sure make them *hombres* back of us wonder how thin air could swallow us so quick."

We tops a rise in the foothills, and ahead of us is a bunch of mustangs. They evaporate quick, leaving a big cloud of dust. They can't do me any good this time; my horse is too far gone; but I thinks of another way and proceeds to act.

I reaches over, takes the hackamore off my horse's head and begins to loosen the latigo. My pony'd took heart to keep up the speed awhile longer, on account of them wild ones ahead and wanted to catch up with 'em.

My saddle cinch is loose and a-flapping to one side; my chance comes as we go through a thick patch of buckbrush, and I takes advantage of it. I slides off my horse and takes my saddle with me; the old pony had nothing on him but the sweat where my saddle'd been. There's mustangs ahead, and with a snort and a shake of his tail he bids me good-by and disappears.

About that time me and my "riggin'" ain't to be seen no more, and when the posse rides by on the trail my horse'd left, there was a big granite boulder and plenty of buckbrush to keep me hid, and looking straight ahead for a dust, the sheriff and his three men kept right on a-going.

But I figgered they'd be back, sometime, and thinks I'd better be a-moving. I hangs my saddle up a piñon tree, leaves most of the grub with it, and, tearing up the gunnysack that was around it, proceeds to pad up my feet so they'd leave as little track as possible. Then I picks up my rifle and heads up towards a high point on the mountain where I could get the lay of the country.

I'm on what seems to be a high rocky ledge, and looking around for some shelter in it from the cold wind, and where I can hole up for the night. I comes to the edge of *nothing* — and stops short!

Another step, and I'd went down about three hundred feet; a fire at the bottom of it showed me how deep it was, and by that fire was two men; maybe they're deer-hunters, I thinks. I keeps a-sizing up the outfit, and then I spots three hobbled ponies feeding to one side a ways, and there amongst 'em was my good old buckskin. I'd recognize his two white front feet and his bald face anywheres.

I'm doing some tall figgering by then, and I has a hunch that before daybreak I'll be well mounted again and on my own horse. Seeing that my rifle was in good working order, I slides down off my perch to where going down is easier and surer of a foothold. I'm down about halfways, and peeking through a buckbrush, I gets a better look at them two *hombres* by the fire. The more I size 'em up, the surer I gets of my suspicions.

I'm close enough to see that one of the men is about my build, and not only that, but it looks like he had on my clothes. The other man I couldn't make much out of — he was laying down on his face as though he was asleep; but I could see he was some stouter and shorter.

Well, all appearances looked a safe bet to me, and beating my own shadow for being noiseless, I gets to within a hundred feet of 'em.

"Stick 'em up," I says quiet and steady for fear of their nerves being on edge and stampeding with 'em. One of 'em flinches some but finally reaches for the sky, the other that's laying down don't move, and I warns him that playing 'possum don't go with me; but threatening didn't do no good there. I'm told that he's wounded and out of his head — I remember the sheriff saying that one of the men had been wounded, which altogether tallied up fine as these being the men *me* and the sheriff wanted.

"Take his hands away from his belt and stretch em out where I can see 'em then," I says, not wanting to take the chance. That done, I walks over toward 'em and stops, keeping the fire between. I notice that the man laying has no gun on or near him; the other feller with his arms still up is packing two of 'em, and I makes him shed them by telling him to unbuckle his cartridge-belt.

I backs him off at the point of my rifle and goes to reaching for the dropped belt and six-guns, when from behind and too close for comfort somebody sings out for me to drop my rifle and reach for the clouds. I

Somebody sings out for me to drop my rifle.

does that plenty quick, and looking straight ahead like I'm told to, I sees a grin spreading all over the face of the man I'd just held up a minute ago.

"Where does this third party come in?" thinks I. My six-shooter is jerked out of my belt as I try to figger a way out, and is throwed out of reach along with my rifle; and then of a sudden the light of the fire in front of me was snuffed out, and with a sinking feeling all went dark. . . .

When I come to again, I hear somebody groaning, and I tries to get my think-tank working; my head feels abut the size of a wash-tub, and sore. Whatever that *hombre* hit me with sure wasn't no feather pillow. I tries to raise a hand and finds they're both tied; so is my feet, and about all I can move is my eyelashes. Things come back to me gradual, and star-gazing at the sky I notice it's getting daybreak.

Hearing another groan, I manages to turn my head enough to see the same *hombre* that'd been laying there that night and in the same position. I hears the other two talking, off a ways. It sounds by the squeak of saddle-leather that they're getting ready to move, and that sure wakes me up to action.

I know I can't afford to let 'em get away, and I sure won't. Raising up far as I can, I hollers for one of 'em to come over a minute. There's some cussing heard, but soon enough here comes the tallest one, and he don't no more than come near me when I asks him to give me a chance to loosen up my right boot, that my sprained ankle was bothering me terrible.

"You needn't think you can pull anything over on me," he says sarcastic. He sizes my boot up awhile and then remarks: "But I'll let you pull 'em both off. I need a new pair."

My arms and feet are free, but awful stiff; he's standing off a few feet, and with rifle ready for action is watching me like a hawk while I'm fidgeting around with my right boot; I gets my right hand inside of it as though to feel my ankle, but what I was feeling for mostly was a gun I'd strapped in there.

(When I started out on the trail of my buckskin I figgered on getting him; I also figgered on running acrost somebody riding him that'd be a gunman, and I'd prepared to compete with all the tricks of the gun-toter. This gun in my boot was what I called *my hole card*.)

My foot is up and toward him, and I'm putting on a lot of acting while getting hold of the handle and pulling back the hammer, but I manages that easy enough and squeezing my finger towards the trigger, I pulls.

That shot paralyzed him, and down he come. He'd no more than hit the ground when I falls on the rifle he'd dropped, and I starts pumping lead the direction of the other feller. His left arm was bandaged and tied up, but he was sure using his right so that our shots was passing one another halfways and regular. . . . Then I felt a pain in my left shoulder. I begins to get groggy — and pretty soon all is quiet once more.

I must of been disconnected from my thoughts for quite a spell, 'cause when I come to, this time the sun is way high. I straightens up to look around and recollect things, and it all came back some as I gets a glimpse of my buckskin feeding off a ways.

My shoulder's stiff and sore, but feeling around for the harm the bullet has done, I finds I'd just been creased, and being weak on account of not having anything under my belt either in the line of grub or moisture for the last twenty-four hours, that bullet was enough to knock me out.

I'm hankering for a drink right bad and starts looking for it on all fours, when in my rambling, I comes across a shadow, and looking right hard I can make out horse's hoofs, then his legs and on up to a party sitting on top of him and looking down at me. The warm sun had made me weak again, and I quits right there.

Somebody's pouring cool water down me, and when I opens my eyes, again, I feels better control of 'em. I'm asked when I et last and I can't seem to remember; then I gets a vision of a pot of coffee, and flapjacks, smells frying bacon, and the dream that I'm eating evaporates with the last bite.

"Well, I see you found your buckskin," says a voice right close, and recognizing that voice makes me take notice of things. It was the sheriff's; the posse'd rode in on me.

"And by the signs around here," the same voice goes on, "it looks like you just got here in time and had to do a heap of shooting in order to get him, but I'm sure glad to see you did, 'cause along with that horse you got the two men we wanted for the robbery, which makes you free to go. No mistake this time."

That last remark brought real life to me, and interested again, I takes a look around. The two men was setting against a rock looking mighty weak and shot up. I looks for the third, and I'm told that he was being took in to the nearest ranch for care he was needing mighty bad.

"How does he come to be with these *hombres?*" I asks.

"He's a Government service man out after these two outlaws," says the sheriff, "and your dropping in when you did is all that saved him — if we hadn't heard your shot, we'd never found this hole, and he'd been left to feed the buzzards."

Not wanting to hog all the credit, I says, "I've sure got to hand it to you too — for camping on a feller's trail the way you do; it wasn't at all comfortable."

"Neither is a piggin' string around a feller's neck," comes back the sheriff, smiling.

It's after sundown as I tops a ridge and stops my buckskin. Out across a big sage and hardpan flat is a dust stirred up by the posse and their prisoners. I watches it a spell, and starting down the other side of the ridge, I remarks: "Buck, old horse, I'm glad you and me are naturally peaceable, 'cause being that way not only saves us from a lot of hard traveling, but it's a heap easier on a feller's think-tank."

The evening star looks near as big as the moon as I glances up to keep my bearings straight; I finds myself gazing at it, and then comes a time when my vision is plumb past it, a vision of two brown eyes and a hint of a smile.

Then the buckskin shook himself and at the same time shook me back to realizing that I was on a horse.

"Some day soon we're going visiting, Buck," I says, coming to; and untangling the knots out of my pony's mane as I rides, I heads him up the trail back to the cow-camp on Arrow Springs.

WILL JAMES
'30

One of them ropes sneaks up and snares him by the front feet just when he's making a grand rush to get away from it.

THE MAKINGS OF A COW-HORSE

A MONTH OR SO before the round-up wagons pull out, the raw bronc (unbroke range horse) is enjoying a free life with the "stock horses" (brood-mares and colts). He's coming four years old marked by the first signs of spring. A few warm days starts him shedding, and just as the green grass is beginning to peek out from under the snow and living is getting easier, why here comes a long lanky rider on a strong grain-fed horse and hazes him and the bunch he's with into the big corrals at the home-ranch.

He's cut out with a few more of his age and put into a small round corral — a snubbing post is in the centre — and showed where, according to the rope marks around it, many such a bronc as him realized what they was on this earth for.

The big corral gate squeaks open and in walks the long lanky cowboy packing two ropes; one of them ropes sneaks up and snares him by the front feet just when he's making a grand rush to get away from it. He's flattened to the ground and that other rope does the work tying him down. A hackamore is slipped on his head while the bronc is still wondering what's happened, and from the time he's let up for a sniff at the saddle he's being eddicated, so that when the wagon pulls out a few weeks later his first promotion comes, and he's classed as "saddle-stock."

From then it's 'most all up to what kind of a head that pony's got whether he'll get on further than being just a saddle-horse. He may have to be pulled around a lot to get anything out of him towards what he should do, or on the other hand, he may take to it easy and get down to learning of his own accord after his bucking spells are over with.

He'll get all the time he needs to catch onto the new ropes of cow work, and only one thing at a time will be teached to him so that he'll

49

not be rattled, but first, his bucking is what the rider'll object to and try to break him out of, and every time he bogs his head for that perticular kind of orneriness that bronc is apt to get his belly-full of the quirt.

But the cow-foreman has no place on the outfit he's running for any such *hombre* what don't treat the ponies right, and if a cowboy is kept on the pay-roll what naturally is rough on horse-flesh he'll get a string of horses cut to him that's just as mean as he is and fight him right back, or even go him one better whenever the chance shows up.

There's horses though that has to be rough handled, born fighters what'll do just the opposite of what they should do to be good; they want to be ornery and them kind calls only for the real rough bronco fighter what'll fight 'em to a finish.

Them's the kind of horses what makes up a "rough-string"; every cow outfit has 'em. Them horses'll range in age from five-year-old colts what craves fighting on up to fifteen and twenty-year-old outlaws; they 'most always keep one man in the hospital steady, and when he comes out the other man is about due to take his place either with the nurses or the angels.

The good, patient "bronc twister" what takes pains to teach the bronc to be good and be a real cow-horse don't as a rule have anything to do with the "rough-string"; his patience and ability with horses is too valuable to the company to have it go to waste on outlaws. So his work comes in on the uneddicated colt (the raw bronc), trying in all ways to hold the good what's in him, at the same time keeping his spirit intact, and talk him out of being ornery, if he can.

Like for instance, that long lanky cowboy and the raw bronc I mentioned in the first part of this writing; they both have a mighty good chance of getting along fine with one another. If they do, that same bronc'll be rode out on circle and learn the ways of the critter, when later on he'll be turned over to another hand. The older cowboy, what's past hankering for "rough edges" on them broncs, will then take him and proceed to ride and help him along with his learning.

Then's when the good or the bad in him will come out to stay; at that time he knows the human enough to tell what to expect, and if he wants to be good he's got a mighty good chance, the same if he wants to be bad, for this older hand is not hankering to get in no mix-up; the pony feels that, and *if* he's bad at heart he'll sure take advantage of it and buffalo the older cowboy to turning him loose or else buck him off in the hills somewhere.

If he succeeds in running his bluff once he'll feel sure that he can do it with every man what tries to handle him, and if he can fight wicked enough it might be hard to show him different. Consequences is, if that confidence ain't taken out of him right sudden it'll take hold on him with the result that he lands in the "rough-string" and the promotion stops there, — one more what has to be tied down before he can be saddled.

But, being as I said before that this raw bronc and the long lanky cowboy had mighty good chances of getting along fine, I'll let the good win out the same as it did with this perticular little horse I been trying to write about ever since I started this.

This little horse weighed around eleven hundred pounds and all in one hunk; what I mean is each part of him knowed what the other part was going to do and followed up according, without a kink nowheres. In bucking, or running, he'd make you wonder if he was horse-flesh or dynamite. Just an ordinary horse to look at though, chunky, short back and short ankles, but with a deep chest, and that head promised a lot either way he went.

That day I run him in, throwed him, and slipped the hackamore on his head, a name for him came to me just as natural as though I'd been thinking of one for hours. "Brown Jug," and that sure fit him all the way through even to the color; also like the jug he had plenty of "kick" in him.

From the first saddling he didn't disappoint me none, for he went after me and sure made me ride; in order to stay I had to postpone fanning him for a spell and thought I was doing real well to be able to

I gave him a good half-hour to think it over.

do that much. It was just my luck that none of the boys was around to see me put up such a ride on such a horse; I told 'em about it, but, to the way it struck me, that was mighty tame compared to how it really was, and the next day when some of them boys happened around just as I was climbing Brown Jug again, the little son of a gun just crowhopped around and acted like he loved me and my rigging 'most to death.

He bucked at every setting each day after that for about ten days; then one day as I was going through the corral gate to give him his daily "airing," he "went to pieces" right there at the gate, and where it was slick with ice he fell hard and flat on his side and smashed one of my stirrups.

Naturally the first thing came to my mind was to hold him down for a spell and see if I was caught anywheres in the rigging. I wasn't. Then I thinks that now would be a good time to teach *his kind* of a horse how bucking wasn't at all nice, so I proceeds to tie him down. That don't hurt a horse, only his feelings, specially so when interrupted that way in the middle of the performance.

I'd whipped him some while bucking a few days before and I found out before I was through that his kind had to be handled different, 'cause he bucked and showed fight all the way through and never let up till he was tired out, then he went to sulking. After that I watched my chance for some other way to break him out of it.

My chance came when he fell and I didn't let it slip by. I gave him a good half-hour to think it over, and when I let him up, me a-setting in the saddle, he was glad to get away from the forced rest and be able to stand on his pins again; but he was sure took down a peg, and when I loped him out sudden he seemed to've forgot that was the time he liked to buck best.

There was twelve broncs in my string, each was getting short rides on "inside circle," or at the cutting grounds. Their teaching came right along with the cattle and the average of them colts was coming fine, but Brown Jug was ahead of 'em all and naturally I helped him all the more.

He'd bucked only once since I tied him down and that second time he didn't get to buck like he wanted to then; he'd only made a half a dozen jumps, when I reached down on one rein, pulled his head up and jerked his feet out from under him, laying him down again just when he wanted to be in action the most.

That fixed him for good, and I figgered if he'd ever buck again it'd be when he got cold and wanted to warm up, or when somebody'd tickle him with the spur at the wrong time. Well, if he did it'd only show he had feelings and the kind of spirit that makes the cow-horse.

It was a couple of weeks since Brown Jug'd bucked last; it was out of his system by now and I was beginning to take a lot of interest in the ways of handling the critter. I kept him in my string long as I could; then one day the foreman, who'd been watching with an eagle eye the work of every colt I'd been breaking, figgered the "raw edge" was pretty well took off them broncs and fit to be divided up amongst the boys for easy work.

The next morning I'm ready to leave the wagon behind, also the ponies I'd broke, and hit back for the home-ranch on a gentle horse, where I'm to round up another string of raw broncs and start in breaking fresh. But before leaving I manages to get the foreman to one side. "Now Tom," I says, "there's one special little horse in them broncs I'm turning over what has the makings of a 'top-horse' and I'd sure like to see a real good man get him, a man that'll make him what he promises to be. I know Flint Andrews would sure like to have him, and I'm asking as a favor if you'd see that Flint gets Brown Jug."

"You surprise me, Bill," he says, squinting over Brown Jug's way, then back at me, "why I thought all horses was alike to you no matter how good or bad they be; but I guess I thought wrong, and if you'd like to see Flint get the brown horse don't worry about it, he'll get him."

"That's the trouble being a bronc peeler and working for them big cow outfits," I says to my horse as I'm riding along back to the ranch; "a feller don't no more than begin to get interested in the way the colts are learning; and just about the time the orneriness is took out of 'em and they're behaving fine they're took away and scattered along in the other boys' strings, and another bunch of green, raw, fighting broncs takes their place."

I'm at the ranch near three weeks and coming along pretty fair with the new bunch when the wagons begin pulling in. The spring round-up was over with, and three of the four "remudas" was being corralled one after another; cow-horses, night-horses, and circle-horses was being cut out and turned on the range to rest up till the next spring, over five hundred head of 'em, and the other two hundred was put in the pasture to keep going till fall round-up. Them was the colts what'd just been "started" that spring along with the "spoiled horses" what belonged most to the "rough-string," and needed steady setting on in order to make 'em good.

Brown Jug came in with one of the remudas and was looking fine. Flint couldn't get to me quick enough to tell me what a great little horse he was, and how near he could come to being human. "Never kettled (bucked) once," he says, "and I never saw a horse getting so much fun out of beating a critter at her own game as he does; he sure camps on their hocks from start to finish."

A few days later I had a chance to watch him at work. Flint was a-talking away to him and that little son of a gun of a horse seemed to understand everything he said and talk right back with them ears and eyes of his. I was getting jealous of what Flint could do with Brown Jug, and it set me down a peg to see that he sure had me beat in teaching him something. I was all right when it come to starting a colt and taking the rough off him, but after that I sure had to take a back seat from Flint.

The boys was rounding up fresh horses and the wagons was getting ready to pull out again, all the corrals was being used and every rider was topping off the horses cut to him; from ten to fifteen head of the big fat geldings is what made a "string," and the company saw that each cowboy had all he needed far as horse-flesh was concerned.

And when the four and six horse teams was hooked on the "chuck," "bed," and "wood" wagons and the big corral gates was opened to let the remuda follow, every cowboy was on hand and ready. "The pilot" (rider piloting the wagon through the roadless plains and breaks) started, the cook straightened out his team and followed with the chuck wagon, then the "flunky" next with the bed wagon, and the "nighthawk" (night herder for the saddle-horses) on the wood wagon took up the swing, then last came the day wrangler bringing up the rear with upward of two hundred head of saddle stock, the remuda.

Fifteen or more of us riders rode along the side, doing nothing in perticular but keeping our ponies right side up till we come to the country where the work begins. The whole outfit moved on a fast trot and sometimes going down a sag you could see the cook letting his team hit out on a high lope, and the rest was more than aching to keep up.

Two more such outfits was to start out soon for other directions and on other ranges. I went along with the first; the broncs I'd just started a few weeks before was in the remuda and on the trail of eddication to the ways of the critter, the same as the bunch I'd took along early that spring.

In this new string of broncs I was putting through the ropes, there was another special little horse what promised to come up along with Brown Jug as a cow-horse. But I was kinda worried, he was *too* good, never bucked once and seemed to try too hard to learn. His kind of a horse was hard for me to make out, 'cause they was few. I always felt they was waiting for a chance to get you, and get you good whenever that chance showed up.

I figgered a horse with a good working set of brains like he had ought to've done *something*, but all he did do was to watch me like a hawk in every move I'd make; and he was so quiet when I was around that I naturally felt kind of nervous, thinking he might explode and tear up the scenery 'most any minute.

But he stayed good and kept a-learning fast, and even though I figgered he might be one example of a horse in a thousand, I was still dubious when I turned him and a few others of my broncs over to the boys. I wished he'd bucked, once anyway.

I kept my eye on him, and every time it was his turn to be rode I was always surprised to see how docile he was. The new hand what was riding him made an awful fuss over "Sundown," as he'd called him (he was too much of a puzzle for *me* to name) and the two was getting along better than I ever expected.

With Brown Jug, he was showing a little orneriness now and again, but that was to be expected, and Flint could 'most always talk him out of it. He done the work though, and was getting so he could turn a "bunch-quitting" critter so fast she'd think she was born that way.

And, if you'd asked me right quick which one of them two ponies, Brown Jug or Sundown, would make the best cow-horse I'd said Brown Jug; on the other hand, if you'd let me think it over for a spell it'd been that to my way of thinking that the two horses don't compare; they're both working fine, but I trust Brown Jug and I can't as yet trust Sundown. Anyway, to put myself in the clear I'd said "let's wait and see."

My broncs being all took away but four, a string of "cut," "circle," and "night" horses are turned over to me and I gets in on circle day-herd and night-guard with the rest of the boys, so now I can watch the colts I'd started get their finished eddication.

Fall was coming on and the air was getting crimpy; the light frosts was turning the grass to brown, and the old ponies was developing a

57

hump in their backs and had to have their bucking space to warm up in before straightening out and tending to business.

For the good old honest hard-working cow-horse does buck, and buck mighty hard sometimes, specially on cold mornings, but he's never "scratched" for it. The cowboy a-setting atop of him will only grin at the perticular way the pony has of unlimbering for the work what's ahead of him on the "cutting grounds." He'll be talked to a lot and kidded along for his "crooked ways," while he's tearing up the earth and trying to be serious in his bucking, and never will either the quirt or the spur touch that pony's hide while he's acting on that way, for him being a cow-horse and at the top of the ladder in saddle stock gives him a lot of privilege.

The cow-horse I'm speaking of here is the *real one*, the same you'd find anywheres, some years ago, even to-day on the big cow outfits to the east of the Rockies and on the plateaus stretching from Mexico to Canada. This cow-horse done nothing but cow work where it'd need a pony of his kind. He never was rode out on circle or straight riding and never was used anywheres outside of on the cutting grounds. All the action, strength, endurance, and intelligence that pony has was called for *there*, and the horse that could do that work and do it well was worth near his weight in gold to the country.

I well remember the time, and not so long ago, when you could buy any amount of mighty good saddle-horses for from five to twenty dollars a head, well-reined horses that could turn a Sonora "yak" quicker than you could wink; and I'll leave it to any cowman what savvies them cattle that that's saying a lot. But there was something them same ponies lacked to make 'em real cow-horses; what they lacked was intelligence, knowing where to be ahead of time when the snaky critter side-winded here or there, and put 'er out of the "main herd" before she had time to double back. Them same ponies depended too much on the touch of the rein; they couldn't see themselves what they should do, and far as they'd get in saddle stock was "dayherd," "circle," or "rope horse."

Where with the real cow-horse, he's the kind what'll work *with* the man, he's got to be able to see what should be done and do it without waiting for the feel of the rein, for sometimes things are done so quick in working a herd or cutting out a critter that the human eye or hand may be too slow, and that's where the instinct of the cow-horse comes in, to pick up the slack. He's got brains enough to know what the cowboy wants done, and he goes ahead and does it.

Man is not all responsible for making the cow-horse what he is; you got to give the pony half the credit, for after all, man only shows him the work and coaches him along some, but the horse himself does that work and will take enough interest in it as to sometimes bite a hunk of rawhide and beef right off some critter's rump if that critter happens to act ornery.

You can see feelings and wisdom all over that pony as he winds in and out through the herd. He goes along with his head straight from the body, not paying no attention to any of the bellering herd around him. The cowboy leaves the reins hanging loose and then, of a sudden the horse is given a sign which is really *no sign at all*, but anyway the pony knows *somehow* that the rider has a critter located and to be cut out; and even though there may be some cattle between him and that certain critter, he has a strong hunch just which one it is; that's enough for the cow-horse to work on.

Such a horse couldn't be bought at all, and many a time I've seen two hundred dollars or more (that was a lot of money then) offered and turned down for the likes, when the other well-reined kind could be got in trade for only a saddle blanket or a box of cartridges. Yessir, you'd had to buy the whole kaboodle, cattle, horses, range, and all, in order to get the cow-horse I'm speaking of here.

And Brown Jug, he was turning out to be just that kind of a horse. That fall after his first summer of eddication with the cow, he showed strong where in a couple more years he'd be a top cow-horse, the kind what's talked about around the cow camps from the Rio Grande to the Yellowstone. Flint was always raving about him and I'd always chip in with "well, look who started him."

Sundown was coming up right along with Brown Jug, and the new hand what was riding him sure used to get into some long sizzling arguments with Flint over them two ponies, but the argument kept neck to neck, same as it did with the horses.

They was both turned out that fall together with the rest of the remuda. That winter was easy on all stock, and the horses was all packing a big fat when spring broke up.

The spring horse round-up brought in near a thousand head of saddle stock, and in one of the corrals with other horses I got first glimpse of Brown Jug and Sundown. They'd been pals all winter and where one went the other followed; if one got into a scrap the other helped him and they sure made a dandy pair.

Flint'd been complaining of getting old and stiff for a week or so past, and when he seen Brown Jug acting snorty he mentioned it again, and a little stronger this time. Finally I took the hint and told him I'd top him off for him if he wanted me to. "Sure," he says, "I don't mind."

Well sir, that little horse gave me a shaking up the likes I never had before or since, and when he finally quit and I got off, I was beginning to feel old and stiff myself, but I rode him again that afternoon and took it out of him easy enough. The next day he was all right and Flint rode him away.

In another corral something was more than raising the dust and soon as I see what causes it, I don't lose no time to climb the poles and

All that could be got of him was buck, fight, sulk, and stampede.

get there. Sundown had "broke in two" *at last.* The new hand was having it out with him but he had no chance. Somehow he stayed on though and when the horse quit he fell off like a rag.

I takes a turn at that horse and tired as he is he sure makes it interesting, and I don't find no time to use the quirt. He finally quits again and I was mighty glad of it. He's standing with legs wide apart, fire in his eyes and puffing away like a steam-engine and when I tries to move him out of his tracks, all I gets is a couple more hard stiff jolts. He's mad clear through and I know there's no use trying to make him do anything just then.

From then on he was just as bad this spring as he was good the spring before. All that could be got of him was buck, fight, sulk, and stampede. He was no more interested in anything else, and after he put a couple of boys in the hospital and come damn near getting me, he was put in the "rough-string."

I wasn't surprised to see him turn out that way; if anything, I kind of expected it. For even though I've seen a *few* what never bucked on first setting and stayed good all the time, I always figgered there was something wrong with 'em and could never trust 'em till I knowed for sure.

I quit the outfit that year, right after the spring round-up was over, and it was a couple of years later when I rode back into that country. The spring round-up was in full swing and a herd was being "worked" a little ways from camp.

I rides over, and there was Flint and Brown Jug working *together,* and doing the prettiest job of cutting out I ever saw. A long-legged and long-horned staggy-looking critter was being edged to the outside of the herd, and I could see that critter had no intentions of being put out of that herd, none at all.

*After he put a couple of boys in the hospital and come damn
near getting me, he was put in the "rough-string."*

Pretty soon an opening shows up and Brown Jug come pretty near seeing it quicker than Flint. Anyway that critter was stepped on from there and put out before she knowed it. She tries to turn back, but the little horse was right on hand at each side step, when of a sudden Brown Jug stumbles. His foot had gone down a badger hole and he come near turning over. Flint quits him, and when the little horse straightens up the bridle is off his head. All was done quicker than you could think and the critter hadn't had time to get back to the herd.

That little horse without man or bridle puts 'er out
of the herd, and heads 'er for the cut.

Then, Brown Jug sees 'er, and, transformed into a lightning streak, he lands on 'er; the fur is flying off that critter's rump and that little horse without man or bridle keeps on as though nothing happened and puts 'er out of the herd and heads 'er for the cut.

Nobody says anything for a spell, but the expressions means a lot. Then the foreman, who'd seen it all, kinda grins and says: "If I had a few more horses like that I wouldn't need no men."

A few days later that same foreman piles his rope on Brown Jug, leads him out, and puts his own saddle on him. That sure set me to thinking, for even the boss is not supposed to ride any horse the company furnishes you with in your string, and still wondering I looks over at Flint, who's leading out the boss's top horse and putting *his* saddle on him.

I finds out afterwards that they'd swapped, and that Flint was to get his wages raised to boot, but I could see that Flint wasn't any too happy over the trade and I says to him, "I guess you feel about the same now as I did when *I had* to turn him over to you three years ago."

"Yes," he answers, "and worse."

But even at that, we was both mighty proud that we'd helped make Brown Jug what he was, *the top cow-horse of four remudas.*

THE YOUNG COWBOY

I 'D JUST STEPPED OFF A BRONC which I'd started breaking. It was hot in the corral, and I figgered it'd be a good idea to hunt shade for a few minutes and puff on a cigarette while giving that bronc a fair deal and a breathing spell.

It'd been my fourth setting on that pony, and he was getting so he really knowed how to buck. He was inclined more on the bucking and not so much on the behaving, and he'd made things some interesting for me that fourth time, till I figgered it'd gone far enough and I started to whip the buck out of him.

War had been declared from the time my quirt layed along his neck, and the fight that followed had been mighty fast and wicked, the pony bellered, swapped ends and had lit into bucking with all his heart and strength, his action hadn't lacked speed either, and there'd been a few times when my quirt had missed him entirely on account he wasn't where I'd figgered he'd be.

The battle hadn't been one-sided, and I kinda showed where I'd been in it plain enough. One of my spurs had been kicked off my heel and sent a sailing acrost the corral plumb on to the top of the log stable, and when all was over and I touched the ground I found that one of my ankles wasn't at all willing to stand my weight.

I was rubbing my ankle and figgering to go that bronc another round, when I hear the corral gate open and sees a young feller, a boy about ten years old coming toward me. He acts awful shy, but what struck me most was the way he sized me up, just as though I was a Santa Claus or any other such person that kids admire and want to get on the good side of.

I could see he wanted to say something, but the words didn't seem to want to come, and he had to swallow considerable before he could finally say:

"By golly, Mister, you sure can ride."

It'd been mighty hard for him to get them few words out of his system, but he showed relieved a heap after it was over with, I guess it all had to come out somehow, and when I grinned at him and told him I was glad he thought so, it seemed to put him more at ease as to what else he wanted to say.

I listened to his talk and kept serious while it went on. It all had to do with what he was going to be when he got big, and I gathered soon enough that his ambition layed on being a bronco buster, a straight-up riding bronc peeler.

"I rode a big weaner calf the other day," he says, and then, as a kind of proof, he pulled up his shirt-sleeve and showed me where some of the skin had been scraped off his forearm. "This is what I done when I roped him in the corral, I couldn't hold him, and he dragged me all over, but I got my turns around a post and *then* I had him. It was no tame calf either, and you ought to seen him fight when I put a rope around his belly so as I could have something to hang on with, and you ought to seen him buck when I climbed him. He throwed me off twice too, but by golly I sure rode him the third time."

In another corral was a bunch of big fat weaner calves from four to six months old, I knowed how strong and kinky them little fellers could be, and maybe as I looked the direction where the calves was corralled I might of showed some doubt as to the kid's ability to handle and ride any of them, for he says:

"Want to see me ride one?"

"No, I don't think I do," I says, "your dad might not like to see you riding 'em for fear you'd get hurt."

"Dad don't mind," says the kid as he picks up a rope, "he just laughs and tells mother that I'm just like he used to be when he was a kid, always riding or roping something. It's mother who don't like it, she

67

says she's too busy to be patching my shirts every day, but I'll be careful not to tear it this time."

There was only one way out for me, and that was to get busy with my bronc. I knowed the kid would want to stay and watch till maybe he'd forget all about the calf riding, and that's what I wanted.

I'd been on the outfit just a few days, just long enough to learn that the kid was the son of the cow foreman, the man who hired me. I'd seen the kid's mother only a couple of times and that was on the way to the grub pile the chink cook had fixed and hollered for me to come and get. Both the foreman and his wife seemed mighty fine cow country folks and I wasn't going to take any chances of the young feller getting bruised up, not while I was around and looking on.

He'd forgot all about wanting to show me how he could ride the minute I got ready to climb my bronc, and as me and that pony went around and around I'd get glimpses of the kid. I had to laugh some at the interest he showed, his eyes was near popping out of his head and then I noticed — his attention wasn't on the horse none at all, he wasn't worried how that pony bucked, he was just watching how I rode, and it was my turn to wonder — that kid was sure out to be what his heart was set on him being.

It was bright and early the next morning when I sees the kid come around the corner of the bunk-house and heading my way, the first sight of him made me want to grin some, he was all togged up like a full-grown cowpuncher and looked ready for anything, a blue jumper fitted him tight around the shoulders and waist, a stetson was pulled down to his eyebrows, and the best of all was a well fitting pair of batwing chaps and a hanging just right; then a neat made to order pair of boots and at the heels of 'em was straight-shanked, silver mounted spurs all a fitting him like the light gloves that was on his hands.

"This is the outfit my dad gave me last Christmas," he says as he grins his way up for inspection. The whole of what he was wearing sure met up with my liking, and as I watched the kid go in the stable, get his rope, and line out for the calf corral I knowed his outfit would show considerable more wear before he'd come out of there again.

I glances over, and sees that the kid has snared himself a big calf, one of the biggest and fattest of the bunch.

I'm working along trying to ease my saddle up on a bronc when I hear a beller come from the next corral, I glances over, and sees that the kid has snared himself a calf, one of the biggest and fattest of the bunch and he was working hard to get his rope around a post before the weaner could begin dragging him too fast around the big corral.

It was about then and when I was getting the most fun out of watching the kid that my bronc started acting up and I had to put all my attention to my own work. I'd just bought me a new pair of flower-stamped tapideros and that pony was doing his bestest a trying to disfigger 'em with his hind hoofs.

The bellering coming from the next corral kept up and my curiosity was doing its daggonedest to make me look, but as my bronc was doing considerable bellering and fighting himself I gradually found it some easier to keep my mind in my own corral.

All finally quietened down, and of a sudden, as I made ready to climb my horse, I knowed the kid had let up on his calf and was peeking thru the bars at me, even my horse had come to a shaking standstill and the way it all felt was like the quiet of the land just the minute before a cyclone hits.

I rode my horse, sashayed him around the corral a few times, and then I opened the gate and rode him out to where there was more room.

On account of me having other broncs to top off I couldn't stay away very long, and as I rode back to the corral a half an hour or so later I see that the kid had somehow hazed his calf on my corral and tied him down. He was standing by his critter seemed like waiting, and when I come closer and where I could get a good look at the goings on I seen the kid take the foot rope off the calf, climb on him as he got up, and start fanning him from there.

The trouble that kid had went to show off his riding ability had me grinning, but my grin soon faded to admiration for the little son of a gun. He was riding loose and reckless, and as I figgered that he'd last only a couple of jumps, I seen where I'd sure figgered wrong, he stuck on like a leach and every chance he got he'd glance over my way to see how I was taking it — I guess I was taking it all with a mighty blank face, mouth open and eyes a staring, 'cause every time the kid looked at me it seemed like he'd go at it all the wilder and a trying to show me what he really could do. I guess my opinion meant a considerable to him.

It was as the kid was doing his best work and the calf bringing in his wickedest twists that something happened which was too quick for

70

eyes to see. In half a second the kid was standing on his head on the calf's withers, throwed against the side of the corral, and before he hit the ground the calf had kicked him.

I was off my horse and into the corral in mighty quick time as I seen the kid land in a heap. I straightened him out and went for water,

It was as the kid was doing his best work and the calf bringing in his wickedest twists that something happened which was too quick for eyes to see.

71

poured it on him, and was just getting him to breathing regular again, when off toward the foreman's house I hear a screen door slam and then a woman's voice calling.

"BIL-L-e-e."

The kid was all right, but daggone it I sure didn't want the lady to see him just then, and I thanked the luck that the corrals was so well hid from the main house. I picked the kid up and packed him away around the corner of the stables and layed him in the shade of a big cottonwood. That done, I took one more glance at him to make sure there was nothing about him that needed rushing attention, and then hightailed it back to the corral and where I'd left my bronc.

I was right busy fooling around with the latigoes of my saddle when the lady turned the corner of the bunkhouse and seeing me, headed my way.

"Have you seen anything of little Billy?" she asks.

I'd been prepared for that question long before she asked it, and had managed to keep my tongue in working order by swallowing a few times, and that way keep my throat moist.

"Why, I think," I says, trying hard to keep from getting tangled up in my words, "that he's down in the big pasture, I seen him ride out on his little sorrel horse not long ago."

The lie seemed to work all right for she seemed relieved considerable as I sprung it.

"Well, if he's out on Concho I won't worry about him."

She smiled, and turned back to the house. I drawed a long breath and soon as she was out of my sight I run back where I'd packed the kid. Billy was laying in the same position I'd left him, but his eyes was open, and vacant like was staring up in the branches of the big cottonwood.

I reached over in the creek with cupped hands and splattered water on his face, and pretty soon he looked at me pretty natural. I grinned at him and he tried to grin back, but somehow it hurt him to do that. There was a swollen lump raised on the bridge of his nose close to his forehead, and it was turning black, so was both his eyes.

"How are your feeling, *cowboy?*" I asks.

Me calling him cowboy tickled him into a pretty prompt answer and he smiled kinda proud as he says:

"I don't know yet, I'll have to feel of myself first."

Then something came to his mind which by the look of his expression seemed mighty important.

"But say, Mister, will you watch out that my mother don't find me for a spell, she gets worried every time I get a scratch."

"Don't be afraid Billy, I'll tend to that. You just take it easy for a spell. I'm going to saddle up another bronc then I'll be over to see you, and if you need help just holler, I'll be listening."

I walked over to the chuck house and talked the chink cook out of a nice piece of raw meat. I had to do a lot of explaining before I could get it, but when I told him I wanted to use it for bait to catch the bob cats that'd been eating his chickens, he never stopped to think that I was using mighty good meat for such a purpose, he just handed me the butcher knife and showed me a hind quarter of fresh beef.

Back to the corral I went and then around to where Billy was stretched out. The little feller seen me come and wondered at the steak I was packing.

"Looks to me like," I said sort of explaining, "that you're due to pack a couple of black eyes for a spell, but that's all that's ailing you, and when I get the rough off of 'em with this hunk of meat, you'll be as good as new."

It was getting near noon, and while I was busy working with my broncs I kept a thinking and figgering on ways so that Billy could be missing from the dinner-table without his mother wondering, and finally I come to something that seemed pretty good.

I suggested to Billy that he get on his horse and ride out, and try to show up in plain sight somewheres on the meadow, and just when his mother would be calling him to come and eat. That suited the boy fine, for he'd been thinking about how his mother would feel when she'd see him with them two "shiners," and he wanted to put off the meeting as long as possible.

I was in the bunk house when the screen door slammed again, close to within hearing distance, and as his mother called, I showed myself natural like, and, walking up to her, told her I thought Billy had found a den of coyotes. I could see the boy out on the meadow about a mile, and as me and him had arranged it, he was moving back and forth the same as he was watching something. The distance was too far for him to hear if she called, but she could see him plain, and that seemed to satisfy her.

"If he's found a coyote den, there's no use me waiting for him to come and eat," she says, and she started back for the house. I headed her off once again, but I sure felt guilty somehow, and I didn't want to think what would happen if she ever found it out on me.

I et my bait, swiped a plate full of grub for the kid and hit back for the shade of the cottonwood where a half an hour or so later Billy met me. I watched him eat, and could see where he felt like a pretty big man to be knocked out the way he'd been and be able to grin and enjoy grub a few hours afterwards.

Ever since Billy had been knee high to a grasshopper and able to navigate by his lonesome, his company, outside of his mother, had been cowboys. His dad was of the bowlegged, sunburnt, and hard riding breed. His dad's daddy had been the same, was one of the first cowboys through the times when he had to make his own chaps out of a green cow hide, and even his saddle from the tree to the stirrups was turned out by his own injun fighting hands.

Billy was a chip off the old block, and if anything, a better chip on account that the blood of the pioneer generation before him had already made it second nature for him to be what he was, he had the start on 'em by inheriting some of what his father and the father before him had to learn through experience. They'd had to find a way to meet odds that was strange to 'em, and finally, after a lot of hardships and dangers, they'd lived to know how to meet and contend with all the frontier country called for, but with Billy, he'd fell heir to a kind of a

WILL JAMES
NM '26

Billy was a chip of the old block—a born cowboy.

sixth sense at birth, that sixth sense was nothing short of what was handed down to him from what all the generations before him had went through, learned, and passed on.

He was a *born* cowboy, the only kind that ever makes the real cowboy. There was as much difference between him and the town or settlement-raised kid as there is between the wild horse that rustles his own living on the open range and the standard-bred horse that lives in steam-heated box stalls, gets rub downs, and a feed of grain twice a day.

And taking all what Billy was, it would sort of set a person to thinking when looking at the country around that *it* hadn't waited, or stayed as it was; he couldn't of followed the trail his forefathers had blazed, and what all the generations before him had went through and the sixth sense which he'd inherited from it was going to go to waste.

Windmills and nester's fences and irrigating ditches and railroads and boosters and all was claiming the land, the range his father was running the Company's cattle on was dwindling away hunk by hunk, and one day when Billy had went to town with his dad he seen a rig, no horses hooked on, but going along and chugging away on two lungs, the first automobile.

"By God," he'd heard an old cowman say, "they'll be flying next."

What cattle, horses, and range that was left was Billy's last straw. If he'd come to earth thirty years or so before, he'd naturally took to hunting wild cattle and buffalo, he'd been learning to use the long rifle, and how to make his own ropes, but as it was, everything was all plain, ready made, and set and before him with no choice.

Being a good rider, a top bronco buster, seemed to him right then the only thing worth while. He didn't know it, but his heart was a hanging on to the last of the life his forefathers had lived, and limited as he was with what little of it that was left, he went at the remains like a drowning man grabs at a rope.

"Feel better now?" I asks the kid after he'd near cleared the plate of all I'd brought him.

"You bet, I feel fine," and then: "Did mother suspicion anything?"

I was back in the corral and had been there for about an hour getting the kinks out of one perticular ornery gelding, when happening to glance toward where the kid had been I noticed he'd moved, come right alongside the poles of the corral and was watching me like a hawk. He was still holding the piece of beef I'd got for his eyes, but he wasn't holding it where it'd do any good, he was peeking underneath, and I had to laugh at the looks of him as he stood there.

He laughed back, and when I tried to get him to go back to the shade of the cottonwood and take it easy, he only laughed some more and said:

"I'll wait till you get through with that pony you got there, dad always said he'd be a hard one to set."

Dad was right, that pony was a hard one to set and Billy watched the performance through them swollen eyelids of his the same as tho his vision was hindered none at all.

"Now it's all over with, Billy," I says as I pulled my saddle off the bronc, "you go on back under the tree and lay down for a spell."

I walked out of the corral to help him on the way and see that he was made comfortable, I'd took a few saddle blankets along figgering to make him a sort of a bed. It was as I was walking along that way with one arm kind of steadying him that I happened to glance on the back of his shirt (as the day was hot I'd took off his jumper to make him more comfortable) and there was dry bloodstains.

I found the little son of a gun had got some skin scraped off his back bone as he was throwed against the corral, but nary a word did he tell me about it. He figgered, like a cowboy, that such scratches shouldn't be mentioned and don't count, and I'll be daggoned if he didn't seem ashamed that I found it out on him.

There was no shaking Billy the rest of that afternoon, I'd no more than got through with one bronc when he'd be right alongside of the corral and watching me saddle up and ride another, and I seen where I had to move his quarters closer and where he could watch me without having to stand in the hot sun. But even that didn't seem to agree with him and there was no happy look on his face as he watched me a trying to make him a comfortable place in the shade of the log stable. Finally he spoke, and I seen then what was the matter, I was making too much fuss over him.

"Aw, I'm all right," he says, "I ain't got no legs or back broke nor nothing, my head just feels a little heavy that's all."

"All right Billy," I laughed, "I forgot you was a big feller."

I let him be as he wanted from then on, and I could see that pleased him a lot. He even tried to show how little the bumps bothered him by playing with a rope and practicing on a few throws and with his hat a hanging on the back of his head wandered around from corral to corral, but he was always on the spot and mighty close whenever I'd bring in and top off a new bronc. The sound of the screen door slamming was the only thing that made him hightail it no matter what was going on.

It was along toward evening and when the day's work was near over that Billy came up to me and, with a worried look, said:

"By golly, I don't know what I'm going to tell mother about this face of mine, she never did agree with me riding them weaners."

We was both figgering strong on the subject when pretty soon Billy's face lit up with a grin, and pointing to a big dust on one of the benches he hollered:

"Dad's coming! Dad's coming! I'm all right now."

He jumped up and down, and I never seen pleasure show so plain on a human's face as it did on that kid's.

It was about an hour later when the foreman (Billy's father) and a dozen cowboys rode up. He was the first to come to the corral and there in front of him kind of proud and a little doubtful stood Billy.

His dad just stayed on his horse at the sight of that son of his and looked, he couldn't do nothing else for a minute but just stare, mighty serious for a spell, but pretty soon as he noticed Billy's expression (what there was of it to see) he looked less serious, then a grin spread on his features and he asked:

"What hit you, Son?"

Billy seemed to draw a long breath, and pointing toward the other corrals he answered:

"One of them weaners did, throwed me off and kicked me before I hit the ground."

"What did your Mother say?"

"She ain't seen me yet."

The foreman got off his horse, and grinning a little was fooling with his latigoes and slowly unsaddling. He was thinking the while and after turning his horse loose in the big pasture he came to Billy, who was waiting, and put his hand on his shoulder. There was a kind of proud light in his eyes as he spoke.

"Don't worry, Sonny, we'll tell Mother that you run into a tree or something — was you out riding to-day?"

"Yes."

"Does mother *know* it?"

"Yes."

"We're o.k. then, Son, we'll just tell her you was chasing a cow through the willows and you hit your head on a limb."

All was fixed, and arm in arm the little cowboy followed the big cowboy toward the house.

Supper was over with, and while we'd been eating, the horse wrangler had reached the ranch and was corralling the remuda, there was near two hundred head of saddle horses in it. I was walking toward the corral to kinda look the ponies over when I hear somebody holler back for me.

I turned and seen Billy leave his dad and catching up with me, there was something he wanted to tell me, and tell me mighty quick, but somehow in his excitement he could only stutter, and finally I could make out something about his dad getting him a new horse.

We'd reached the corrals before he'd quieted down enough to speak and there I was informed again that his dad had brought him a new horse.

"Dad says," went on Billy, "that I can have him if I can break him. By golly, I've *always* wanted to break in a horse. That'll be lots of fun."

The foreman caught up with us and pointed out the gelding to Billy. It was a little black horse, not much bigger than a good sized shetland and pretty as a picture. Billy went wilder than ever at the sight of him and into the corral he run to get as close a view of the horse as he could.

"Bought him from an injun for ten dollars," says the foreman soon as the kid was out of hearing distance. "I knowed the kid would be tickled to death with him, had one of the boys try him out and he can't buck very hard, there's not a mean hair in him either, just a little spooky."

"Say, Daddy, can I catch him now?" Billy hollered, — he had a rope in his hands.

The foreman grinned, "Just like I used to be," he says, "couldn't get on 'em fast enough" — and then to the kid:

"You'd better wait till you heal up a little first, Sonny, you'll need all the skin you can get together to handle that pony."

Billy looked mighty disappointed. "Well, when *can* I ride him?"

It seemed, though, the next morning, that Billy had won out, his eyes was still black, and the raw place on his back had nowheres near healed but the sun hadn't been up very long when I found him in the round corral with his new horse.

"Well, I see you're busy right early, Billy."

"You bet you," he says, and then remarks, "he's some horse, ain't he?"

"He sure is," I agrees, "and your first bronc too."

I watched him a spell while he worked his way on up the rope and tried to place a hand on the pony's head, and as I watched a hunch came to me that a little advice right at the start wouldn't go bad, and I says:

"Now, Billy, I've found out that the best way to get along with a green colt is to allow that he's got lots of brains, and give him a chance to reason things out once in a while without rushing him."

Billy looked back at me, seemed to figger a while, and then says:

"I'd never thought about that, but now that I do think of it it seems to me like I've *always* took that for granted."

"Pretty daggone good," I says to myself. I grinned and had no more advice to give after that.

An hour or so later Billy had his saddle on the black and cinched to stay. By that time quite a crowd had gathered around, a bigger crowd than I'd ever drawed even if I'd been about to ride the worst horse in the world, the foreman, the cowboys, all the ranch hands, and even the chink was present and watching through them slanting eyes of his. I looked the crowd over to see if the lady of the outfit was around too, and the foreman knowing who I was looking for gave me the wink and says:

"She don't know this is going on — and I hope she don't find out."

All was set but taking the hobbles off the horse's front feet and climbing on. Help was offered to do that for Billy but that young cowboy refused it, he wanted to do it all himself, it was *his* bronc.

For a kid of his age Billy'd already had lot of experience with horses, and even though the others he'd rode had been well broke and gentle, he'd made a many a long ride and followed his daddy many a time on "circle." He could saddle a horse in the dark as well as in plain daylight and never get a string twisted, and taking that knowledge and stacking it up with the experience he'd had a trying to stick on the kinky backs of the weaners or whatever was around that could shake him, the young feller sure wasn't climbing the black gelding without knowing what he was up against, nor without being able to put up some fight.

Billy gathered his hackamore rope, a hunk of mane to go with it, grabbed the saddle-horn with his right hand, and sticking his foot in the stirrup, eased himself in the saddle. He squirmed around till he was well set, and like an old bronco fighter seen that the length of the reins between his hands and the pony's head was just right, then he reached over and pulled off the blindfold.

Billy's lips was closed tight, he was ready for whatever happened. The pony blinked at seeing daylight again, looked back at the boy setting on him, snorted, and *trotted* off.

A laugh went up from all around. It was Billy who'd caused that laugh, for soon as he seen that the pony seemed to have no intentions of wanting to do anything but trot around, his set jaw relaxed and disappointment showed plain. He turned a blank face toward his father and hollered:

"H—, Dad, he won't buck!"

Another laugh was heard, and when it quieted down some the foreman spoke up.

"Never mind, Son," he says, while trying to keep a straight face, "he might buck yet."

The words was no more than out of his mouth, when, of a sudden the little black bogged his head and lit into bucking. Billy was loosened the first jump on account that he'd been paying more attention to what his dad had been saying than what he'd been setting on. The little pony crowhopped around the corral and bucked just enough so as to keep the kid from getting back in the saddle, Billy was hanging on to all he could find, but pretty soon the little old pony happened to make the right kind of a jump for the kid and he straightened up once again.

Billy rode pretty fair the next few jumps and managed to keep his seat pretty well under him, but he wasn't satisfied with just plain setting there, he grabbed his hat and begin fanning —. All went fine for a few more jumps and then hell broke loose. The pony brought in some *reserved* twists, Billy dropped his hat like it was a hot iron and made a wild grab for the saddle horn.

But the holt on the saddle horn didn't help him any, he kept a going, up, and up he went, a little higher every jump, and pretty soon he started coming down. When he did that, he was by his lonesome. The horse had went another direction.

"Where is he?" says Billy trying to get some of the earth out of his eyes.

"Right here, Son," says his father, who'd caught the horse and brought him up.

He handed him the hackamore reins, and touched the kid on the hand.

"And listen here, young feller, if I catch you grabbing the horn with that paw of yours again, I'll tie it and the other right back where you can't use 'em."

Them few words had hit the kid pretty hard. He looked my way from under his hat brim to see if I showed I'd heard. There was a frown on his face and his lips was quivering some at the same time, he was both ashamed and peeved.

His father held the horse while Billy climbed on again.

"Are you ready, *cowboy?*" the foreman looked up at his son and smiled.

After some hard efforts the kid smiled back, and answered:

"Yes, Dad, let him go."

The pony lit into bucking the minute he was loose this time and seemed to mean business from the start. Time and time again Billy's hand reached down as to grab the horn, I could see it was hard for him, but he kept away from it.

The little horse was bucking pretty good, and for a kid Billy was doing mighty fine, but the horse still proved too much for him. Billy kept a getting further and further away from the saddle till finally he slid along the pony's shoulder and to the ground once again.

The kid was up before his dad could get to him and he begin looking for his horse right away.

"I don't think you'd better try to ride him any more to-day, Sonny," he says as he brushed some of the dust off the kid's clothes. "Maybe to-morrow you can ride him easy."

Billy sneaked a glance my way. Maybe he was only trying to get a hint from any expression (if I had any) as to what he should do. Anyway, as he turned and seen the horse, challenging him, seemed like, — the kid crossed the corral, caught the black, blindfolded him, and climbed him again.

It was then I figgered again that another little hunk of advice wouldn't go bad, I walked up to the kid, touched his chap' leg before he'd reached to pull off the blind, and I says to him so as nobody else could hear.

"You go after him this time, Billy, and you just make this pony think you're the wolf of the world and paw him the same as you did that last calf you rode."

"Y-e-e-e-p," Billy hollered as he jerked the blind off the pony's eyes, "I'm a wolf."

Billy had turned challenger and was pawing the black from ears to rump—"Y-e-e-e-p," he hollered, "I'm a wolf!"

Billy *was* a wolf, he'd turned challenger, and was pawing the black from ears to rump. Daylight showed a plenty between the kid and the saddle, but somehow he managed to stick on and stay right side up as he fanned and reefed. The gelding, surprised at the change of events finally kinda let up on his bucking, he was getting scared and had found a sudden hankering to start running.

After that it was easy for Billy, he rode him around the corral a couple of times and then, all smiles and proud as a peacock, he climbed off.

Billy had rode and fanned his first bronc.

I was unsaddling one of my ponies that evening when the foreman came into the corral.

"The kid's got an idea that the black will never be able to throw him again," says the foreman smiling. "I figger to wait till he rides him some more and see, but that's a good horse for Billy, bucks just hard enough for his first one."

He was quiet for a spell, and he smiled kinda proud when he spoke again.

"It sure done my heart good the way he went after that pony that third time. . . . "

WillJames
'30

CATTLE RUSTLERS

R AGGED, BEWHISKERED, narrow-brained, cruel, and mighty dangerous to all folks, specially women, unscrupulous, with a hankering to kill and destroy all what he runs across, leaving nothing behind but the smoke and a grease spot, is the impression folks get thru the movies and other fiction of the cattle rustler and horse thief.

I don't blame them folks for shivering at the thought of ever meeting such a bad *hombre*, but they can rest easy, 'cause there is no such animal in the cattle rustler. Picture for yourself a man sleeping out under the stars, watching the sunrise and sunsets, where there's no skyscrapers or smoke to keep him from seeing *it all*, acting that way or being what *they* say he is.

When I speak of cattle rustlers, I don't mean them petty cheap crooks what's read dime novels and tries to get tough, steals some poor old widow's last few "dogies" cause they ain't got guts enough to get theirs from the big outfits what keeps riders the year 'round — them kind don't last long enough to be mentioned anyhow — and I always figgered the rope what kept 'em from touching the earth was worth a heap more than what it was holding.

To my way of thinking anybody with a lot of nerve is never real bad all the way, whether he be a cattle thief, or cattle rustler — the excitement he gets out of it is what he likes most, and you can bet your boots that even tho' he may be dealing from the bottom of the deck, he's taking his from them what won't suffer from the loss, or maybe even miss it; you're plumb safe when that kind rides up to your camp to leave your silver mounted spurs and bits scattered around as usual, and most likely if he sees you're in need of a fresh horse he'll be real liberal in offering you the pick of his string — only danger is, if you're caught riding one of them ponies, it may be kind of hard to explain just how you come in possession of said animal.

There's cases where some cowboy what's kind of reckless and sorta free with his rope might get a heap worse reputation than what he deserves; and he gradually gets the blame for any stock disappearing within a couple of hundred miles from his stomping ground. Naturally that gets pretty deep under his hide, with the result that he figgers he might just as well live up to his reputation, 'cause if he gets caught "going south" with five hundred head he won't get hung any higher than he would for running off with just some old "ring boned" saddle horse. Consequences is when the stock associations and others start to keep him on the move, he's using his *long rope* for fair, and when he's moving there's a few carloads of prime stock making tracks ahead of him. In Wyoming a few of the feud men tried to even scores that way; the hill billy was on horseback and toting a hair-trigger carbine.

I don't want to give the impression that the cattlemen started in the cow business by rustling, not by a long shot — they're plum against it in all ways, and most of 'em would let their herd dwindle down to none rather than brand anything lessen they're shure it's their own. But there is some what naturally hates to see anything go unbranded wether it's theirs or not, and being the critter don't look just right to 'em without said iron, they're most apt to plant one on and sometimes the brand don't always fit.

Like for instance, there was Bob Ryan riding mean horses all day and a lot of the night in all kinds of weather for somebody else at thirty a month and bacon. It wasn't any too interesting to him; he kinda hankered for a little range and a few head of stock of his own, and come to figgering that some outfits he'd rode for had no objections to their riders picking up a "slick" whenever it was safe. There was no reason much why them slicks couldn't just as well bear his own "iron,"

The hill billy was on horseback and toting a hair-trigger carbine.

and that certain "ranny," being overambitious that way and sorta carefree, buys a few head of cows, calves, and yearlings, wherever he can get 'em and takes a "squatter" in the foothills, his weaning corrals being well hid higher up in some heavy timbered box canyon, and proceeds to drag a loop that makes him ashamed, at first.

There's the start of your cattle rustler — it's up to how wise he is, or how lucky, wether he keeps it up till he's really one or not. If he can get by till his herd is the size he wants it without getting caught, most likely he'll stop there and no one will know the difference, but if some inquisitive rider gets wind of his doings, and that wind scatters till it begins to look like a tornado, why it's liable to leave him in bad humor and make him somewhat more reckless.

A few months after Bob started on his own, a couple of riders out on circle was bringing in a bunch to the "cutting grounds," and in the "drags" noticed four cows with big bags bellering their heads off — and no calves. In another drive there's two more. Next morning, the range boss takes two riders with him, leaving the straw boss to take the others out on first "circle" — the six cows with the full bags was turned loose the night before and the boss finds 'em by a little corral in the brush still bellering (a cow and calf, if separated and losing track of one another, always return to where they'd last been together and wait for days till the one missing returns). There'd been a lot of cattle there and 'most impossible to track any special critter, so he goes up on a ridge toward the high mountains and "cuts" for tracks. A few miles to the north he runs across what he's looking for, and by the signs to be seen they sure must of been travelling and a horse track was there on top of the rest, looked a few days old.

Up a canyon it leads a ten or twelve miles, and they pass by Bob's camp, not seeing it. It was well hid and what's more, tracks is what the boss and the two riders was keeping their eyes on most — up a little

The end of a wrong start.

further there's a corral and if it wasn't for them tracks it'd never be found. There'd been cattle there the night before, it was plain to see. They kept quiet and listened. Off into the timber higher up a calf was heard and single file they climbed toward where it sounded to be from. When figgering they was close enough, they scattered and went three ways and on past around where the cattle was feeding till they got up above 'em, then joined one another; and getting off their horses they climbed a high point, squatted, took their hats off, and looking thru the cracks of a red rock, they could see a few of the cattle below 'em. Bob had 'em on feed and under cover during the day and in the corral at night till the brands healed. Nothing of *him* could be seen anywheres, but he was there keeping his eye on what he could see of the back-trail and at the same time standing "day herd" on the cattle.

Bob knew 'most any one would ride right up into the cattle, if in case they was looking for him figgerin' he'd be there, but he would of fooled 'em by just dropping off his perch into the other canyon and making distance — by the time they'd got thru looking for him he'd been in the next county. The boss reckoned on all that, being quite a hand on them sorta tricks himself at one time; so calculates the best thing to do is keep out of sight, circle around back to the corral, hide and wait till Bob brought the cattle down and put up the poles at the gate. Along about sundown, the cattle is coming and Bob is with 'em, drives 'em into the corral, and he's putting up the last pole when from three different places at close distance he hears the command "Put up your hands," "'Way up there!" Bob reaches for the sky, knowing better than try to do different.

The next morning to the boss's surprise, there's no weaners in that corral; all grown stock mostly cows, and calves too young to be branded, but them cows had fresh irons and earmarks on 'em just beginning to heal. What was the original iron on them critters nobody could make out, it was blotched so bad and the ears cut so short that there was nothing to be seen but the *new iron*, that being sure visible and stretching from shoulder to hip-bone.

It was plain to see what Bob had been doing, but he had cattle of his own bearing the same iron, and he could prove it was of the first branding, and them weaners disappearing was a puzzle. The boss had a strong hunch he had 'em hid somewheres, but where? And how could he prove Bob did it?

Bob not being caught red-handed just lands into court and with his lawyer wins the fight; the judge and jury pronounces him "Not Guilty," and the lawyer takes the cattle for the fee. (It's 'most impossible to convict any one of cattle rustling, and that's why "necktie-parties" was so popular.) When the sun shines on his freedom again, the first thing that stares him in the eye is cattle once more, cattle everywhere on the hillsides and brakes — he knows it's his move, so calculates to make the most of it while moving. His idea is to clear enough to get him started in some new country, where he ain't branded so well.

He knows he'll get the blame for all that disappears in that territory, so he goes to work and takes pains to let everybody know in the town and country that he's hitting the breeze. He wants to let 'em understand that there'll be a whole State, maybe two, between him and those what suspicions. He sticks around for a week or more, straightening out his affairs, and the while telling the folks about him what a paradise this new country is where he's going to, that he wouldn't come back again on a bet.

The stage-driver takes him and his "thirty years' gathering" to the railroad-station and comes back telling the storekeeper and livery-stable man that he's went for sure. He'd seen him buy a ticket for some town a thousand miles away, and everybody kinda draws a long breath saying something like "good riddance of bad rubbish."

Sure enough, Bob had went all right, and arrives at this new country unknown and walking kinda straight. The sheriff ain't ever heard of him and he inquires 'round at the stable where the headquarters for the Blue River Land and Cattle Company might be found. The superintendent, upon his asking for a job, informs him that he's full-handed excepting that he could use a good man "snapping broncs."

A few days later you could see Bob inside the breaking corral of the home ranch; four broncs are tied up and getting "eddicated" and another's saddled ready to be "topped off." He's standing there rolling

The stage-driver takes him and his "thirty years'
gathering" to the railroad-station.

a smoke, his mind not at all on the hobbled glass-eyed horse standing alongside him with legs wide apart and tipping the saddle near straight up with the hump that makes the boys ride. His eyes are on over and past the other broncs tied to the corral, and sees only away across the valley some fifteen miles. Timber out there draws his attention, and Bob wonders what the range is like at the perticular spot.

It's quite a ride for a green bronc, but not many days later you could see him winding up, following the cow trails to that timber and

*He's rolling a smoke, his mind not at all on the
hobbled glass-eyed horse standing alongside him.*

waterhole. He passes two "alkali licks" and rides on thru the aspens to the mesa — white sage, grama, and mountain bunch-grass everywhere, shad-scale on the flat and wild peas in the gullies higher up. There's a line of troughs at the waterhole and a few head of the Blue River cattle are watering there.

That night at the bunk house with the boys, Bob hazes the talk to drifting on about the springs and holdings of the company and by just listening, asking no questions, he finds that the little range he'd rode into that day was held by the outfit. He had a hunch they was holding it with no rights, and every one in the country had took it for granted it was theirs, never bothering about finding out.

A few months later the broncs are all "snapped out," a paycheck in Bob's chap pocket, and then pretty soon a log house is up and the smoke coming out of the fireplace thru the timber where the line of troughs and alkali licks was located. There was a howl from the company about somebody "jumping" one of their springs, but that don't do no good; saying they owned that range and proving it was two different things; and Bob stayed on, taking in horses to break at ten dollars a head and making a big bluff as to how much he's putting away, every so often.

One day Bob disappears and is gone for 'most six weeks; his place being out of the way of any riders nobody knows he'd went or returned, and if you'd asked him where he was keeping himself he'd said, "home." Anyway, in a few days after his return, he buys a hundred head of mixed stock, and some kinda wondered where he'd got the money to buy stock with, figgering even if he did make a good stake at breaking horses, it wouldn't buy one-fourth the cattle he'd paid cash for. He disappears once more without any one knowing of it and buys another little bunch of "dogies." Bob was getting bolder every time and the big outfits a thousand miles to the north and east was putting out a big

*He'd camp on the critters' tails till they'd use all
the energy they had to get out of the way.*

reward for a cattle thief they didn't have the description of. They'd
plumb forgot about Bob, knowing him to be south somewhere and
doing well, as they'd hear tell from the riders travelling thru.

He got so he could change a brand on a critter, and with a broken
blade and a little acid of his own preparation make that brand to suit
his taste, and in fifteen minutes appear like it'd been there since the
critter was born. You could feel the scaly ridge in the hide where the
iron was supposed to've been and even a little white hair here and
there; it would sure stand inspection from either the eye or the hand.

Bob knowing every hill, coulée, flat, creek, and river of that country,
was a great help to him. He'd rode every foot of it for a hundred miles
around. It was where he'd stood trial and lost his first herd. He knew
the folks there had forgot him and that's what he wanted. It left him a
clear trail out of suspicion; the train would take and leave him at some
neighboring town. At night getting a couple of ponies and hitting out
on "jerky," a little flour, and salt before sun-up, he'd skirt the foothills
and never would a rider get sight of him. Laying low by day and riding
by night he'd locate the herds with the best beef and camp within a few

miles of 'em so if they drifted he'd know their whereabouts and, soon as the weather permit, fog on behind 'em.

At the first sign of a strong wind, when tracks a few hours old are sifted over with fine sand, or before a first snow, you could see Bob getting his "piggin' string," unlimbering his ropes and testing his acid; his copper "running iron" was always with him too, hid between his saddle skirting and the lining; his 30-30 well cleaned and oiled and the old smoke wagon under his shirt and resting on his chap belt, he'd hit out on the best horse the country had for the herd he'd been watching, and go to cutting out a couple of carloads of the primest stuff he could get. Of course, by the time he'd get 'em to the shipping point, or market, they'd only be "feeders," but that brought a fair price.

The first night he'd camp on the critters' tails till they'd use all the energy they had to get out of the way. (In some cases it's been known of some cattle rustlers covering over forty miles single-handed with fifty some odd head in one night.) Bob had figgered a long time ahead the best way to take his cattle out, the hiding places for the day, and water to go with it, keeping shy of fences and ranches. At first sign of the rising sun his cattle was watered and taken up in some timbered canyon, the brands was worked over and a few hours later the herd was bedded down or feeding. The next night would be easier on both man and stock, and by the third, Bob felt pretty secure, but never would you find him with the cattle during the day. The cattle being too tired to stray away was left soon as watered and taken on feed. When they'd be hid, Bob would "back-trail" a mile or so, where he could watch his cattle and see any riders what might be following him. In case there was, he had plenty of time before they got to his cattle and had 'em identified to make a getaway; for even tho' an "iron" may be worked over into another, the rustler ain't going to take a chance. There may be a "marker" in that bunch that only the owner, or the riders familiar

A man with a critter down, his horse standing rope's length away, is a good thing to keep away from—unless you want to get your Stetson perforated.

with the cattle, would recognize; and that's enough to entitle the rustler to the stout limb and a piece of rope if he's caught.

When once out of the stolen cattle's territory and a hundred miles or so farther the cattle are loaded into the cars. (It's done at night if there is no inspection in that particular State.) Bob's going to stick to the finish 'cause he figgers his iron is going to stand the inspection of the stockyards inspector — he can show you where that brand is recorded and that they're his cattle unless you have reason to be real out of the ordinary inquisitive and want to know too much — but even then Bob has cattle bearing the same "iron" on his range to the south, and it may be mighty hard to prove they're not his. Furthermore, nobody knows or can prove he's been out of the country or whether he's shipped some of his own cattle or not — and no one had seen him around where the cattle was stolen.

It was getting real interesting, and he did not realize that he was taking a liking to stealing cattle and making clean getaways. The herd at his home camp was getting to be just a bluff, bearing half a dozen different recorded irons and earmarks. He was beginning to use them to fall back on in case investigation was made and traced back to his "hangout." He'd made three trips to Chicago and was just thinking of settling down to steal no more. He knew this good luck wouldn't last, and besides, picking up a few "orejanas" now and again around his own little range to the south might prove just as interesting; but the fever had him, with the result that he found out no matter how close you figger there's always something you'll overlook what'll give you away.

He started north for another raid, and thought he'd take his own saddle horses along this time, being that good horses are hard to pick up everywhere that way. There was one horse especially he hated to leave behind. It was a big blood bay, bald-faced and stocking-legged, and when he got to his destination to the north, and the stock car was being switched at the yards, one of the old timers recognized the horse and kept mum till Bob came to the stock car and led him out with his other horse. Ten minutes later Bob was feeding up at the "open-all-night" Chink restaurant and watching the front door. The sheriff comes thru the kitchen and when Bob turned around to his "ham and eggs" there was the muzzle of a "45" staring him in the eye.

He lost his second herd to the same lawyer and faced the same judge of two years before. He'd only stole one horse where he'd got away with over two hundred head of cattle in that country, but that one horse put the kibosh on him. There was no proof that he'd stole any cattle, but they suspicioned mighty strong; and they couldn't of handed him any more if they could of proved it. So figgering on killing two birds with one stone, the judge, not weeping any, throws the book at him, which means he gives Bob the limit.

If Bob would of had better luck the first time he tried to settle down in the country where he'd made such a bad "reputation" for himself, most likely by now he'd been just a prosperous cowman and kept his "long ropes" to home. I don't figger Bob was bad, just a little too anxious to have something, and later on getting too much satisfaction in outwitting others. Any stranger was welcome to Bob's camp to feed and rest up; a fresh horse, or anything else he had, was offered to them what needed it, and it wouldn't matter if your pack horse was loaded with gold nuggets they was just as safe in his bunk house, or maybe safer, than in the safety vault. His specialty was cattle and he got to love to use his skill in changing irons.

He was just like a big average of the Western outlaw and cattle rustler; his squareness in some things made up for his crookedness in others. There was no petty work done: saddle, spurs, and chaps was safe hanging over the corral, but there was one thing you had to keep away from in the rustler's doings; if you saw at a distance a smoke going up, one man with a critter down and a horse standing rope's length away, it's always a good idea to ride 'way around and keep out of sight, unless you want your Stetson perforated. If you was interested and had company, why that's another story.

I used to know a big cowman, who'd been fairly free with the running iron at one time and had done a heap of rustling. Many a head he'd lost in the same way afterward. Those he caught was dealt mighty hard with, and he'd expected the same if he'd ever made that fatal mistake, but he was lucky enough not to.

One day a "nester," what had drifted in from the other side of the plains and settled on one of his creek bottoms, finds himself and family run out of bacon or any sort of meat. He ups and shoots a fine yearling, takes the hindquarters, and leaves the rest in the hide for the coyotes, or to spoil. One of the riders runs onto the carcass, and lucky there was no proof of who done it, for that kind of doings sure gets a "rise" from a cowhand. A little over a month later, another yearling is butchered the same way, but the hide is gone and that's what makes it interesting.

It was found under the nester's little haystack. There's nobody home just then. The cowman finding this evidence had changed many an iron and earmark in his early start (as I've mentioned before) but never had he played hog and left any perfectly good beef to spoil on the range, and he figgers to teach that country spoiling *hombre* a few lessons in range etiquette. About sundown, he catches up with him and family just when the wagon and team reaches the musselshell bottoms where there's fine big cottonwoods. A carbine stares the nester in the face, and at the same time the cowman produces a piece of the hide bearing his iron and asks him to account for it. The man on the wagon is too scared to speak or move, so is the rest back of the seat.

A little "wild cat" loop settles neat and around that waster's neck, he's jerked off his seat and drug to the nearest cottonwood.

The cowman uncoils his rope, plays with it a while, and pretty soon a little "wild cat" loop settles neat and around that waster's neck, he's drug off his seat and close to one of them natural gallows, the rope is throwed over a limb, picked up again on the other side, and taking his "dallies" to the saddle horn, the cowman goes on till that farmer's big feet are just about a yard off the ground, a squawk is heard from the wagon and the whole family runs up to plead for the guilty party. They plead on for quite a spell but the cowman acts determined and hard of hearing. When it's gone far enough and that nester gets blue 'round the gills, the rope slacks up and he sprawls down to earth; the cowman is right atop of him and tells him he's got his family to thank for to see the sun come up again, "and if I ever catch you leaving meat of my stock to spoil on the range again I'll get you up so far you'll never come down, family or no family"; and he winds up with "*you can kill all of my beef you need*, but just what you need and no more, do you hear? And I want you to produce the hides of them beeves too, every one of 'em."

With that he rides off, and the nester's family is still trying to figger out what kind of folks are these "cow persons," anyway.

MIDNIGHT

RUNNING MUSTANGS had got to be an old game for me; it'd got so that instead of getting some pleasure and excitement out of seeing a wild bunch running smooth into our trap corrals I was finding myself wishing they'd break through the wings and get away.

Now that was no way for a mustang runner to feel but I figgered I just loved horses too well, and thinking it over I was kind of glad I felt that way. I seen that the money I'd get out of the sales of 'em didn't matter so much to me as the liberty I was helping take away from the slick wild studs, mares, and specially the little colts. Yessir, it was like getting blood money only worse.

I may be called chicken-hearted and all that but it's my feelings, and them same feelings come from *knowing* horses, and being with 'em steady enough so I near savvy horse language. My first light of day was split by the shape of a horse tied back of the wagon I was born in, and from then on horses was my main interest.

I'd got to be a good rider, and as I roamed the countries of the United States, Mexico, and Canada, riding for the big cow and horse outfits of them countries I rode many a different horse in as many a different place and fix. There was times when the horse under me meant my life, specially once in Old Mexico, that once I sure can't forget, and then again, crossing the deserts I did cross, most always in strange territory and no arrows pointing as to the whereabouts of moisture, I had to depend altogether on the good horse under me wether the next water was twelve or sometimes forty-eight hours away.

With all the rambling I done which was for no reason at all only to fill the craving of a cowpuncher what always wanted to drift over that blue ridge ahead, my life was pretty well with my horse and I found as I covered the country, met different folks, and seen many towns, that the pin-eared pony under me (which ever one it was) was a powerful friend, powerful in confidence and strength. There was no suspicious question asked by him, nor "when do we eat." His rambling qualities was all mine to use as I seen fit, and I never abused it which is why I can say that I never was set afoot. Sometimes I had horses that was sort of fidgety and was told they'd leave me first chance they got wether they was hobbled or not but somehow I never was left, not even when the feed was scattered and no water for 'em to drink, and I've had a few ponies on such long cross country trails that stayed close to camp with nothing on 'em that'd hinder 'em from hitting out if they wanted to.

A horse got to mean a heap more to me than just an animal to carry me around, he got to be my friend, I went fifty-fifty with him, and even though some showed me fight and I treated 'em a little rough there'd come a time when we'd have an understanding and we'd agree that we was both pretty good fellers after all.

And now that things are explained some, it all may be understood why running mustangs, catching 'em, and selling 'em to any *hombre* that wanted 'em kind of got under my skin and where I live. I didn't see why I should help catch and make slaves out of them wild ones that was so free. Any and all of 'em was my friends — they was horseflesh.

The boys wasn't at all pleased when I told 'em I'd decided to leave and wanted to know why, but I kept my sentiments to myself and remarked that I'd like to go riding for a cow outfit for a change. That seemed to satisfy 'em some and when they see I was bound to go they didn't argue. We started to divvy up the amount of ponies caught so as I'd get my share, and figgered fourteen head was coming to me. There was two days' catch already in the round corral of the trap and from that little bunch we picked out them I was to get.

There was a black stud in that bunch that I couldn't help but notice — I'd kept track of him ever since he was spotted the day before. He

It was early the next morning when the black and the other ten horses I still had left was started away from the trap.

was young and all horse, and acted like he had his full share of brains. I wondered some how he come to get caught, and then again I had to size up the trap noticing how easy a horse, even a human, could be fooled, so well we'd built it.

The big main corral took in over an acre of ground; the fine, strong woven wire fastened on the junipers and piñons wasn't at all to be seen, specially by horses going at full speed, and the strength and height of that fence would of held a herd of stampeding buffalo.

Knowing that trap as I did, it was no wonder after all that black horse *was* caught. Nothing against his thinking ability, I thought, and as I watches him moving around wild-eyed seeming like to take a last long look at the steep hills he knowed so well I finds myself saying, "Little horse, I'm dog-gone sorry I helped catch you."

Right then I wanted that black horse, and I was sure going to get him if I could. I maneuvers around a lot and finally decides to offer the boys any three of the wild ones that'd been turned over to me as my share in trade for the black. It took a lot of persuading, 'cause that black stud ranked way above the average, but the boys seeing that I wanted him so bad and me offering one more horse for him which made four, thought best to let me have him.

It was early the next morning when the black and the other ten horses I still had left was started away from the trap. Three of the boys was helping me keep 'em together, and as the wild ones all had to have one front foot tied up, it hindered 'em considerable to go faster than a walk, but that's what we wanted. We traveled slow and steady. The ponies tried to get away often, but always there was a rider keeping up with 'em on easy lope, and they finally seen where they had to give in and travel along the way *we* wanted 'em.

Fifteen miles or so away from the trap and going over a low summit, we get sight of small high-fenced pasture, and to one side was the corrals. There was a cabin against the aspens and as I takes in the layout I recognizes it to be one of the Three T's Cattle Company's cow camps.

I decided we'd gone far enough with them horses for one day, so we corralled 'em there, and the boys went back after me telling 'em the ponies was herd-broke enough so I could handle 'em the next day by my lonesome, but they was some dubious about one man being able to do all that, even *if* the wild ones was tired, one foot tied up, and not aching to run.

The cabin was deserted, and I was glad of it, for I wasn't wanting company right then, I wanted to think. I went to sleep thinking and dreamt I was catching wild horses by the hundreds, and selling 'em to big slough-footed "hawnyawks" what started beating 'em over the heads with clubs. I caught one big white stud and he just followed me in the trap. It all struck me as too easy to catch 'em, and the little money I was getting for 'em turned out to be a scab on my feelings compared to the price freedom was worth to them ponies.

I woke up early next morning and the memory of that dream was still with me, and when I pulled on my boots, built a fire and put on the coffee, I had visions of that black horse in the corral looking through a collar and pulling a plow in Alabama or some other such country.

I went outside, and while waiting for the coffee to come to a boil I struts out to the corral to take a look at the ponies. They're all bunched up, heads down, and ganted up, but soon as they see me they start milling, all heads up and a-snorting. I looks through the corral bars at 'em and watches 'em.

The black stud is closest to me and kinda protecting the mares and younger stock, there's a look in his eye that kinda reminds me of a man waiting for a sentence from the judge, only the spirit is still there and mighty challenging the same as to say, "What did I do?"

A little two-year-old filly slides up alongside of him and stares at me. I can see fear in her eyes and a kinda innocent wondering as to what this was all about, this being run into a trap, roped, a foot tied up, and then drove into another place with *bars* around.

All is quiet for a spell in the corral, a meadow lark is tuning up on a fence post close by, and with the light morning breeze coming through the junipers and piñons there's a feeling for everything that lives to just sun itself, listen, and breathe in.

Then it came to me how one time I'd got so homesick for just what I was experiencing right then, the country, and everything that was in it — I'd been East to a big town and got stranded there — that I'd given my right arm just so I got back.

When I come to and looked back in the corral, the black horse was looking way over the bars to the top of a big ridge. Out there was a small bunch of mustangs enjoying their freedom for all they was worth. So far there was no chance of a collar for them, and wether it was imagination or plain facts that I could see in that black stud's face, I sure made it out that he understood all that he was seeing was *past*, the shady junipers, the mountain streams, green grass and white sage was all to be left behind, even his little bunch of mares was going to be separated from him and took to goodness knows where.

Yessir! Thinking it all over that way sure made it hard to take. I didn't want to get sentimental, but dag-gone it I couldn't help but realize that I was the judge sentencing 'em to confinement and hard labor just for the few lousy dollars they'd bring.

Sure enough, *I* was the judge and could do as I blamed pleased. It struck me queer that it didn't come to me sooner.

I wasn't hesitating none as I picked up my rope and opened the gate into the corral, I worked fast as I caught each wild one, throwed him and took off the rope that was fastened from the tail to the front foot.

They was all foot-loose excepting the black. I hadn't passed judgment on him as yet, but I knowed he wasn't going to be shipped to no cotton fields, and the worst that could come his way would be to break him for my own saddle horse.

I opened the corral gate and lets the others out, watches 'em a spell then turns to watch the black. "Little horse," I says to him, "your good looks and build are against you —"

But it was sure hard to let the others go and keep him in that way, it didn't seem square and the little horse was sure worrying about his bunch leaving him all by his lonesome, in a big corral with a human, and then I thinks of all the saddle horses I already had, of all the others I could get that's been raised under fence and never knowed wild freedom.

Then my rope sings out once more, in no time his front foot is loose, the gate is open, and nothing in front of him but the high ridges of the country he knowed so well.

For a second I feel like kicking myself for letting such a horse go. He left me and the corral seemed like without touching the earth, floating out a ways then turned and stood on his tiptoes, shook his head at me, let out a long whistle the same as to say "this is sure a surprise" and away he went, right on the trail his mares had took.

My heart went up my throat for a minute, I'd never seen a prettier picture to look at than that horse when he ambled away. The sight of him didn't seem to fit in with a saddle on his back, and a heap less with a collar around his neck and following furrows instead of the mountain trails he was to run on once more.

I felt some relieved and thankful as I started back for the cabin. The coffee had boiled over while I was at the corral, and put the fire out, but I finds myself whistling and plum contented with everything in general as I gathers kindling and starts the fire once again.

It was a few days later when I rides in on one of the Three T's round-up wagons, gets a job, a good string of company ponies, and goes to work. The wagon was on a big circle and making a new camp every day towards the mustang territory.

I was trying to get used to riding for a cow outfit once more, and it was hard. I'd find myself hankering to run mustangs but the I'd see them wild ponies crowded into stock cars and my hankering would die down sudden.

One day a couple of the boys rode up to the *parada* (main herd) from circle with a very few head of stock and it set me to wondering how come their horses could be so tired in that half-a-day's ride, but I didn't have to wonder long, for soon as they got near me one of 'em says, "We seen him!"

"Seen who?" I asks.

"Why, that black stud Midnight. Ain't you ever heard of him?"

"I don't know," I says, but it wasn't just a few minutes till I did know.

From all I was told right then it seemed like that Midnight horse was sure a wonder. It was rumored he was at least a half standard, but nobody was worried about that, the main thing was that he could sure run and what's more, keep it up.

"We spotted him early this morning," says one of the boys, "and soon as we did we naturally forgot all about cows. We took turns relaying on him. We had fast horses too, but we'd just as well tried to relay after a runaway locomotive."

I learned he had been caught once and broke to ride, but his mammy was a mustang, he'd been born and raised on the high pinnacles of the wild horse country, and one day when his owner thought it was safe to turn him out in a small pasture for a chance at green grass the horse just up and disappeared. The fences he had to cross to the open country never seemed to hinder him, and even though he was some three hundred miles from his home range, it was but a week or so later when some rider spotted him there again.

A two hundred dollar reward was offered for anyone that caught him. Many a good horse was tired out by different riders trying to get near him, traps was built, but Midnight had been caught once, and the supposed-to-be-wise fox was dumb compared to that horse.

I was getting right curious about then, and finally I asks for a full description of that flying hunk of horseflesh.

I'm holding my breath some as I'm told that his weight is around eleven hundred, pure black, and perfect built, and a small brand on his neck right under his mane, a "C."

Yep! that was him, none other than that black horse I turned loose.

I started wondering how *we* caught him so easy, but a vision of that trap came to me again. It wasn't at all like the traps other mustangers of that country ever built, and that's what got Midnight. We had him thinking he was getting away from us easy, when at the same time he was running right inside the strong, invisible, net fence.

A picture of him came to my mind as he looked when I turned him loose that day now a couple of weeks past, and then I thought of the two hundred that was offered to anybody who'd run him in. That was a lot of money for a mustang, but somehow it didn't seem to be much after all, not comparing with Midnight.

It was late in the fall when I seen the black stud again. Him and his little bunch was sunning themselves on the side of a high ridge. A sarvis-berry bush was between me and them, and tying my horse to a juniper, I sneaks up towards 'em, making sure to keep out of sight. I figgered I'd be about two hundred yards from the bunch once I got near the berry bush, but when I got there and straightened up to take a peek through the branches, the wild bunch had plum evaporated off the earth. I could see for a mile around me but all I could tell of the whereabouts of Midnight and his mares was a light dust away around the point of the ridge.

"Pretty wise horse," I thinks, but somehow I felt relieved a lot to know he was going to make himself mighty hard to catch.

The winter that came was a tough one, the snow was deep and grass was hard to get. I was still riding for the Three T outfit and was kept mighty busy bringing whatever stock I'd find what needed feed, and as I was riding the country for such and making trails out for snow-bound cattle I had a good chance to watch how the wild horses was making it.

They wasn't making it very good, and as the already long winter seemed to never want to break I noticed that the bunches was getting smaller, many of the old mares layed down never to get up, and the coyotes was getting fat.

Midnight and his bunch was nowheres to be seen, and I got kind of worried that some *hombre* wanting that two hundred dollars right bad had started out after him with grain fed horses, and the black horse being kinda weaker on account of the grass being hard to get at might've let a rope sneak upon him and draw up around his neck.

I knowed of quite a few riders that calculated to get him that winter, and I knowed that if he wasn't already caught, he'd sure been fogged a good many times.

I often wished that I'd hung on to him while I had him, and give him as much freedom as I could, just so nobody pestered him. I'd forgot that the horse already belonged to somebody else and I'd have to give him up anyway, but that pony had got under my skin pretty deep. I just wanted to do a good turn to horseflesh in general by leaving him and all the other wild ones as they was.

Winter finally broke up and spring with warm weather had come, when as I'm riding along one day tailing up weak stock, I finds that all my worries about the black stud getting caught was for nothing.

I was in the bottom of a boggy wash helping a bellering critter up on her feet. As luck would have it my horse was hid, and as for me, only my head was sticking up above the bank, when I happened to notice the little wild bunch filing in towards me from over a low ridge. I recognized Midnight's mares by their color and markings, but I couldn't make out that shaggy, faded, long-haired horse trailing in along behind quite a ways. He was kind of a dirty brown.

I stood there in the mud up above my ankles and plum forgot the wild-eyed cow that was so much in need of a boost to dry ground, all my interest was for spotting Midnight, and my heart went up my throat as I noticed the faded brown horse. That couldn't be Midnight, I thought, Midnight must of got caught some way and this shadow of a horse just naturally appropriated the bunch.

But as I keeps on watching 'em trail in and getting closer there's points about that shaggy pony in the rear that strikes me familiar. He looks barely able to pack his own weight, and his weight wasn't much right then for I could see his ribs mighty plain even through the long winter hair. All the other ponies had started to shed off some and was halfways slick, but not him.

The bunch was only a couple of ropes' length away from me as they trailed in the boggy wash to get a drink of the snow water, and I had to hug the bank to keep out of sight and stick my head in a sagebrush so as I could see without them seeing me.

Then I recognized Midnight. That poor son of a gun was sure well disguised with whatever ailed him, and when I got a good look at that head of his I thought sure a rattler had bit him. His jaws and throat was all swelled up plum to his ears, but as I studies him I seen it wasn't a snake's doings. It was distemper at its worst, and the end was as sure as if he'd been dead unless I could catch him and take care of him.

I'm out on my best horse the next morning, and making sure the corral gate was wide open and the wings to it in good shape I headed for the quickest way of locating Midnight. I had no trouble there, and run onto him and his bunch when only a couple of hours away from camp.

I thought he was weak enough so I could ride right in on him and rope him on the spot, but I was fooled mighty bad. He left me like I was standing still, and tail up he headed for the roughest country he could find, me right after him.

My horse was grain-fed, steady, strong, and in fine shape to run, but as the running kept up over washouts, mountains, and steep ridges for the big part of that day, I seen where there was less hope of ever getting within roping distance of the black.

Dag-gone that horse anyway. I was finding myself cussing and admiring him at the same time. I was afraid he'd run himself to death rather than let any rider get near him, and I thought some of letting him go, only I knowed the distemper would kill him sure, and I wanted to save him.

I made a big circle and covered a lot of territory, my horse was getting mighty tired, and as I pushed on the trail of Midnight and got to within a few miles of my camp, I branched off and let him go. I was going to get me a fresh horse.

I was on his trail again by sundown, and an hour or so later a big moon came up to help me keep track of the dust Midnight was making. That big moon was near halfways up the sky when I begins to see signs of the black horse weakening. I feels mighty sorry for the poor devil right then, and as I uncoils my rope and gets ready to dab it on him I says to him, "Midnight, old horse I'm only trying to help you."

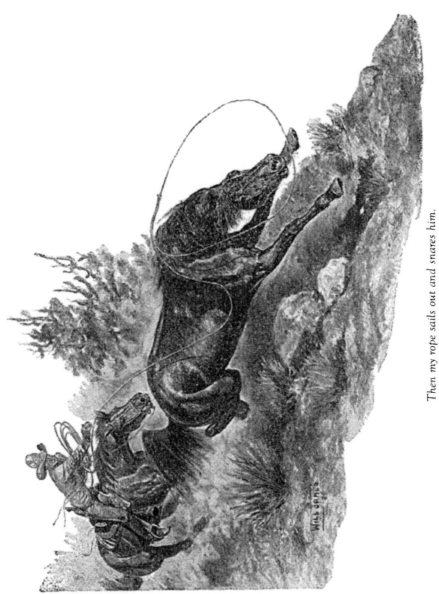

Then my rope sails out and snares him.

Then my rope sails out and snares him. He didn't fight as I drawed up my slack and stopped him, instead his head hung down near the ground and if I ever seen a picture marking the end of the trail, there was one.

It was daybreak as we finally reached the corral and sheds of my camp. In a short while I'd lanced and doctored up his throat, good as any vet' could of done, made him swallow a good stiff dose of medicine I had on hand for that purpose in case any of my ponies ever got layed up that way, and seeing he had plenty to eat and drink in case he'd want it I started towards the cabin to cook me a bait. That done and consumed I caught me another fresh horse and rode out for that day's work.

I'd been doctoring up on Midnight for a week without sign he ever would recuperate. He was the same as the day I brought him in and I was getting scared that he never could come out of it. Every night and morning as I'd go to give him his medicine I'd stand there and watch him for a spell. He'd got used to that and being that my visits that way meant some relief to his suffering he got to looking for me, and would nicker kinda soft as he'd get sight of me.

If I could only get him to eat the grain I'd bring there'd be a chance but he didn't seem to know what grain was, and from that I got the idea he hadn't been treated any too well that first time he was caught. I'd kept sprinkling some of that grain in the hay so as he'd get used to the taste and begin looking for it, but he wasn't eating much hay and it took quite a long time before I begin noticing that the grain I'd put in the box had been touched. From then on, he started eating it and gradually got so he'd clean up all I'd give him.

There was the beginning of a big change in the little horse after that. The powders I'd mix in the grain started to working on him, the swelling on his neck went down, his eyes showed brighter, and he begin to shed the long faded winter hair. After that it was easy, a couple of weeks more care and he was strong as ever again, all he needed was the green grass that was all over hills by then. It was time for me to turn him loose — and that's what I did.

It was near sundown when I led him out from under the shed, through the corral where I'd let him out of once before near a year past, and on out to where he'd be free to go. I took the hackamore off his head — nothing was holding him — but this time he just stood there, his head was high and his eyes was taking in the big country around him.

He spoke plainer than a human when, after taking long appreciating breaths of the cool spring air, he sniffed at my shoulder and looked up the hills again. He wasn't wondering or caring if I understood him so long as he understood me, and that he did — he knowed I was with him for all the freedom these valleys and mountains could give him.

It was a couple of months later when one of the cowboys rode up to my camp on his way to the home ranch, stopped with me a night, and before he left the next morning dropped me some information that caused me to do a heap of thinking.

It appeared like some outfit had moved in on this range and was going to clean it out of all the wild horses that was on it. They had permits and contracts to do that and seemed like the capital to go through with it. Most of 'em was foreign *hombres* that craved for other excitements than just jazz, and getting tired of spending their old man's money all in one place had framed it up to come West and do all that *for a change.*

They was bringing along some fast thoroughbreds, and I couldn't help but wonder how long them poor spindle-legged ponies would last in these rocks and shale. They'd be as helpless as the *hombres* riding 'em. If it'd been only them high-bloods I'd just laughed and felt mighty safe for the wild ones, but no such luck, they was paying top wages and hiring the best mustang runners in the country.

As I heard it from that cowboy it was sure some expensive layout, there was big wagon loads of fancy grub and fancier drinks, air mattresses and pillows, tents and folding bath tubs and tables, perfume and chewing gum, etc., etc. — Yep! they was going to *rough it.*

"But I'm thinking," says the cowboy as he left, "that with the wild horse hunters they hired, that black stud Midnight is going to find hisself in a trap once more, and somehow I'd kinda hate to see them catch that horse."

For a few weeks that outfit was busy building traps. I seen they was going at it big as I rode through one of 'em one day, and as I talked to one of the pilgrims who I'd found busy picking woodticks out of his brand new angora chaps, I also seen they had big visions of cleaning this country of the mustangs along with making a potful of money.

"And it's the greatest sport I know of," says that *hombre* as he reaches for another woodtick next to his ear.

"Yeh," I says to myself as I rides away, "I'm not wishing him harm, but I hope he breaks his neck at it."

There was in the neighborhood of a thousand head of mustangs in that country, and it wasn't long when the hills and white sage flats was being tore by running hoofs, a steady haze of fine dust was floating in the air and could be seen for miles around, and at night I could see signal fires. Some greenhorn had got lost or set afoot.

The hired mustang runners was having a hard time of it, one told me one day they'd of caught twice as many if them pilgrims wasn't around. "Two of the boys was bringing in a nice bunch yesterday," he was saying. "They had 'em to within a few yards of the gate and as good as caught, when up from behind a rock jumps a pilgrim and hollers, 'That's the good boys, step on 'em!' Well, the ponies turned quicker than a flash and *they* done all the stepping, a good thirty head got away."

I was glad to hear that in a way, but I was careful not to show it, I was thinking that after all Midnight and his little bunch had a chance at their freedom, and I finds myself whistling a pretty lively tune as I rode on.

I hadn't seen Midnight only once since I turned him loose that last time, and I had a hunch that he'd changed his range on account of these mustangers keeping him on the dodge, but then again this wasn't the only outfit that was out for the wild ones. The whole country for a hundred miles around was full of riders out for the fuzztails (mustangs), and I couldn't figger out where that horse and his little bunch could go where they'd be safe.

But nobody had seen the black stud, and everybody was wanting him. I was asked often if I'd seen any sign of him, and as I'd go on a-riding the country keeping tab on the company's cattle that was on the same range as the wild ones, I was watching steady for him, but he couldn't be seen anywheres.

Come a time when it was easy to notice that the mustangs was fast disappearing. I could ride for a week at a stretch without seeing more than a few head where some months before I could of counted hundreds. I'd run acrost little colts, too young to keep up and left behind. Their mammies had stayed with 'em long as they could but as the riders would gain on 'em fast, fear would get the best of 'em, and the poor little devils would be left behind to shift for themselves before they was able to and keep a-nickering and a-circling for the mammy that never came back. She'd be in the trap.

Carloads of wild ones was being shipped every month to all points of the U. S. wherever there was a market for 'em. They was sold to farmers and drug to the farm back of a wagon, the trip in the stock cars, not mentioning their experiences in the trap, took most of the heart out of 'em, and there was no fight much as the collar was slipped around their necks and hooked up alongside the gentle farm horse — a big change from the tall peaks, mountain streams near hid with quaking asp, bunch grass, and white sage.

It was late fall and the air was getting mighty crimpy when the mustang running outfits started pulling up their tent pins and moving out, the country looked mighty silent and deserted and all the black dots that could be seen at a distance wasn't mustangs no more, it was mighty safe to say that them black dots was cattle. . . .

I rides up to the pilgrim camp one day just as one of 'em is putting away his cold-cream and snake-bite outfit, and inquires how they all enjoyed the country and mustang trapping.

"Oh, the country is great, and mustang trapping is a ripping sport," I'm told, "but we lost a few thousand dollars on the deal which don't make it so good. Besides our blooded horses are ruined.

"And by the way," goes on that same *hombre*, "have you seen that black stallion they call Midnight anywheres? I see by the San Jacinto *News* that the reward on the horse is withdrawn, also the ownership, so he is free to anyone who catches him I understand."

"Yes," I says, tickled to death at the news, "but there's a catch to it and that's *catching him*."

"Free to anyone who catches him," stayed in my mind for a good many days, but where could that son-of-a-gun be? I tried to think of all the hiding spots there was, I knowed 'em all well I thought, but I also knowed that all them hiding spots had been rode into and the mustangs there had been caught. I was getting mighty worried that Midnight and his little bunch might by now be somewheres where the fences are thick and the fields are small, a couple of thousand miles away.

It's early one morning when I notices one of my saddle horses had got through the pasture fence and left. Soon I was on his trail to bring him back, and that trail led through the aspens back of my cabin and on up to a big granite ledge where it was lost on the rocky ground. Figgering on making a short cut to where I can spot that pony, I leaves my horse tied to a buckbrush and climbs over the granite ledge. When I gets up there, there's another ledge, and then another one, and by the time I gets to the top of all of 'em I'm pretty high.

I was some surprised to find a spring up there, fine clear water that run only a short ways and sunk in the ground again, but what surprised me most was the horse tracks around it. How could a horse ever get up here, I thought, but they was here sure enough. I noticed the feed was awful short and scarce and I wondered if it was because them horses couldn't get down as easy as they got up.

Investigating around and looking over big granite bowlders I can make out horses' backs a-shining in the sun. They're feeding in their small territory, and I can tell they're feeling pretty safe, but as I moves around, a head comes up, ears pointed my way, and wild eyes a staring at me.

In that second I recognized the black stud Midnight.

There's a loud snort and whistle, and like a bunch of quail Midnight and his bunch left that spot for higher ground and where they could see all around 'em, but a man afoot was something new and not so much to run away from, and finally they stood off at a good distance and watched me.

The surprise of finding Midnight, and so close to my camp, left me able to do nothing but set where I was and do my share of watching. In a little while I started talking to him and I could see he sure remembered and recognized me. His wild look disappeared and he made a half circle as if to come my way. I wished he'd come closer, but I hadn't broke him to that. I hadn't broke him to anything, I'd only tried to give him to understand that he was safe of that freedom as long as he lived.

I knowed he understood ever since that second time I turned him loose. The proof of that was him picking his hiding place as close to my camp as he could get while the mustang runners was in the country. I know he'd been there all the last few months, and I know there was many a time when he looked down on my cabin, which was only a half a mile or so away, while I was wondering where he could be.

I seen him looking down at me that way the next morning. He was hard to see amongst the scrub mahogany, but it's a wonder I thought, why it never come to me to look up there.

Somehow or other, Midnight and his bunch got down off their hiding place. The mustang runners had all left the county, and as I rode up on the small bunch of remaining wild ones one day and watched 'em lope away toward the flat, I knowed they was safe.

I knowed they'd come back if they ever got crowded, and to that hiding place which nobody else knowed of but us 'uns.

First Money

ACCORDING TO THE POSTER that Gill Bradson had jerked off a telephone pole, the Rodeo of the coming Fourth of July was going to beat any Rodeo that was ever held there previous.

It was announced on the poster that Jim Colter from across the state line had contracted to furnish the association with his string of thirty man-eating outlaws kept in shape and picked for their fighting and bucking qualities. It was claimed that three of them ponies had been tried by the best riders of the West and so far had never been rode past the judges. They was professional buckers.

Cowboys from that part of the country was to follow that ornery string of buckers to Romal and try 'em again during the events. A few trick ropers, trick riders, chariot teams and bucking bulls was also to be furnished by that same Jim Colter.

"Looks like to me," remarks one of the boys breaking in on the middle of the reading, "that we don't stand no show there with that crowd. They'll have two judges to our one and them boys know by heart just how any of them buckers are going to perform, they'll know how far they can scratch on this or that horse and still be safe of the saddle being under 'em, where with us not knowing any of them ponies, we're apt to keep a wondering what the horse is going to do next which'll hinder us some to reaching the finals, and I'd bet not one of us would even get third money on bronc riding."

Five thousand dollars was the advertised cash prizes, that was to be divided up in daily money on ten events and the final three prizes for each of them ten events of the last day. The first prize for bronc riding was five hundred dollars, and that we figgered was sure worth riding for.

There'd been two annual Rodeos already pulled off in Romal and this was the third. Me and Tom Sands who I thought was the best rider in the world was present on the first and second year; we entered for everything that carried big enough purse and after each spending thirty dollars on entrance fees all we got back out of it was mount money, five dollars for every horse or critter we forked. Of course that let us break a little more than even, but mount money ain't what we was after, we wanted to ride off with first prize.

We was willing to ride anything in the world for that first prize, but somehow the ponies we drawed didn't buck hard enough and we had no chance to show the judges *how* we could ride. As it was we didn't even make the semi finals.

In bulldogging they handed me a wampus of a steer, short heavy neck and short horns and was taller by a hand than the horse I rode up on him with, me being a light weight I made a nice decoration for that steer till I finally got the right dig and my boot heels felt the earth again. According to the rules you had to stop your steer and throw him from a standstill, but so much meat all in one hunk wasn't easy for me to handle and when my little weight happened to get that packing house out of balance I couldn't help but take advantage of it. I hoolyhanned him on the jump and busted him right there.

A howl was heard, and a rider who so far had made the best time and was seeing the money slip away from him was doing a heap of objecting. The judges rode up and I was told that if I wanted to compete I'd have to let the steer on his feet again and throw him according to rules.

But me being out of wind as it was, I knowed I could never throw that steer if I had to stop him first, I also knowed that there wasn't any more than one man in that arena who could do it, not with *that* steer, but I kept that to myself and grins to the cheering crowd as I lets the steer go.

Yessir, with all our hard work me and Tom didn't get as much as a peek at prize money them two years. We felt that we was nowheres given a fair chance, and I for myself had a hunch that the outfit what contracted to put on the show wasn't taking chances of giving first money to any outsiders like Tom or myself, so concluded we was handed stock we wouldn't get anywheres with.

But this year's Rodeo might be different, and Tom and me figgered on trying 'er once more. We felt sure we could ride, rope, and bulldog along with any of the professional contestants what came with Jim Colter and his stock, and if the judges was halfways square, and we got the average of bucking horses we'd make the rest of the boys work to keep up with us.

The Rodeo was a month off, and that give us plenty of time to add on a little more practising even though we was getting plenty of it every day, all but bulldogging, and being that don't come in on range work we had to practise up on that when the boss wasn't round.

Tom and me was on day herd in the morning of every third day, and when we'd see the cow foreman line out on circle with the rest of the riders we'd get to work. Another rider that was with us would be our lookout and watch that the foreman didn't ride in on us, as the boss had often made it plain, unnecessary roping or handling of stock wasn't allowed on the range, and any rider caught at it would most always get paid off on the spot.

But we had to have *some* practise, and some of them ornery bunch-quitting critters more than called us on to do our damnedest, which kinda cleared our conscience even if we did roll 'em over. We'd straddle 'em as they'd get up and they'd give us a fair shaking, some of the orneriest we'd bulldog. After we'd let 'em go they was contented to graze on and stay in the middle of the herd. Tom and me figgered it done 'em a heap of good but we was careful not to hint to the boss that we thought so.

A couple of weeks of that and we notice some improvement, the critters go down easier, and one day when we borrowed a watch to kinda time ourselves we wasn't surprised to see that there was only one minute or so between us and record time. We figgered that we'd soon be up with it and maybeso break the record that was made by a Texas cowhand, none had ever got within reach of it so far, and we was sure that none of the crowd following Jim Colter could even hold a candle to it.

And far as bronc riding was concerned, both Tom and me was getting plenty of that, I was kept mighty busy on the rough string that I'd hired out to ride, and Tom was also kept interested in just taking the raw edge off the colts he was handling and scratch out the orneriness that was bound to crop out on some of 'em.

In my string, which as I said before was rough, there was one perticular gelding I was finding hard to set at times. He was a big black horse by the name of "Angel Face," and looking at him you'd swear he belonged to some place where it was hot and the angels had horns. He'd throwed many a rider and he got me too, once, but I finally got on to the hang of his style and as it was now I could scratch him some at his best, and even look over my shoulder while I'd tickle his ear with my spur.

I saddles him up special one morning to see how wild a ride I could put up on that horse. Tom is acting as judge, and from the time I reaches down and tears off the blind I know that according to *that* judge's expression I'd won the championship of the world as a bronc rider.

"Bill, old boy," he says soon as he can get to speak, "if you or me could only draw a horse like that for the finals at the Rodeo, the purse would be sure to come our way even if the judges *was* against outsiders like you and me."

So we're feeling a heap of confidence when as the wagon camps within some twenty miles of Romal we finally talks the foreman to letting us go a couple of days ahead. We wanted to see who all had come to enter, what was the rules, and most who the judges was going to be or where from.

We get some information soon as we ride into the livery stable where we put our horses, and we was glad to learn that one of the judges was none other than Pete Worth. He savvied good riding when he seen it cause he'd been there hisself aplenty and we knowed we'd sure get a square deal from him. Another judge was with the Colter outfit and there to argue over the points with Pete, who was for the local riders of the country, such as me and Tom. The third judge, and the one what give the decision on whichever side he agreed with, was from nobody knowed where, and there we figgered was the snake in the grass.

We was willing to bet everything down to our boots that Jim Colter sure knowed which riders that third judge would be most inclined to decide in favor of, but hoping for the best, we was going to take a chance of getting a fair deal, and we signed in our names on bronc riding, bull riding, bulldogging and steer roping.

There was still two days to kill before the opening day, and Tom and me was making the rounds seeing who all had come in for the events, and if there was any present that we knowed and was afraid of in beating us to the purse. So far we didn't see any that worried us excepting maybe one, he was no better rider than either me or Tom but he was more of a favorite and a drawcard to the crowd, and as he was advertised a lot along with them buckers that was claimed couldn't be rode, it kind of give him a head start on us.

We was making use of our spare time sticking round on the Rodeo grounds and getting a peek at the bucking stock and busting ourselves getting at anything that was led in with a claim it could buck. We was figgering to be in trim when we're called on to ride and show our ability on the side-winding ponies, and Tom even borrowed a work horse off a team that was hooked on the water wagon used in sprinkling the track. That horse had the reputation of never being rode over one jump, so Tom took the harness off of him, put his saddle in the place of it and without anything on that pony's head climbed on. That horse lost his reputation right there and then, and we rode on looking for more of them what couldn't be rode.

But we found some hard ones, and them was what we wanted — so, when the day come for all riders to compete we was ready to take on anything that was led out.

Everything started out fine that first day. Tom was up to ride that afternoon and from all accounts the horse he drawed was a mighty good bucker, but I had my doubts, as it was a big roan mare called "Ragtime," and mares as a rule can't be depended on to do the right thing, but on hearing all her good points I was glad to hope for the best.

She bellered like a steer when she found herself cornered in the saddling shute and tried to climb over the high wall. I had more hopes for her then than ever and I could see by the smile Tom was packing that he sure expected to have something to ride that was worth riding.

I saddles 'er up while Tom is putting on his chaps. A rider is next to me and helping by slipping the bucking strap round her. "Not so tight on that strap," I hollers at him as I notices him pulling on it. "We want that mare to buck, not kick," and pushing him away I fixes it myself. I wasn't taking any chances on any of Colter's outfit spoiling things.

"Say, cowboy," one of the rail birds remarks to Tom, "better lean on that mare when you go out, she's a kicking bucker."

And when Tom climbs over to get in the saddle I whispers in his ear and I says, "You just do the opposite, Tom."

"I'm riding this horse," Tom hollers as he gives me the wink and looks back.

"Let 'er go," and open flies the gate. A roan streak of horseflesh comes out and in a running buck lands right amongst the judges and there she breaks in two, the earth shakes and the judges scatter like a bunch of quail.

That was one of the hardest jumps I'd ever seen a horse do, one that'd throw most any rider, but Tom was still there and when the dust cleared he was still a raking her and looking at any old place but at the horse under him. I could see though that first jump jarred the mare worse than it did Tom for after that she was just crowhopping.

I was sorry that them hard jumps like the first didn't last, for as it was I was afraid Tom wouldn't make the semi finals, not on *that* horse. Tom is working hard and riding reckless and the mare thinking she sees a chance to put in some crooked work makes another one of them hard jumps after which she acts like she's going to fall over backwards.

Tom is still fanning her and I noticed that his hand and hat went down to the saddle as if to push himself away in case the mare did fall back but that wasn't it, I know. The gun was fired and the judges rode away to watch another contestant that was ready to come out, and right then that daggone mare started to do some pretty work just when it didn't count. That's a mare for you, you can't tell nothing about 'em.

But Tom was sure taking it out on 'er, and right up to the minute the pick-up men came and caught 'er that cowboy was busy making that mare think she couldn't buck a saddle blanket off.

It ain't but a short while after when I'm called on to do some bulldogging, and as luck would have it my steer happened to fall as I quit my horse and landed on him. I had to let him up again so I could throw him according to the rules, but that first fall took enough seconds so as to put me back out of the money for the record of that day.

When Tom was up to get his steer I didn't want to think how luck was going to treat him, I was trying to interest myself by looking across the track into the grandstand. Something white and cool looking as the foam on a beer mug caught my eye, it was the fluffy dress of a girl setting up there and looking mighty comfortable and interested. Nothing of what went on was worrying her and if the way she clapped her hands meant anything she sure was enjoying all she seen. I was beginning to think that there was the best place to take in a Rodeo after all. Them folks up there wasn't taking no chances of getting skinned up or mashed flat, like some of the boys do trying to get first money and finally getting nothing but pains.

A streak of something went by and I figgered it to be Tom after his steer, but I wasn't interested there as much as I was in watching the girl in the white dress, she'd tell me by her actions all I wanted to know anyway, and somehow she seemed easier to look at.

A cloud of dust came between me and where I'd been staring, Tom and his steer had butted in. About that time the crowd and everybody is cheering and a whooping and I gets a glimpse of a steer going down.

Tom made her think she couldn't buck a saddle blanket off.

My interest came to earth sudden, and in a second I'd jumped the railing between the arena and the track and I was right there alongside of Tom, I'd also got a peek at the stop watch one of the judges was holding and my spirits came right up with the sight of it.

Tom's shirt had been tore off him and as the steer was let up part of it still hung on a horn. "Good work, Tom," I says to the old boy as I escorts him out of sight and where there's possibilities of getting something that'd do as a shirt for the time being, "I knowed that soon as I kept from watching you'd bring home the bacon."

At the Rodeo headquarters that night we learn that Tom had won the first daily prize for bulldogging — fifty dollars. The sound of that done us a heap more good than the money, but sometime later our spirits are dampened down considerable when it was announced that Tom was disqualified on Ragtime.

Tom was supposed to know why, and figgering there was no use arguing we stepped out, but we wasn't going to let it go at that — we knowed that Colter's pet judges had took advantage of that time when Tom touched the saddle as the mare was going backwards and called it "grabbing leather," and being that two carried the points against Tom, Pete was left a lone judge and his argument didn't go.

And what's more, we find out the next morning that Tom had been "switched" horses. We was talking to a cowboy who knowed all of Colter's bucking stock and as we're walking round the corral Tom points out the mare he'd rode the day before and says "there's that damn imitation of a bucking horse, Ragtime."

The cowboy that was with us looks the way Tom is pointing.

"That ain't Ragtime," he says. "There's Ragtime over there. He's the best bucking horse this outfit's got and if you're lucky enough to draw him and *cowboy* him to the finish you're pretty near sure of first money."

But Tom managed to spread a good loop in steer roping.

That information caused Tom and me to look at each other with a lot of understanding. We was both grinning but not in the way that showed good feelings for the trick that had been pulled on us, for the horse that cowboy showed us was a big bald face bay. It was plain to see the Colter outfit wanted us out of the way quick as possible and they was afraid to let Tom have the horse for fear he'd put up the best ride, but right there Tom said we was sure going to make 'em run to keep us away from the money.

The second day was going to be a mighty busy one for me. My name was up for four events and I was glad to be in the "tryouts" in the morning which give me more time in the afternoon. I drawed a pot gutted runt by the name of Big Enuff and Tom helped me cuss the luck, but somehow that little son-of-a-gun could buck and he was making hisself mighty hard to keep track of. I was real surprised at the showing he made and more so when I learned that I'd made semi-finals on him.

Tom had bad luck in bulldogging that afternoon. His steer headed for the railing and went through it, leaving Tom a hanging on the remains of the fence. He was scratched up some, but his feelings is what was hurt the most.

My steer was better in a way, only he was too fast. He came out like a shot and kept agoing at the same speed, and when the gun was fired that marked the time neither me or the hazer could catch up with him for quite a stretch. When we did and I finally got him down it had taken too much time. The record of that day was way out of my reach.

In bull riding, our bulls just bucked in an average and the judges hardly noticed us, but Tom managed to spread a good loop in steer roping and that brought him first, where with me I only caught one horn and that don't count.

"It strikes me queer," I says to Tom that night, "why we can't do things here like we did on the range while we was practising for this

Rodeo. Why I'd bet that we made better time out there in roping and bulldogging than has ever been made here. Yessir, I'm sure we have."

Tom agrees to that and is kind of wondering too. Finally we conclude that it's because there ain't room enough, too many people to scare a critter to turning sudden and just when it shouldn't.

But we was still mighty hopeful for the next and third day we felt ready and able to bulldog the devil himself. We was going to make a harder try that day than any time before if that was possible, and *ride*. Old Steamboat would of been my favorite horse, for a real horse is what I wanted, a horse that'd carry me to the finals.

"Bill," Tom says, "you're going to ride in the semi-finals today, and you've just got to scratch your horse into the finals, that's all," and getting confidential he adds, "I know the horse you drawed and they say he's pretty good, so there you are, work on him, and if you make it inter-esting enough so that you'll be put in the finals I'll—" But there he stops and thinking I had an idea of what he wanted to say I tries to help him along.

"Listen, Tom," I says, "if the horse I get to-day can buck hard enough you know that I'll put up a ride on him."

"Sure, I know that," he says, "but you got to do even better than put up a good ride, you just got to not only qualify for the finals, but in them finals you also *got* to show the judges that you're the only one entitled to first money, and to make that plain to 'em you know *how* you'll have to ride. There's a lot of competition against you and not only that but there's only one judge to our side, the other two are for their own imported riders, so when you fork your pony this afternoon don't forget *that* and show 'em that you are the wolf of the world."

Well I *didn't* forget it, had no chance to 'cause Tom was right there steady tagging along wherever I went, and he kept a thumbing me right up to the time I forked the pony that was to bring on the decision as to wether I make the finals or I don't.

Tom gives me another dig in the ribs just as I hollers for the judges to "watch me ride," the shute gate flies open and out we go, the pony abellering "I want you" and me awhooping to him "you got to go some."

That pony was a good bucker, he tore up the earth in good shape, throwed sand in the judges eyes and kept me wondering some. There was nothing monotonous about him and everybody seemed interested, and I calculated when the shot was fired and my horse was "picked up" that I was due for the finals.

I made a good catch in steer roping afterwards which brought me first money on that, and Tom kept his steer in the track this time on bulldogging, he made good time getting up to him and I could tell by the sour look on two of the judges and the grin on Pete's face that Tom had made the best time of that day.

It was natural that we was feeling pretty good when we walked in the rodeo headquarters that evening and hear the reports. We got our "daily money" and then we holds our breaths while we listen who all so far had qualified for the finals. There was only three and *I was one of 'em.*

Tom near went through hisself when he heard my name was on that list and a grin spread on his face that sure disguised it.

"Good boy, Bill," he hollers, at the same time gives me a slap on the back that give me to understand he meant all what he said.

The eight or ten riders left what hadn't competed for the finals and due to ride the next day was drawing their horses and I edged in to draw my "final" horse, I closed my eyes and near prayed as I reaches in the hat, gets one envelope and steps out where Tom and me can read it together.

We pulls the paper out of the little envelope like it was going to be either real bad news or else information that we'd inherited a million, and hesitating we unfolds it. — "Slippery Elm" is all that little piece of paper said, but that was enough and meant a plenty. It meant that to-morrow I was to ride a horse by that name and that nine chances out of ten it was up to that horse wether I'd win first, second, or third money or nothing.

We'd seen that horse bucked out on the second day. He was a big black and reminded me some of Angel Face, back there on the range. His mane was roached and from what we'd seen of him he wasn't near as good a bucking horse as our old Angel Face, he wasn't as honest and we remembered that he throwed himself a purpose and near killed a good cowboy on that second day. What's more we learn that he can't be depended on to buck every time he's rode, sometimes he just stampedes and it was told that one time he run through two railings and halfways up the grandstand, where he broke through the steps and near broke his neck.

Putting all that together and thinking it over, me and Tom was looking mighty solemn. Of course, chances was that he might buck and buck good but the biggest part of them chances was that he'd just stampede and crowhop and then fall, and we knowed if it happened the imported judges would take advantage of that and instead of giving me another horse they'd just grin and put a line across my name.

Tom ain't saying nothing, but I can see he's doing a heap of thinking instead, and watching him I can't help but grin a little and remark that everything may turn out all right. "Can't tell about that horse, Tom," I says, "he might buck like hell."

"Yes, he might and he might *not*," says Tom looking gloomy, "and I sure hate to see you take a chance on a scrub like that horse after you getting as far as the finals. If you'd a drawed a good one like that Ragtime horse for instance, I don't mean the one I rode and got disqualified on, I mean the one they cheated me out of, well, if you'd got a horse like that you'd have a chance for your money, but who do you suppose has drawed that horse?" he asks.

"I don't know," I says, wondering.

"That pet cowboy of Colter's got him — and do you think he could of drawed that horse on the square? Not by a damn sight! That cowboy is a good rider and being he is Colter's drawcard same as some of his horses he advertises and claims can't be rode, Colter is naturally going to see that that cowboy wins first. It's a safe bet so far cause when he drawed Ragtime he drawed the best bucking horse in the outfit."

"Now I'll tell you, Bill," says Tom all het up on the subject, "it's not the prize money nor the honors we're after so much, if they can outride us and do it on the square we'd be glad to shake hands with 'em and congratulate, but they're trying to put something over on us and on all the riders of this part of the country. Other outfits like Colter's done the same thing last two years and got away with the money when there was boys from here that could of outrode 'em two to one, and it looks like the same thing is going to be done this year, but if you had a good horse, Bill, we'd sure make them circus hands look up to a cowboy."

It's after supper when Tom, still looking mighty sour, tells me he's going to the stable to get his horse and go visiting out of town a ways. I can see his mind is still on the subject as he's saddling, and giving the latigo a jerk remarks that he can lose on a square deal and laugh about it, "but I'll be daggone," he says, "if it don't hurt to get cheated out of what's yours, have it done right under your nose and not have no say acoming."

The next day was the last day, the big day, the grounds was sizzling hot and the dust that was stirred up stayed in the air looking for a cooler atmosphere. It was past noon and Tom hadn't showed up yet. I was beginning to wonder of the whereabouts of that cowboy and started looking for him. I was still at it when the parade drifted in and the

The critter kept me up for a good airing.

Grand Entree was over, every kid that could borrow a horse was in it, some wore red silk shirts and they sure thought they was cowboys far as the clothes was concerned.

The riders what still had to ride for the finals went hard at it and I was busy watching and judging for myself how many of them would make them finals. I hears when it's over that only two had qualified and them two was of Colter's outfit, that made six of us who are still to ride for the grand prize, four of Colter's men and two of us outsiders and by that I figgers that Colter is sure making it a cinch of *keeping the money in the family*.

"All you bulldoggers on the track," hollers the Rodeo boss, and knowing that Tom is in on that event I takes another look for him, but I can't see hair nor hide of that son-of-a-gun nowheres, so I was getting real worried.

My name is called and I rides up to the shute. My steer is let out and for the time being I forgets everything but what I'd rode up there for. I done good time, the best time of that day so far, and I sure did wish that old Tom was there and seen it, cause I know it'd tickled him.

A half a dozen or so other bulldoggers are called on to take their chance and then Tom's name comes, but he's still among the missing and I see no way out but offer to substitute for him. I had a mighty hard time to get the judges to agree to that, but with Pete on my side and me atalking my head off, they finally decide to let me take his place.

I glances towards the shutes and notices a steer *just my size* already there and waiting to come out, and I also notices that they're trying to drive him back and put another steer in the place of him, a great big short-horned Durham. I rides up there right now and begins to object, remarking that I'd take on any steer as they come but at the same time I wasn't letting any skunk stack the cards on me by going to special trouble of picking me the hardest steer they can find. I object so strong that they finally let me have the first steer.

I was mad, and when that steer come out I figgered there was something to work my hard feelings out on, I made a reach for them long horns that I wouldn't of made if I'd been normal. The critter kept me up for a good airing, but when my boot heels finally connected with the sod the program wasn't long in ending. I stopped him good so there wouldn't be no danger of being disqualified and imagining that I was bulldogging a Rodeo boss or a judge instead of a steer, it wasn't long till I had him down.

"Old critter," I says to the steer as I lets him up, "you play square which is more than I can say for some folks."

I shakes the dust off myself, locates my hat, and being I was through on bulldogging I struts out round and toward the saddling shutes trying to get a peek at that long lean pardner of mine — a vision of his expression as he was leaving the night before came to me, and I'm beginning to wonder if he didn't try to even scores with the Colter outfit. "But daggone it," I thinks, "he should of let me tag along."

"You'll soon be riding now, Bill," says one of the local boys breaking in on my thoughts, "and if you don't bring home the bacon with first money you better keep on a riding and never let me see your homely phizog again."

"Bet your life," I says, "and that goes for two judges, too."

Comes the time when they're introducing Colter's pet cowboy to the crowd in the grandstand, and telling all about his riding abilities on the worst horses, etc., etc. A few bows in answer to the cheers and that same *hombre* rides to the shutes graceful and prepares to get ready.

The Ragtime horse (the one Tom drawed and didn't get) came out like a real bucker, he wiped up the earth pretty and Colter's top hand was a setting up there as easy as though he was using shock absorbers.

None of the hard hitting jumps seemed to faze him and his long lean legs was a reefing that pony from the root of his tail to the tips of his ears and a keeping time with motions that wasn't at all easy to even see.

I felt kind of dubious as I watched the proceedings. If I only had a horse like that, I thought, for as it was I didn't see no chance, and things was made worse when I hear one of the riders next to me remark: "You know, Bill, we got to hand it to that feller. He may be with Colter's outfit and all that, *but he sure can ride.*"

A couple other boys came out on their ponies and they done fine, but it was plain to see who was up for first money. I didn't put much heart to the job when I gets near the shutes to straddle that roach maned scrub I'd drawed. But I figgers to do the best I can, there was no use quitting now and maybe after all that horse might buck pretty good, good enough to get me into second or third money. But dammit, I didn't want second or third money. I wanted first or nothing, and it was my intentions to *ride* for that.

The judges, all excepting Pete, didn't seem interested when it was announced that I was next to come out and I reckoned they'd already figgered me out of it, as they knowed I'd drawed Slippery Elm.

"Judges," hollers a voice that sounds mighty familiar, "watch this cowboy ride, he's after first money."

The shute gate was about to be opened, but I had to turn and see who'd just spoke — and there, a few feet back stood Tom. A glance of him kept me from wondering or asking where he'd been. His features was kinda set, and I finds myself listening mighty close as he looks at me and says — sort of low: "Careful of the first jump, Bill, and ride like you would if old Angel Face was under you."

I had no time to talk back, and that got me to setting pretty close, but I had to grin at the thought of the scrub I was setting on being

WILL JAMES
M ~ 24

*I hear a snorting beller that sounds away off and I gets a glimpse of the roman-
nosed, latern-jawed head that was making it . . . old Angel Face was under me!*

anything like the good bucker old Angel Face could be, but I was going to play safe anyway and get ready to *ride*. If this horse bucked good, all the better — then, the shute gate flies open.

That horse came out like the combination of a ton of dynamite and a lighted match, I lost the grin I'd been packing, I kinda felt the cantle crack as that pony took me up to I didn't know where and I was flying instead of riding.

Instinct, or maybe past experience warned me that somehow and mighty soon we was going to come down again and natural like I prepares for it. A human can think fast sometimes, and you can tell that I did by the fact that all I've described so far of that pony's movements was done in about the length of time it took you to read a couple of these words. That roach mane horse was sure surprising.

When that horse hit the ground I felt as though Saint Peter and all the guards of the Pearly Gates who I'd been to see just a second before, had put their foot down on me and was trying to push me through the earth to the hot place. The saddle horn was tickling me under the chin and one of my feet touched the ground, my other one was alongside the horse's jaw.

I hear a snorting beller that sounds away off and I gets a hazy glimpse of the roman-nosed lantern-jawed head that was making it — I'd recognized the whole of it in hell and instead of Slippery Elm, *old Angel Face was under me.*

Right there and then the tune changed. The spirits I'd lost came back along with memories of first money. A full grown warwhoop was heard. Angel Face answers with a beller and all the world was bright once more.

The judges had no chance to direct me when to scratch forward and back, I was doing that aplenty and they was busy turning their ponies and just keeping track of me. I'd look over my shoulder at 'em and laugh in their face, at the same time place one of my feet between that pony's ears or reach back and put the III (hundred and eleven) spur mark on the back of the cantle of the saddle.

All through the performance old faithful Angel Face kept up a standard of that first jump I tried to describe. He was wicked but true, and it was a miracle that his feet always touched the ground instead of his body. There was none of that high rearing show stuff with that old boy, only just plain honest to god bucking that only a horse of his kind could put out — one in a thousand of his kind.

I got to loving that horse right then. He was carrying me, kinda rough of course, but straight to my ambitions, and even though my feet was in the motion of scratching and covering a lot of territory on his hide, my spurs didn't touch him nor leave a mark on him nowheres, he was my friend in need.

There's cheers from the grandstand, cheers from the cowboys and far as I can see in my wild ride everybody is up and ahollering, everybody but the Colter crowd. The shot is fired that marks the end of my ride and Tom is right there to pick Angel Face's head up out of the dust, that old pony hated to quit and tries to buck even after he's snubbed.

"He's *some* horse," says Tom real serious, "and Bill you're *some* rider."

Late that night finds me and Tom leading Slippery Elm and headed for the grounds, we was going to steal back Slippery Elm's double, Angel Face.

"Too bad," I remarks, "that his mane had to be roached to get him to look like this scrub we're leading. The boss'll have seventeen fits when he sees that."

But Tom didn't seem worried. "What I'd like to know," he says, "is how come I was handed the championship on bulldogging. I wasn't even there the last day."

"I was there," I says, "I substituted for you, and even went and broke my own record doing it, but," I goes on before Tom can speak, "if you hadn't brought in Angel Face I'd never got first money. If the Colter outfit hadn't switched horses on us we wouldn't of switched horses on them, so there you are, Tom. Turn about is fair play and that goes all round."

BUCKING HORSES AND
BUCKING-HORSE RIDERS

IN MOST COUNTRIES a mean horse is got rid of or broke of his meanness by either kind or rough handling. He may be given away to some enemy or shipped and sold at auction — that ornery devil, dragging all the bad names after him, will keep on drifting and changing of scenery till he's too old to be shipped or traded any more. He's a mighty expensive animal, figgering all the buggies he kicked to pieces, the harnesses he tore up, and the stalls he broke down, not counting injury to them what tried to handle him. But there's a place for such horses.

It's anywheres west of the Laramie Plains. If you've got a real ornery, man-eating, bucking, striking, can't-be-rode animal of that kind, he's sure worth a lot, and if he's worse than that he's worth more.

Fact is, there's people out looking for them kind of ponies, and they'll give from a hundred on up for 'em. They're the *hombres* who's responsible for these "Frontier Day Celebrations," "Rodeos," "War-Bonnets," "Reunions," and "Round-ups," and they must have mean horses, the meaner the better. They must have horses that'll give the boys what's rode in for the events a chance to show what they can do, 'cause if the rider "up" gets a bronc that just crowhops, it don't matter how easy he rides, or how much he fans him, and how loud the crowd in the grand stand cheers and hollers, the judges of who's the best rider won't notice him, being he has nothing hard to stick. That's where a good, hard, mean, bucking horse is wanted, he's got to have enough wickedness in him for that cowboy to work on — I've seen mighty good riders left out of the prize money on account of the horse they drew, just because that pony wasn't mean enough; and that old boy a-setting up there with taped spurs and fighting mad, blood in his eye and a-wishing something would blow up under his bronc so he

What the cowboy wants is a head-fighting, limber-back
cross between greased lightning and where it hits.

could show the world and the judges what a wolverene he is on horse-flesh.

Nobody gets credit for riding easy in a rocking-chair. What the cowboy wants is a head-fighting, limber-back cross between greased lightning and where it hits — a horse that'll call for all the endurance, main strength, and equilibrium that cowboy's got — just so he can show his ability and scratch both ways from the cinch, as the judges may direct. There's when a mean devil of a horse is wanted; he gets a chance to show how mean he is with free rein, and the cowboy has something worth while to work at.

I've knowed some great horses in that game — there was Long Tom, Hammerhead, Old Steamboat; that last was a great old pony, eleven hundred pounds of solid steel and action and a square shooter. They say he never was rode, but I know he has been rode to a standstill. They was real riders that did it, tho'. I figgered that horse was part

And scratch both ways from the cinch, as the judges may direct.

151

human the way he'd feel out his rider. He'd sometimes try him out on a few easy jumps just to see how he was setting, and when he'd loosen up for the last, it's safe enough to say, when that last would come and the dust cleared, there'd 'most always be a tall lean lanky bow-legged cowboy picking himself up and wondering how many horses he'd seen in the last few seconds. I've seen Old Steamboat throw his man with his head up and four feet on the ground, but what happened before he got in that peaceful position was enough to jar a centipede loose — and a human's only got two legs.

A horse is not trained to buck, as some folks think; out there on the open range he already knows how; sometimes the bronco-buster encourages him at it for either fun or practice for the next Rodeo, and the bronc, as a rule, is more than willing and might keep on bucking every time he's rode whether the rider wants him to or not. Close as I could figure it out, the blame for originating the bucking, striking, and biting in the Western horse goes a heap to the mountain-lion and wolf — them two terrors of the range, mixed with instinct and shook up well with wild, free blood, kinda allows for the range-horse's actions. The bucking was first interduced when that stallion "Comet" got away from the Spaniards with his few mares, years before Texas was fought for; he started a wild bunch that kept multiplying, till all of Old Mexico and the Southern States was a grazing country for his sons, grandsons, and daughters — they are the real mustang — more horses were brought in from Spain, and Comet's sons would increase the little bands by stealing mares from the pastures; some would get away, join whatever bunch they could, and in no time be as wild as the rest.

Them old ponies had a lot to deal with. The mountain-lion was always a-waiting for 'em from his perch, where he could easy spring down on his victim; he'd fall on their necks, grab holt with front claws and teeth, a foot or so from the ears, then swing his hind quarters

The "lobo" wolf was another to help develop "nerves" under the mustang's hide. He worked from the ground up, and got the pony to use his front and hind feet mighty well. The teeth came in handy, too.

down with all his strength and clamp his claws under the horse's jaw close to the chin, jerk the pony's head up, and, if the cougar's aim was good, he'd break the mustang's neck most as quick as he lit. Once in a while the pony would shake free, but there'd be a story plain to see as to how Mr. Lion worked. The chin was gone and there'd be gashes in the neck that'd leave scars many inches long and plenty deep.

The "lobo" wolf was another to help develop "nerves" under the mustang's hide. He worked from the ground up, and got the pony to use his front and hind feet mighty well. The teeth came in handy, too, so all in all after his enemies got thru edicating him, there was a new nerve took growth and spread from the tip of his ears to the tip of his tail — that nerve (if such you would call it) commanded action whenever anything to the mustang's dislike appeared or let itself be known in any way. And when the cowpuncher's loop spreads over the mustang's head and draws up, he's fighting the same as he would with the cougar, he's a bucking, striking, kicking, and biting hunk of horse-flesh to anything that's close.

The mustang made a mighty fine cow horse and was good enough till, about forty years or so ago, the stockmen started buying blooded horses from the East and Europe to breed up bigger saddle stock. The stallions were mostly French coach and Hambletonians; some registered mares were bought, too — the cross between the hot-bloods and mustangs brought out fine big horses — but, man, how they could buck!

The mustangs kept a-getting chased and caught; they were fence-broken, some "ham-strung," and turned into big pastures where they could range winter and summer, year in year out. In each bunch you could see a thoroughbred, and the herds were showing the blood more every year — but the bucking was still there and worse than ever, the colts never saw a human from the time they were branded till they were four-year-olds, and some never saw one till they were ten. If they did, it wasn't for long, a snort, a cloud of dust, and the rider was left behind a ridge, unless that perticular rider had intentions of catching some, and he sure had to be mounted for that.

As a rule, when a bunch of broncs was wanted out of the "stock" horses — there'd be a "parada" (herd of about 100 broke horses) held together by a few riders — the wild ones would be hazed (not drove) toward the "parada," the riders holding the milling herd would hide on the side of their horses and let the wild ones get in — then there'd be a grand entrée fast and furious into the big corrals, and before the broncs knew it they were surrounded by a good solid stockade of cottonwood poles, ten feet high.

The thoroughbred stallion which was so gentle a few years before was as wild as the herd with him, he'd never show any symptoms of ever having seen a human or ever wanting to see one, he'd forgot his warm box stalls and his feeds of grain, the freedom he'd experienced

And when the cow-puncher's loop spreads over the mustang's head and draws up, he's fighting the same as he would with the cougar, he's a bucking, striking, kicking, and biting hunk of horse-flesh.

was worth more to him than what man could give him. He was proud of his band, his colts were big and slick even tho' not better or tougher than the mustang already was.

And to-day when the bronco-buster packs his saddle into the breaking pen, takes his rope, and catches his bronc to break, he finds that the Comet strain is still there some — it's blended with the "blue dog" of Texas along with the Steeldust, Coach, Standard Bred, etc., and scatters all thru the Western States, the Canadian prairies, and Mexico. The imported thoroughbred can't kill that strain; fact is, they make it worse; for, even tho' the pure blood would never buck, the cross forms a kind of reaction, with the result that the foals sure keep up the reputation of the mustang that was, and then some. The freedom of the open range and big pastures the Western horse gets is all he needs, and he'll always be ready to give his rider the shaking up he's expecting.

I wouldn't give "two bits" for a bronc what didn't buck when first rode, 'cause I figgers it's their mettle showing when they do. It's the right spirit at the right time — every horse what bucks is not a outlaw,

And to-day when the bronco-buster takes his rope into the breaking pen, he finds the Comet strain is still there, some.

not by a long shot. I've seen and rode many a good old well-broke cow horse what had to have his buck out in the cold mornings, just to kind of warm hisself up on the subject and settle down for the work ahead.

The outlaw (as some call him) he's the horse that won't quit bucking and fights harder every time he's saddled; it's his nature, and sometimes he's made one by too rough or not rough enough handling, and spoiled either by the bronc peeler what started to break him or else turned loose on the range before he's thoroughly broke, to run for months before he's caught up again. A colt can be spoiled in many ways, and reckless riders what are good riders have spoiled more horses than the poor ones have, 'cause the good rider knows he can ride his horse whatever he does or whichever way he goes, whereas the poorer rider is kinda careful and tries to teach his bronc to be a cow horse; he won't let him buck if he can help it.

There's a difference in horses' natures and very few can be handled alike. Some are kinda nervous and full of life, them kind's got to be handled careful and easy or they'd get to be mean fighters as a rule. Then there's what we call the "jug-head"; he's got to be pulled around a heap, and it takes a lot of elbow grease to get him lined out for anything; and there's another that as soon as a feller gets his rope on him makes him feel that either him or the bronc ain't got far to go. He's the kind of horse with a far-away look; some folks call 'em locoed. But whether he's that or not he'll sure take a man thru some awful places and sometimes only one comes out. Such doings would make a steeplechase as exciting as a fat man's race; that horse is out to get his man and he don't care if he goes himself while doing the getting. He's out to commit suicide and make a killing at the same time. I pulled the saddle off such a horse one time after a good stiff ride; of a sudden he flew past and kicked at me with his two free legs, snapping and biting at the "jakama" (hackamore rope), heading straight for the side of the

He'll make his cowboy shake hands with Saint Peter, and won't worry
whether the ground is under or on the side of him when he hits.

corral, when he connected with it and fell back dead, with a broken neck. I felt kinda relieved 'cause I knew it was either him or me or both of us had to go; he'd tried it before. There's a lot of them used at the round-ups and rodeos being that they mean business that way — that kind most generally can sure buck and will give a rider a chance to show his skill; but they 'most always wind up a-straddle the grandstand's fence with a piece of broken timber thru 'em, and the rider is lucky if he comes out with just bumps.

And again there's the horse what keeps his brain a-working for some way to hang his rider's hide on the corral or anywhere it'll hang, and save his own hide doing it. He's crooked any way you take him, and will put so much energy in his bucking that when he's up in the air all twisted up, he don't figure or care about the coming down. He'll make his cowboy shake hands with Saint Peter, and won't worry whether the ground is under or on the side of him when he hits. When he falls, he falls hard, and the rider has little chance to get away. That pony seldom gets hurt, he's wise enough to look out for himself; what's on top of him is what he wants to get rid of, and he won't be on the square trying it.

Out of every hundred buckers of the arena there's only about fifteen that are square and will give a man a fair battle. Old Steamboat was that kind, he was gentle to saddle and handle, but when he felt the rider's weight and the blind was pulled off, it was second nature and fun for him to buck, and he knew as well as the boys did that he could buck.

Horses have a heap more brains than some folks would like to give 'em credit for, and if they want to be mean they know how. The same if they want to be good; the kind of interduction they get with man has a lot to do with it.

Most any bronc is a ticklish proposition to handle when first caught; it's not always meanness, it's fear of the human. They only try to protect themselves. Sometimes by going easy and having patience according, a man can break one to ride without bucking, but even at that, the meanest bucking horse I ever saw was gentle to break, and never made a jump till one day he got away and run with the wild bunch for a couple of years. When caught again, an Indian with the outfit rode him out of camp, with the old pony going "high, wide, and handsome." The Indian stuck, but along about noon he comes back, afoot. It was during fall round-up when that horse was caught once more; his back had been scalded by the saddle and all white hair grew where it had been. He took a dislike for saddle and men with the result that the next year he was sold to a Rodeo association for the Cowboys Reunion.

To-day there's more buckers like that in the hills waiting to be brought in, buckers as good as Old Steamboat or any of 'em ever was. They're fat and sassy and full of fight, and in them same hills and range there's riders what keeps their eyes on 'em a-figgering to bring 'em in and "buck 'em" for first money when the Rodeo is pulled off. If the association's got harder buckers, them is what they want; for as long as there's fighting broncs, there's going to challenging riders, and in all the cowboys I've met and buckers I've handled and seen on the open ranges or arenas of U. S., Canada, and Mexico, I've still got to see the rider what couldn't be throwed and the horse what couldn't be rode.

WILL JAMES
'30

HIS WATERLOO

"YOU KNOW DAVE SIMMONS, don't you?" asks the cow foreman as he drags a chair towards where I'm setting away to one corner of the bunk house and rolling a smoke to kinda put the finishing touches on the good supper I'd just had.

"Never heard of him," I says as I lights my cigarette and leans back. "I'm a stranger around here."

"You sure must be a stranger and from far away not to've heard of Dave," he says, looking at me sort of surprised.

"Why," he goes on, "Dave is as well known in this state as our governor, and not only in this state either, folks know him plum up to the Canadian line; of course his reputation has died down some these last couple of years on account of new folks dropping in steady and grabbing all the honors, and you being a young feller and after Dave's time kinda excuses you for not knowing of him.

"But what I'm getting at is this, about two days ride north from here is the prettiest camp this outfit's got. Well, Dave's up at that camp and keeping tab on some thoroughbred Hereford cattle. He's had that job now for some time; and there's where you'll be going with the broncs I hired you to break. We've rounded up near a hundred head of colts around here from three years old on up, that's to be rode, and I think that'll keep you busy for many months. You'll be staying up there with Dave, that's why I asked you if you knowed him. He'll be glad to help you whenever you give him the chance, and being there's good corrals there and a fine country around to ride broncs in, you two sure ought to be able to enjoy yourselves.

"Now, being that you and Dave will have to batch it together you ought to know some about him. But I sure can't get over the fact that you never heard of that old boy, and it makes me ask, where are you from, young feller?"

"Montana is my home state," I says, "but I'm from most anywheres along the Rockies."

"Sure queer you and Dave never crossed trails — and when I first set my eyes on you riding that ornery gelding back of McAllister's stable at Miles, I thought of Dave and how he'd like to seen you ride that horse; your riding reminded me of him, so slick and free and easy it was. That's what made me ask if you wanted a job snapping broncs. Dave always did admire good riding.

"I remember one time when Dave was a younger feller, he'd met a duke or something up in Canada what claimed there was a stallion back in England that no human could ride; there was a few thousand dollars put up by the owners of that horse that said the same thing, and that got Dave all riled up. He was rarin' to go and see that pony and it wasn't but a few weeks when he did cross the water, his little saddle right with him, too.

"Well, a good two months went by and nary a word did we hear from that *hombre*. We'd got to thinking that stallion had got the best of him and just about decided to investigate when we get a letter from him and a clipping of newspaper telling about the wonderful horsemanship of Dave Simmons that American cowboy. It went on and told of the fight between brute strength and human skill and cunning, the desperate chances Dave was taking to curb down the viciousness of that outlaw horse, and how for a spell it looked like the stallion was going to come out victorious. But finally and after a hard fight the iron muscles of that horse had to give in under the steel brawn of the cowboy that was a-settin' on top of him, the earth-shakin' bucks slowed down gradual to crowhops, and head down, nostrils a-quivering, sweat a-dripping from all over him, the horse stopped, the cowboy dismounted with a smile and crowds cheered the victor.

"'The worst horse ever known had been conquered,' says the paper, but here's what Dave said in his letter: 'That pony could buck pretty good all right, but he was nothing much compared to Old Sox.' Old Sox was a horse Dave had started to break before he left, but Dave had seen many a harder horse to ride than even Sox ever was.

"Anyway Dave went on in his letter and said how he wished he had Sox along so as he could show them folks what real fighting horseflesh acted like, 'but they was satisfied,' he says, 'and they was all good to me. Even when I was handed the three thousand dollars reward they congratulated and remarked that the show was well worth the money.'

"Dave was hoping there was more easy money like that hanging around and even thought of shipping some of our own ponies over there so he'd get a chance to ride 'em, but it took him a lot of money to get back and when he reached Chicago a few months later he was broke flat. He rode a few mean horses that'd been shipped there from the range and by manouvering around he got enough money out of it to get back to the outfit.

"'Well,' he says as I met him at the train, 'I sure had a lot of fun anyway and seen plenty of sights. I think I'll go to work now and be good, but it sure gets under my skin when I think of the ponies I got to ride here for fifty dollars a month. I figger at the rate I'm riding here which is ten broncs a day I only get seventeen cents per mount, that's not much compared to three thousand dollars, and any of these broncs are as bad as that English stallion, and many are a heap worse, besides there's no folks sticking around these bare corrals to cheer when I put up a good ride.'

"But Dave was too much of a cowboy to let any brass band spoil him, and with all the lamenting he done there was a grin following. I could see he was glad to get back, and it was no time when England and the 'chaps' over there was only distant memory.

163

"Dave was born and raised in the Buffalo Basin country. His dad had a nice bunch of cattle and from the time Dave was fourteen years old he was kept busy riding. He started breaking horses at home and it wasn't long when he was breaking 'em for neighbors and using 'em on

"Many a horse throwed him at first."

his dad's range. From the time he was fifteen Dave was never seen riding a gentle horse and soon as the pony under him quit his fighting and bucking he'd turn that horse over as broke and run in another green bronc.

"He started in like all cowboys do, only he got to be a way better rider than the average. There was many a horse throwed him at first, and many a shirt his mother had to mend, but never did I see the horse Dave was afraid of.

"He was along about eighteen when he came to work for this outfit, and a more reckless rider I've never seen. Many is the time I've watched him get on a raw bronc in a winter day. He'd get the barefooted horse on a slick patch of ice and climb on him when it was all the horse could do to stand up.

"'That's a fine place to see how good this bronc is on his feet,' he'd remark, and as luck would have it the horse would seldom fall. If I'd tried a stunt like that I know I'd never come out of it without a broken leg.

"I've often seen him take his rope down on a colt when it'd be the first time that colt was rode, and rope some full-grown critter — it didn't matter to him what kind of country he was in at the time either, and whether it was open flat or rocky steep ridges covered with timber, it was all the same to Dave.

"His rope was always tied hard and fast to his saddle horn when he snared anything, and that I think is the most dangerous thing a man can do on an unbroke horse; he'd get in mix-ups that way that couldn't be watched for the dust that was stirred, but the first thing you'd see when that dust settled was Dave's head a-smiling and watching the conglomeration of a horse and critter all mixed with a rope.

"Why one time I seen him rope a little calf that'd broke away from the herd, and as usual he was riding a mighty mean horse. That little calf was sure running for a ways and when Dave caught him it was quite a distance back to the herd. The little calf was only a week or so old and of course he didn't want to drag him back all the way — well sir, that daggone fool just pulls on the rope and hoists the calf right up in the saddle with him.

"His horse started to bucking, and believe me, stranger, that horse could sure buck, too. But Dave didn't want him to, right then, and that pony having had previous experience with that *hombre*, straightened up and lit out a-crowhopping and running. I bet that was the wildest ride any calf ever had, but he was took back to his mammy all right even though the horse that packed him did have murder in his eye.

"Of course we all know that a cowboy, to be one, has to be mighty reckless and carefree as regards to life and limb; I've had many a good cowboy on this outfit; that's all I'd ever keep. But I don't expect none of 'em to carry on the standard that Dave has set. I've knowed many riders that tallied up pretty well with him, but somehow Dave was always a leetle bit better.

"I've stood and watched Dave handle green broncs by the hour. The way he'd go at it always done my heart a lot of good. He was so quiet that you wouldn't know he was around unless you seen him; he never petted a horse, but he done better: he treated 'em like they knowed something. And it'd always wind up by them ponies just a-busting themselves to do things they knowed Dave wanted 'em to do.

"Yes sir! he was a great hand. He never made a horse buck but he never was so happy as when some pony would buck with him. The harder the tossing the more he'd grin, and I never seen a feller so disappointed as when he'd get on a fat, kinky, raw bronc and that horse didn't bog his head and buck good on first setting. He'd always pass this remark as he'd pull off his riggin': 'That horse'll never be worth a damn.'

"But few ever disappointed him that way. He believed that all horses had some buck in 'em and the time to get it out of their system was on first saddlings; and he'd often say: 'Look out for the horse that don't jump when he's first rode, he'll break in two just when you think you're riding something gentle. And when them kind of ponies do break in two in that stage of the game they're most generally hard to set, and a lot harder to make 'em quit it.'

"As for the horse that never no time bucked, he'd wave his hand and say: 'Take 'em away, feed 'em sugar and sell 'em off to some livery stable.'"

Right about then I broke in on the foreman and asked: "Did Dave ever run acrost any horse that was too much for him?"

166

"No, sir," says he, "not since he was fifteen and while he was *riding*. Of course, like the rest of us he finally had to quit, but I'll come to that later, and as I was going to say —

"One spring we'd bought a carload of Oregon horses. We'd got 'em cheap and figgered they'd make fine saddle stock. They was all well built ponies and averaging around eleven hundred with just enough daylight under 'em to make 'em good anywheres they was put. Their age run from three to ten and even twelve years old, and none of 'em was supposed to've been rode.

"But soon as we got 'em in our own corrals we found that about half of 'em had been tampered with and turned out to be real outlaws; that's why we got 'em cheap. Of course we never worried much about that cause we knowed we had a man that'd be glad to get a chance at 'em. He enjoyed that kind, and we felt mighty sure that he'd make good ponies out of the worst of 'em.

"And that's what Dave did. He lit into them broncs and whistled a tune while they fought and bucked and tore the buttons off his shirt with their front feet. Dave had a way of always being where them broncs didn't want him to be, and when they'd strike or kick there was always a hair's breadth between the hoof and what that hoof tried to reach.

"Dave let 'em buck and fight all they wanted, and when they'd quit he'd make them broncs feel like they hadn't done anything. It sure got under their hide to see that their efforts to orneriness didn't faze that human none at all; instead he seemed to like it and called for more.

"Like one morning Dave walked into the corral, roped the meanest one of the bunch and saddled him while that pony was near tearing hisself apart a-trying to outdo that human and take the grin out of his face with new tricks. He was a big powerful 'gruller' horse, tall and rawboned and all muscle. But with all his strength, action, meanness, and size, Dave was never interrupted no time, and while the big gray was a-standing stary-eyed for a second and wondering what to do next, Dave climbed him and unloosened the foot rope.

"It all was done so neat and quick and easy that the horse didn't even know where his man went till he looked back and seen him a-setting there right on his middle and a-grinning — well, sir, that horse was desperate. You could see it in every inch of his long frame; he didn't know whether to just stand still and quiver or just leave the earth for good.

"A beller came out of him that made every animal within hearing distance stop grazing and stand still with head up and a-wondering. Such a beller had been heard before, but only in mountain lion countries and when the big cat had jumped down on his victim. If it'd been a mountain lion that big horse could of shed him off, maybe, but it was sure aggravating how that human could stick and laugh at him through the hard crooked jumps that'd jarred loose every other rider.

"I know that horse bucked then like he never did before; he was gone crazy, and he didn't care how he went up or hit the ground or even if he broke his own neck so long as he could loosen up that grinning rider and scatter him in the dirt.

"As cow foreman of this outfit, I've seen many a horse buck and many a good cowboy ride. I've seen so many and got so used to it that came a time when I wouldn't even turn my head to see the performance. It was only part of the work; but if I lived to be five hundred I'd never forget what I seen that morning with Dave and the big gray.

"It was that horse's heart and life *not* to be rode; every muscle along his backbone was against the feel of saddle leather, and many is the time (as we heard later) he throwed both saddle and rider and made 'em hit the ground together. He was an outlaw natural and his pride was on keeping his back clean of any human that tried to set there. His

No rider had ever been able to make fun of him that way before.

ambition was to kick at 'em as they fell off and step on 'em as they measured their length on mother earth.

"He'd had good luck, and his head was up and mighty confident when he first was run in our corrals, but he hadn't met Dave then and he still had that feeling that he could throw any rider faster than they could climb him.

"So as I was watching that horse that morning I caught myself feeling kinda sorry for the ornery son-of-a-gun. I could see how he was hurt by at last running up against a rider he couldn't shake. And worse yet, that rider was making fun of him.

"But the hardest was still to come; the big gray was bringing in some of his fancy twists, saddle leather was a popping and a machine gun couldn't of kept time for the speed that pony was using in hitting the ground. I was standing inside the log stable which made part of the corral and looking thru one of the windows, and do you know by God I'd even feel that solid log stable shake, so hard did that horse land each jump.

"It was along about when the big gray was doing his best work when I seen Dave do something that sure took my breath away for a spell. That daggone fool leaned down on one side of the saddle, his face came right down alongside the horse's head and looked like he was whispering something in his ear; then he straightened up again, one of his hands went in the air, and in that hand he was holding the hackamore.

"The big gray's head was free, not a string on it; he had more chance to buck than ever before, and that rider a-setting up there was calling him on to do his best. . . . Right then I think something snapped in that bronc's heart strings; that last was too much.

"He quit; legs wide apart he stood there, while Dave sat on him and rolled a smoke. Dave was serious now and pretty soon his hand was running along the gray's mane untangling it some as it went, and then he says to him, 'Never mind, big horse, you sure can buck just the same.' He petted him along the neck a couple of times and climbed off — the horse never moved.

"I think I've told you that I've never seen Dave pet a horse, but I take it back — he did it *that once*.

"Well sir, you wouldn't believe it if you'd seen them horses when Dave started on 'em, but in three months he had 'em all to behaving so as you could do anything with 'em; none of 'em had any buck left — that was wore out of their system by Dave letting 'em have all they wanted of it and a little more. They got so they just naturally hated to buck.

"The big gray? Why, he never bucked since that morning I was telling you of, and he never fought no more either. Instead of that he got to be real attached to Dave and Dave had took such a strong liking for him that he decided to keep him for a 'snubbing' horse and use him to break colts to lead with. Dave often remarked that was one of the best horses he'd ever rode.

"But there's no end of telling what Dave could do and has done with a horse or what a rider he was. It was natural talent with him, and I know that if he'd been born and raised where there's no horses he'd a been a sure and bad failure at anything he'd ever undertook.

"Many is the time when he used to leave me flat and disappear just on account of him hearing about some horse that couldn't be rode. It didn't matter to him whether that horse was in this state or in the next, he'd just up and go; and he'd always come back with a smile.

"Yep! he got real popular that way, and sometimes somebody would even send him a ticket and a request for him to appear at some 'doings' and all they'd have to say to be sure of him being there would be that they had a horse for him nobody in that territory could set — Dave was sure to be present.

"There's not so many riders that can go to any cow or horse outfit with the feeling for sure that they can ride anything that's pointed out to 'em, and as long as I've been with this outfit no strange cowboy has ever come up to me with the remark that they could. It's a wise remark *not* to make and nobody but a greenhorn would pass it; but if there is one man entitled to pass such a remark I don't think there's any what can live up to it like Dave Simmons.

"I know that feller has enjoyed the feeling that he could ride any horse at any time longer than any cowboy I've ever knowed. He could walk in a corral full of ornery outlaws and feel that none of 'em could

Dave was still in the game at thirty, which is when most of us are ready to quit the rough ones and start looking for the gentler kind.

shake him off, and better than that, he knowed he could ride the worse one in the bunch and laugh at him while that one would near bust hisself a-trying to get him down.

"He was a top rider at eighteen and still one at thirty, which as every bronc rider knows is a mighty long time to ride rough ones; but Dave seemed past human that way. He wasn't a big man, either; never weighed over a hundred and fifty. But he was pretty tall and wiry, and the way he could handle himself around a mean horse would make a cougar seem kinda awkward, he done it all so easy. No matter what move a horse made, it looked like Dave was always ready for it, and you know, stranger, that a mean horse is never slow in his movements that way, and you also know that them movements come fast and with no thinking spell between.

"There was no main strength and awkwardness with Dave; his was all skill, balance, quick thinking and quick acting; still he never seemed to hurry, either. Everything a horse done seemed to come his way, and the more a horse did do the more he was interested. The son-of-a-gun sure enjoyed action!

"Dave was still in the game at thirty, which is about when most of us are ready to quit the rough ones and start looking for the gentler kind. But that wasn't the way with him. He kept right at them rough ones and it ain't that he always got away without a scratch either. No, sir; he'd got in many close arguments with the hundreds of different horses he'd rode.

"And as we all know, few mean horses play square; hardly any are what you'd call honest, and sooner or later they get their man. Many will buck out a ways and then throw (not fall) themselves over backwards; others will go up in the air and let their feet go out from under 'em and turn a somerset; sometimes two or three, before they stop rolling. A man ain't got much chance there.

"Then there's these stampeders that take a man thru some awful places. Barb wire, cut banks, hundred-foot cliffs, heavy timber and all is just the same to them. A day of that would put ten years of the prize-fighting game in the kindergarten.

"Them ponies' hoofs are not padded either, and I'd sure like to carry the punch that's back of them hoofs, not mentioning the lightning speed that's with 'em. Even Dave got a wee bit too close to one of them hoofs one time. That was a little while before he quit riding — anyway

Some will go up in the air and let their feet go out from under 'em as they come down, and turn a somerset; sometimes two or three, before they stop rolling. A man ain't got much chance there.

he layed in the hospital with a broken jaw for quite a spell, and when he come out he was packing a full set of false teeth. A ten-dollar horse had done the damage.

"A while before that another pony had wrapped one of his front legs around Dave's neck and kinked it. He was unconscious when we found him and stayed that way for a few hours. But the next day Dave was out on that same horse and roping bulls with him. Dave couldn't look over his shoulder for a month afterwards.

"I won't mention the bones that's been broke in his body nor how he's all twisted up inside nor how it all happened; that'd make a big book and maybe too close to real life to make good reading. But right now that old boy is packing a silver tube that's running from his knee to his ankle. That leg had been broke so often it was past mending.

"Yessir! Old Dave has sure been through the mill, and you'll say he looks it when you see him. But things wouldn't maybe been quite so hard on him if he hadn't hunted around and looked for a horse he *couldn't* ride. You and me and all cowboys have seen men like Dave; even some of us may've been like him, but for myself I don't care to take that much credit.

"And as I was saying, Dave might of got along better if he hadn't been always looking for a horse he couldn't ride. For fifteen years he tried to find one. Maybe it was just to see if there was such a horse, but anyway he kept a-hunting. Of course, in that time he did run acrost some that made things interesting for him; and a few — mighty few — throwed him. But it wasn't done on the square, and when Dave would climb on 'em again he just made fools out of 'em.

"Then one day we run in a bunch of horses right off our own range. In the bunch was a big brown gelding and a few other colts that Dave was going to keep to break. It was just like Dave to pick on the worse horse first, and the brown gelding seemed about *it*.

"He frontfooted him, throwed him, and I helped slip the hackamore on his head. Dave tied up one foot as I held the horse down, and when that's done we let him up.

"Nothing seemed out of the ordinary with that horse till Dave eased his saddle onto him, and then it struck me right between the eyes, that horse wasn't acting natural. He didn't fight enough, and seemed altogether too cool. But what struck me most was them sunk eyes of his. You couldn't tell by looking at 'em what was going on between his ears, and them ears of his drawed my attention too. They stuck straight out from both sides of his head and moved neither back or forth; they seemed dead, the same as his eyes. But somehow I didn't want to think just what that combination of ears and eyes and brains was hatching out between 'em just then.

"That horse gave me a hunch that the end of something had come and I come pretty near telling Dave to turn him loose; but before I could think of an excuse the foot rope was off and Dave was on him.

"The big brown just stood in his tracks and shivered for a minute kinda like feeling if his muscles was all answering, and then Dave stirs him by the flat of his hand on his neck. It was just like putting a flame to a keg of powder, and hell broke loose right there.

"I seen Dave get loosened from the first jump, and that never happened before. I didn't want to look no more but somehow I just had to stand there and watch. I couldn't follow the action of that horse, it was too fast, high and crooked, and wicked. His front legs would bend back to a half circle so hard he hit the ground, and his hoofs would sink to the hair in a ground that'd been tamped for years by thousands of other hoofs.

"The saddle on his back was twisting and turning like it was on a pivot, and sometimes even stand straight up on end, the cantle toward the skies.

Their hoofs are not padded and a day of this would put ten years of the prize-fighting game in the kindergarten.

"By some miracle, Dave was staying there and riding, and he *sure* had to be *riding* to be there, let me tell you; but pretty soon my throat began to get dry, old Dave was loosening up more and more every jump, the saddle was steady getting away from him; but the old boy was still a-riding as though he was sure of his seat. His left hand was on the hackamore rope and his right was up in the air and in fanning motion the same as he'd always done. But there was no grin on his face, and believe me, stranger, you don't know how it hit me or what it meant to see that grin fade away.

"Then the end came; the big brown gelding made a leap in the air and for height it broke the record. Then he just seemed to float around up there for a second, both hind feet shot out in a kick that seemed to make the saddle horn and cantle touch, and when he hit the ground he was facing the opposite direction from where he started up. That horse bucked right out from under Dave and left him in the air to come down by himself.

"Well sir, from that day on it was sure some pitiful to watch Dave. None of the boys felt like or wanted to kid him and all was carrying a long face for quite a spell. Riding had been Dave's life and ambition; he done a mighty good job of it and lasted longer than the average, but he'd forgot that a human can stand just so much of that and no more, and he couldn't see why his body had to give out on him when his brain 'was just beginning to function good,' as he'd put it.

"And every day afterward as I'd see Dave going from the bunk house to the corrals, it'd come to me how the tables had turned on him. I remembered that time some ten years back when he took the bucking out of that big gray; how he'd near broke the pony's heart when he just laughed at him and rode him easy and let him buck to his heart's content. That pony had throwed many riders and never been

Both hind feet shot out in a kick that seemed to make the saddle horn and cantle touch.

laughed at before that way; it was his pride not to be rode, but Dave took that pride away and made a good saddle horse out of him.

"And now a big brown horse had done the same thing to Dave. It was Dave's pride not to be throwed and he had got to thinking no living horse could do it, till he met that gelding. That gelding maybe couldn't buck much harder than the gray, but then Dave was past being the same rider. Too many rough ponies of that kind had jarred the life out of him and put him in the discard.

"That was bound to come some time, and I was kinda thankful that big brown horse done such an honest job of it. Dave tried him often, and that pony gave him all the chance he wanted, and stood still till he was well set. But when Dave would let him know he was ready, that pony sure transformed hisself into a full-grown hurricane.

"There was time when as Dave kept a-trying, where he showed indications that he was going to stick to the finish; but always when the dust cleared and settled he'd find himself on the ground and getting dirt out of his ears. The brown horse would be to one side all quiet and sort of challenging for him to try again.

"And Dave would try again; he'd try him every day. But every time that pony bucked a little harder, if that was possible; — that horse was fast learning the tricks of the trade while poor old Dave was fast going downhill at it.

"But it was no disgrace getting bucked off that horse, and every man that seen him in action, good riders and all, wondered how many jumps *they* could of stayed. None tried to offer to ride him for Dave; they knowed better for two reasons. One was that Dave wanted to ride that horse himself and without no help; the other was that none of 'em felt at all sure they could ride him and a heap more knowed damn well they couldn't.

"So that's the way things stood. As Dave's friend I tried to talk him into letting that pony and all other broncs go to younger fellers, but he wouldn't listen to it and he'd always come back at me with the remark:

"'I can ride as good as I ever could, and I can ride that brown horse, too. You'll see me do it some of these days, and you'll see me fan and laugh at him the same as I used to do with the others.' But he'd never look me in the eye when he'd say that, and somehow I didn't look up much either.

"It was a month or so later when Dave had to be took to the hospital. Past internal injuries had been stirred up by the brown horse and hemorrhages had started. He layed in the building all that winter, and many is the time we wondered if he'd come out straight up or feet first.

"In his delirious spells he'd lean down on the side of the bed, one arm in the air the same as if he was fanning a bronc; his head would near reach the floor and he'd laugh the same as he'd used to laugh in a bucking horse's ear, and tell the brown horse to do his damndest.

"'I'm with you, you son of a sea cook,' he'd holler at him. 'Let's see if you can shake this cowboy off that brown hide of yours.' The nurse would bust in about then and we'd help her straighten him out.

"The superintendent came along to see him with me one day. He's a stern-looking sort of old feller and always struck me hard as stone; but when he seen Dave act up that way I caught him wiping the moisture off his eyes. It may be that he just realized something he'd never thought of before, but anyway, I sure liked him a heap more after that.

"And while we was hoping for the best for Dave that winter we framed up on him and tried to fix things so there'd be no more broncs for him to ride. There was one man in the country we figgered could ride the brown gelding. He wasn't as good a rider as Dave had been in his prime, but we hired him, thinking he could ride the horse and have him broke before Dave came back. But that horse didn't break so easy as all that, and he threw his man pretty often — too often for that horse to quit his bucking.

"In the meantime, Dave's constitution, which wouldn't say 'die,' was the cause of him coming out before we expected. He rode up to the ranch one day as big as life and straight to the corral where the new rider was finding himself busy with the brown horse, Dave's Brown horse.

"Well sir! Me and the superintendent sure got hell for a few minutes, and we tried to explain; but there was no explaining much to Dave right then. We had to wait till that night before he cooled down so we could talk reason with him, and then we had to give conditions before we could bring the argument to a wind-up.

"The conditions was that we let him have the brown horse and let him try him again soon as he was well recuperated. 'And when I ride him,' he says, 'and make a good job of it, I'll quit and never look at another bronc. But I want to quit knowing that I've rode every horse I ever mounted.'

"That settled it. We raised his wages and gave him an easy job keeping tab on the thoroughbred herd up near the foothills. He'd earned all of that, and we was mighty glad to see him accept. He rode away on a gentle horse, the first gentle horse Dave had rode for fifteen years, and he took his brown horse with him on the end of a rope.

"'Some of these fine days,' he says, pointing at the brown gelding as he was leading him away, 'you'll see me ride him in and right up on the front porch of the superintendent's house.'

"That's been two years ago now and Dave ain't showed up on the superintendent's porch as yet, not riding the brown horse, anyway. But I know Dave's been trying to ride that horse again. He may not of been trying very often on account that it takes him too long to get over the

182

effects afterwards, but it ain't over a month ago when I rode up there and seen the brown horse in the corral, and seen by the way the hair was laying on his back that the saddle had just been pulled off.

"Dave was lying full length on his bunk when I got up to the cabin, and when he heard me coming he straightened up as though he'd been caught rustling. He hee-hawed around for a spell and finally remarked that them thoroughbreds had sure kept him on the jump that morning, how some broke through the fence and all, but nary a word did he say about that brown horse in the corral. He was mighty careful not to.

"And stranger, that's the way things stand now. You know Dave and his feelings and when you get up there humor the old boy. And if you can frame it up so that Dave can ride that brown horse, or else make him quit and be satisfied, you got a good job here for as long as you want it.

"All of us that knows Dave thinks a powerful lot of him, and we know that if his talent had turned to politics instead of broncs he'd been President of the United States and busted the two-term law all to hell."

The foreman got up from his chair, pointed to a bunk and says, "You can unroll your bed in there for the night if you want, and I'll get some of the boys to help you start out with them horses in the morning."

It was a couple of days later and near sundown when I hazed my bunch of broncs into the corral of the camp Dave was holding down. On the trail over I'd been thinking steady of what the foreman had told me about him, and I was right anxious to see that *hombre*.

I was unsaddling my horse when glancing through the corral bars I spots him making tracks towards me. I took in all about him and looked for familiar signs, and even though he was like a lot of cowboys I'd seen and knowed I could see he was a plum stranger to me. I'd been hoping him and me had run acrost one another somewheres before.

But as he got closer and put out his paw for me to shake, I felt right then that I wouldn't of gained anything if we had exchanged the "makings" before. With all what the foreman had already told me about Dave and what I could see myself from one squint at him, not mentioning the feel of his handshake, made things mighty easy for me to know that old boy, and I knowed right there that if I'd broke horses in the same corral with him for the past ten years we wouldn't be no more acquainted than we was in that short spell we'd met.

"I heard a considerable about you," he says as a starter, "and I'm mighty glad to notice by the string of broncs you brought here to break that you're going to be with me for quite some time. Bring your pack-horse on up to the house and we'll put your bed inside while we're at it."

That evening and part of the night was mighty well used up with all we had to say. We talked most of what was past and the countries we'd been in, the ponies we'd rode and the times we'd had here and there. Many things was made to happen again by the old box stove that night, and as the time slid by I gradually edged out of the talk and was finding a lot of pleasure in just listening to Dave.

I could see that *hombre* had sure took bronc riding to heart and as he talked it was plain to see his heart still layed that way. It was hard for him to quit and the two years he'd been away from the rough ponies only left a hankering that was all the stronger.

"You know, Bill," he says, "it's sure been pounded to me a-plenty that it's high time for me to quit, but I still have the craving for setting on the kinky ponies and hearin' 'em snort back at me as I ride 'em out of the corral. These I'm riding now don't kick at my spurs like them others use to and I kinda miss that; and another thing, it sure worries me to feel that I'm now a 'has-been.'

"But I know it's no use, and that's been proved to me often. It took only one horse to prove it, but that pony sure persuades strong and without a doubt. He took all the conceit out of me and done it easy. That was a hard jolt and not at all gradual and that's one reason why I want to ride that horse. I'm going to ride him, too, and when I have him broke into a good saddle horse why then I'll be ready to quit, not before."

I could see there was no use arguing with Dave on that subject. All I could do was to try and help him win out that once. But he wouldn't stand for no help and every time he'd run in the big gelding and try his hand once more at setting him to a finish, that day would be sure to wind up mighty disappointing for both Dave and me.

"But I'll get him next time," he'd always say.

As the days and weeks wore on and once in a while Dave would try again with no better result, I kept a-trying to figger some way so as that brown hunk of horse meanness would sort of tame down and let Dave stay on for once. There was some ways that it could be done, but I didn't want to think of the consequences if I'd ever got caught trying 'em. It would spoil everything for Dave, for I knowed he wanted to ride that horse as he was and wouldn't want anybody to interfere that way.

Every minute of spare time he had he'd be in the corral watching me ride my colts, and from the way he took in everything I understood why I was sent there to do the horse breaking. The owners of the outfit, respecting Dave's feelings, didn't want him to break away too soon from what he'd been raised to seeing and doing and made a success at. They figgered it'd help some even if he couldn't mix in no more, to just watch some other feller do it and let things wear off gradual that way. Not many outfits, I thought, would do that for their riders that got "stove-up" on their range, riding their horses.

I climbed off a pretty "oily" bronc one day and thought I'd rode him slick enough considering the crooked work he put in his bucking. Dave had been watching the performance as usual, and when I walked over to where he was standing by the snubbing post to get my hobbles he says to me:

"You know, Bill, there was a time when I could ride like you rode just now."

I noticed his voice was trembling as he spoke, and I looked over his way. His hat kept me from seeing his face, but the way his hands was shaking as he tried to roll a cigarette told me plain which way his thoughts were running.

A few days later Dave was finding himself busy trying to keep some of his thoroughbred stock under fence; a few was bound to be out and straying away every day when Dave would have to track 'em down and bring 'em back to the big fields. I'd be by my lonesome for the biggest part of the day, and that's what I wanted.

Soon as Dave would disappear and was gone long enough so I was sure of him not turning back on account of forgetting something, I'd run in the big brown gelding, saddle him up and mount him on the fly. We'd go around and around and pretty soon I'd have the feeling that we'd run up in a stone wall. He'd break in two, and from then on is when I had to ride.

He was a rough pony, that boy, and sometimes would suggest mighty strong that I should grab the "nubbin," but somehow I kept my hands free from leather and managed to sideswipe him along the ears with my hat every once in a while. He never liked that, and as I'd hand him that kind of medicine every time I rode him he soon learned that the only way to keep me from doing it was to carry his head up where it belonged and trot around the corral peaceable.

But I didn't want to take all the bucking out of him. I had to leave some for Dave or else that *hombre* would be sure to see that all wasn't well. So, with a lot of work and hard riding, I finally broke that gelding to ease up on his bucking the minute I hollered at him. He'd took a lot of persuading to show that I could *make* him do that, but before I turned him loose one day I had him where all I had to do was to let out my war whoop and his head would come up like it'd been shot out of the earth by a cannon. I had him ready.

I wanted Dave to put in his work on that gelding the next morning, while I had him under my thumb, and Dave wasn't slow in taking up my hint that it was about time for him to try again. I run the brown horse in with the other colts I was breaking; Dave roped him, saddled him, and was pulling down his hat and pulling up his chaps ready to straddle him when he turned to me and says:

"This pony don't seem quite so spooky to-day."

"Maybe he ain't feeling well," I says, as I picks up my rope right quick and make tracks away from there.

I stopped at a safe distance from any more such remarks and watched him ease up in the saddle and get well set. He was mighty serious as he done that, and I could see what he expected was the same as he'd always got in trying to ride that horse. Then the big gelding went into action.

Gradually his jumps got higher and crookeder and each time he hit the ground harder, till I got a glance at Dave getting loosened up again, and I hollered. The horse remembered that holler and come damn near queering things by quitting all at once. I breathed some easier when he went to bucking again; that break in the performance had saved Dave. He'd got his seat back under him once more and then his features lit up into a grin. He was riding him, and daggone it he was even fanning him off and on.

And when the horse would get too rambunctious again I'd just holler out, but not quite so loud as the first time. Finally the doings quieted down, the gelding slowed down to crowhops and then high loping around the corral. Dave was a-setting up there proud as a peacock and grinning from ear to ear.

He was like a kid on Christmas morning when he finally climbed off and went to unsaddling. He was a-jabbering away at me and the gelding and petting him on the neck the while remarking that they'd get along yet. Then he turned on me sudden and asked:

"What t' hell made you holler like that when I was riding?"

I'd been expecting that from him, and my answer was ready.

"That was just my war whoop," I says. "I just can't help but let it out when I see somebody put up a good ride."

But it seemed like he never heard me as I explained, he was thinking of something. Something which showed on his expression as mighty important and sort of cheerful, too, for pretty soon he come out of his trance and says:

"Tomorrow, Bill, I'm going to ride the brown horse right up to the superintendent's house, and right on the front porch. I tole 'em I would do it some day."

Tomorrow came, Dave rode his horse again with the help of my war whoops. Then I opened the corral gate and let 'em go, old Dave a-riding like a cyclone and the brown horse carrying him on.

I sure wished him luck as I watched him top a ridge and disappear on the other side full speed ahead. I knowed what it meant for him to be able to ride up on *that* front porch with *that* brown horse, and somehow as I closed the corral gate I was finding myself hoping that I wouldn't take things so hard when the time came for me to quit the rough ones.

It was my life, too; I enjoyed the feeling that I could ride any horse and I liked them ponies for their orneriness, for the fight they'd put up and how interesting they made things, till they'd finally give in and do as *I* wanted 'em to.

I picked up my rope, packed my saddle by the snubbing post and went to work. There was ten head of broncs in the corral. It was my day's work to "uncork" all of 'em and give 'em each a spell under me and my saddle.

I was saddling up a second horse when I noticed a dust coming back over the same ridge Dave had took. A horse with a saddle on him was making that dust. Stirrups was flapping on each side and nobody was on him. Then I recognized the horse. It was the big brown gelding.

In another second I was on my bronc and headed from where the brown gelding had come. The bronc under me wanted to slow down some and juggle me a little, but I wouldn't give him time. He'd have to do it on the run.

I run onto Dave a mile or so from the corrals. He was all doubled up and leaning against a sage brush and I don't think he knowed I was there till I was near on top of him.

"Are you hurt, Dave?" I asks.

"No, just got the wind knocked out of me a little," he says. "I'll be all right in a minute."

But I knowed the symptoms, and knowed it'd take him quite a few days to recuperate. Dave was mighty quiet the rest of that day. He was doing a lot of thinking and would only grin sort of foolish when I'd look at him. It was after supper before he loosened up and decided to tell how it happened.

"I never was so surprised in my life as when that horse throwed me," he says. "He had me loosened up from the first jump, and I don't remember anything about the second."

Then he's quiet again for a spell, and finally he goes on:

"I guess it's no use, Bill. I've got to quit — I've met him."

"Met who?" I asks.

"My Waterloo," he answers, grinning.

"Jake Adams, Sourdough"

OLD JAKE WAS A BACHELOR, the folks around called him a confirmed bachelor, which I guess means that there was no hopes of his ever being anything else. He was a little over twenty when he first started batching, which was when he left his home grounds in New Mexico and rode north into Wyoming to start in the stock business for himself.

On the banks of Willow Creek which runs into Green River, Jake had took a Squatter's right and built himself a two roomed log house with a stone fireplace in the centre, bought a lot of grub and proceeded to accumulate a herd. From then on, Jake's meals and bed had been of his own making, all excepting when he joined some cow outfit during round ups, or went to town once or twice a year for a load of grub or such. In town the restaurant and hotel bed had to do.

Of course there was such other times too when he went to different doings or "shindigs" at some school-house on the river, but that was only during his first few years of batching. Folks tell of how Jake had come pretty close to tying to one of the fair sex a couple of times then but somehow something had happened each time that made him coil back the loop that only needed a flip. The words "will you" had never come — For some reason, that only Jake knowed, he'd shied clear of the double harness and settled down in a rut, which even tho it didn't lap over with all life has that a feller can gather, it all seemed to hold what he wanted and he'd never looked for more.

He had his place, and range, his cattle and his horses. Once or twice a week he'd ride twenty some odd miles to the post office and he'd ride back with a sack full of newspapers, and magazines. Them was his company, and by the fireplace of evenings and following the printed lines he travelled in strange countries and got the slant on other people

Folks tell of how Jake had come pretty close to tying to one of the fair sex.

and lives. Old Jake could talk on any subject with any man and stump many men on many of them subjects.

But with all his knowledge and wise views on things in general which he'd accumulated, Old Jake, in his thirty years or more of batching, had never somehow hankered for anything other than what he had, maybe there's the proof of his wisdom, but anyway, his pleasure in life was to have things the way he wanted 'em. He had sense enough not to want too much, so that was easy. His idea of real living was in seeing a bunch of his cattle in tall feed. Another one of his weaknesses was in riding fat saddle horses thru his range, his own little country. What little fencing was on his place was up tight and no wires was sagging, his gates was tall and made of peeled poles, and it was another pleasure to him to see how easy they swung open or shut.

Everything on the ranch had been made by Jake's own hands, the stables and sheds was of hewed logs and grooved in a way that'd make a cabinet maker look at 'em twice and wonder, the corrals and outside mangers sort of blended in amongst the cottonwoods by the creek and all made a picture that only added on to the beauty of what nature had already put there.

Then a hundred yards or so up a grassy slope stood Jake's two roomed log house. It looked like a safe bet against any kind of weather and there was something about it that'd invite a feller in wether it was hot or cool. No tin cans was seen on the way up to it, and if a feller was to look around, which he'd be bound to do, the first thing that'd attract his attention would be a water wheel on the creek which, by some idea of Jake's, pumped the water out of a little spring by the hillside into a tank by the house. The surplus water went to irrigate a little weedless garden, that garden was all the ploughed soil on Jake's land — the sourdough wasn't much on disturbing the natural sod.

He was a little over twenty when he left his home grounds in New Mexico and rode north to start in the stock business for himself.

Anybody looking at Jake's place and studying it a spell would know what sort of a man he was. There was everything about it all that showed how the sourdough was a crank in the way he done things. His pleasure was in doing 'em well and pleasing to the eye. Not only that, but handy and everything working perfect from the squeezer where he branded his cattle to the rack in the stable where his saddle layed. He could of saddled his horse in the middle of the night without a light and not miss the touch of his riggin' by half an inch. It was the same with everything else about Jake's place and like most of the bachelor cowmen of the range countries. They have to know where things are because there's nobody around to tell 'em if anything is lost or mislayed, but the advantage there is that once a thing is put it stays put.

Things was in the same order in that house of Jake's. He could of come in there out of a bone chilling blizzard, closed the door, and in a half a minute have a roaring fire to thaw out by. There was always pitch kindling topped with a big armful of wood in the fireplace and it was always ready for a match any time. It wasn't only for himself that he'd have things ready that way, there was others who might ride in and be in need of some warmth mighty quick.

Any other sourdough (bachelor) or passing cowboy could of found things in Jake's house near as quick as he could find 'em himself, all have about the same lay. Any rider could of come and warmed up and cooked hisself a meal with one hand and both eyes shut. As for old Jake he could of been blind and found everything without fumbling once. Then again with all so handy for them what knowed where to look there was a cleanness about everything that'd make many a lady wonder about her own kitchen. There was no starched tablecloth on the table but the oil cloth looked just as clean, so did the baking-powder cans with the holes in the lid that was used for salt and pepper shakers. There was no paint on the wide cottonwood-board floor, no paint on the windows, and no curtains, the bedspread on the bed in the little room adjoining was only a big tarpaulin canvas, and glancing at it all a feller wouldn't get no feeling of the kind that mahogany and overstuffed stuff would give but there was something about the whole of it that'd invite a feller to rest without fear of scratching a polished surface or upsetting the fish bowl, and all was clean, all was where Jake could put out his hand and reach for whatever he wanted without wondering where it was.

With all that was his, his place, his cattle, his horses and everything the way he wanted it to be, Jake had let the world slide by and enjoyed things the way he liked best. He shipped a little bunch of beef every fall and they always topped the market, and his earnings was so that when the income tax came in style he had to hunt up somebody to help him fill out a blank, the taxes he paid evened up well with what one of his steers would bring.

That's the kind of rut, if it can be called a rut, that Jake was into when a neighbor cowman rode up one day and caught the sourdough figgering from a calendar and taking 1874 from 1927. The neighbor helped him out on the figgers and the both of 'em allowed 53 was the difference. That was Jake's age and close as he could remember, that day was his birthday. A little brown jug was drug out from under the tarpaulin covered bed and the two lived back many years for many hours.

"Sure a nice little place you got here Jake" says the neighbor as he saddled his horse to leave late the next day. "You sure done a powerful lot of work on it too, but" he added on "don't you hanker to travel around a little bit once in a while? You sure could afford it now it seems to me like."

"Yep, I reckon I could afford it" says Jake "but all my hankerings are right here. There's no place else in the world where things are the way I want 'em and I've seeded down here so that if I was to budge out it'd be like as if both my arms and legs would have to be cut off and my heart out. I belong to the place that much — then again" he went on "if I went any place else I'd only get restless for the want of things that suit me. I've got 'em here and there's nobody around to disturb what I've planted or built, and say" says Jake sort of wanting to change the subject, it was all too deep even for him to figger out, "I wish you'd seen that last bunch of steers I shipped out."

"I know now why Old Jake never got married" says the neighbor grinning to himself as he rode away. He opened the big gate and looked back at the place and shook his head "sure is a pretty place." But the thoughts of Jake and the place all went out of his mind soon as he turned his horse towards home, something else had come to him sudden and which would need considerable figgering, and that was to explain to his wife how come he was gone two days instead of one.

He was letting his horse pick his own way towards the home grounds and thinking deep on the subject, when from his right a ways came the purr of a motor and looking the direction where the sound came from he spotted an automobile stopped at the creek crossing, a man was out waving for him and the cowman rode over to see what was wanted.

He noticed as he rode closer that there was two ladies in the car, one sort of stocky setting in the back seat and the other, a younger lady setting in the front one. He figgered at a glance that the youngest one was the man's wife and the oldest to be the mother of either one or the other.

"Well what can I do for you?" says the cowman as he spurred his shying horse closer to the car.

It seemed like there was nothing much he could do only to tell them where was the closest place they could put up for the night. A boulder at the creek crossing had bent the axle till both front wheels was near running into one another. The boulder had went on thru, cracked the battery and stripped a few other things before the car could be stopped.

"Better shut off your car till you see if you have any oil in the crank case, John" says the lady in the back seat.

That done, the cowman told 'em of Jake's place, "It's about three quarters of a mile up the creek, and most likely he could haul your car to town with a team for you."

"Lucky we don't have far to walk anyway" says the man John after the cowman rode away.

So, that's how come that Jake, while bringing in some kindling that evening, seen three people walking up the trail along the creek towards his house. He just had time to put his kindling away and touch things up a little inside when the three came to the door. Jake was about to say "howdy" and kindly invite the folks in when he was interrupted by the stocky lady who'd clasped her hands, rolled her eyes, and remarked:

"My, isn't this a charming little house."

Then getting a glimpse of Jake standing in the door she smiled and introduced herself and the others, she followed that up with telling how their car broke down, then she went on to ask if he could put them up for the night, they hadn't brought no camp nor grub with 'em.

"I expect you folks are powerful hungry" Jake chips in, "and if you'll all wait a spell I'll have the best I can gather up on the table for you."

Jake went inside after telling 'em to make themselves at home and to come in or set on the porch as they wished. In two minutes Jake had the old stove throwing a cooking heat, the coffee was on, then he sliced some bacon, put it in the pan and out of some cool place, which was arranged from the spring, he brought out half a dozen good sized speckled trout, rolled 'em in flour and sizzled 'em in bacon grease. Adding on warmed over sourdough bread, a dish of prunes and some tomato preserves it all tallied up to what Jake called a meal. He could of done better he thought, but maybe the folks was too hungry to wait.

As it was he called 'em to the table fifteen minutes after he started his fire. He escorted 'em to the home made chairs around the home made table and told 'em to "go to it."

"Gracious" remarked the stocky lady "I never expected anything like this, and trout too, so crisp and nice." Then she looked up at Jake and says, "John is right at home where there's trout, he's a regular fiend when it comes to fishing."

"Yes" says John taking a mighty mouthful of said trout "I like to eat 'em but I'd rather ten to one fish for 'em, where there is any. I expect there's lots of 'em out here tho."

"Not so many" says Jake "this creek's been fished out long ago, but I've been planting some here in a pool up the creek every year and I manage to get a few once in a while."

"Well, that's good" says John, then "I don't suppose you'd mind if I went to catch a mess of 'em early in the morning."

"Oh yes, do that John" chips in the chunky lady "and I'll cook 'em myself."

Old Jake could only smile in favor of all of that, there was nothing else he could do.

After a lot of compliments on Jake's cooking and how good the trout and sourdough bread tasted the meal finally come to an end. Jake then told 'em to make themselves at home some more and to take it easy, he'd wash the dishes, but Mrs. Potter, which was the stout lady's name, begin to argue with Jake on that subject and said she'd wash the dishes and her daughter could wipe 'em.

"Well, I don't mind doing dishes" says Jake getting busy with the dish pan as he talked "I sure hadn't ought to anyway, I've been doing 'em for about thirty years now."

"Have you really?" says Mrs. Potter. "Gee, you must of been widowed young."

"No maam" says Jake squirming a little "I've never been married."

"Haven't you? — well" — Then after a while she went on, "I've been widowed nearly ten years, and now all I have left is this married daughter of mine, but I'm afraid" she glanced at the girl and smiled a little, mostly to Jake, "I'm afraid now" she said once more "that they're trying to get rid of me, you know how young married folks are."

Mrs. Potter grabbed a dish towel and went to wiping dishes. Jake had beat her to the job of washing 'em, and he seemed awful busy and interested in that dish pan, specially when John and his wife got up and walked out, as they said to watch the sunset.

Being left alone with a talkative lady wasn't Jake's idea of a too pleasant time. There was many other things he'd rather look forward to, and the dishes begin to rattle out of the pan in pretty fast time. The lady talked on not at all hindered by Jake's record speed. When things got too hot there by the sink he'd have an excuse of going to the stove for something or other and then the table.

The dishes was no more than done and put away when he begin to fix up places for the folks to sleep. He rolled his bed and set it out on the porch, got clean blankets out and fixed up the one big bed he was using and a couch in the kitchen, then he managed somehow to chip in a few words edge-ways to tell Mrs. Potter where they was to sleep. The young folks was still missing.

"In the morning" Jake went on, after he'd managed to get a holt with a few words "I'll ride over to a neighbor of mine about fifteen miles from here and telephone for a tow car to come and get you. I'd take you in myself but it's pretty slow work with a team, and besides all my work horses are out on the range and it'd take time to get 'em."

"Don't go to putting yourself out too much for us Mister Adams" says Mrs. Potter. "We don't mind staying here a day or so." She smiled at him. "That is, if you don't mind our company."

"Sure not, glad to have you" says Jake. He edged on out to the porch, grabbed his roll of bedding, and saying good night walked on down the path towards a big cottonwood by the corrals where he unrolled his bed, pulled out the makings for a smoke, and after a while, as darkness came over the land he crawled in to stargaze at the stars.

It was along about the middle of the night, and Jake was dreaming that John was cutting down his corral poles for fire-wood, then along came Mrs. Potter with a basketful of squirming trout that splashed water all over his face, and Jake woke up. It was raining and not a star could be seen.

It was still raining when daybreak come, and as the sourdough cowman stuck his head out from under the tarp' to investigate the sky, he seen where there was no chance of it quitting, not for that day anyway. Jake listened for any sound from the house and a hoping somebody would be up so he could go in and have his coffee, but no sound come, and pulling the tarp' back over his head he tried to go to sleep some more, but it was his time to get up and the best he could do was to doze off and on till Mrs. Potter moved. Her bed was on the couch in the kitchen and there was no going in for Jake till he knowed for sure she did move.

It was, what seemed to Jake, a couple of hours later when he stuck his head out from under the tarp' once more and still no sound come that'd tell him Mrs. Potter or the young folks was up, but he couldn't stand to be in bed any longer so he dressed under the canvas and got up, then went to get the "wrango" horse that was picketed in tall grass, saddled him up, and rode out to run in a few saddle horses. He roped himself a big brown horse, led him in the stable, and while that pony took on very unnecessary mouthfuls of bluejoint old Jake puttered around and finally went to saddling him. He even brushed the slick hide of that pony, and that was sure unnecessary too, but Jake liked to see the brush over the big dapples, and besides he was trying to kill time.

He killed some more time by going down to the corral to give a look at them ponies that was still in it, a big yellow slicker over his shoulders, he gave them all a good look, that satisfied him some, after a while he opened the corral gate and let 'em out and gave another long look as the good feeling ponies played and bucked thru the rain to their feeding grounds. He then led the little wrango horse, which had been tied up, back to the picket log, he picked up the long rope that was fastened to it and fingered one of its strands, it was wearing out close to the knot and Jake cut out the weak part and tied a new "turkshead." He stood and watched the pony graze a while and then walked down to the creek where he took off his slicker and begin to wash up. There was a little bridge close by and he noticed as he reached down with cupped hands for water that one of the timbers underneath was beginning to rot. He'd have to get another peeled log to put in the place of it soon.

A few minutes later found Jake heading back for the stable again, he stood in the door and watched the rain come down and once in a while he'd turn to look at the big slick brown horse a chewing away on the good hay. All with the looks of that pony, the clean dry stable, and then the smell of good clean moisture outside which promised more tall grass, it all was to Jake a picture with a feeling of peace and plenty.

Jake was sniffing at the air and letting his eyes complete things up when from up towards the house came sounds that made him stop his sniffing and looking, instead he begin to listen, and pretty soon the sound came again.

"Yoo hoo — yoo hoo — Mister Adams."

Jake mumbled something as he came out of the stable on towards the path to the house. When he got up there he found the door part open and as he walked in he come near running into the smiling Mrs. Potter.

"Good morning," says Jake. "I hope you all had a good sleep."

"Oh yes indeed," says Mrs. Potter. "I never slept so well in my life, and in a strange place too."

Jake hadn't heard what Mrs. Potter said, he'd smelled coffee, and sure enough there was the steaming coffee pot on the stove and seemed like waiting for him, and better than that, the table was all set and ready, a steaming hot breakfast was also waiting, and at the sight Jake's eyes sort of lit up.

Mrs. Potter had watched his face and seemed mighty pleased.

"I thought of surprising you with a taste of somebody else's cooking" she says "you know even the best of cooks get tired of their own cooking, and being that John caught such a nice mess of trout I couldn't help but cook them. Just think" she went on "John had been out fishing ever since six o'clock and in this rain too, my! ain't this weather just simply awful?"

Jake grunted, and after all the others had set down he took his seat and begin reaching for his coffee cup, he was over two hours late on it and he was aching for a swallow, but Jake was due for disappointments, the first swallow he took of the coffee made him think of the rank sulphur spring that was up in his pasture, his horses never touched it.

"Gee mother" says John's wife "you certainly outdone yourself in making coffee this morning, I never tasted such good coffee."

Jake come near snorting at that, but instead he just looked at the young lady to make sure she wasn't joking, she sure enough wasn't, and then he got to thinking most likely it was his taste which might be altogether different than other folkses'. To him it tasted like it had too much coffee and not enough boiling or else too much boiling and not enough coffee, but anyway there was sure something wrong and he sure didn't enjoy it. Then he got to thinking, it must be his taste, because he didn't remember of going anywheres and getting coffee that suited him, not unless it was at some cow camp or of his own making, but anyway it was too late for him to change his taste now even if it might be different than others, so he swallowed the coffee the best way he could and let it go at that. He thought once of having one of them good looking biscuits to help along, but that only made things worse. "She must of put baking powder in the sourdough," thought Jake.

The trout and fried potatoes was nearest to his liking than anything and after a little helping of each, no more coffee, Jake allowed he had enough, and got up from the table remarking that it was the finest breakfast he'd ever et.

"If you folks will excuse me now" he went on "I'll ride over to that neighbor of mine and see if I can get a car to tow you folks back to town, I don't reckon I'll be able to get back till tonight, but you folks make yourselves to home, and most likely you can pull out of here by to-morrow if you want."

"That's mighty good of you helping us out that way Mr. Adams" says Mrs. Potter "but couldn't John here go in place of you?"

Jake thought of his big brown horse with a green stranger on him who didn't know how to ride, and says "Thanks Maam, but on account of him being a stranger around here I don't reckon he could find the place."

"Fine" says John "I can go get another mess of trout."

With that ringing in his ears old Jake walked out of the house to the stable, a big bear trap was hanging on the corner of that stable and as he walked by he spotted it and stopped, then grunted and went on to get his horse.

It was late in the afternoon when Jake, after riding thru heavy rains and flooded creeks, got back to his place. He'd got the long distance call to town o.k. but he was told there at the garage that on account of swollen creeks and many bridges washed out on the way they couldn't possibly send a tow car out for many days, maybe a week.

Jake had hated to come back with that kind of news, but as he walked in the house and begin to spread the meaning of 'em, he seen that his fear of disappointing 'em had been for nothing. Mrs. Potter didn't seem at all mournful about it and didn't want to even waste a breath on the subject. Soon as Jake came in she dropped a magazine she'd been reading and begin to make a place by the stove for Jake to set and dry. Even his telling her that he was dry as powder didn't check her none.

John's wife was setting by a window and showed a little interest as Jake came in but she soon turned back to her task again, she'd also been reading a magazine, it must a been a magazine they brought with 'em because Jake couldn't recognize the cover. On it was the picture of two young people, looked like they was making love or something. Jake's gaze sort of wandered around some from there till it came to the table. On it was a big panful of trout, his raising, all cleaned and ready to fry. At the sight of them he begin to wonder where the other party was, but he didn't have to wonder long, there came a sort of rumble from the next room and then a choking noise like you hear when a rope tightens up on a critter's wind pipe.

"Oh John, John, turn over." It was the good wife speaking. John turned over and all was quiet.

Things was so quiet that, between spells when Mrs. Potter tried to start a conversation, Jake could hear the clock ticking. He sort of listened to the ticking in a hazy way, and then it came to him that the sound didn't come from the usual place. He glanced at the shelf in the corner where the clock had been and spotted a looking glass there instead, the clock was on top of the home made cupboard, and that cupboard, he noticed there was something wrong with it. It was all decorated up with fancy cut newspaper a hanging over the shelves, just right, he thought, to lap in the gravy bowl as it was put in there.

The dishes was all piled up in there in neat ways sure enough, but daggoned hard to get at, and he wondered what was the idea of tipping some of them dishes on edge like it'd been done at the back, they'd sure slide to the floor and break sometime, and them cups a hanging by their handles to little hooks, what happened to them what had the handles broke off? —

All the cans Jake had saved to keep things in and labelled, had disappeared and after a lot of looking around he found 'em in a box in a corner, seemed like ready to take out and dump. The whole inside of the house seemed transformed, it was good to look at in a way, but it sure wasn't handy, not to his way of thinking. The atmosphere of the place was changed and he figgered that the company around had something to do with it, but somehow it didn't look like his place no more, he sort of felt like he was in a stranger's home, and the more he looked around the more he seen how it'd take him a powerful long time to set things to right again and the way he wanted 'em.

It looked awful dark inside too, even for a cloudy rainy day like it was, and the reason of that he seen was curtains on the windows, he had to lean ahead on his chair to make sure they was curtains, and they was. A big bolt of sheeting which he'd bought to line the ceiling of the place with had been found and some of it cut up for that purpose. "Well" thought Jake "I can use 'em for dish towels after they're gone, I need some new dish towels anyway."

Jake wondered what they'd done in the other room, but he figgered he'd seen enough to do him for a while, as it looked now even, it seemed like he was out of a house and home. He thought on the subject for quite a spell and then it came to him that after all the lady sure must of meant well. Yep, too well. Anyway he figgered maybe he ought to show some appreciation of the work they done on the place wether he liked it or not.

He noticed Mrs. Potter a setting there reading and like she was sure enough waiting to hear a word from him and Jake swallowed a couple of times so he could speak.

"Quite a change in this place" he says.

Mrs. Potter kind of jumped up at that, turned in her chair, and faced old Jake with a smile.

"Well, it's about time you noticed it" she says. "Here, I've been working like a slave all day so to have things all done before you got back. You men keep things in such funny places," she went on "but I don't expect you have time straightening a house much when you have so much outside work to do — and nobody to cook for you."

That all was quite a blow to Jake because he'd sure always prided hisself on keeping his house always in shape.

"Too bad I didn't know of your intentions, or I'd tried to talk you out of the work, it's pretty hopeless fixing this place up because it was only built for an old bachelor like me. It wouldn't be much of a place for a woman."

"Oh, I think it's a dandy place" comes back Mrs. Potter. "I had lots of fun fixing it up."

"I'm glad you got some fun out of it, but I wouldn't do any more because it ain't worth it, and besides you better rest up, you must of had a hard trip before you got here."

Jake had no more to say after that, but Mrs. Potter wasn't thru yet, she hadn't even started, she went on to tell of the beauty of a home when all is in harmony and everything is fixed right. She even brought her dead husband to life so as to back up her talk on what a home should be and all it meant. She painted a mighty pretty picture before she got thru, but to Jake the picture soon turned to wax and the colors begin to run like as if a lighted candle had been near. He was a *Confirmed* bachelor.

It rained all the next day after Jake's ride to the neighbor, that night it tried to clear up, but Jake prophecized that it'd rain some more the next day, "the sunset wasn't promising good weather yet," and Jake was right, it rained the next day as hard as ever, but as the sun went to setting that evening it looked like the storm had come to a long-winded end.

Jake took a long breath at the sight of the clear sunset, he'd never seen such a pretty sight he thought, and it was the first time in his life, specially at that time of the year when he'd wished for a rain to quit. The two days' heavy rain had been mighty hard on the bachelor, he'd seen his home changed into somebody else's and he'd been helpless to say anything against the changes. If anything he felt he had to make 'em think he liked it. Hospitality was a sacred thing to the sourdough, it was a Western law he lived up to more than any law ever made in courts, and he wouldn't of dreamed to do a thing that was against that law.

So Jake'd had to bear it all and smile. One day he seen Mrs. Potter raise a lid on the stove and put one of his frying pans over the flame, getting the bottom of it all black, then again he seen her washing the frying pan that evening and she didn't wash the bottom nor the handle. That was something he was always careful of doing well, and when he looked at the paper against the wall where the frying pan hung he seen grease spots on them, grease that'd been dripping from them same pans. That never happened when *he* washed 'em.

But he was out of that job of washing, he'd been edged out of it for as long as they'd be there the same as he was edged out of lots of things that was his ever since they come. There was only one chair which he could come to in that house and use, it wasn't his old favorite cowhide chair either, John had appropriated that one. Everything else had been appropriated by either Mrs. Potter or her daughter till Jake felt the only place left for him was in one of them box stalls in the stable.

He'd come in one afternoon, while it was raining and after he'd stayed outside as long as he could, and found both of the ladies going thru his stack of books and magazines. They smiled and said they was straightening them up, but when he tried to find a certain book the next day he had to give it up. It was in that pile somewhere, but where?

Jake didn't want to get peeved at 'em because he knowed they was only thinking of doing him a good turn, but daggone it, he wished they wasn't so willing, and he wished Mrs. Potter would quit her hinting and telling on what all a bachelor missed in life and home and so on. That part of it was getting the best of him and he was for hitting the breeze often only he was afraid of what all they'd do to that place of his if he left.

Like one day he caught John bringing in an armful of pitch pine, something he used for kindling, Jake didn't say nothing, but the stove got awful hot and the next day it had to be all cleaned out of the soot that'd accumulated in there. Every day John kept a bringing trout, sometimes twice as much as could be used, and then one time that same gazabo went out with Jake's shot gun and brought in two sage chickens, one of them Jake recognized as the pet he'd had for two winters and which used to come and eat bread crumbs off the porch.

So, with all of that, it was no wonder that Jake drawed a long breath when the rain finally quit and the sun begin to dry things up, there was hopes of his getting rid of 'em then, he hoped, without having to tell 'em, but he would never tell 'em to go, that was against his religion.

Two days of sunshine along with a good breeze followed up. The creeks went down to normal again and the roads dried up plenty fit for travel in a car. On the morning of the third clear day Jake, figgering that the washed out bridges would all be repaired, saddled up his brown horse and went to start out for the neighbor again to telephone for the tow car, but Mrs. Potter met him at the corral gate.

"You seem awful anxious to get rid of us Mr. Adams" remarked Mrs. Potter sort of shy-like and smiling, after Jake told her where he was headed. "And," she went on, "I was just going to ask you where was the best place to pick berries. John says there lots of 'em here, and I was going to pick some and make you some good jelly."

So it wound up that Jake, instead of riding over to the neighbor, escorted Mrs. Potter to a berry patch. She remarked on the way how she'd like to get on a horse some time, if he had one gentle enough for her, "she hadn't rode since she was a little girl." Jake left her in a thick patch of berries, saying that he had to ride on to take a look at his stock.

The way it was now, and according to the way Jake felt about it, he wasn't to go for a tow car to get the folks out till they said they wished to go. The sourdough didn't want to have it seem that he'd like to have 'em go, not as much as he wanted to get rid of 'em, and it seemed like there was nothing for him to do only to wait and hope that they'd want to go soon.

But clear bright days followed on one after another and no sign came from Mrs. Potter or the young folks that they was anywheres near wanting to move. They'd settled down to stay seemed like. Jake had made 'em feel so welcome, and they all figgered that by bringing sunshine to the bachelor's, what they thought dreary, life they was doing a plenty to feel right in taking on the hospitality he offered.

Every day John kept a bringing trout till Jake thought sure no more was left in the pool. The wife would go with John sometimes on walks or hunting, they was having a fine time, and one evening they brought another one of Jake's pets full of shot, it was a big wild duck, one of 'em that'd been coming to the pool every year and bringing others. Jake had fed 'em and they'd all got so tame that they'd hardly notice him when he'd come to watch 'em.

Jake had got red in the face and come pretty near exploding at the sight of the dead duck but somehow he held himself and only wished something would happen that'd make the visitors vamoose before they done more damage. For days Mrs. Potter put up wild fruit and jelly, then the sugar run out, and on investigating, Jake seen where he'd also run out of other things, he'd have to go to town soon and stock up.

But all them things, as much as they disturbed the peace of the sourdough, wasn't what aggravated him most. He could of stood that maybe for a long spell but he sure couldn't bear the stand Mrs. Potter had took towards him. That lady was out to get Jake, and she'd got so bold in her hints towards the last few days that Jake didn't hardly dare come in the house, only at meal time. She'd cornered him one day, and holding a jar of jelly to the light, had made him look thru it to see how clear it was, then she'd say smiling her best as usual:

"If the way to a man's heart is thru his stomach this sure ought to get you Mr. Adams."

But that didn't faze Jake none at all, instead, as he layed in his bed under the big cottonwood that night and stared at the stars, he hoped they could help him plan a way out. Finally, after a lot of hard thinking one plan sort of shaped itself, but Jake didn't like it much. It struck him a whole lot like he was fighting prairie fire and him doing the "back-firing," fighting fire with fire and so on.

When that plan came to him again soon as he woke up the next morning he was less for it than the night before, and he was for forgetting about it and all other plans, he'd decided to play "freezeout" and let the folks stay till they was ready to go. All would of went well maybe and Jake would of stuck to what he'd decided, but the well meaning Mrs. Potter went and made another big mistake, a mistake that Jake couldn't make himself overlook. He'd seen the lady take his sourdough crock and scour it out, the fine thick dough he'd been so careful to let accumulate on the inside of the crock, and which all added taste to the biscuits and flapjacks, was scraped out clean and soapy water took what was left.

The sight of that near broke Jake's heart, it hurt him even more than when John killed his pet sage chicken and duck, fished his trout stream dry, and many other things which had been none at all to Jake's liking.

All them things capped with the sight of the sourdough crock finally got under Jake's hide, he felt that he had to do something and mighty quick, and at breakfast that morning Mrs. Potter noticed that Jake was even quieter than usual. The truth of it was Jake was afraid to say anything, one word might start the landslide of the others which had accumulated and was aching to be off his chest, and the sourdough was still chewing on his last bite when he excused hisself and went out. The pile of tin cans that'd been scattered to one side of the house and which he sighted only speeded him on to the stable and his brown horse. Five minutes later he was riding out and as he rode he begin mapping out the plan which had come to him the night before.

Jake was gone all that day, Mrs. Potter went to work doing some more changes and surprising things which she figgered would be bound to show the sourdough what a change there was between batching and having somebody around who could make things homelike. She was at her busiest transforming one thing into another that afternoon when she heard footsteps on the porch. It couldn't be John, she thought, him and his wife was out hunting and wouldn't be back till dark, then she heard spurs ringing, and she thought of Jake, but it couldn't be him because Jake's spurs had a different sound. She left her work, and hitting for the door she came face to face with a lady there in riding skirt.

Mrs. Potter's heart missed a beat as some kind of hunch made her size up the strange lady. She noticed that stranger was not near as stout as she was herself, that she was younger, and she had to admit that she was pretty to look at, specially in that riding outfit.

The lady introduced herself as Mrs. Farrell and said she'd rode over to see Mr. Adams. When she was told Mr. Adams was gone and nobody knowed when he'd be back, she remarked that she'd wait for him as she wanted to find out if she could throw her steers in with his when shipping time come.

Mrs. Farrell was invited in and it was only a short while later when, by hinting around, Mrs. Potter found out some disturbing things about the newcomer. She learned that Mrs. Farrell was also a widow and lived with a son up on a small ranch a few miles away, that she thought a great deal of Mr. Adams, how her and him run their cattle together and shipped at the same time. "He's certainly been a good neighbor" Mrs. Farrell had added on.

Mrs. Potter hadn't liked the sound of her voice when she said that, and when she glanced her way she noticed that Mrs. Farrell was sizing up the place in a sort of surprised look.

"I see there's quite a change here," says Mrs. Farrell. "It's not at all the way Mr. Adams usually keeps things" she smiled and looked at Mrs. Potter.

"Well, you see" says Mrs. Potter "Mr. Adams has been so good to us that I thought I'd fix the place up for him, men so seldom have time or know how." Then she went on to tell how their car broke down at the creek crossing, and how they had to impose on Mr. Adams till they could get back to town again.

"I'm sure Mr. Adams must like your company" says Mrs. Farrell "and he appreciates anything anybody ever does for him, like for instance the way you fixed up the house, it looks very home-like, but" she hesitated some and smiled "knowing Mr. Adams like I do I'm afraid he would like it better the way it was — These bachelors out here are so particular about their cabins, more particular I think than most housewives, and their ideas how a cabin should be fixed is very different."

The talk between the two ladies went on for a while and then it begin to lag, came a time when words was few and far apart and Mrs.

Potter went to finish up the work she'd started before the interruption come. Somehow she had no heart to keep on with the job no more, she wished she could quit, but most of all she wished that lady hadn't come, because with her around she'd of a sudden felt sort of uncomfortable and put out.

She was glad when as evening come her daughter and son-in-law walked in the house. Fixing up supper kept her busy then, and when Mrs. Farrell asked to help her she took pleasure to let her know in her own way that she didn't need none of her butting in.

Supper over with, Mrs. Farrell walked out and in the dim light of the evening strolled around by the water wheel and down the creek to Jake's well kept corrals and stables. Jake was sure a crank on the way his place must be, and she had to smile a little at the thought of how the transformation of his cabin must of struck him. It was dark when she went back to the house. Mrs. Potter and the young folks was reading by the lamp and not one raised a head or offered a chair as she walked in.

Not a one suggested any help as she hunted for blankets or a place to bed down for the night. But Mrs. Farrell only smiled at that, she didn't need no help, and went on to fix herself a bed in the best way she could.

But, on account of the bed not being any too comfortable, Mrs. Farrell didn't sleep any too well that night. She was up an' around before any of the others when morning come and begin to make breakfast. The coffee grinder made a noise at an unreasonable hour for Mrs. Potter and the others, and when all of 'em come up to take a hand there was nothing for 'em to do but set down and eat.

They was hardly thru eating when Mrs. Farrell followed up her lead and proceeded to wash the dishes. Mrs. Potter wasn't much for helping her but she finally did and she noticed as Mrs. Farrell put away the dishes and things that they was being put away in places where Jake had been keeping 'em, not where Mrs. Potter had moved 'em.

The house was being swept up when Mrs. Potter begin talking to John who was setting on the porch and whittling. As she went on she remarked how she wished the car was fixed so they could get back to town.

"You and Jennie had a pretty good vacation now" she says "and I think we better go."

But John wasn't anxious seemed like, there was such good fishing and hunting around. They maybe would of decided on staying even longer but Mrs. Farrell who'd overheard the conversation came in on 'em about that time, and seeming anxious to help, offered to ride over and telephone for a car to come and get 'em.

Mrs. Potter hadn't figgered on being heard, but she wasn't put out much by that, she only smiled sarcastic like at Mrs. Farrell and said:

"Very good of you, my dear — I wish you would."

So, that's how come when along about noon the next day, a tow car with room for passengers drove to the door at Jake's place. Mrs. Potter seemed mighty glad to see the car come, she'd been waiting and ready. She'd even talked John into sticking around and not go fishing no more, and after a hurry-up noon meal Ma Potter piled in the tow car followed by Jennie and John. Mrs. Farrell waved an unanswered good-by to them as the car started away and then she went into the house and worked the whole afternoon a trying to put things back to the way she remembered Jake having 'em.

It was along about the middle of that same afternoon that Jake himself topping a ridge, seen two cars, one pulling another, a heading the direction of town. The sourdough shook his head in wonder and smiled, then reined his brown horse the direction of his place on a high lope. When he got there and walked in the door he shook his head again, smiled, and wondered some more. Mrs. Farrell was taking off the

It was along about the middle of that same afternoon that Jake himself topping a ridge seen two cars, one pulling another, aheading the direction of town.

finishing touches and Jake's place very near looked like his own once more.

"Daggone it" says Jake losing his smile "I sure don't feel any too proud of myself for putting you to so much trouble, Mrs. Farrell, your posing as a widow just on account of an old sourdough a wanting to get rid of a designing old woman and her brood, but I was desperate Mrs. Farrell. I was desperate, and" he looked around the place "I never figgered you'd go as far as to even fix up the house like it was, I —"

"Now, Jake you keep quiet and stop your apologizing" interrupts Mrs. Farrell. "I had a lot of fun out of this, and come to think about doing anybody a favor, I guess you never go to no trouble for anybody, do you? I guess you forget the time you practically saved all our cattle by letting my husband have the hay he needed so bad that hard winter a few years ago. You didn't have any too much hay for your own cattle that year if I remember right, and I guess I can remember many other good turns you done us Jake, and if you don't keep quiet I'll tell you about 'em."

Jake did keep quiet, that is as far as that subject was concerned, but he talked on pretty well about the wonders of the performance and all the way while he escorted Mrs. Farrell to her home and husband, the trip was slow because back of the two saddles on both horses was gunnysacks full of jars filled with jellies and preserved wild fruits. Jake had insisted on Mrs. Farrell taking 'em, for as he'd remarked, his sweet tooth didn't allow no such stuff.

"And sometime" says Jake winking at Tom Farrell, after they both got at the cowman's home, "sometime Mrs. Farrell if you ever do happen to be a real widow why — I'll see that you'll never got *too* lonesome."

"A Home Guard"

"IT'S DAGGONE QUEER how come some folks are born with everything and never make use of it."

That remark floated on the desert breeze from one Flint Spears, a cowboy, acrost to one Don Evans, another of the same breed.

The two riders had left the round-up wagon that morning and was poking along behind a little herd of mixed stuff, headed for a low range of juniper hills which looked hazy in the distance. The mixed stuff which had been gathered during the round-up, or Rodeer, as they say in that country, was to be drove and turned loose at the springs amongst them juniper hills, after which the cowboys was to ride back and join the round-up wagon again.

It was a three days' trip, and in that time, riding pretty well side by side, the two cowboys would let pass many an opinion or remark, for the slow trailing, mile after mile of it, seems to give air to many thoughts which any other time would stay asleep in a man's think tank.

There's no danger of being interrupted, and it seemed like, according to the remark already passed, that Flint had found a long winded subject to harp on and waller around in to his heart's content while he kept the drags on the move.

Don knowed from past long rides with Flint that many words was due to skim along the heat waves to his ear, that last remark of Flint's suggested that, and as was natural with Don, he prepared to meet the attack and weaken it all he could by finding flaws in it. That was his way, a way which aggravated Flint often, but which was sure to stir him always to win on whatever argument or subject he might bring up.

This time tho, Flint seemed to have more than just an ordinary subject on his mind, and there as more reason for his bringing it up than just to make talk. Something was worrying him, and Don knowed that soon now he'd be hearing about it.

And sure enough . . . Flint flipped the end of his rope at the tail of the closest drag and then looking thru the dust at Don, went on to ask.

"Did you ever see a home guard that was any good?"

That question was kind of sudden for Don, it wasn't what he expected, but in such a case he was always ready with a neutral answer.

"W-e-l-l," he says "it seems to me like I have. . . . You know" he went on "there's some good in everything."

"That may be so in most cases but it didn't work that way with any home guard *I* ever seen, and if there's any good in 'em it's sure well hid under a lot of worthlessness."

"Now, what home guard made a victim of you lately, Flint?" says Don grinning at him.

"None . . . and that ain't all," says Flint mighty serious like "but since that new 'Rep' (rider representing a neighboring outfit) joined this spread I got a hankering to chew up on my finger nails to keep from thinking. He reminds me strong of one home guard I used to know and had dealings with a few years back. Not that he acts like him, because this feller seems to be a real hand, but he sure looks like him, and that's enough to remind me."

"Remind you of what . . . what the home guard done to you?"

"No, not what he done to me, nor to anybody else, for that matter. And that's just it, he never done anything, nothing good or real bad, and the shame of that was he had everything to start with.

"But," Flint went on before Don could edge in a word "what got me under the skin wasn't how worthless he was, as how I figgered his dad must of felt about it, and how such can happen when it seems like all is set to bring out nothing but the best.

"His dad was one of the biggest cowmen in the state and started in the business with nothing but a saddle and a half-broke horse under him, now he's got as nice a spread as you want to see, good grade of cattle, and as fine a bunch of saddle horses as you'd find anywheres, not mentioning the good camps that's all over his range, a palace of a home on one of his ranches, and another such a place in town for when he has to spend a little time there.

"He gathered all of that from nothing, made a big name for himself as an all around man, and could of been elected governor of the state if he'd wanted to, . . . and then he turns around after all that and brings to the world a son, such a thing as this home guard I'm raving about, a scrub that ain't fit to scrape the gumbo off the old man's boots."

"That's nothing," Don chips in, "you see the same happening every day."

"Maybe so" says Flint "but that fact don't keep it from being a daggone shame, specially if you knowed Old Nye Roswell, that's the boy's father's name. That old timer, being a real cowman, was natural like dead set in starting that son of his in that game and making a real cow hand of him too, for there was nothing Old Nye thought more of, as a profession for a real boy, as that being a rip-snorting, bronc-scratching, all around cowboy, and after that cowboy's play was over with and the boy got less rolicky, that same profession was open for bigger things, that boy could begin gathering cows for himself then, and start a little outfit of his own and grow along those lines to the standard Old Nye himself had set.

"To give his boy a better chance than he himself had had, Old Nye sent him to school. Every summer the boy was on the range with his dad, and every fall he went to some house of eddication.

219

"All went pretty till the boy finally got the idea that he could do some thinking for himself, I don't know how that idea ever originated, but somehow it did, and then Old Nye's dreams of his son going thru life with spurs jingling at his heels begin to get a few shocks.

"For one thing, a thing Old Nye was most afraid of and which he hated to take for a fact, was how Young Nye seemed to take no interest in horses or stock in general. The boy was a pretty good rider but he didn't seem to take no pride in breaking any new broncs. He'd started a few and managed to break one or two, but most of 'em he'd started turned out to be too much for him, and once, for fear of being shamed on account of not being able to break one horse he'd started, he deliberately let that horse, a mighty fine colt, choke himself to death, just so he wouldn't have to ride him any more, the horse either had him buffaloed or he didn't want to be bothered with him.

"Old Nye never did find that out and maybe it's a good thing he didn't, but the way he acted for a while I think he must of had his suspicions. In fact I know he did because he'd come over to the corral a few times and tried to pump me on the subject.

"I was working for Old Nye at the time, breaking a string of horses which his son should of been breaking himself. He was big enough, bigger than I was, and just at the age when he should of been good at that, but he didn't have the gumption, no more than any home guard ever has. I seen him kill the horse, and gave him the beating of his life right there on the spot and kicked him over to the bunk house to hide from his dad while I drug the dead horse away with a team and covered up the signs.

"When Old Nye came to me the next day I lied as no man ever lied before. It's hard to lie to that old timer, too, let me tell you, but I managed it somehow, and I didn't do it to save the hide of that son of his, not by a long shot, it was the old cowboy's heart I was thinking of.

"I got by with that pretty well, and then the old boy comes back at me with something else which I wasn't expecting none at all.

" 'How come that boy of mine to be all battered up?' he asks. 'He looks like he's been run thru a sausage grinder.'

" 'Well . . .' I says looking down at the ground 'him and me was running horses yesterday . . . and . . . I guess he got in trouble with his horse and was throwed or something, and maybe was drug thru the brush a ways.'

" 'That's what the boy told me too,' says Old Nye, 'but I didn't know wether to believe him or not.'

"That sure relieved me a considerable because I didn't know what that kid had told him, and I sure didn't want that old boy to catch me in a lie.

"Things went on pretty well the same as usual for a few days, only me and Young Nye wasn't what you'd call on speaking terms, none at all. He packed a sort of murderous look and I noticed he started toting a gun in his belt.

"Just like that scrub, I thought, he was going to try and throw a scare into me, but I figgered that was a game two could play at, and I too unlimbered my old six-shooter and begin packing it around. I had to laugh as I turned the cylinder of my smoke-wagon to make sure she was well loaded and in working order, because there was nothing I'd rather done right then than just make a sieve out of him and roll his worthless carcass right alongside of that horse he'd killed. I figgered I'd been doing his old dad a big favor."

"Yes," Don adds on, "and get a rope around your fool neck."

"Most likely,' agrees Flint, "but if I'd got my credits for doing such a stunt I'd been handed a medal instead.

"Anyway," Flint went on "the shooting scrape daggone near come to a head one day. That galoot had come in with a bunch of saddle horses, and he was corralling 'em when one broke out right at the corral gate and hit back for the hills for all he was worth. Well, I claim I'm pretty fair at cussing myself when I have a reason, but at my best I was nothing but a beginner compared with the line of cuss words that feller spit out when that horse broke back, and then, looking his direction to see why all the noise, I was just in time to see him pull out his gun and aim for the runaway horse.

"I hate to think now of the consequences if he'd killed that horse, but as luck would have it he just nicked his withers, and when he fired again the horse had disappeared over a knoll.

"Mind you, him a shooting at a good old gentle horse too, and just because he was a little ornery to corral sometimes.

"But that was just his caliber, and all I've got to say now is that I'm mighty glad he didn't kill him, because to me, feller, a good horse amounts to the same as a good human.

"Well, I worked on for Old Nye for another month or so. I broke a nice string of ponies for that son of his to maul around, now that the rough was took off of 'em. I even gentled them same horses which that boy had got too scared to ride, and when I was ready to leave, I'd rode the buck out of every one of 'em.

"And say, cowboy, I sure hated to leave them ponies too, but they wasn't mine, my work was done, and there was nothing for me to do but turn 'em over.

"Of course I could of stayed on the outfit, and the boy by that time had got over his intentions to take a shot at me, but I got sort of fed up on the sight of him. I got to hate him so much for the things he'd do that I begin to feel leary of what would happen if I got my hooks on him once more, so, for the old man's sake, and being I was born to drift, I run in my private horses one day, bid Old Nye good-bye, and hit out for new territory.

Well, I worked for Old Nye for another month or so.

"But I didn't get to drift very far. The fall works was starting and the wagons was beginning to pull out for the range, and two days' ride after I left Old Nye's spread I fell in with another outfit.

"The round-up wagon was out a week and all hands was tying on an average of three new hondoos a day, when what do I see one evening but my friend the home guard, Young Nye, a riding in to the wagon with his string of ponies. His dad had sent him out to 'rep' for him.

"Well, I don't know why, but I was sort of glad to see him come, maybe it was on account that at the sight of him I sudden like got to thinking on what a fine chance I had now of knocking on him and finish up on his edducation or else break his neck.

"This outfit I was working for was a mighty rough one and most of the boys was pretty reckless, good ropers, good riders, not one home guard amongst 'em, and all top hands ready to tackle anything. That outfit wouldn't hire nothing else, and I thought here was the place for Young Nye to learn *something*."

"You was sure taking a lot on your shoulders, wasn't you?" says easy going Don. "How come you should take it on yourself to edducate people, it was none of your business how that boy acted, was it?"

"There's lots of things that's none of my business which I stick my nose into," says Flint, "but that's me all over. I guess I was born with a natural hankering to try and set things to what I think is right, and I never cared how bruised I got in trying.

"Like one time I yanked a blanketed Injun off his horse and set him afoot, that was none of my business either, but if you'd seen that horse and how lame, leg weary, and sore footed he was, just skin and bones and that daggone Injun a pounding on him, I think you'd of done the same thing, unless you was blind or dead from the neck up.

"There was two things which I had against Young Nye, and either one of 'em was enough to give me indigestion when I thought of 'em.

224

One was his caliber. He reminded me of a pop gun, all air, and he was a disgrace to the name he was packing. The other was in the way he treated horses, and that was enough to make me see red at any time.

"So, as I said before, I was glad to see him come to the outfit. He'd give us all something to play with and knock on without feeling that we should be ashamed of ourselves or that we was taking advantage of anybody. He was sure entitled to all we could hand him, for he had it coming to him and then some.

"Like every flusher, he rode into camp kind of wild and loud, and tried to show off on the good gentle horse he was riding. I noticed the horse's mouth was bleeding a little, and right then I figgered it was high time for that home guard's edducation to begin.

"I watched him ride by to the rope corral and noticed the string of ponies he'd brought with him to follow the works. There was ten head of 'em, not counting the one he was riding, and I never seen a prettier string of horses in my life than they was. All slick and shiny and built perfect, and fat too. But it wasn't his fault they was fat, because Old Nye had so many saddle horses that that boy of his couldn't begin to ride 'em down even if he rode two hundred miles a day.

"But the boy had no special pride in them ponies, I knowed he didn't appreciate 'em, and far as he was concerned it'd been just the same to him if they'd been all Injun cayuses.

"That sure sort of hurt me too, more so because I knowed all of them ponies so well. I'd broke the most of them myself and savvied every one of 'em like as if they'd been of my own raising. Well, I was going to see that that *hombre* treated them ponies right, even if I had to break a picket pin over his head."

"Kind of tough, wasn't you?" says Don.

"Not so's you'll notice, just alive and interested that's all.

225

"Well, it was early the next morning when the edducation begin on the home guard. It was just daybreak and we was roping our horses for the first circle. I caught the horse I wanted, snaked him out, and started saddling when I noticed Young Nye catching a little trim built black. That horse was one of the last I'd broke and he was still fidgety to handle, nothing mean, just sort of nervous like, but that pony had a lot of brains and would make a bear of a cow horse if handled right.

"But I seen right away that he wouldn't be handled right, not by that home guard anyway. That daggone fool was trying to show off with him and making him act up so as the boys would think he had a bad one. Maybe you think that made me feel good after me doing my daggonedest to gentle that pony and make a good horse out of him.

"I begin to boil up, but I kept the lid on somehow because, as I figgered, time wasn't ripe yet.

"That feller went on aggravating and exciting the little horse till, when the time come for him to climb on, that pony was ready for fight and he had a hump in his back. That was sure a surprise to me because that horse hadn't offered to buck with me the last few times I'd rode him at the ranch and he'd behaved like the good one he was.

"Well, there was nothing for me to do but watch and hope for that four flusher to get bucked off and stepped on. I climbed on my own horse, yanked his head out of the ground where he'd been bellering things at me, and scratched him out of his first bucking spell to a crowhopping standstill. I wanted to be up and setting where I could sort of watch, without letting on, what that little black horse would do the grandstander.

"But I was disappointed, and disappointed two ways. One was that the little horse bucked, and the shame of it was that he wasn't the kind that wanted to buck, he could of been 'talked' out of it. The other was that when he did buck he didn't buck hard enough, and the result was that Young Nye stuck on the saddle, which made it so that he was all the more stuck on himself.

"Yep, it was sure disappointing and, as we all lined out for the morning circle, that kept a eating on me, so much that I finally had to haze my bronc alongside of Young Nye.

" 'Daggone queer,' I says to him, 'how that little horse come to crow-hop with you. He was all out of that notion the last time I rode him.'

" 'That so?' he says, 'well he's bucked with me every time I got on him, and this is the third time now.'

" 'Well,' I comes back at him, 'all I can say to that is it's a shame to have him buck, but it's a good thing he don't buck hard or you wouldn't be setting on him.'

"I said that last so all the boys around could hear, just for that four flusher's benefit. The boys laughed, and that done me good.

" 'If you feel kind of wild,' I goes on, 'I'll accommodate you all I can and trade you something that will buck. I'd be glad to accommodate you right now and let you have this horse I'm riding in the place of yours, he might make it interesting for you, and you wouldn't have to aggravate that gentle horse you're setting on.'

"I know I wouldn't get nothing out of him that way, and all he said was that he wasn't swapping horses with anybody, that he had all he could do to ride his own horses and so on, and to mind my own business.

"But I piled on some more remarks which I think suited the occasion pretty well, anyway the boys laughed some more off and on, and I thought of working along that line till maybe there'd come a time when Young Nye would sort of feel small and start to maybe realizing something.

"I pecked at him for quite a ways and till I figgered he was about ready to crawl my frame, then I let up on him, thinking I'd said enough and wanting to let that soak in.

SUN UP

"But if what all I said to him had soaked in that brain of his, it sure didn't show no effects, and he'd no more than got away from me when he begin to want to show off again. I seen him reach down and run his thumbs alongside his horse's neck and 'goose' him. The horse bucked around a little bit, and that sure made me mad.

"I got so mad that I thought of knocking on him some more, but I knowed that wouldn't of done no good, so I thought of another way. I didn't think that other way to be so good either because I hated to make that little black horse mean, but something had to be done or I'd just swell up and bust.

"My chance came when he rode up on a knoll where we stopped while the boss scattered the riders. The men was being sent off two by twos in all directions to comb the country. Young Nye was setting there on his horse waiting to be called when rider who I'd picked on to help me rode up close to him, about ten feet of the end of his rope was dragging.

"I took my place on the other side of Young Nye's horse, staying pretty well behind, and then I winked acrost at the rider to let him know I was ready. About that time the rider flipped his rope under the little black horse's belly and I caught it on the other side, brought it up over the black's rump and swapped holts with the rider acrost me. All that was done quicker than a flash, and at that same speed we drawed the rope around the touchiest part of the pony's flanks, and yanked.

"Well, that pony shot up like as if he'd come out of a scatter gun, and the home guard doubled up so that he daggone near kissed the saddle horn. The rope around that pony's flanks, and taking him by surprise, had acted about the same as if you'd slid an icicle down somebody's back, only this brought better results and a heap more action.

"The black horse hadn't been the only one that was taken by surprise either, the home guard had been another and he'd bobbed up and down on his saddle like he'd been setting on springs, but daggone it,

228

that little scheme of mine didn't work out right. I'd figgered he'd get bucked off the first jump, and he didn't, and being we had to let the rope go, after that the horse didn't buck so hard and that feller gradually got to set his saddle in pretty good shape, and stayed.

"I will give that home guard credit for being a pretty good rider tho, when he *had* to, but that's what'd spoiled him, he didn't have to ride, and far as that goes he didn't have to do anything hardly unless he wanted to, he could most always frame up some excuse and good Old Nye would let him off easy. That's what makes a home guard worthless.

"But that little trick I played on him done some good, even tho things didn't turn out the way I wanted 'em to. He didn't know how the little black come to buck, and buck so hard, and for a while he didn't know if he could stick him or not. So, all of a sudden, he'd developed some respect for that horse and he didn't aggravate him no more.

"That helped some, but I sure wished he'd bucked him off, because he'd had still *more* respect for him.

"Anyway, his edducation wasn't over yet, it hadn't hardly started, and when he caught up another good horse for the afternoon and started to aggravate him and make a fool out of him the same as he done with the little black that morning, I made up my mind that I was going to camp on his tail some more and steady till my feelings was eased and I figgered him to be well done over.

"The only thing that worried me was the length of time I'd have to do all that in. I didn't expect Young Nye to be with the round up for more than two weeks because by that time we'd be moved plum out of the territory where any of his dad's cattle might of drifted. So I had to act fast.

"Two or three days went by when nothing happened that gave me much chance for a dig at him, only little ones. Like one time one of the boys begin to cuss the luck on account one of his best horses getting kicked pretty bad and which daggone near crippled him for good.

" 'Aw, don't mind that,' says the home guard, 'there's a lot of good horses and plenty more where he comes from.'

" 'Yeh,' says the cowboy, 'and if we had to depend on the likes of you to get them good horses we'd sure all walk.'

" 'I'll tell the cock-eyed world,' I joins in, 'and I'd sure hate to have to ride any horse you'd break, he sure wouldn't know anything.'

"I went on a lot more on that subject, but pretty soon I shut up because I knowed I was just getting riled up for nothing. The only way to edducate him was with action not with words.

"Two more days went by when I had nary a chance to bring in any of that said action, and I begin to fret considerable. Time was getting short and I figgered in another week or so he'd be going back to his mother's apron strings and the comfortable bed she always kept neat and clean for him.

"Then one night I stumbled on an idea. I went to the foreman with it to see if it'd be all right for me to pull it off, and that old boy, hating a horse killer as much as I did, got a big laugh out of the idea and he didn't only agree but said he'd help me along if I wanted him to.

"Well, the next morning, and in some mysterious way, Young Nye's horses had all disappeared, not a one was in the remuda, nor to be found nowheres in the many miles of big country that was covered in looking for 'em. Young Nye figgered then that his horses must of slipped away from the nighthawk during the night and hit straight for home. That was the natural thing for a feller to think, and he was for borrowing a horse from the outfit and try to get 'em back soon as he could.

"But the foreman headed him off there, and in a nice way told him there was no use of him trying to get them horses back now, because he only had a few more days with the round-up and then he'd be going back anyway, besides he'd be losing two or three days getting them horses, and by that time there'd be no need of him being with the outfit any more as it'd be out of the territory and where none of his dad's cattle ever strayed.

" 'The boys will be glad to chip in a horse a piece and make you up a string that'll do you for the next few days,' says the foreman, mighty obliging like, 'and I'll even let you have one out of my own string.'

" 'Sure,' chips in one of the boys, 'I'll let you have Rocket, he's a good circle horse.'

" 'And I'll let you have Tombstone,' says another, 'he's crippled a few men but he ain't killed none as yet, and I know he'd be pickings for you.'

"All the boys kept on a being obliging that way, and there was nothing Young Nye could do but feel obliged himself and accept, for after playing wild like he had he couldn't of backed out and felt graceful about it.

"I kept sort of quiet till all the boys got done contributing to the good cause because I didn't want to scare that home guard away from the start by offering one of my horses, none of mine was what you'd call nice and gentle, and he knowed it.

"But the foreman helped me out on that, and to make it seem natural like, he says to me.

" 'Ain't you going to chip in a horse, Flint?'

" 'Sure,' I says, 'I was only wondering which one I could trust with him . . . How would Hornet do? he's about the gentlest one I got.'

"I was aching to hand him a big roan I had which was called Rowdy but I figgered that would be carrying a good thing too far, that horse *was bad*.

"Funny how I get soft hearted when I get the upper hand and do get a good chance to soak somebody I been aching to soak. Well, anyway, I let him have Hornet, and even tho he wasn't so bad I felt that Young Nye would sure at least respect him.

"Everything was all set and that home-guard's first real edducation was about to begin. We was hoping to fix him so that when he straddled a good gentle horse again he'd be wanting to love him to death, because with this string we handed him it would be hard to get a rougher bunch of ponies together. They'd most of 'em strike at their own shadow, and stampede, and buck, and fight, and for no reason only that it was their nature. Them ponies was sure tetotally different from them willing ponies that got away, things had been reversed, and if there was going to be any mauling and pounding done now, Young Nye was going to be at the receiving end of all of that.

"It all started to our taste with the first 'company horse' he piled his rope onto. That pony had to be snaked out and then front-footed before the hackamore could be put on his head, and even handicapped that way he managed to kick Young Nye on the leg as that feller was putting his saddle on him. It was lucky that kick didn't land square too.

" 'He's a little mean to handle from the ground,' one of the boys says to him, 'but once you get in the middle of him he ain't so bad, can't buck very hard.'

"But he did do a pretty fair job of bucking when Young Nye finally did get up on him, and we felt confident that here was one horse which he sure wouldn't aggravate none. He didn't put on no wild nor reckless airs on that pony, and he seemed mighty pleased to be able to set there and just ride.

"That was one point to our credit, and we figgered that a week or so of him riding that kind of horses would bring on many points towards that edducation which we set out to hand him.

"What surprised me tho, was that Young Nye was a pretty fair hand out there amongst us, a lot better hand than I ever seen him be when he was at the home ranch, and I know he wouldn't been riding no such

232

as that company horse if he'd been there. He'd just left him for some other feller to ride, some feller like myself who'd be working for his dad.

"Two days went by with everything going hunkydory. Young Nye was getting it right and left, and it seemed like every horse we'd handed him was in cahoots with us in shaping out his edducation. He was bucked off twice in that time, his shirt pawed off of him once, and mauled around pretty regular, and at every change of horses, that boy got quieter and more serious, maybe he was thinking of his own horses and how good they'd been, and maybe he was getting to appreciating 'em. Anyway, he got to be a lot better in many ways them last two days, and we figgered now if we only had a week more we could make something out of him which old man Nye would be proud of.

"Things went along good again all the next day and the boy's edducation was piling on thick, when what do we see that evening but a rider coming into camp with Young Nye's string of horses. Them ponies, after I'd cut 'em out of the remuda a few nights past and sashayed 'em a ways had trailed straight for their home range. That rider had found 'em there, and being he was working for Old Nye, he'd been sent back with 'em to locate the round up wagon.

"Well, I sure called that tough luck, here we was just going good when we run up against a snag which ripped all our good intentions like they'd been cheese cloth.

"Young Nye stayed with the wagon a few days more, and before he left for home with the few cattle that'd been found we seen that our start in edducating him hadn't took much holt. We didn't have enough time.

" 'Too bad,' says the foreman as Young Nye was saddling up one of his own horses to leave, 'that that feller's got such a good home or we'd sure make a cowboy out of him.'

"That's the last time I got to see that home guard, and when I left the country that fall I heard rumors that Old Nye asked him to get off his range and hit out. It appeared like he'd wanted the boy to take charge of a camp for the winter instead of going to college, and the boy hadn't agreed to it.

"That's a home guard for you every doggone time, they're all right when everything is soft, when they can sponge on the old man and go to mother for this or that, but when they're asked to take a holt or make hand of themselves they're not interested."

"I don't know about that" says Don who'd been waiting for a chance to chip in a word "I've seen home guards that took holt and run things in pretty good shape."

"Yep, run 'em down hill. If a corral pole breaks they'll patch it up with wire instead of putting a new one in the place of it. If a roof sags they'll let it sag, and that way with everything the old folks work to build and gather. Buildings, stock, and all will go downhill and then the bank most generally gets it all.

"Why? because the home guard ain't never felt the responsibility. He ain't never built these things himself, and when they're handed to him he don't know how to appreciate 'em. He don't know what the word appreciate means, he takes what the old folks sweat to give him, asks for more, and plays around not interested in anything to speak of, and the worse part of it is that they're spoiled into thinking they're precious things, how smart they are and everything, when they really don't know nothing, and ain't worth the powder that'd blow 'em to the hot place."

"How long ago has it been since you seen this Young Nye?" asks Don.

"Aw, not too long, about three for four years I guess."

"Well," Don goes on, "he might be amounting to something by now."

Flint laughed, and he didn't say no more.

The remuda.

It was three days later when Flint and Don, after turning their cattle loose at a spring amongst the juniper hills, returned to join the round-up wagon and went on with their work there.

A big circle was made the next day. A big herd was brought in, and being it was middle afternoon before that herd was worked no second circle was made that day. All the riders gathered at the camp and to do different little jobs of their own. Some had horses to shoe, others went to the creek by the camp and begin to do their washing, while a few had nothing in perticular to do much only stretch in some shady place or fix up a saddle or mend a pair of chaps.

Flint and Don was together as usual, and seemed like to have nothing to do only set by a shady willow and talk. But Don was doing most of the talking this time, for Flint had all his attention on one of the riders who, off a ways, was busy doing something or other. That rider was the new rep' who'd stirred Flint's memory, and he was so interested in watching him that he hardly heard a word Don was saying.

"By golly," says Flint kind of like to himself, "it sure looks like him."

"Like who, and who're you talking about?" asks Don.

"That new rep' over there, looks like Young Nye."

"But it can't be," Flint went on. "I couldn't imagine Young Nye ever doing what that feller is doing just now."

It seemed like the rep' had ordered and just received a new pair of spurs, and like all new spurs, the rowels had sharp jagged points on 'em which would tear a horse hide at the least touch. That feller was busy with a file at dulling the point of them rowels and filing all sharp edges off, and that's what had drawed Flint's attention.

"Young Nye would never done that," says Flint, "too thoughtless."

But just the same, Flint kept his eyes on that cowboy, and when he got the chance he looked at his saddle to see the name of the maker on it, and he wondered at that because the name of the maker was that one of Young Nye's home territory.

A couple of days went by when Flint watched every move that cowboy made, and the more he watched him the more he wondered, because as much as that feller looked like Young Nye and with other things that went to prove it, his actions and all he done didn't at all tally up with the Young Nye he used to know.

There was nothing four flushing about this feller, nothing wild. And then again, Flint noticed that he rode his ornery horses the most and gave his good horses all the advantage. That sure wasn't like Young Nye, he thought. He seen him loosen a curb strap once when it seemed too tight on a horse's chin, and time and again he also seen him uncinch his saddle and raise it to air his horse's back, he done that even with the ornery horses.

All that, and with the likeness of him to Young Nye, got to be too much for Flint, and one day he rode up alongside of the boss of the outfit, and asked.

"Who is that young feller over there on that spooky gray?"

"I don't know for sure," says the boss, "but I think his name is Roswell, Nye Roswell. He's repping for the Aravacas', good hand too, specially with young horses."

"Yeh, I noticed that," was all Flint could say.

But Flint had sort of expected that, only he couldn't account for such a transformation in Young Nye, and it was hard to believe. Flint had no more questions to ask, he was thinking, thinking on the big change that'd come over the boy, and what a great favor his dad had done him in asking him to hit out. . . . Knocking around on his own, amongst strangers, and having to take things as he found 'em without being able to go to his mother and cry about it had made a man out of him. The strange lands had showed him no favors. It all had shaped out his edducation, and made him realize, and appreciate a lot of things he would never thought of or noticed before.

The change that'd come over the boy in the way he handled his horses and took care of his riggin' was a plenty for Flint to go by, because if a man is perticular and thoughtful in one thing he will be the same in other things, and Flint, in judging a man by the way he treated a horse, had never been wrong.

The main herd was being slowly grazed to the bed-ground that evening when Flint found himself paired off at one side of the herd with none other that Young Nye Roswell. Flint had his eye on him as usual, and when Young Nye of a sudden turned in his saddle and looked back he was staring right into Flint's face, there was a big long grin on it.

"Expect you don't recognize me young feller," says Flint, "but I do you, *now*."

"Sure I recognize you," says Young Nye. "I recognized you long ago."

"Why didn't you say something?"

"Well, I didn't know if I should, because as I remember you and me didn't used to get along so good."

Flint didn't have nothing to say to that, instead he held out his hand, and the two shook hands, for the first time.

"You're kind of far away from home ain't you?" Flint went on.

"Pretty long stretch all right," says Young Nye, "but I guess it's a good thing to get away from the home grounds once in a while. Been away now ever since that year you worked for Dad."

"Where you been all the time?"

"Pretty well everywhere, been knocking around and working for different outfits all the way from home down here. Was acrost the Border for a while, riding line on an outfit down there and watching Yaquis. I been kind of keeping my eyes peeled for a little spread lately too, thought I'd kind of like to start on something of my own."

"Don't you figger on going back home some time?" asks Flint.

"Well," says Young Nye, gazing over the herd, "I kind of think about that, but me and Dad had a sort of falling out, and I don't think he'd maybe want to see me much any more. . . . I don't know as I can blame him either."

Flint was quiet, the herd grazed and begin to scatter, and neither of the riders made a move to turn 'em, then finally Flint spoke.

"You're wrong to think that your Dad wouldn't want to see you," he says, "because I know for a fact that he'd be mighty doggone glad to. . . ."

Young Nye looked square at him, "How do you know?" he asks.

"Well, I know," says Flint acting mighty sure of himself, "and don't deprive that old boy of the pleasure he'll get in seeing you."

Young Nye was quiet a spell a trying to find something to say to that, and when he did finally speak it was only to say, "Thanks Flint." But the expression that was on his face as he looked at Flint said a lot more, and the two shook hands once again.

FILLING IN THE CRACKS

A BRONC KICKING ME IN THE JAW is what started me to looking for a altogether different country than what I'd been used to, and away to where there's more folks and specialists, jaw-bone specialists mostly.

A kick is something you can't always dodge, wether it be from a human or a horse. And this bronc maybe meant no harm and was only acting according to his instinct towards the human, but anyway I underestimated his reach by an inch, with the result that the boys had to straighten me up and lay me in the shade of the chuck wagon to recuperate some.

A few days of shade, soft grub, and pain and I'm trying to think of some place to go where I can get my grinders tended to, when one of the boys suggests Los Angeles, remarking that he knows one *hombre* on the outskirts of that town who could sure fix me up good as new.

That sounded kind of promising; — besides I wanted to see Los Angeles. I thinks it over careful for a day or so and finally decides to head that direction. I asks for my wages with a few months in advance throwed in, sells my two saddle horses that was laying around at the home ranch, and with the few hundred dollars in my pocket I hits for the nearest railroad and buys me a yard of ticket for Los Angeles, two thousand miles to the south and west.

I'm getting good and tired of soft grub by the time I see the smoke of that town and I don't lose no time hunting up the specialist and putting him to work. He tells me after looking things over that it'd take a couple of months to fix me up; and when I steps out and looks around, I wonders what I'm going to do with all the spare time I'll have.

I runs across a saddle shop where I fingers saddle leather, looks over the silver-mounted bits and spurs and wishing all the time I was a millionaire; then sashays out the beach where they all tell me it's the place to go to have a good time and see the sights; but it didn't interest me none and after going over there every day, covering twenty miles of beach country and not seeing what I calls a good time or sights, the time and days are dragging along mighty slow.

I'm there about a week and getting awful homesick for the range, when, roaming around one day I gets the real surprise of my life and runs across a altogether different atmosphere, the likes of which sure set me blinking and staring. — A cow town it was; and right here at the edge of the tall stone and brick buildings of Los Angeles, instead of automobiles was buckboards, ponies was tied here and there, and cowboys, the same I'd seen up in the Montana town I'd just left was sticking around and taking it easy.

It was sure good for sore eyes, and I even forgot about my bum jaw. I parades around and takes in the best sights I'd seen for quite a spell, and when I turns a corner and comes face to face with two real pretty cowgirls I come near giving myself away and saying, "Aw."

I goes on a little further and doubles back on my tracks, for I sure didn't want to lose the whereabouts of that spot that really belonged up in Montana or Wyoming somewhere. I passes corrals full of horses and longhorned Mexico cattle. There's stage coaches and prairie schooners by the stables and in the shade of them was the old-time Cherokee and Sioux bucks and squaws all in war feathers and paint.

Daggone it, the whole kaboodle sure looked mighty good to me, and when a little later I struts by the saloon and hears a argument between a "dally" and a "tie" man I begins to feel right at home. One of the boys arguing has his back turned, and that back looked familiar to me and his voice I'd heard before somewhere. The argument goes on good-natured and I'm listening, at the same time trying to place just where I'd seen that back and heard that voice. It all comes to me of a sudden just as he moves his arm to illustrate his point in the argument, for I'd often seen that arm in the same motion at throwing the rope.

"What the hell do you know about a tied rope, Sam?" I asks, breaking in on the confab. I'm ginning at him when he turns around to see who's making all the noise and I see he don't recognize me in my store clothes; I waits a while then I says, "Remember the Z-X and Slivery Bill?" That was enough, and Sam Long just busts hisself getting down off the saloon steps over to me. I missed my appointment with the Doc that day.

I finds while I'm getting introduced to the boys around that this little cow territory I'd run into was called Edendale, that it was the place where all the moving picture producers got their men when they wanted real cowboys for Western pictures, there was studios right close and Hollywood or Universal City was a short ride on horseback. The boys was kept busy most of the time and when they wasn't, they'd be practicing up on bronc riding, steer riding, steer roping, or bull-dogging and getting in shape to compete in rodeos wherever they was held; they was professional contest hands and mighty hard to beat.

There was plenty of stock to practice on, and amongst that stock was anything a picture director could call for and any amount from the meanest bucking horse down to the bob-tailed roach-maned english thoroughbred; all was used in pictures along with the boys and none had a chance to get rusty.

I'm told a lot about the inside of the picture game and I'm all interested. Then Sam suggests that I join the crowd: "you just got to" he says "and with that face you got there's all the chances of you being a leading man, if any time a good horse-thief character is wanted."

Anyway I sticks around for a spell and one day comes news that a big "western" is going to be filmed, — they'd need a hundred riders and most all the bucking stock and steers around Edendale besides a

And afterwards us boys was called on to do our bit on bucking horses.

hundred saddle horses. Before I know it, Sam has my name on the list and I'm one of the extras at five dollars a day for a month steady — you can bet your boots I didn't kick, for I couldn't found a better way to make my expenses; besides being with my own breed of folks was a plenty to keep me agreeable.

"Six-guns and Ropes" was the starting name of this picture where I introduces myself to the screen. It was supposed to've been of the days when most everybody wore red flannel shirts and was overweighed about twenty pounds with guns and ammunition. Us boys had to mash down the crown of our hats to make 'em match up with them times and a few was picked out of the crowd to wear full beards, — about that time Sam and I was missing and didn't show up till everything was safe.

A "Fiesta" was pulled off, and afterwards us boys was called on to do our bit on bucking horses, steer roping and the like. There was no rehearsing on our stuff and the director was tickled the way we went at it.

Then, I gets a vision of the leading man strutting in the arena. I'd seen him on the screen many a time and thinks to myself "here's where I'm going to see some bronc riding that'll make our efforts look sick." The director is walking along with him and heads over to us fellers setting by the chute; they both give us the once over, and I'm wondering what for when that same director crooks his finger at me asking me to come over.

I'm lined up alongside the leading man, sized up one side and down the other and then I'm asked if I can ride — I'm thinking maybe I was picked on to show the world what a bum cowboy I am compared to that leading man and I'm not hankering for such, so I says, "I can ride, *some.*"

Then the director comes back at me with, "aren't you the fellow that rode that Graeagle bucking horse a while ago?" and I says "yes." —

"Well then you'll do fine," he says walking away and telling me to come along.

I tags along doing some tall wondering till we get to a big car on the edge of the grounds, and there I'm told I'd get five dollars extra if I'd ride another bucking horse like I did Graeagle and wear the leading man's clothes, "and if you can get your horse in front of the camera and pull him over backwards when I give you the sign, I'll give you twenty dollars more," says the director.

I begins to see light as I accept the terms, I'm all dolled up and prances out following the director to where a big brown horse is snubbed

I'm lined up alongside the leading man, sized up one side
and down the other and then asked if I can ride.

and blind-folded, the camera is off a ways and ready for action and I'm to start from there, saddling the brown, mounting him and do my bestest to follow the instructions.

I'm warned not to let the camera see my face any more than I can help and I keeps that in mind as I pulls off the blind, let out a war whoop and begins fanning said bronc.

The show is on, the camera is grinding, the bronc is a bawling, tearing up the earth and scattering himself all over creation and universe; I'm fanning him, and every time the horse faces the camera I covers

The director gives me the sign and when my chance comes I sets down on the rein and pulls that horse over backwards.

my face with my hat, at the same time making it look natural as I can and in fanning motion.

Then the director gives me the sign and when my chance comes I sets down on the rein and pulls that horse over backwards as pretty as you please. Down we come, all in a heap but I took care to see that I was in the clear and when the bronc starts up again I'm right in middle of him, and finishes the grandstand ride in good style.

The director acts mighty pleased the way I done it and tells me that I couldn't done better if I tried, which after thinking it over means a whole lot. Then the leading man steps up, does a heap of congratulating and wants to give me an extra twenty dollar bill for the good work, as he put it.

But some way I'm disappointed in him, and I tells my feelings to Sam. "From seeing him in the picture," I says "I thought this *hombre* was a top 'ranahan,' a he wolf on a horse, and it sure gets me deep to learn that he couldn't ride in a box car with both doors shut, and couldn't throw a rope in the ocean, if he was in the middle of it in a rowboat. He admits that himself and still, they keep on fooling the people to thinking he's a real cowboy."

"Now wait a minute," Sam says, "you're pawing at the hackamore without knowing what's hurting you. Stick around for a spell and I can talk to you better about it, but for the time being let me tell you that this leading man is getting a thousand to your thirty dollars a week, that if he was to get hurt the whole company would be held up till he recuperated, the picture would be delayed, his wages would have to be paid along with others, and the bed rock of it is that his contract reads where he's not to take any chances on anything dangerous and where he can be 'doubled.'

"What's more," Sam goes on, "he's got talent, he can act and people want to see him for that most. They're not worried much wether he's a real cowboy or not so long as he can roll his eyes right and at the right time. Put yourself in his place and try to act, how far would you get and how much would you be drawing from the company? — your expression is just the same wether you're eating a plate of 'frijoles' or riding a bronc; fact is you ain't got no such thing as expression and far as you'd get is what you done to-day; or as I said before, if a good horse-thief character is wanted you might shine there."

"Hold on there, Sam," I manages to squeeze in between breaths, "I think I understand, and before we go any further on this subject I'll wait and do as you say, I'll stick around for a spell and when I get enough information to start another argument I'll get you over to one side and have it out with you."

I walks off, rolls me a cigarette and thinks it all over. No doubt Sam was right, but to me it didn't strike me right, that one man should do all the dangerous work and have the other feller get all the credit for it, when all he did was congratulate after all was over — of course nobody cares about the credit much, but there was something about it that hit the wrong spot, with me.

We're working along up in the hills, taking the part of outlaws one day and being a posse chasing them same outlaws the next day. We're taking some mighty steep hills and coming down off 'em hell bent for election and the leading man is *trying* to ride with us, but he finally has to be doubled again for the reason that he couldn't stay in the lead where he was supposed to be. Instead of that he'd be so far back that it'd take him a half hour to catch up. He'd rode in the cavalry and at chasing foxes but this was different. A heap different.

A few days later the director asks me if I wouldn't double for his leading man again, and jump my horse over a twenty foot cliff they'd located for the picture; *that* set me to thinking for quite a while before answering, but I finally agrees.

It had to be done twice being we didn't fall good enough the first time, but I got twice my price and outside of a sprained ankle and a skinned elbow felt pretty good.

I layed around camp for a few days rubbing my ankle with liniment and Sam was taking every chance he had to come over and pester the life out of me; like one time I see him riding up packing a grin a mile long, I knew right away he had something good to spring on me, and I got ready. "Now Bill," he begins, "do you see the difference between a man what works with both his feet and hands, and another man what works with his head?" — He turns his horse and tries to get away, but one of my boots caught up with him and left him serious.

"Come on, Sam," I hollered at him, "spring another one."

Then one morning, the director walks up to me and asks when I'll be able to ride again, remarking that he'd like to give me a small part in the picture and he begins to explain what I'm to do, I'm to be one of the boys what's to help the hero round up that bunch of desperate outlaws he's after, we're to do most everything but rescue the heroine, and as the director tells me it's just something extra and of his own thinking to give the picture more punch.

"I'd like to have you do a little bulldogging too," he says, "and maybe some more wild horse stuff, if we can chip it in along the story."

I finds that Sam is in the outlaw gang we're supposed to corral, and something hatches up in my mind that's too good to leave go, wether it makes a hit or I get fired off the lot for it, anyway, I'm not worried.

We're chasing Sam and his crowd of horse thieves all over the country, over hills and across washouts for a whole day, and when the last close-up of the chase comes along I begins to get ready. So far, we'd been doing nothing but chasing and swapping shots and when this time the director hollers "get ready — cam-e-r-a" instead of getting out my six-gun as I was expected to do I uncoils my rope, builds me a loop and away I go.

Sam is way ahead with his bunch of desperadoes, but in this last shot we're supposed to corner 'em, and we sure do. I passes 'em all like they was standing still and heads for one certain party who's supposed to be the only one getting away (according to the story) but I'm out to spoil his plans. I shakes out my loop and spreads it right around that *hombre's* middle, jerks him off his horse right where the camera can get it all and at close range.

Sam is real surprised, — I'm off my horse before he can come out of it, and moving picture style I lets him stare into the business end of my six-shooter. He's staring alright, and wondering what's up, but I keep up my acting, and real sarcastic, at the same time having a hard time to keep from laughing I tells him that *he sure makes a dandy character of a horse thief.*

About that time, the director who's doing a heap of wondering and staring himself had let the camera grind, and when he comes to himself orders the camera man to "cut."

I'm feeling kinda foolish and expects to get fired right there. Then I sneaks a peek at the director again who's looking at the ground like he was going to bore a hole through it, and somehow by the way he's thinking and trying to grin a little I have hopes.

In the meantime Sam'd shook off the dust he'd gathered, turns on me real vicious and asks what the hell I'm trying to pull off. "Nothing much, you jughead," I answers, "just trying to even scores on the bright remarks you passed off and on. I was real easy with you," I goes on, "I could of drug you all over these hills if I wanted to."

Sam thinks it over for a spell, and pretty soon he begins to see light and says, "All right, Bill, we're even now and let's stay that way."

I shakes out my loop and spreads it right around that hombre's middle.

The director picks up the megaphone and hollers "get ready folks, we'll take this last scene over again, and everybody do as directed *please*"; — that last was meant for me I know, and when I looks over his way to make sure, he gives me the wink like as to say he'd forgive me this time.

I'd been over to see the dentist pretty regular, my appointments was changed for evenings, and I was getting in fair shape to be able to laugh again without hiding my face with my fist. I was glad of it cause I didn't want to get to work on the little part the director gave and run chances of showing a toothless grin.

I played some pony express, a few close-ups by my lonesome, and others with the leading man showing where I'm delivering some important papers; then again where my horse breaks a leg in a badger hole and how I catches me a wild horse as he comes in to water, saddles him when he's down, gets on and proceeds, riding a bucking streak of greased lightning and delivers the important message at the other end.

I does the bulldogging stunt and saves the fair heroine from an awful death; but in this one I'm wearing the leading man's clothes and I'm congratulated again, but I wasn't the only one to be congratulated and wearing such clothes as the leading man's, there was two other boys (ham actors) called on to double for him: one to rescue a dummy supposed to be the heroine and come down on the outside of a twenty story building; — I thought it was a pretty ticklish job myself, and I couldn't blame the leading man much if he was glad to be out of it. The other boy done a high dive, about fifty feet into the ocean to rescue that very same heroine once more, and I didn't want that job either, — diving or coming down off tall buildings was plum out of my line, and I didn't hanker for it, none at all.

252

Riding a bucking streak of greased lightning.

We sure put 'er on wild, every horse had a fall and some two.

Well, the picture went on, we corralled all the outlaws, Sam with 'em and put 'em all in jail, — the heroine was rescued once again out of the clutches of a villian and she decides to marry the hero.

Another big fiesta was pulled off and everybody was having a great time, and celebrating on the good work of ridding the country of desperadoes (who all was enjoying themselves right with us and dressed for the occasion as we were), the leading man and lady was married right there and that ended the stirring photoplay of "Six-guns and Ropes."

It took five weeks to grind that picture, and on the last day when everything is being took off the sets and put away in the "prop" rooms, the director gets me over to one side and tells me about the time I roped Sam and drug him off his horse. "That was the best piece of work I ever looked at" he says "and when I saw it in the projection room, I found it so much better than plain acting that I'm going to try and make it fit in the story somehow, the expression on Sam was great, he wasn't expecting that and he sure registered surprise without trying, which makes it good." And you he says "sure looked as though you meant it."

He winds up by telling me to be sure and be around when he starts on his next western.

The rainy season was with us and the cameras wasn't being used much, I'd been laying around for near three weeks when the weather shows signs of clearing and I gets some work from another company. Sam and me and a few other cowboys went and rode for a few days in a steeple chase as jockeys, and we sure put 'er on wild, every horse had a fall and some two; four riders went to the hospital for a while, and one of 'em doubling for the leading lady who according to the story was supposed to win the race got the worst of it and stepped on a whole lot, but that was in the story and that horse was supposed to fall; he only "pulled" and throwed him when he was told to. It was exciting alright and the leading lady thought it was grand, till she found out how badly hurt the rider was.

But none of the boys kicked, they took their own chances and accepted the consequences the way they was dealt, and the rest of us boys what was still altogether kept on riding the postage stamp saddles, and putting our horses over the hurdles and water holes the same as before till our work was thru.

It started to cloud up and rain again, and kept up a steady fog and drizzle day after day, the movie folks stayed inside with the camera, and us boys hung around the stables and tried to pass the time away the best we could. We was mighty glad when the weather cleared up again and most tickled to death when we hears that one of the big companies was going to start in on a seven reeler western drama.

We all hung around the phone at the stable like a bunch of ants, waiting to hear the good words of "get ready" — finally it comes. They'd need a hundred riders to make up as the early days man on horseback, such as the injun fighter and scout in buckskin, trappers and spaniards, and two hundred Injuns with teepees, ponies and squaws all in full war paint. They'd also want twenty prairie schooners all fixed up with ox teams, some with mules or horses, along with about a hundred head of loose stock, mostly cattle: — could we fix 'em up? "We sure can" Curly Jones answers "and if you need any hogs or geese and chickens and goats and burros and —," but about that time the receiver at the other end was hung up and Curly turns around to tell us "get ready boys, and tell the other fellers down the line to sashay right over here if they want to get work on this one, it'll mean about six weeks and maybe more."

Well, we're ready in no time and stringing out on location a few miles out in the hills, it sure made some outfit, and you wouldn't think the way all of us boys was mixing with the Injuns and kidding along that soon there'd be a terrible fight between them reds and us whites, — well, there was and we was all massacreed, all but a little orphant what was hid in the blankets that the fire didn't get, — *and there was the story.*

There was a heap of acting in that picture, a few running fights and the burning of a frontier town. Us boys was used mostly to fill in the cracks in the background, making things look natural, outside of that we didn't figger much.

It got monotonous, that is for me anyway cause I was one of the bunch what was entirely willing to let the other feller "hog the foreground."

We'd been at it near six weeks and the picture wasn't over half done, the rain and fog kept a driving us in every once in a while and there was a lot of time lost on that account. And every time we'd come out again I'd keep a noticing how nice and green the country was getting to be, that old phony, petrified looking grass that covered the hills when I first come had disappeared and instead of it there was great long stems of that green new grass.

But it all looked too pretty to suit me, and gave me the feeling that here was a country the likes of which you'd find after crossing the Great Divide and your boots was pulled off for the last time.

April come along, and I was finding myself doing a lot of dreaming, picturing in my mind just how that country to the north and east would look at this perticular time, I could kind of see the snow most all melted away leaving the big patches of green where little white faced calves are sunning themselves and everything all quiet. The boys back there would be getting ready for the spring round up soon and running in the "remudas."

Daggone it, I was getting homesick, and when one day a letter is handed out to me and I reads the few words it said, I know right away I'm going and "poco tiempo."

A little bunch of green buffalo grass was in the letter and that alone was enough, the few words only made me act all the quicker saying "come and get it or I'll throw it out" (meaning the cook's holler to grub pile) and, "we'll be pulling out soon for the spring works, will you be with us?" It was signed by Tom Rawlins, cow foreman of the "circle dot."

Would I be with 'em? — I sure would, or else break my neck trying. I showed the letter to Sam, and it pretty near got him too, for awhile, but he'd been in the picture game too long to quit so sudden and after thinking it over decides to stick it out for a spell longer, "I don't think I'd be much good on the range any more" he tells me "but I hate to see you go, Bill, cause you're the only one around here I like to argue with; — anyway, I think you'll be back again soon and I'll try to stick around till you are."

"All right, Sam," I says, "but don't stand on your head all that time, will you?"

My bridle teeth and grinders being all fixed up and good as new, I feel pretty good as I pack up and grabs the first train going out, and the next morning when I wakes up, goes out to the rear of the train and sees sage brush again, I feell considerable better. The sight of the cottonwoods and real he-mountains on the way sure made me perk up my ears and take a long breath, and the thought of just living and knowing just where I was headed was a plenty to keep me more than contented.

As the train traveled on I'd find myself wondering how them broncs I'd started to break last spring was going to pan out this year, how many of the boys I know will be back to join the outfit and how the stock pulled thru the winter.

I figgered it kind of queer that it didn't bother me to leave the movie game and the good folks I'd met there, but I layed it to the fact I wasn't cut out to be a actor anyway. I'd found it easier living there in a way and more fun than we'd have on the range, but I didn't get no satisfaction out of that and got to hankering for something more real and what I was raised to doing.

I wanted to stand night-guard again with the snow or sleet flying by, and hear the range critter's beller without the camera being near, — I wanted the *real thing*.

And the real thing was right there, seemed like waiting for me when the train stopped at Malta, it was the old "circle dot" chuckwagon and the cook who'd just drove in to get a few months' supply of grub to carry the outfit through the round up. The first thing struck my eye was the brand, made with a "running iron" and burned deep on the fresh rawhide covering the side jockey box of the wagon.

The sight of the whole layout brought a lot of things back to memory, for I'd et many a meal alongside of it in all kinds of weather and with many different riders. I remembered the time I layed in the shade of that same old wagon for a good two months with a busted leg, and how I'd pester the cook to make us some "son-of-a-gun-in-the-sack" for a change.

Them happenings was all the real thing, no acting about it, and it didn't get under your hide like the other did in time.

It seemed to me like I'd been gone four years instead of months and when I run across some of the boys and Tom Rawlins a little while later, I think the way I acted made 'em get the hunch that I'd been abused while down in Los Angeles.

I tells 'em of me working in the movies, careful not to mention Sam, being I didn't know how he stood with the sheriff here. They was surprised that a common looking *hombre* like me could get in the movies at all (I was too at first but I didn't say so), and when they ask me what all I done in the line of acting, I says "nothing much, just stood out in the background and filled in the cracks."

My string of company horses was turned over to me, twelve head of 'em; Tom tells me they hadn't been rode since I left and they sure looked it, all fat as butter and full of kinks, and I saw where I'd sure have to ride close to my saddle if I didn't want to walk. But I got along all right, this was something I was raised at doing and knowed how to take.

I stayed with the outfit all thru the spring and summer. We was done with the fall round-up, put the weaners under fence and on the way to the shipping point with some of the beef herd, three thousand head of fine big three year olds; — we are taking 'em slow and letting 'em graze as they go.

The fourth night out, and about half way to the railroad a double guard was put on, six men instead of three, and by all indications in the sky which was sure threatening I had a hunch that all of us six riders would have our hands full long before the time for the next "relief."

And my hunch was right, only it come quicker than I expected. The stiff wind, rain, lightning, and thunder didn't follow one another as it usually does in such cases, they all came together fast and furious and trying to beat one another, seemed like.

And the cattle didn't fool with preliminaries of milling around before starting out; they all got up at once and went from there, every single critter as quick as the other and moving the same as one, three thousand head of 'em and stampeding down the draw, — not a beller was heard and we all saw where *we sure had to ride.*

Our six-shooters was a smoking and tearing up the earth in front of the leaders trying to scare 'em into turning and milling and about the time we'd get some control of 'em a few streaks of chained lightning would crash down on some big boulders in the rear and send 'em a flying to little pieces, making the herd worse than ever to handle.

I'd rode in a few stampedes that was wild, but this one was wilder than any I'd ever been in before, the steers'd been rearin' to find an excuse to run for a couple of days past, and now that they had it was sure making use of the chance, and I couldn't help but think and wonder even as I was smoking up the leaders, how much a stampede like this, reproduced on the film as I saw it, would be worth to any moving picture corporation.

But I had to laugh at the thot of a camera getting that stampede as it was, even though I know how good they are with that machine. The lightning was playing on the steers' horns, and there was spells when it was light as day. It could of been photographed, *maybe,* but I couldn't picture a camera around taking it all, there was too much real life and, somehow it didn't strike me as tho it'd belong on the screen cause the real good of it would be lost there, the life of it couldn't be reproduced.

The rest of the riders at the camp finally caught up with us as we had the herd slowed down some, and with the twenty cowboys circling 'em in it wasn't very long till we had 'em milling on one spot, we held 'em there for a while and when they're quieted down a little we starts 'em back careful and easy for the "bedground" they'd left so sudden.

I wondered how much a movie outfit would give for such a stampede as I was seeing.

The herd stayed spooky all the way into the railroad, and the double guard was kept up every night till we got 'em in the stock yards. We loaded 'em thru the night and at daybreak the carloads of beef pulled out headed for Chicago.

We was thru, and after resting up during the day and cleaning up towards sundown we was ready to take in the sights of what the cow town could offer.

The first thing that caught my eye as I steps out of the restaurant where I'd been feeding was the electric lights decorating and advertising The Palace, moving picture theatre, and I strolls over to it just to see what was on.

I hardly believed my eyes when I saw that the main attraction that night was no less or other picture than "Six-guns and Ropes." I near had a fit right there and it was all I could do to keep from doing a little stampeding of my own.

I reads all about the daring horsemanship of the leading man, and then I thinks a while, and thinking, it comes to my mind that it'd be a good idea to get the boys over to see it and not say anything about how I acted in that perticular picture.

I remembered the part I had in it as pony express rider along with the few close-ups, how I caught that wild horse at the water hole and finished my ride. As far as the doubling I done for the leading man was concerned I thought I'd best keep that to myself, but I was anxious to see how I looked when I pulled the horse over backwards, and when I jumped the other horse over the cliff or done the bull-dogging all in that leading man's clothes.

I cornered about ten of the boys, pulled a few out of bed and tells 'em that I'm going to treat the whole bunch to the show. That sounds kind of tame to a few, but I finally hazes 'em in and in plenty of time to all get good seats together.

I wasn't interested in the comedy that came ahead of the picture, but the other boys sure got a laugh out of it. As for me I was anxious to see what they'd all think when they see me doing my bit on the screen.

The comedy finally run out, then, daggone the luck, they went to showing all about how automobiles was made, and it lasted too long. Finally, and at last I see the fimiliar title flashed on the screen, and right there I changes to a better seeing position.

It started out pretty with the fiesta, I saw myself way in the back a couple of times and again when I rode and scratched out the gray horse, but I didn't say anything or give myself away by asking the boys if they'd seen me. I wanted to wait till they saw plenty more of me and hear 'em say, "by God, there's Bill."

The picture went on and come to where I rode the brown bucking horse in doubling for the leading man, and pulled him over backwards, and I hears remarks such as, "that boy can sure ride."

I was aching to see that scene where I roped Sam and pulled him off his horse, but that wasn't supposed to appear till near the end. Then come to where I jumped the horse over the cliff, and later on, the bull-dogging which all drawed something good.

I kept a waiting and waiting for my little part to come along, but the picture went on, and before I know it comes to the last fiesta and the end, — *I was left, and entirely cut out.*

I remember Sam telling me one time that they sure do plenty of that in the cutting rooms, and that sometimes they do it just so there wont be nothing going on in the picture that'll draw the people's attention away from the hero. Anyway it seemed to me like they should of left some of it. Why in the hell did they waste all that film on me if they wasn't going to use it, then I happened to think, and wonder; *Was there any film in that camera when they used it on me so free?*

Or was they doing that just to encourage me, and make me break my fool neck doing stunts doubling for that daggoned pink leading man.

I wasn't saying much when I walked out, but I still could hear the boys talk about the good stuff that leading man pulled off. Then one of 'em turns towards me and asks if I'd met him while I was in the pictures.

"He's sure a wampus-cat on a horse," he says, "and the way he pulled that pony over backwards and got up with him, you could sure tell that he's been there before and plenty of times. I'll bet that boy is a real cowhand off the hills, ain't I right Bill?"

"Yes" I answers "some."

I'm doing a heap of thinking, and then it comes to me that I'd like to see Sam again, I'd like to get him over to one side and resume that argument with him about the leading man and them what doubles for him.

THE LAST CATCH

I'D BEEN AT SAND WASH CAMP for near a week before I noticed that up on one of the high ridges and hiding amongst the junipers, sunning themselves, was a bunch of wild ponies. They was backed up against a high rocky ledge which not only sheltered 'em from the cold spring winds but reflected the heat of the sun on 'em.

Then again it was a fine place for 'em to doze and sun themselves on account that the only thing that could very well get up there was mountain goats; they was safe enough from mustang runners, and if any ever did ride toward 'em they could always see 'em first.

I'd noticed how they'd be at that spot near every morning when the sun shined, and also noticed their tracks where they come to water at night, a mile or so above my camp. — An old corral was up there and showed, the way it was built, that it was a mustang trap at one time. Many had been caught in it I could see, and when the mustangs was thick, but now it was down in spots and I noticed it'd been neglected for quite a spell.

The water came out of a spring right inside of that corral and sunk in the ground a few feet away, still inside, and that's where that little wild bunch was watering.

My mustang-running fever raised up again when I thought how easy I could trap that bunch by just fixing up that corral and close the gate on 'em as they came in. I'd run and caught many a wild horse and still remembered the thrill, but now I was punching cows for a big outfit once again, had a steady job, lots of good bronc's, good camp and good grub — and I tried to forget mustangs and how easy it'd be for me to catch that little wild bunch that was up on that ridge, but they was always up there reminding; I felt the wild-horse fever getting me and I was trying hard to keep it down.

And most likely I could of kept it down too, only, one day I happened to get a closer view of the black stallion that was in that bunch and the mustang fever had a hold of me once more — I wanted that black horse, I never stopped to think *why*, but I wanted him.

The days was long, and after my day's ride was over I'd go to the corral and try to fix it up so it'd hold the black horse and his bunch. I was mighty careful in the fixing too, on account that a too big a change in the corral would be noticed by the mustangs and if they got suspicious they'd go and water somewhere else.

But with a few live junipers and pinons with the branches and all still on, I managed to make everything look natural, and strong enough to hold any wild horse. — In a few days I was ready, fresh tracks showed that the mustangs came in to water as usual every night, and one night I took my stand by the trap and waited.

It was along about the middle of the night when I heard the wild bunch coming up the sandy wash, the sound they made brought back many memories and my heart was thumping again. Right on up they came and acted like they would walk right into the corral without any hesitating. That would be too easy, I thought — but there they stopped and bunched. I could tell by the snorts they was suspecting that all wasn't well, but as nothing stirred and all seemed as usual, they finally lined in.

I could make out the outline of the black horse as he stood with head up while his bunch was drinking, that long heavy mane, curved neck, and pointed ears was easy identified. All was inside and I was about ready to pull the rope that'd close the gate when, for no reason that I could see, the band stampeded and scattered out like a bunch of quail a-snorting and shying. I could near touch some of 'em, so close they passed by.

I figgered right there that my chances for catching the black horse that night was gone, but he hadn't drank yet and maybe he'd come back. He was out there with his bunch and I could hear him nicker, the same as to ask if everything was all right as he scouted around 'em. — Then when all got quiet once again and I kept a-waiting, I finally heard a horse coming; pretty soon I could make out a black shape, the stallion was coming in to have his drink, alone.

That's just what I wanted — the black stallion alone, for I didn't care for any of the rest — and when he put his head down to drink I pulled on the rope and closed the big pole-gate with a bang.

I couldn't sleep very well the rest of that night on account of wanting to see that black at close view and with the sun a-shining on him, the first light of day found me awake and waiting for it. A hunk of pitch pine soon had the little stove a-roaring, the coffee pot begin to sing and by the time I'd went and caught me a saddle-horse and came back, the coffee was boiling; a cup of that and a cigarette and I was riding up the wash toward the trap corral and the black horse.

I'd no more than got sight of the top poles of that corral when a long whistle and a snort told me he was still there, and as I rode up I found a quivering picture of horseflesh that was sure good to look at, and that's all I did for a while was look; the more I looked though, the less I liked the idea of putting a rope around that black shining neck, for sometimes a rope sure does take the hair off in spots.

But I was too excited just then to worry about what a rope could do to a horse that fought it, and as I kept a-watching and admiring every move that black was making, and noticing the deep heart, the short back, and the long sloping hip that was some of his good points, I was natural-like uncoiling my rope, and making a loop.

He fought like a wild-cat when that loop settled over his head and drawed up back of his ears, but I was riding my best rope-horse that day and, with the brand new rope I'd saved for such a purpose tied hard and fast to the saddle-horn, I knowed I had him for keeps. Being careful of keeping the slack out of the rope, so as none of us would get tangled up in it too much, I edged my horse toward the corral gate and opened it. — I was going to take him to another corral close to my camp.

The distance to that corral, with the black horse pulling on the rope for all he was worth, was sure covered plenty quick, but when he got sight of the new corral, he started another direction from there and I had to do considerable manœuvring to get him through the gate and into it. Next was to put the hackamore on him and tie him up.

I'd planned to start breaking him right away, but I wanted to take my time at it and do a good job, and as luck would have it, cattle begin scattering and straying away right about then, my time was all took up with 'em and I'd hardly ever get back to camp till away after sundown. As it was, the only chance I had to see my black horse was early in the morning and before I started out for a day's ride.

Things went on like that for quite a few days, and then I begin to notice something wrong, the black horse was ganting up pretty bad, wouldn't eat and wouldn't drink and I was getting worried. I'd give him plenty of fresh hay and even turned him loose in the corral, thinking it'd help, but all that attention didn't seem to better things any with him; the only thing that seemed the same was his spirit, he'd show plenty of that every time I walked in the corral, but there again I could see what kept that up. I'd often caught him looking up toward that big rocky ledge where him and his little bunch used to sun themselves — and that finally got to working on me.

I'd think of that often as I rode along through the day and somehow the more I thought on the subject the less satisfaction I was getting out of the idea that I'd caught the horse and had him in my corral, all safe

The distance from the trap to the corral was covered in no time.

for whenever I wanted him. And then soon enough I realized —, it wasn't owning the wild horse that made me want to go after him so much, it was the catching of him that caused a feller to get the mustang fever, and after the mustang was caught and the fever cooled down — well, I'd kinda wished they'd got away.

I'd quit running the wild horse on that account, and here I was with another one I'd just trapped and took the freedom away from. I had more horses than I could use as it was and what would I do with this one, sell him? not hardly. I was too much married to them ponies I already owned and I knowed it'd be the same with the black horse, I'd never sell him even though I had no use for any more.

I'd been running them thoughts through my mind for quite a few days and had come to no conclusion, and every morning found me making tracks toward the corral where I'd smoke a cigarette and watch my black horse — the hay I'd give him would hardly be touched.

Then one morning I started the fire as usual, put on the coffee pot and walked out toward the corral. I figgered on coming back before the fire died down, but as I set by the corral I forgot everything but the little horse there with me and the country around us. All was quiet excepting for a meadow-lark tuning up on a juniper close by. I felt like just setting there breathing in and listening — and I was thinking, thinking as I watched the black horse. He was standing still as a statue and looking up where his little bunch of mares and colts used to be at this time of the day. Finally I stood up, took in every line of him, like for the last time, and then I leaned against the corral gate and opened it slow and steady and *wide*.

The black horse seen the opening, and maybe it's a good thing he took advantage of it right then, for a minute afterward I felt like kicking myself for letting such a horse go; but that feeling didn't last long and instead, it done me good to watch him pace away, head and tail up, and seemed, like hating to touch the ground for fear another trap would spring up and circle him once more. Then, as I watched him disappear out of sight, I felt relieved — Somehow, he was better to look at that way.

The coffee had boiled over, put out the fire, and scattered grounds all over the stove when I got back to camp, but I felt sorta cheerful and whistled a tune as I rebuilt the fire and put on fresh coffee.

A few days later I tore down the mustang corral by the spring and snaked the posts away with my saddle-horse. Then one morning I seen the black stallion and his bunch again; they was up by the big rocky ledge and just a-sunning themselves.

"Cupid, the Mustang"

IT WAS EARLY SPRING, the mustangs was getting a taste of the first short blades of green and getting perticular, the white sage and dry grass wasn't good enough no more, and you could see the "fuzztails" keeping up on the sunny side of the buttes where the green grass had a head start, nibbling it down to the ground. Sometimes even the roots was pulled up, dirt shook out, and et down. They was getting just enough of a taste to make 'em weak and the warm sun helped along making 'em weaker, all but the few, mighty few little colts and they was strong, always a bucking and kicking, teasing and biting the older horses and sticking their noses into everything what looked strange.

But even tho the mustangs was weaker at that time of the year, you couldn't tell it on 'em much, and they'd give us as hard a chase then as any other time, they had a lot of nerve to make up for the weakness and they'd run on that. We had a blind trap in the junipers and luck was pretty well with us, we'd caught over a hundred head in fifteen days. But the trap was getting wore out and the "broomtails" was getting wise as to its location, for, the last couple of days we'd done a lot of running and no catching.

It's near sundown when I look out on the flat a few miles, and sees a couple of riders "making signs" (by riding a couple of circles) for all hands to hit camp. Seemed like the wild ponies couldn't be hazed nowheres near the trap and I knowed where we'd have to put in another month's work finding a new trap site and putting it up. I'm riding along heading towards camp thinking deep of spots I'd seen around what would be best to put a new trap in, when out from behind a Sarvis berry bush comes a little bay streak of horseflesh a nickering for all it was worth, ears pointed straight ahead and not even touching the tall sage brush. My horse answers and the little feller runs up alongside acting awful tickled on seeing another of his kind, and follows.

He was a little mustang colt with a blaze face and trim as a deer and I feels mighty sorry for him cause I knowed what happened. I knowed some of us had been running a bunch he and his mammy was in. I knowed how his mammy must of stayed back when the little feller got tired and winded and how she tried to keep him with her, but fear must of got a holt when she seen a rider closing in, and then she just stampeded forgetting all about the poor little devil. I'm not what you'd call soft hearted but it always did get me pretty deep when I'd see some of them little fellers losing their mammies that way, cause its just one chance in a thousand they'd ever find one another again, and the poor little colt would just mope around over the deserts and mountains looking and nickering for that mammy of his, he wouldn't know how to find water and the green grass would never take the place of his mother's milk, consequences is after a month's suffering he mostly lays down never to get up no more.

I looks down at this little orphant keeping pace alongside my horse. He was too young to realize that close to him was a human, one of them two legged mean devils what was responsible for him hitting the trail by his lonesome that way, what he wanted was company and horseflesh to run alongside of, any kind would do for a spell. And tired as he was when he was resting in the shade of that Sarvis berry bush the sight of my horse made him use his legs without him knowing of it.

I noticed his little Blaze face, the deep little chest, short back and sloping rump. I figgers him to be about ten days old and knows that with some help he might pull thru' even if away from his runaway mammy, and after sizing up his little roman nose and glass eyes along with the other good points I already mentioned, and him being a little

273

hunk of horseflesh needing care mighty bad, I concludes to find a place for him. Us riders at the camp was not able to take on any orphants, we wanted to bad enough but daggone it we had no place to keep 'em being we was on the move most all the time, besides they'd be needing warm cow's milk.

The little feller is getting too tired to keep up even tho' I'm going at a mighty slow walk. It's after sundown and getting real dark when I cross a little stream, figgering he might want a sip of moisture even if it was weak compared to his mammy's milk. I stops on the other side and when he steps in the water and hears it splash, down goes his head reaching for a drink, but his neck being so short and his legs so long he can't quite make it. I'd like to hand him some in my hat but I know he'd scoot away. Finally he spraddles his legs far apart as he can, bends his knees a little and takes on a few swallows of the flat thin drink, but I guess it must of tasted a heap better than none. It's good and dark by the time I climbs on my horse again and away we go slow but sure towards the light that's our camp.

"What's kept you so long Bill, did you 'jigger your horse'?" is the first I hear when the boys make out its me showing up. "No," I says, "I picked up a orphant and the poor little devil is all in." I dilutes a can of condensed milk with warm water and the boys help me pour it down him, he's too tired to fight much and after I get thru taking some of the shyness out of him and watching his little glass eyes roll I turns him loose with our saddle horses, knowing he won't leave 'em, not that night anyway.

The next morning I throws a "Bait" of fried sage chicken and afterwards I holds a confab with the boys as to where would be the most likely place to take the colt. We was all strangers in the country and didn't know one ranch from the other so I finally concludes to take the colt and drop him at the first place where they'd like to have him. The closest ranch is a few miles down the "sag" and telling the boys I'd circle and shove the mustangs ahead on my way back I started off taking the little "fuzzy" with me. I have a little trouble at first and have to kind of easy drag or shove him away from the sight of the other horses and when at some distance he don't see no other but mine he's willing to try and not lose sight of that one. "Poor little Blaze (as I called him) I hope I find a good place for you, where you'll get took good care of."

In an hour or so I'm getting into a lane dividing two fields, that lane leads on up to the first ranch where I'm going to try and get somebody to adopt my orphant and I'm squinting my eyes for a glimpse of what kind of folks may be living thereabout, but I don't see none. The stock around are in good shape and the fences are up neat which says a whole lot. I rides on keeping a look out on everything I see, I'm but a few yards from the bunk house skirting around the big corrals when here comes a bunch of dogs barking and showing their teeth, down comes my rope figgering on snaring me a few and wrapping 'em around some post in case they got too familiar, one of the hounds is sneaking up behind little Blaze and I'm just about ready to spread my loop over his snoot when from past the corrals and stables and out of the big ranch house somebody hollers "Stop it, Spot" then I looks up. A girl is walking up, I guess just to make sure them dogs will behave, or maybe to see I'm not dragging any of 'em around, and I spurs up to meet her.

She ain't looking at me none at all when I ride up, seems like little Blaze took all her attention and before I can lift my hat or say a word she looks up and says without any preliminaries, "I hope you're not taking this little colt very far, he seems tired out." That kinda blazed a trail for what I wanted to say, and I needed some kind of a lead mighty bad for as soon as she looks up at me I feels like I had a frog in my throat and I couldn't keep my eyes off the first freckles I ever saw on any human what looked good, there wasn't over a dozen of 'em and I think I was trying to count 'em when I come to and realized I ought to be saying something. Finally I comes out with "Beg your pardon lady, but this little feller lost his mammy and I'm just trying to find a place where somebody would be glad to have him, he's needing care mighty bad."

With that out and over with I feels more at ease specially when she looks up again and says, "Oh! can I have him?" "You sure can" I says and even tho she acts mighty tickled I know she wasn't any more than I am, for I knowed I couldn't of found a better person to turn little Blaze over to, not if I'd hunted over a half dozen territories. "If you'll tell me where you want to keep him" I says "I'll put him in for you." "Sure" she says "but put your hat on before you get more sunburned than you already are and we'll look in the stable, maybe we can find some empty box stall." I got off my horse and led him toward the stables little Blaze bringing up the rear. I was walking right alongside of her, and funny I'd never noticed before how much noise them chaps and spurs of mine made when I was on foot that way.

The sun is way high and it's getting near noon by the time little Blaze was made comfortable, a box stall was cleaned out and little as I knowed about milking cows I tried my luck anyway and squeezed enough out of an old "Dogie" to keep the colt kinda contented till the chore boy done the regular milking. Little Blaze was getting real gentle, he was tired and hungry, and a place to rest and eat seemed to suit him fine for the time being. We, the girl and me kept on a talking about the fine points of the little horse, what she missed I made her see and the confab went on for quite a spell, lucky there was horseflesh to talk about for I know with any other subject that frog in my throat would of showed up again and the conversation would of been dragging some.

I mention something about it's time I was going when she says "You must stay for lunch Mister ah." "Bill is my first name, the last one I don't use enough to keep a shine on it but if you'd rather know that one, it's Saunders, and as regards to staying for lunch, I'd like to mighty well but I'm a few hours late now meeting the boys out on circle and I've sure got to travel to make up." "Well Mr. Saunders I'm sure obliged to you for bringing me this dear little colt and really now" she says "do you think your horse can carry you fast enough so you'd be able to get there in time to be of help? and besides there is no use your running away when the cook has dinner so near ready."

About that time the dinner ring busts out, and the chink is playing a reglar tune on the big triangle steel. No backing out now, and with the swishing of my chaps and the ring of my spurs chipping in on the harmony, we start out toward the other noise. We step up under some big cottonwoods past the little gate and pointing at some basins on a bench she says to me, "if you care to wash Mr. Saunders."

With that she goes on up to the house. My chaps are took off pronto and hung on the picket fence and my spurs went with 'em, it's queer how relieved I was on taking them off, they'd never bothered me that way before and I was always glad to have 'em on, far as that goes I'd never went nowheres without 'em and it got me why I should feel different now. I looked the outfit over, my spurs was big silver inlaid one pieced steel with a two inch rowel. I know any cowboy would of been glad to have 'em for they was made to order and something to be proud of. As for my chaps, they was nothing fancy and showed a little wear but they was neat fitting and not at all sloppy, so I figgers there's nothing wrong with my outfit and it's just me getting kinda self conscious in different company that's all.

Anyway, I feel better when I struts in the door where the victuals was spread. The chink walks in packing ribs of beef on a platter and tells me to sit down. There's four plates on the table and I wonders who they can all be and I'm wondering pretty strong when thru the door I'd come in walks a man I figgered to be about fifty, I sized him up right away to be the girl's father, he was a big man with white hair and moustache, small around the hips and bow-legged as they make 'em. By his spurs and boots, his talk and looks I was sure for him to be of Texas and I was right as I finds out afterwards.

"Howdy stranger" he says as he looks at me and classes me up right there and then with one glance. He walks on past. Talks to the chink a while and turns to tell me to make myself comfortable that dinner will be ready soon. With that he opens a door and goes into another room. Now I says to myself, there's one more to be accounted for, I takes a peek out towards the corrals but I don't see nobody and I'm just turned back around in time to see the door open again and in walks the girl and what I'd already figgered to be her father. A introduction proves I was correct and we all sit down to partake of a "bait" the likes I'd never tasted before, I had to size up the cook a couple of times to make sure it was a chink what was responsible for such.

I finds the empty chair at the table was for the girl's brother what'd been riding the "starvation" field and was expected back most any time. I'm digging up all the manners and table etiquette I can think of and figgers I'm doing fairly well when the old gentleman hits me on the blind side with, "My daughter Alice was telling me you brung her a mustang colt to raise." "Yes" I says "I just didn't want him to suffer and die and figgered somebody would like to have him, and your place is the first I run onto."

"I don't mind it" the old man says "but it's only a mustang after all and there's hundreds of 'em up in the hills." This time the girl cuts the rope and saves my neck with "but father you ought to see him, he's so different than any I ever saw and I like him so much that I nearly asked for him before I knew what Mr. Saunders' plans were or where he was going to take him." The old man smiles a little at both of us and looked kinda good with his face that way. He turns to his daughter and says "Oh well, if you like him Alice that settles it."

After the meal is over, me and him heads for the porch to roll a smoke, the girl excuses herself and vamoses the other way leaving us to the average talk of the weather, stock, feed, and mustangs. When it begins to lag, I figgers it's time for me to be going and shaking hands I paces out toward my horse picking up my chaps and spurs on the way. I'm watering my horse at the trough and hoping the girl comes out so I can try and say how glad I am to've met her and all that goes with it, but it don't look like I'll have any luck and it don't strike me quite right to go at the door and tell her. I'm taking all the time I can putting on my chaps and spurs even straightening my saddle when it didn't need it, and after waiting a spell and figgering there's no use I finally straddles my roan and starts out, when I hear a screen door slam and I turns. Here she comes and I whirls my horse back to meet her halfway. "Mr. Saunders," she says putting out her hand, "I'm awfully glad I met you and sure appreciate your giving me the little Blaze faced colt. I hope when you come by here again that you'll stop for we'll always be glad to see you."

I'm up halfways back to camp and letting my horse poke along when I gets to wondering what the boys will be thinking happened to me for not showing up when I should of, and maybe they lost a bunch all on account of me not being where I was expected to be. I tickles the roan with my spurs and heads up a pinnacle where I can look over the other side to see if I can locate any dust from running mustangs, but on getting up there everything is quiet and settled, not a stir nowheres within a good twenty miles around, a little bunch of "fuzzies" are sleeping standing up about half a mile below me and I wonder if instead of "running" they been looking for me, for I know many a bunch was let go on account of a missing rider, thinking that *hombre* had a fall, horse holding him down or something. So instead of fogging in behind the little bunch I'd located, I shashays toward the trap on a good long lope and gets up there in time to see at least forty head of wild ones fresh caught and gates being closed on 'em, and all the boys are there.

That relieves me considerable and when they see me riding down the trail into the trap, they're all packing a smile remarking they was glad to see me show up just then being it'd save 'em the trouble of lining out and looking for my carcass. "Well," I says, "it don't look to me like you missed my help much come to figgering how many you all run in without it, and I might try to be among the missing again soon being it worked so good this once." They didn't get the drift of that, and so tickled they was of the day's catch they forgot to ask me who adopted the orphant or what about it. I was kinda glad they did 'cause I'd had to went around some of the details.

In the next few days we catch around ten head, then a few more days with no luck at all. We figger it's about time to try finding another trap location and we spread out from camp early one morning starting every bunch we see and letting 'em go to suit themselves. Along about noon we had close onto five hundred head lining out at a stiff trot, they took a whole side of a mountain the way they was scattered but they was sure heading straight for some place, and a place where the canyons came to a pinch or where ever we could hide a trap was what we was looking for. The mustangs are still fogging on and about ten miles further we came to the spot where according to the way the ponies was running *now* would make a sure bet trap site. We do a little figgering as to just how we was to lay it and about sundown we also find a place to put up our camp. It's way into the night when we get back, with nothing under our belts since early morning, not even water, and after the horses are all grained and we're thru eating we hit our soogans mighty quick for we all know it won't be long before old Sol peeps over the ridge and a big day's work ahead with moving camp and starting on our new trap.

I'm trying to find excuses to be amongst the missing but I figger if I did, what reason would I have to go by or stop where I'd left little Blaze, I was hoping we'd run out of grub or something, just so I could go by and say "howdy" to the lady who'd adopted the orphant, but no chance that I can see and worse yet we're moving a good twenty miles further on up in the mountains, so when I see there's no escape I try and make the best of it and being my part of the job is snaking junipers off the side of the mountain, I sure make the rope sing and smoke and it looks like with the early start we got on this trap, and the good location it's in that we ought to make a good catch in this one.

One morning, about the time we're at our busiest and crowding the work, a rider shows up and asks if we'd seen any cattle south of the mountains, he stays on for a spell and naturally the talk drifts to mustangs and before he goes he remarks as how he's wishing they was all dead. "They're a lot trouble" he says. "We can't turn our horses loose on account of 'em and they're taking a lot of good feed from our cattle. Somebody rode in the other day and give my sis a colt, just as tho there wasn't enough of them dam broomtails around without raising any. Of course the colt won't live cause it's getting weaker all the time and she's pretty near sick herself over it." With that he rides off and one of the boys says pointing to the rider, "He's the kind what'd shoot a mustang just because he can't catch 'em."

That night I tells the boys I'm hitting out for town early in the morning, being I was out of smoking and needing other things. I'd took care to see that the other boys needed smoking too cause I'd hid most of it and by the time they was willing to let me go they see plenty of good reasons that somebody should go plenty quick and with a pack horse too. So, long before dawn I'm pulling the pack horse into a high lope and rides into the ranch a couple of hours before noon. The same dogs make the same noise, a screen door slams way over by the cottonwoods and this time the girl Alice is running up and even tho I see she's mighty glad to see me, most of the gladness is for the help that little hunk of horseflesh in the box stall might get. Without any "howdy do" much and me not acting as tho I already knowed, we heads towards the stables my chaps a swishing and spurs a ringing but they don't bother me this time.

Little Blaze is all in a heap in the corner of the box stall and near too weak to even raise his head. "What you been feeding him?" I asks kinda easy. "Nothing that I thought would hurt him," she answers, "just warm cow's milk twice a day and a little green grass I'd cut for him with a little alfalfa. Nobody but father would help me with him and he's so busy I didn't want to bother him, I'm glad you came for I'd hate to lose little Blaze." "So would I hate to see him go" I says "and if you have a little fenced in place around where there's a little green grass for him to pick on and so he can get a little sunshine, we'll take him over to it." True enough she sure felt bad about the little colt being so near gone, and mighty glad I was to see her so interested in that helpless little orphant. I picks him up and carries him, long legs and all and it wasn't long till we had him in an old stack yard, I steadies him a while and helps him navigate. When I think the stiffness is out of his legs some and he's beginning to notice things again I lets him go, and I see the mustang blood is putting up a hard fight, for shaky in the legs as he is, there's no laying down for him. I tried my luck once more at milking a cow, asked the girl for some cottonseed lumps and mashing a few in the warm milk we gives little Blaze all he wants which wasn't much but it helped him some.

We stick around for a spell, her watching the colt and me watching both the girl and the colt, and it's doing me a lot of good to watch the girl cheer up to what I had to say for little Blaze. "Don't worry at all" I says "I've seen 'em in worse fix than him come out of it and be fine little horses, in another couple of weeks he'll be playing all thru here, you watch." Queer, but that little feller was getting under my own hide, pretty deep too, and I finds I'm doing some worrying about him myself on my own hook, I'm kinda dubious when I make a move to go wether he'll pull thru or not and I'd hate to have the girl know.

I refuse when I'm asked to stay for a bite with the excuse that I still had twenty miles to go to reach town and that I had to get back to camp quick a possible the next day (which was the truth). Far as that goes I should of been working on the trap but then I thought I was doing what was just about right by being here, I was mighty pleased anyway and when she tells me that I must stop on my way back and eat with them, why I says, "thanks mam I'll be here," and gets on my horse and rides away telling her not to worry, he'd be fine in a few days.

"Now Eagle" I says, talking to the gruyer I was riding towards town "I suppose I'm making a lot of fuss over that little colt and making some long rides on account of him, not mentioning how I got to kinda beat around the bush with the boys back to camp, but lissen here old top horse that same little mustang was the cause of me meeting such a lady, the like I never seen before and I'm kind of took up with that colt being he's such a good hand playing cupid and seeing how I'm to be expected around every so often that way on his account. And being she thinks so daggone much of the little son of a gun too, even naming him Blaze without her knowing I'd already named him that myself, all kinda breaks a trail for me to get acquainted. Of course I'm expecting a lot of disappointment and all that and maybe she don't like me at all, but anyways I'm on speaking terms with her and who's the blame for it? just a little Blaze, and I sure hope he don't go and die and stop playing the game for me 'cause I'd never find another such little horse to take his place, not with both the lady and me."

The next day finds me back to the ranch plenty early, the girl is out in the stack yard keeping company to little Blaze and watching every one of the few moves he makes. The little feller looks up when he sees my horses coming and he tries to nicker but he didn't do a very good job of it. "He seems a lot better this morning," the girl says, "he even nibbled at a little grass." The way she said it sure showed how tickled she was and I was afraid a lot that it was just his last lively spell before keeling over for good.

I tied my horses to the feed rack, loosened up the cinches and pack, and spraddled down where I can watch the girl talk. She tells me how little Blaze is the first little colt of all she's seen at the ranch what seemed to talk, what really showed how he needed sympathy and care and how by that she thought more of him from the start than any of the fat slick little fellers her dad was raising. The talk got more or less general and pretty soon branched out on wild horses when I joined in the conversation more often, a little was asked as to how I come to be running mustangs, some about where I was born and where was my folks to which I answered direct with nothing added much. Then between remarks passed on as to some perticular moves of the little feller we was watching she started on to tell of how her dad drifted into Nevada from Texas years ago before she and her brother was born, of how her mother died sudden while she was away to summer school and left her the only lady on the ranch, and then before I can catch my breath she tells me that she has to leave soon for what she figgers to be her last time to college.

"I'd rather stay here at home" she says "but it's my last term and thought I ought to finish if I can. There's so much to keep me here" she goes on "my books, my ponies, the river bottoms and mountains."

"Well she's too good for him too," I thinks out loud, "and I bet I can whip him."

"How long do you figger on being gone?" I asks, trying not show my feelings.

"I'll be away about eight months or more," she says.

It was getting near noon, and my appetite that generally speaks up about that time had nothing to say, far as it was concerned it didn't care when we et.

"And when are you going?" thought I'd just as well know now and have it over with.

"In about a week" she answers, and I figger it served me right for asking. I kept my nose on my plate pretty well during dinner and after it was thru' I didn't lose no time much cinching up my outfit and getting out, I pets little Blaze over the rump as I leave and tells him that "he's got to do better than that." The big gate squeaks as I push it open and the girl comes out to meet me, telling me to come over again if I can spare the time and see how little Blaze is pulling thru before she leaves. "Yes mam," I says, "I'll sure try."

I'm not singing any or talking much on the trail back to camp, but I'm doing a heap of thinking and not of the kind what puts flowers on sagebrush either. But what's the use, what right have I got to think a girl like her could want a feller like me and besides she might have her own pick waiting for her at college town. "Well she's too good for him too," I thinks out loud, "and I bet I can whip him."

I'm back to camp a couple of days when the boys start calling me "Gloomy Bill," but I make such a hand of myself that it'd take two of 'em to keep up with me, I'm snaking junipers down six and eight at a time, setting 'em up and wiring 'em fast an' furious, nobody sees me grin any more and as I heard the boys say when they thought I was too far to hear that I was working a grudge out on the trap the way I as going at it, even big Larry was side stepping and stopped his joking when he'd see me coming. "Suffering jehosafat" I thought "I must be a mean looking crethure." And then I begins to grin again some, more every day till the time comes nearer when I'll be making another fast ride down the valley.

When that day breaks, I'm up and gone before the boys know it, chewing away on a cold biscuit with bacon between and taking the washout on high run, I'm just touching the blue ridges and never sees the flats, I'd picked on a spoilt horse what always wanted to stampede and run blind, he got all the running away he wanted that day and kept a looking back to see when I was going to try to stop him, but I gives him his head on up to within a couple of miles of the ranch where he was kinda glad when I settled him down to a jog trot. "Well old boy" I says "did you get enough?"

On hitting the ranch and seeing the girl again, I know everything ain't going just right, and it's as I thought, little Blaze is down to nothing and couldn't get up. I watched the girl a while and it don't take me long to decide what to do. Telling her I'd be back in a short while I jumps on my horse and hits out for the horse pasture I'd passed, I cuts out about twenty head of horses mostly mares with young colts and hazes 'em back towards the corral. The girl is there to open the gate, I asks her if any of the mares with colts are broke to lead and she points me out a couple, it don't take me long to spread my line around one of 'em's neck, jerk up my slack and pull her to, takes my dallies and out we go again leading the mare on a stiff trot towards where little Blaze is counting his last chips.

The mare sure objects to nursing a strange colt that way, but when I lifts little Blaze up again all I have to do is point my finger at her and she's still as a petrified tree. The girl catches up out of breath and says with lot of feeling "Will he live Mr. Saunders?" And by the time I get thru telling her of all the good chances he has, specially now with the natural fluid he's getting, why she's smiling again.

"I know how you want to save little Blaze" I says. "So you just keep this mare up, she's got a lot of milk and her colt won't be able to use over half of it for a couple of weeks or more and nursing little Blaze twice a day for that length of time would sure put him on his feet to stay. Get the chore boy to do it for you. But I forgot that you're going away in a day or two."

"It may sound silly to you Mr. Saunders" she says "but I couldn't leave while little Blaze is like this. I don't care if I am late getting there."

"I don't call that being silly mam, none at all. And I'm sure grateful to little Blaze for keeping you here this little while longer."

I make a couple more early sneaks out of camp, am gone all day and manage to get back late enough to find all the boys asleep, so there's no questions asked till the morning comes and then there ain't much time for we got to be out and going. The trap was near done and the way she was setting sure promised a lot, the mustangs hadn't been run for near a month and they was getting to feel safe, besides there was new bunches coming in from other parts of the country where the mustang runners was keeping 'em on the move. A couple more days and the rag wings would be done. The next day there'd be a big circle, all the boys riding low on their ponies necks and over washouts, cut banks, and thru timber sticking close to the mustangs tails, turning 'em and bringing 'em in the big rag wings where other riders would be hid, ready to take up the slack the tired horses are leaving.

I know I've got to be on hand with the rest of the boys that first day and that I ought to be there every day after that so I've only got two days left to do one more sneak in, and I pick on the second, the day before the big run.

The girl tells me when I'm tying up my horse at the ranch that she's been busy packing up and she don't look a bit happy over the idea of leaving either "but little Blaze is getting real strong now, and I really ought to get a little education," she says trying to laugh. We're making tracks towards the stack yard. Seems like that's been where we had all our talks, and where we'd both watch the little orphant sink or recuperate, this time he's recuperating and chewing on the green grass like he'd been looking for it, and never noticed before that it'd been right under him all the time. We're both sitting on a log watching the young 'un, neither of us saying much but both doing a heap of thinking and I wonders if her thoughts are running along on the same trail as mine.

Maybe they are, for in a few minutes we both turn and look at each other kinda smiling like we understood what we thought but didn't want to say, then little Blaze lifts up his head, nickers, and walks towards us, his little knees still shaky and near rubbing together. "Mr. Saunders" the girl says "you've saved his life, and now I still hate to leave him, he's only a little horse, but he means more to me and I'm worried as to what kind of care he'll get when I'm gone." She's looking at the ground mighty hard and I'm kind of bogged down as to what to say. If the little feller could travel I'd take him to camp and take care of him somehow, and she knows that when the big run starts I won't be able to ride down only once in a long while.

"My brother went away," she says still staring at mother earth. "He's left for some city where he plans to learn a trade, he was restless here but I think he'll be glad to come back some day. Anyway, father is needing a good man mighty bad, there's fifty head of broncs to be broke to ride or work and I hope you'll forgive me Mr. Saunders, but I thought you'd like to take the job. Father would pay well and when I spoke to him of you he said he'd be glad to have you but is afraid you like to run mustangs too well. I mentioned you because I thought you *might* want such a job, and then again I'd feel so relieved to know that little Blaze would be taken care of right."

I'm doing a heap of thinking and no interrupting while she's telling me all this. Sure enough, I liked to run mustangs better than anything when it come to doing something, but then breaking horses is no slow man's job either and what'd I care about the jobs, she was wanting me here and that's enough said. I know I'll have to do some tall parleying with the boys before I can break loose but I got to manage it some way, for the little lady is not going to be wanting of anything for very long, if I can give or get it for her. "You thought right" I says. "And bank on me to be on hand whenever you want me, and if I can suit or help little Blaze and your dad, I'm plum satisfied even if the job was milking cows." "Yes" I says "I'd even herd sheep in a case like this."

"We have no sheep" she says laughing, and I'm sure glad to see how happy she is on account of me taking the job. "But Mr. Saunders," she goes on, "I don't want you to take the job for our sake. I wouldn't like to impose on you that way and if you want to stay with mustangs why believe me there won't be no hard feelings. I know your kind, but I thought you'd like breaking horses and having your meals reglar for a change." "Sure," I says, "You're right I don't care for mustang running any more, and believe me lady I'm glad to take this job, if your dad'll have me."

Too bad I have to be on hand for the big run, for the girl was leaving that same day and there's no saying as to how much I'd like to been around up till when the train pulled out. But then again I thinks it best for me not to be present cause I might just be butting in some way, so after talking things over with her dad who looked real glad at me taking the job, I gets ready to leave, telling him I'll be back to stay soon as the first three days run was over with. The girl is at the hitching rack where my horse is tied, her head is down and she's working away with the toe of her shoe making little mounds of sand and flattening 'em out, she don't hear me coming and as I come near I gets a hunch of what her thoughts might be. I hopes I'm right but maybe I'm wrong for when she looks up she says "let's go see little Blaze once more, together."

Little Blaze comes up to meet us nickering kinda soft, the girl rubs him between the ears, the while telling him that he'll be well took care of now being that I'm going to be around. "It may be a long time before we see you together again little horse" she says. "But I know you won't forget me no more than I'll forget you." I chips in a couple of rubs on the little orphants neck and we starts back to the hitching rack.

She puts out her hand and says, "Mr. Saunders, don't let any of them big broncs get you under, 'cause I'd want to see you too when I come back." I know there's a lot back of that and I think I understand but that makes me all the more helpless and all I says is, "Don't worry mam, you'll sure see me, and if any of them broncs get me down, as you say, I'll sure pick 'em up and shake 'em." I'm still holding her hand when I says that little Blaze and I will sure be glad to see her again, and not doing what I'd like to do, only the next best I gives her a final shake wishing her all kinds of good luck and that she enjoys herself while away. With that, I climbs on my horse and rides away before I say something what wouldn't be just right, and looking back when I turns by the corral, I see she's standing where I'd left her.

Something tells me to go back and do things right, but then I'm not sure of my footing and the way it all seems to look just leaves me wondering. She waves a good bye and I do the same, and like a dam fool I rides on, headed for the most lonesomedest trail I ever knowed.

When me and the rest of the boys lined out for our big circle and run the next day I was glad to find that the mustangs was kind of scattering and hard to haze the direction of the trap, it gives me something to use my mind on and I'm riding reckless, taking short cuts with ten foot drops trying to turn the bunch I'm after. I'm riding the best horse in my string and he's sure coming up to all whatever I knowed him to be.

In two days we trap a little over sixty head, it's all the small corral at the point of the trap will hold and being the next day they have to be roped, throwed and with one foot tied up, drove to pasture, I figger it's high time I was going and taking my new job. The boys all think I'm "loco de cabeso" when I tells 'em I hired out to break broncs for somebody down the valley, and they don't see why I want to quit running mustangs when it all looked like we'd had so good a chance to come out with more broomtails than we wanted. They see there's no use arguing and they know better than to ask the reason, besides I think they had a suspicion of what's up, ever since that day when Alice's brother rode up and passed the remark of somebody giving his sis' a mustang colt to raise.

I gives all my ponies away to the boys excepting a couple of "tops" I'd shipped down from the north, and with my belongings all "squaw-hitched" on one of the horses, I tells the boys adios, and that I'd be up once in a while to see how they was getting on with the wild ones. I sure hated to leave them boys, they was all good hands and the kind what'd tackle the devil hisself and pull his eye teeth out for him in case he got in the way. I'd been with 'em for months, we'd cussed and laughed together, worked and rode together, and all helped cook and eat the same grub. It was hard for me to go, and if only the girl would of been at the ranch I'd felt a heap different, but there was only little Blaze. Then I stops and thinks again, what if I'd never seen little Blaze?

I'd been to work in the breaking corrals for a couple of months, and was getting along fine. I'd got little Blaze two more mammies in the meantime for when one little colt would grow up and want all the milk that left the little orphant out in the cold, so I'd hunt him another

And all helped cook and eat the same grub.

mammy out of the stock horses, put her in the chutes and let the little feller nurse thru the bars twice a day, he was coming fine and growing like a weed, he was losing his leppy look and getting real playful and when a couple of times I'd got letters from the girl asking how the little orphant and I was getting along all I could say was "fine." I'd start an answer back and when I'd get past "These few lines to let you know" I'd be stuck, there's a lot I wanted to say but just what to say and how to say it tangled me all up, besides I was wondering if she wasn't writing just to be sociable, or wanting to know about little Blaze.

I figger its near five months yet before she returns. And every once in a while when I sees little Blaze in the shade of the cottonwood half asleep, I runs my thumb up his neck and tells him to wake up and do something if he don't want to be a orphant again but he just stands there looking wise, and he sure can do that well, I keep noticing how big and strong he's getting to be and then I gets to wondering if my time ain't up, if I shouldn't corral my two ponies and go back with the boys and mustang running. I'm kinda dubious as to how everything is going to hatch out, and rough or mean and kinky as these broncs are to handle they don't come up with mustang running with me, it gets kinda monotonous and I'm mighty lonesome at times. I'm getting more restless every day and having a hard time to decide wether to come out and tell her what's on my mind or just pick up and hit for the mountains, I know her letters say more than mine but I don't know enough about reading between the lines to be sure about what might be, or is she just waiting like I am, but I don't know.

It ain't long when I gets to thinking things had come to a showdown, she ain't wrote for over three weeks and I makes up my mind to hit out. That afternoon I corners the chore boy and asks him to turn little Blaze out in the pasture a few days after I'm gone, I stops by the stack yards to watch the little feller buck and play, he's sure got a kinky little back and I know some day he'll make somebody grab the nubbin.

The next morning when I'm heading toward the corrals to get me a wrango horse I glance over to the stack yards and noticed little Blaze with his head down and standing on three legs, one is limp. I rushes over to him and finds where he'd got one front foot caught (while playing I guess) and broke the front leg a ways below the knee, looked like it'd just been done and I forgets all about my wrango horse, my outfit all packed, and that I was ready to go. I'm working till way late setting little Blaze's leg, putting on the splints and fixing up a rigging with a wide canvas belt to hold him and hold his front feet up off the ground while the bone is mending. I got on the good side of Charlie the chink and had him cooking barley and bran, and with green alfalfa

I'd cut for him, along with real good care I was giving him three times a day, he slowly but surely started to recuperate again and now I'm sure glad I stayed for what if I'd went and he died?

A few days later I gets a letter from Alice asking why I don't write, telling me how she'd sent me two letters and wondering what was the matter with me and little Blaze. She goes on to say she misses us, the ranch, the hills and meadows and wondering how she's going to stand it to be away from all she loves till fall. I wonders if I'm included in what *all she loves.*

It's late afternoon, but I catches me a bronc (an ornery one) and proceeds to make tracks a long ways apart, figgering to get them two letters out of the post office or else wreck the place looking for 'em. We finds 'em in the box of another outfit to the west and lucky it was they hadn't called for their mail lately 'cause I'd still be looking for them letters. An' reading them, I gets a new look on things in general for even tho they don't say so much I have an inkling as to where I'm standing. I buys a tablet right then and there and does my best to write something what'll tell her some as to how things are going with me, little Blaze don't figger in this letter much only that he's getting big, fat and sassy. I forgets on purpose to mention he'd got hurt and when all this is done and the moon sees me hitting the short cut back to the ranch, I'm singing and whistling my head off, I lets the bronc pick his own gait and I'm not worried if I don't get back till morning, for I don't remember of ever before seeing such a pretty night, and enjoying being out in it.

All is quiet and peaceful when I gets under the big cottonwoods at the gate of the ranch. I turns my bronc in the feed corral and walks over to where little Blaze is, he nickers as usual when he hears me coming and I tries to make him as comfortable as I can. "Too bad I can't lay you down little feller," I says. "But I know you wouldn't lay so this is the best I can do." I talks to him and keeps him company for quite a spell telling him to cheer up being he could get out and play again in about three weeks and that he'd be better than new when the lady comes back.

The girl's dad was plum satisfied the way I was turning out the broncs, he'd shipped a carload of 'em, and now I was in the thick of the breaking the rest to ride, but I'd seldom ever stop whistling no matter how big and strong they come or how hard they could buck, there was always a grin on my face and if my saddle was kicked out of my hands I'd be grinning when I picked it up, and I'd be grinning when I'd screw it down on that bronc's kinky back, climbed on, pulled the blind and "scratched" him out. And why shouldn't I grin? The mail was coming in regular from the little girl back there, she was aching to come back and I knowed or had a mighty strong hunch that she'd never leave again when she did come back.

Summer was with us, a few ranch hands was put on the pay roll and the old gent with a couple of extra riders had the cattle up the mountains. Little Blaze was in the shade of the orchard and on four legs once more picking up fat every minute on green clover and alfalfa mixed, I was still working in the breaking pens and had most all my broncs lined out, outside a couple of ornery devils what had the fight born in 'em.

One Sunday afternoon I'm putting up a grandstand ride, the audience is four ranch hands, a chore boy, and the chink. I'd drug out one of them fighting broncs figgering to scratch the raw edge off of him for fair and not letting up on him till he quit, for that I wanted room and when the corral hindered him from doing what he wanted to do worst I hollered "open the gate and let us out." We're going so high wide and crooked that I could of touched the top pole over the gate and the sides of it near at the same time, the bronc is bawling like a mad critter and every time he hit the ground a little hunk of fur shakes off my spur rowels and floats in the air.

I'm getting real het up on the subject when of a sudden I hears the "honk" of a automobile horn and right there in front of me, not over ten yards is a big red car full of people. I gets a glimpse of the one person in the world I wanted to see most, she's waving and laughing and I want to pull up my bronc so I can say something, but no chance, the only thing that devil under me is interested in is to get me off and step on me if he can. When I know there's no use trying to call the fight off for the time being I stretch both legs over his neck and burries my spurs both sides of his mane, which makes him act as I wanted for when he hits the ground again, instead of going ahead every jump he just drags backward and when my chance comes where I'm clear I lets him buck out from under me, which leaves me standing up with care my hat in my hand and making a bow to a certain person in that car that would make any duke want to practice.

I'm only using the rest of the crowd for a background when I steps up, all I can see is Alice and I'm afraid if I take my eyes off her that big red car might disappear taking her along and leaving me just the "honk." Then I realize I'm getting introduced to so and so, and for the first time notices a young feller setting at the wheel and looking me over, I'm doing the same when he says "Mr. Saunders I congratulate you on the way you rode that horse." "Thanks," I says and looks at the back of the car, there's two older folks setting there and I learns afterwards that they're his father and mother.

I'm trying to be sociable and answering questions fast as they come, when the girl touches me on the arm and tells me she'd like to see little Blaze, and asks if I'd come along. I see how glad she is to be back, and for once I gets real jealous of the little orphant for the way she's hugging and talking to him, but it does me a lot of good to watch and see how happy they both are. After a while she looks my way and compliments me a lot for taking so good a care of him. "He's so much bigger," she says. "And his hide is so smooth and shiny."

After a spell she tells me how she just had to come and wanted to surprise us, then put the damper on it by saying that she could visit only for a few days, and I see then how she'd like to stay, by the way she looks at the mountains, the meadows and big cottonwoods, she's rubbing the little feller back of the ears and her eyes are taking in everything on the ranch and range she knows so well. "I've only been gone four months, but is seems more like a year," she says. I'm mighty glad to hear that and keeping it all to myself I sure agrees with her.

There's nothing said about the young Mr. Williams what drove her in, and I'm not asking no questions, but after supper that night when I walks past a ways and sees her setting on the porch with him and a talking away by themselves I'm thinking a lot of things what I don't want to. I'm headed for the corral and seeing that the gates are all closed so none of the broncs get away, I'm taking long time at it and it's dark when I goes back to the orchard. It's cool there and with little Blaze around I'm hoping everything will come out all right.

I'm there quite a spell feeling kind of left out in the cold, when I see the girl coming, straight towards little Blaze and I'm not five feet away from him. She's not at all surprised to see me there for she says "I know I'd find you here," then she asks me how everything's been with me and my work and the little horse, how I like the ranch and if I was surprised to see her so soon, to all of which I ain't got much heart answering. There was one thing worrying me and that took all my thoughts, but I done my best to hide it and tell her all she asked.

I tells her how glad I am to see her again, and that's as far as I can go for my footing feels kinda shaky right then.

The next day I am in the corral the same as usual far as the place and the time is concerned, but I'm not whistling any, my feelings are some different, and when I see her riding away in the meadows with this Mr. Williams I find myself picking the wrong ropes. The old folks come over to watch me top off a few but that don't help things any, even if I see they're a heap interested.

When the chink rings the big steel, I'm walking towards the house more as a force of habit than because I wanted to eat, but when I see Alice across the table looking at me kinda quiet and smiling I perks up again and manages to be real sociable being careful not to eat with my knife or putting my elbow on the table, 'cause as I says to myself it wouldn't be nice in front of these people, they'd think it was wrong being they don't look as they'd ever missed a meal or been hungry in their life the fancy way they was handling the grub.

That afternoon I closes my eyes to everything but horseflesh and about when I'm getting real good at it here she comes with that feller tagging alongside, the girl is nice as can be and acts the same as ever but I'm wondering, and when I opens the gate to take one of the broncs out for an "airing" tops him off and sashays out in all ways but straight I find time to look back and wave some.

But that evening me and the girl are both in the orchard with little Blaze again, seemed like that's where we'd both hit for when things was kinda hard to make out or when the trail was hard to follow. There was something about that little orphant and his whereabouts what settled things and knowed that when we lost track of one another in anyway, that little Blaze faced horse would put us together again.

Somewhere, sometime, and a long time ago, I remember reading something about "faint heart never wins fair lady" and that evening with just her and me and little Blaze struck me just right, to see how it'd be to follow the lead of them few little words. In my mind I runs over all what's went on with her and me since we met. I know she likes me some, but how much is what I'm wanting to learn. And the closer to bedrock I gets the more I see where things's got to come to a showdown. And with a strong heart I proceeds to try and tell the fair lady what'd been in my mind ever since that day she looked up at me the first time I rode in, and asked me if she could have little Blaze.

One of her hands is resting on the little horse's withers, and remembering about "faint heart" again, I takes that hand. She looks at me kind of wondering, but I don't keep her guessing long. "Alice," I says, "I think the world of you, I never really knowed what want meant till I seen you, and if you could care enough for such as me . . . I'm asking you, would you marry me?"

I'm still holding of her hand, all's quiet and I'm not able to think much but I'm waiting and holding my breath, her head is bent a little. And then before I know what's happened my free arm's around her and her head is on my shoulder.

Time was lost track of, and many a word was said, the old moon was shining and making things look prettier than I'd ever seen 'em before, and when after a spell little Blaze rubs his head on my arm I kind of come to the fact that I'm wanting to say something. We're both taking turns at running a hand and smoothing the hair down on the little horse neck, when I asks her if she's going to leave me and little Blaze to our lonesome again.

In another week the big red car is loaded and the folks are all ready to go, but there's two suit cases missing, young Williams is at the wheel and setting with him is a preacher going back after his work is done. There's congratulations, good wishes along with handshakes passed all around and when the dust of the leaving car settles the girls' father had disappeared too.

Little Blaze sees us heading his direction and comes up to meet us nickering on the way, he's feeling real playful, and when we get near he turns, his head up, neck bowed and handling his tail like a fan, he trots around stiff legged, and snorting every jump gives us a exhibition of his breed, the mustang. He's active as an antelope and I wonders how the little fence around the orchard can keep him in.

The next morning I see by tracks, where a bunch of mustangs had come and stuck around close to the outside fence, and my first hunch was to look towards the orchard, there's no little horse there to be seen, and thinking he might be laying down in some corner I walks over to investigate but I only see where my hunch was right, he'd jumped the fence and I follows his tracks on thru where he'd went over the high fence too and mixed in with the others. Yep! the mustang blood held and little Blaze had answered, he'd got in with the wild bunch all right. Cupid, the mustang, had done his work.

SILVER-MOUNTED

"HOWDY!" We turned at the voice of a stranger who, outside and setting on a good-looking bay horse, was looking at us through the camp's only window, and smiling.

Strangers was mighty scarce in that country, and mighty welcome; and when Long Tom, our foreman, returned that stranger's "howdy," it was natural-like followed with "Turn your horse loose and come on in."

It was a while later when a shadow was throwed acrost the door and the stranger walked in, and still a-smiling begin unsnapping his bat-wing chaps.

"We just got in a few minutes ago," says Long Tom, "and the cooky's got 'er all ready. Go ahead and wash up; we'll wait for you."

The stranger had gone to the wash-bench outside, when Little Joe leaned my way and in a low voice asks: "Say, Bill, did you see the boots that *hombre's* wearing? And look at them chaps," he goes on while fingering of 'em. "Soft as silk, and with silver mountings."

I sure had noticed them boots; they was the kind any cowboy would glance at more than once. The flower design that was on 'em, in inlaid colored leather and bordered with many rows of fancy stitching, would attract a blind man. The soft kangaroo vamp, with the well shaped, not too high heel, sure had my eye too. The chaps was of gray soft leather, the wing covered with leather designs, and pure silver ornaments on the belt and more along the wing.

"It'd be a shame to use an outfit like that in this sunburnt lava and sage brush country," says Joe. "It'd sure skin the pretty spots off it in no time."

The stranger, all washed and hair combed, walked in again, and all of us trailed over to the long table to partake of the last meal of the day. The talk was as usual, and not ruffled any by the presence of the stranger. Once in a while he'd inquire some about the country, and his talk fitted in well. Before the meal was over, and without asking any questions, we had him figgered out as a rider from the prairie countries, but we wasn't sure. A few days would tell, and we hoped he'd stick around, for we'd sort of took a liking to his ways, fancy outfit and all.

It was early the next morning when a few of us boys was at the corrals and rolling that day's first cigarettes. The *remuda* hadn't got in yet, and while waiting, we run acrost the stranger's rig. A real fancy saddle it was, all hand-carved and weighed down with silver, and on the *"rosaderos"* was letters saying: *"For First Prize in Bucking Contest."*

Them carved letters sort of identified the stranger to us, but there was other things about the outfit that was a puzzle and which didn't match none at all. Like for instance, there was a real honest-to-God-well-made saddle with a neat little silver horn, bare and for tying, and instead of having the hard-twist grass rope coiled up on the side of that saddle, and which was the only kind that belonged there, there was a sixty-foot rawhide *reata*, plumb useless, and not at all fitting with it nor the slick horn that was on it.

His bridle didn't agree no better; the head-stall belonged to Wyoming, the bit to Mexico, and the rawhide reins to the California Spanish. None ever go together, and it was sure a puzzle to us how that waddy worked or where he was from.

But we was soon to know. The *remuda* was being drove in the big corrals, and about that time we spots Long Tom coming down with the stranger. Our hopes that he'd stick around went up to the top as we seen the foreman pointing out a string of ponies for him to ride; and seeing it was settled that he was going to be with us for a spell, we all went after our ropes and begin snaring our ponies for that morning's ride.

Our ponies was all caught, saddled, and ready to "top off" when we see the stranger circling a rope over his head and trying to run the horse he wanted, with a "Missouri throw." He was using a braided cotton rope, the kind that's used in spinning, and we figgered the rawhide *reata* that was on his saddle was only for an ornament.

To begin with, we seen he was no roper, not while he was on the ground, anyway. Long Tom watched the proceedings of the whirling rope for quite a spell; he didn't want to tell the new hand not to whirl his rope in a corral full of horses, on account he figgered the stranger ought to know that without being told, but he didn't like to see the ponies getting all jammed up and skinning their hips on the corral-poles, either. He was just about to flip his rope and catch the stranger's horse for him, when he stopped and seen that *hombre* do a funny thing. The stranger, after missing three or four throws in the "Missouri swipe" fashion, had coiled up his rope and built another loop; and instead of whirling it this time, he begin to spin it. He kept a-spinning it till the horse he wanted circled around the corral and came within roping distance, and about that time the spinning loop shot out, never losing its circle, and caught that pony under the chin, and then the loop settled over his ears.

Long Tom and all of us grinned, looked at one another and shook our heads. The throw the stranger had just made matched well with his fancy boots, chaps and saddle: it was fancy too. But it seemed like there was no end of puzzling things about that stranger, and the next to happen was after we'd topped off our ponies and all of us was ready to line out of the corral gate. I was somewhat surprised, after I made my horse quit sweeping the corral with his foretop, to see that the new hand hadn't saddled his horse yet; he was just a-hanging on to him, wondering what to do, and seemed like looking around for something he couldn't find. Finally, he looked at Long Tom, who was setting on his horse and waiting.

"Is there a chute I can saddle this horse in?" he asks.

The horse he'd caught was a spooky little sorrel and a fighter, and he wouldn't let the stranger come any closer than a safe ten feet from him. He wasn't the worst horse that outfit had, not by a long shot, but he wasn't the gentlest, either. The foreman sized the stranger up for a spell and finally says:

"We saddle our horses in the middle of the corral or anywheres we get 'em — *out here*."

I looked at Long Tom as he said them last two words, and had a hunch right then that he knowed what kind of man he was talking to. That was more than the rest of us could figger out.

Having no time to waste, Long Tom got off his horse, walked over to the stranger and told him to get his saddle. While the stranger was gone, the foreman flipped the loose end of the rope around the spooky sorrel's front feet and hobbled him; then he reached for the saddle that'd been brought up, put it on the slick back and cinched 'er up.

We felt sort of sorry for the stranger as that went on, for we could see that he didn't know what to do with his hands, and he just sort of kept fidgeting around, careful not to look at any of us; but he brightened up some as Long Tom handed him the bridle-reins and told him, "It's up to you now."

The stranger seemed glad of it, and the way he climbed that pony showed he was aching to prove that he was some entitled to that fancy outfit of his.

It was when the little sorrel bogged his head and went after the stranger that we got another surprise, and which made the puzzle all the harder to figger out. The stranger had seemed at home from the time the horse side-winded out of his tracks, and it was then we understood how it was he brightened up when Long Tom handed him the reins and told him to go ahead. That boy could ride.

He reefed that pony and made a fool out of him as well as Little Joe could, and Joe was about the best rider in the outfit. It made a mighty pretty sight too, to watch that new hand ride on that fancy outfit. The silver was a-shining to the sun at every curve of the horse's body; the long hand-carved tapaderos, along with the wide wings of the rider's chaps, sort of made the movements of the horse and man mighty easy to watch; and even old bronc'-fighting Long Tom had to stand there like the rest of us and admire.

Finally the show was over, and a little too soon to suit us, but we figgered there'd be some more later, as that outfit sure had plenty of mean ponies. We all filed out of the corral, and the stranger amongst us, a-riding along like he was sure a credit to that outfit he was setting on.

We loped out of camp, Long Tom in the lead and never looking back. Three or four miles out, the ponies was brought down to a walk; the gait was kept to that for a mile or so, and into a long lope we went again. A knoll twelve miles or so from camp was reached, and there Long Tom "scattered the riders" different directions — two up a creek, two more over a ridge, and so on, till all the boys was scattered in fan shape to hunt and run in whatever horses was in that country.

The "Double O" was a horse outfit, and run over ten thousand head of the finest horses a man wants to see. It took a big range to run that many horses, and the proof that it was big and also good was by the kind of horses that was raised there. They showed they had all the chance in the world to develop and grow full size, and they was wild, as wild as any horse ever gets, and if it wasn't that they was corralled once or twice a year, they'd soon turn into renegades, for even as it was, it took a mighty good hand who knowed horses, and he had to be well mounted, before he could turn a bunch of them and bring 'em toward the corrals.

As Long Tom scattered the riders, I'm thinking that most every one of us wished to be "paired off" with the stranger: he was such a surprising cuss, and if he could sashay horses like he rode the sorrel, that'd sure be another show well worth watching.

It made a mighty pretty sight too to watch that new hand ride on that fancy outfit.

Most of the riders rode away two by twos, till there was only me and Joe, the stranger and Long Tom left. Then the foreman spoke again.

"Bill," he says, "you, and you" (pointing to the stranger) "take Lone Mountain; and me and Joe here'll skirt around Rye Patch."

I grinned at Joe and rode away, the stranger for my pardner. We rode along a-talking of nothing in perticular and everything in general. I was wanting awful bad to get an inkling, so as to clear the puzzle he was to me and all of us, but no hinting would make him give any information, and it sure never came to me to come right out and ask him, 'cause you can never tell what a feller's hiding in his upper story or what he's trying to keep as *past*.

To sort of make him feel that I wasn't wanting him to talk on himself unless he wanted to, I turned the confab toward the present and says:

"You want to watch that sorrel you're riding; he ain't through with you yet, and is apt to bog his head and go after you just when you least expect or want him to. But," I says afterward, "I guess you don't mind that."

I expected him to grin at me in a way that'd show he wasn't caring what the sorrel done or when he done it, and there is where I got another surprise; for the stranger instead of grinning as any cowboy would at my remark, seemed to turn pale, and then I noticed how he wasn't setting straight up and free, as he had when first leaving the corral. He was setting close now, and with a short tight holt on the reins.

We skirted the foot of Lone Mountain and then wound our way up it; it was a steep and high old mountain and could always be depended on for a couple of bunches of wild, highland-loving ponies. We was half-way up, and I was keeping my eyes peeled to see the wild ones *first*, when on a ridge that run to the mountain, and away up, I spots the buckskin rump of one horse, and I figgers there's a bunch with him.

I stops my horse and points his whereabouts to the stranger and asks: "See that horse up there?"

"Yes," he says, and he was looking away to one side of where the buckskin was; he wasn't seeing him at all.

"Well — anyway," I says, "you keep about the middle of this mountain, and when I start the bunch, I'll head 'em down your way, and you can keep 'em going on down toward the flat."

"All right," he says.

"Dag-gone queer," I says to myself as I rode away. "He's a top hand in some things, and a pure greenhorn in others. Now, he's never hunted stock much, or he'd sure seen that horse up there; and then again, his acting scared on a horse he *knows* he can ride, sure is past me figgering out."

I manœuvered around till I got on the other side of the bunch I'd spotted, and when I got to the right place, I showed up sudden and fogged in on 'em so quick that them ponies just got scared and flew straight away to where I wanted 'em to go — they didn't have time to stop and parley on how would be the best way to lose me; they just went.

There was about fifteen head in the bunch, and one "marker" amongst 'em identified 'em as Double O horses. I camped on their tail for a ways and till I made sure they was headed past where the stranger should be; he'd keep 'em from doubling back up the mountain, I figgered, and fog 'em on down to the flats as I'd told him to.

Taking another look at the bunch so as to make sure of their going straight down the mountain, I sat on one rein, brought my running bronc to a crowhopping standstill, and then made him head back, up the mountain. There was another bunch I'd spotted up there. I circled around and on up, losing no time, 'cause I wanted to get that second bunch and throw it with the first so as I could help the stranger in case he needed it; but realizing what a big head-start he had on me, I had no hopes much of seeing him and the first bunch till I reached camp.

It took me quite a while to reach the top of that mountain; it was steep and high, and I didn't want to rush my horse too much on account of the run I figgered I'd have to make to get that bunch in. I let him take a good breathing spell when the top was reached, and while I uncinched my saddle and cooled his back a little, I took a look down the flat away below me for a sign of the dust the first bunch I'd started would be making. I had a mighty good view of the country from up there; it all looked like a big map a-stretching with the edges petering out into atmosphere. I could see the fringe of cottonwoods by the camp we'd left that morning, and the creek a-shining in the sun, but in all that landscape I couldn't see no dust. I wondered if the stranger could of got his bunch to camp already and while I was climbing the mountain; it could happen easy enough, 'cause there was nothing slow about them ponies once you got after 'em, and then again that stranger was so surprising, he might be a wizard at running wild ponies.

I got on my bronc and lined him out in a fast walk toward the other bunch. I didn't see no more chance of having the interesting company of the stranger, and I was sorry for that. Anyway, I kettled the other ponies from the right side and fogged 'em on down a long ridge that stretched away out on the flat. It was a fine place to run, and my horse was a-fighting his head to get in amongst the bunch that was raising the dust ahead of him. All was going fine and to order, and I figgered at that speed I'd be in camp in a short spell, when in the canyon to the left I sees a big dust and another bunch of running ponies. They was headed straight up the mountain and the opposite direction I was going, and then I got a glimpse of the buckskin horse, the one I'd first spotted, and then the marker, which told me plain that there was the bunch I'd turned over to the stranger.

"What t'hell, now!" I says as I rode off the edge of the ridge I was on and into the canyon. I was hoping to turn 'em and throw 'em in with

The next half-mile I covered was sure no bridle-path.

my bunch. The next half a mile I covered was sure no bridle-path, and the speed I made it in went to show what a dag-gone fool a feller can be when getting het up on the subject. I'd turned my horse off into a straight down run, and the little shelves of shale rock that was here and there was all that kept us from going down faster than we did.

But I got in the canyon before the bunch passed me, and that was the cause of my hurry, for if the bunch had ever got above me, I'd just as well waved my hat at 'em and let 'em go. I'd never been able to turn 'em.

As it was, they'd had to go through me to get away, and they'd been handled enough so they didn't try it. They turned, went down the canyon a ways; then, when the sides of the ridge wasn't so steep no more, I turned 'em once again and up on the ridge where the other bunch was still going strong and the right direction.

Both bunches'd had quite a bit of running; they wasn't so hard to handle no more, and I had no trouble much getting 'em all together. All was going fine once more; my bronc had quit fighting his head and a-trying to get in amongst the horses; he was glad to just lope along behind a ways and just follow 'em.

I loosened up on the *mecate* (hair rope) reins and rolled me a cigarette; then it comes to me: "What's become of the stranger?"

I looked at the country around as I rode, but no sign of him was anywheres; then I looked at the bunch which was keeping ahead of me about a quarter of a mile, and running my eye over 'em, I thought I seen something a-shining to the sun and on one pony's back; something else was a-flapping on each side of him. And doing some tall wondering, I rode a little faster so as to have a closer look.

It was hard to make out through the dust, but as I looked on and squinted I finally made out the shape of a saddle; but what bothered me was them things a-shining on top. Then I come near kicking myself for forgetting and being so dumb: them shining things was *silver*; it was

312

the stranger's saddle, and under it was the sorrel he'd rode so well in the corral that morning!

I stopped my horse as the thought came to me that somewheres was the stranger, afoot, and maybe with some bones broke; for when a rider sees a horse packing an empty saddle out on the range, it sure sets him to thinking. A man can petrify out there and never be found only maybe by coyotes or magpies. Fifteen or twenty miles is a long ways with a smashed-up leg.

Of course the stranger might be all right, I thought, but there's no telling where he may be laying and crippled from a fall. There was only one thing for me to do; I fogged in on my bunch and took 'em as fast as I could. Halfways in, I could see the dust of other bunches being brought in by other riders, and I turned my bunch to meet one of the closest.

Throwing my bunch in with 'em, I stopped just long enough to tell the two boys that was hazing 'em in that the stranger's horse was in the bunch I'd brought in and he was afoot somewheres. Then I headed on the back-trail to look for him.

I picked up his trail where I'd left him and followed it along a ways. I seen where he stopped his horse and waited for me to head the first bunch down his way. From there on, the tracks of his horse was far apart: he'd been running him and, as I figgered, taking after the bunch as they come.

I followed that trail for quite a while; it was doing a lot of zigzags, and I could see that the bunch was somehow getting away from him and back up the mountain; then of a sudden I seen a patch of tore-up ground. It'd been tore up by the hoofs of the little sorrel, and in the middle of that patch was something that made me get off my horse for a closer look. There, as pretty as you please, was the print of the stranger's body where he'd connected with mother earth and measured his length. The stranger had been throwed off.

That was hard for me to believe, but there, and right in front of me, was plain proof. I took another long look at the tore-up patch, then got on my horse and went to cutting for tracks which would tell me where the stranger went. One thing I was mighty glad for, and that was he wasn't hurt, and when I run onto the trail he'd left with them neat heels on them pretty boots of his, I could see he was walking straight up and not staggering any, far as I could make out.

His trail crossed a creek, and there I felt better some more, for he'd had water anyway, in case he needed it. Acrost the creek, a few miles wide, many miles long and running toward camp, was a strip of lava rock. No earth was there to follow a trail, and I lost track of him, but I figgered he'd be following the lava strip back to camp, on account it might be a little easier walking there.

I rode on back toward camp following it, and feeling sure I'd run acrost him before he got in, but I rode many miles, and no stranger was seen. A little ways further, I spots the boys riding up; they'd started out looking for him too.

After I told 'em where I left his trail, they rode on to look for him; my horse was tired, and I went on into camp. The boys didn't get back till away after dark, and no sign of the stranger had been found. We built a big log fire by the camp that night and where it could be seen for miles around. It would burn a long time, and if the stranger was within ten miles, he couldn't fail but see it. We couldn't do no more.

The fire burned down; morning came, and still no sign of the stranger. Two riders was sent out to look for him that day, and when night come and they rode back, the disappearance of that *hombre* was still as much of a puzzle as ever. It seemed like the earth had just swallowed him. Another day went by, and it was as the mountains was throwing long shadows that Joe points out to a dust acrost the flats. A rider was making it.

The last horse had been unsaddled as the rider came up to the corral gate and got off his horse. It was the stranger, but a very different-looking stranger than he'd been a few days past and when he'd made his first appearance at the horse camp. There was a stub growth of whiskers and hollow cheeks on a face that'd been round and smooth, and the alkali dust that covered him from head to foot sure done the work of disfiguring all he'd been to look at.

We all greeted him as though nothing had happened, and not a question was asked; we didn't have to ask, on account that there was everything about him that told us all we cared to know and plainer than words. It was all easy reading, the same as the print he'd left in the foothills and where the sorrel throwed him off.

The horse he'd rode in wore the brand of a neighbor outfit which was some thirty miles away, and knowing he couldn't of caught him on the range with a saddle on him and all that way, it was easy to see he'd rambled on afoot for some time till he come to one of that neighbor outfit's camps, borrowed the horse, and got his directions to come back on from there. Yes sir, the stranger had went and got lost.

It was sure a mystery to us how a man that could ride like he'd rode the sorrel, and do such fancy roping as he'd done, could turn out to be such a freak. "How and where," we'd ask one another, "can a man learn to ride like he could, if it ain't on the range?" Nobody could answer that, and the mystery instead of getting any clearer with reasoning, kept a-getting deeper.

The next day came, and a long ride was ahead for that morning. The stranger showed up at the corral and we seen him make his spinning loop with a lot of interest. That interest went up many notches as we seen that same loop settle around the head of a tall, rawboned brown horse. That horse was one of the meanest buckers in the outfit and didn't belong to his string none at all; but he'd mistook him, amongst the two hundred ponies, for one that'd been pointed out to him that first morning.

"I guess you don't want him," says Long Tom, riding up. "He ain't in your string, and besides, he's sure hell on wheels when it comes to bucking."

"Whose string is he in?" asks the stranger.

"Nobody's; we take turns at him once in a while, and he's for anybody that wants him."

"Well, I guess I'll try him, then, if can get somebody to help me saddle him."

He got all the help he wanted, and in less time that it takes to tell it, the saddle and bridle was on the big horse, and the blindfold ready to take off soon as the stranger was well set. That *hombre* climbed on not a bit ruffled, and when ready, he told us so in a way that would make us put our money on him.

The blindfold was yanked off, and it was no more than done when the tall gelding called on his wiry frame to do its duty. Two spurred heels went up in the air about the time the horse did, and when that pony buried his head in the dirt in a hard-hitting jump, them spurred heels came down on his neck and played a ringing tattoo there.

Between the bellering of that horse, the ringing of the spur-rowels, the sound of that pony's hoofs hitting the earth — all a-popping, and keeping time — it sure made a sound worth sticking around for by itself; and even if a man couldn't of seen the goings-on, he could of told by them sounds that here was a hard horse to ride, and on top of him was a hard man to throw.

The stranger seemed in the height of his glory; he was setting up there, and fast and crooked as the jumps came, he wasn't caught napping at any of 'em. He met that pony halfways in all he done, and when finally the big gelding seemed to have enough and held his head up, we'd forgot that the man on top of him had let a little sorrel horse buck him off, we'd forgot that he'd let a bunch of horses get away from him on the range, and even his getting lost and roaming straight away from the home camp seemed away in the past. The stranger was one of us again.

We filed out of the corral and strung out on the morning's circle. Me and the stranger was riding side by side and by ourselves a ways; I expected that brown horse to go to bucking again most any time, and sure enough, Long Tom had no more than started us out in a lope, when I glimpses a brown hunk of horse-flesh transformed into a cloud-reaching and then earth-pounding whirlwind. I heard the beller of the pony, but I didn't hear no spurs ringing, and when I looked for the reason, I was surprised to see that them spurs wasn't at all where I thought they'd be — on the horse's neck. Instead of that they was buried in the cinch with a staying holt, and I thought for a second that I seen the stranger grabbing for the horn.

Little Joe, who'd been to one side a ways, rode close about that time, and I noticed the blank look on his face, like he didn't believe his eyes; and my face must of showed about the same look as I stared back at him, 'cause I know I was sure as surprised as he was.

Somehow I was glad when the brown horse quit bucking and lined out on a lope with the stranger *still* on him; I sort of hated to get disappointed in that feller, and I could see that Joe felt the same about it; but we both could see that it was pure luck the stranger hadn't been bucked off — he'd rode his horse like a rag and hung on with a death grip.

"That feller seems like a different man outside a corral," Joe remarked as we rode on, a-trying to figger out the puzzle.

Long Tom done a mighty fine job of scattering the riders that day; most every man wound up by hisself, and none of us got to see one another again till the circle was made and we was within a few miles of the corral wings. Every man had a bunch, and some two, and when the gate closed on the last bunch that was run in, we all natural-like begin to take a tally on one another, to see if any was missing.

It was then that Long Tom points at me and Joe and says: "You two better change horses; take an extra one along and go look for the stranger. I'm thinking he's afoot again." Yep, the stranger was amongst the missing once more!

It was pure luck when we found him, near sundown. Joe had spotted an object up on the ridge that first looked like a prospector's monument, and when we rode up on it, it turned out to be the stranger a-setting on his saddle. His clothes was near all tore off of him, and the fancy saddle looked like it'd run up against a buzz saw; it was all twisted out of shape and caked with dirt.

The stranger's spirit was sort of low too, but he managed to smile as he seen us, and half-hearted-like told us how the brown horse had bucked him off.

"But what happened to your saddle?" asks Joe.

"Well, I guess that's my fault," goes on the stranger. "I never figgered that a cinch gets loose as a horse runs and ga'nts up. I'd been running him up a slope and the saddle slipped back. After he bucked me off, it turned under his belly, and, as you see, that pony sure done a good job kicking it apart."

We all rode on back to camp, not saying much. I'd glance at the stranger once in a while, and I could see that feller was thinking about something mighty strong. I wished he'd let us in on his thoughts, but it wasn't till we'd near reached camp that he seemed to want to loosen up.

"I can't figger it out," he says.

"What's that?" asks Joe.

"Well," he goes on, "it's the difference in my riding, and why there is such a *big* difference between riding a bad horse out of a chute where there's a band playing and folks cheering, and riding that same horse out where there's not a soul for miles around. I seem to lose my confidence out here by myself this way; and then riding along, not knowing just when the horse is apt to go to bucking, sort of gets on my nerve. I've come to find out that it sure ain't like riding that horse in front of the grand-stand. I *know* he's going to buck there, and exactly when. I'm prepared for it, and when he's through, I'm through riding him too.

"You notice," he says after a while, "that I ride very different when inside of the corral than I do when out of it. . . . I guess that only goes to prove I'm a show-hand, and not a cowboy. I followed circuses and Wild West shows as a kid, and learned to ride there. Afterward I took on contests, but I never rode a bucking horse outside of corrals or show-grounds before. I don't have to tell you that I never rode outside of town limits either — you can see that; but it's sure surprising to me how much there's to contend with out here, not only with the kind of horses a feller rides, but the country is so daggone big, and there's so much a man has to know, to work in it and qualify."

We was saddling up as usual the next morning when we notice the stranger had picked his own horse. He tied a few belongings on the saddle and then turned toward us all as we was getting ready to file out for that day's riding.

"I'm not riding with the outfit to-day," he says, walking toward us and smiling. "And you boys wont have to look for me after the day's ride is over, 'cause I'm going back to where I can ride my bucking horse inside a fence, where there's people around to watch me, and a brass band playing and keeping time with my pony's hoofs as they hit the ground."

He started to get on his horse and ride away. We watched him the while and noticed what a change had come over the fancy rigging that'd been so pretty and shiny just a few days past. The neat boots was et up with alkali, the fancy stitching all unravelled, from the ramblings he'd done afoot. The saddle was all loose and tore apart here and there.

"The country sure put its mark on that outfit," says Joe as we rode out of the corral. "Dang shame, too; it was sure pretty."

A month went by, and then one day Long Tom received a letter from the stranger; inside the envelope was a newspaper clipping and telling some of the winners of the prizes at some rodeo. Heading the list was a name underlined; the man packing that name had won first prize in the bucking horse contest and first in rope-spinning also. At the bottom of the strip was handwriting which said: "The name underlined is yours truly, *the stranger*."

We all read the strip; after which Long Tom poured a little syrup on the back of it and pasted it to the wall. On the top of the strip, and to sort of decorate and identify, he nailed a twisted piece of silver which the brown horse had kicked off the stranger's saddle. It had been found that day out on the hardpan flat.

WHEN IN ROME—

"THINGS ARE SURE A-POPPING NOW, COWBOYS."
Them words skimmed over the prairie sod to where twenty or more of us riders was "throwing the last bait" of the day; and as one and all looked in the direction the talk was coming from, we glimpsed the smiling features of a long cowboy, the straw boss, a-riding in on us and acting like something had sure enough popped. But the grin he was packing had us all sort of guessing; it hinted most to excitement and nothing at all to feel bad about, but there again a feller could never tell by looking at Bearpaw what really did happen. He was the sort of feller who'd grin at his own shadow while getting away from a mad cow, and grin all the more if he stubbed his toe while on the way to the nearest corral poles.

The grin spread into a laugh as he got off his horse and walked into the circle, where we'd been peacefully crooking elbows and storing away nourishment, but now, and since that *hombre's* appearance, all forks was still and all eyes was in the direction of that laughing gazabo and a-waiting for him to tell.

"You don't seem anyways sad about whatever it is that's a-popping," finally says an old hard-faced Tejano.

"No, I don't," answers that cowboy between chuckles. "I take things good-natured, but *you'll* feel sad, old-timer, when some foreigner drops into camp some of these days and *orders* you to roach the manes of your ponies, and brand calves afoot, and tells you that ropes and stock saddles ain't necessary in handling range stock."

The old Texan just gawked at that, and couldn't talk for quite a spell, but finally, after his thoughts got to settling down to business on what Bearpaw had just said, his opinion of such proceedings came to the top and kicked off the lid.

"Any time I get off my horse and begins to pack myself around on foot after a slick-ear," he howled, "I just don't — not for no man. And as far as anybody coming around and ordering the manes of my ponies to be roached, that wouldn't be orders; it'd be plain suicide for the other feller."

There he stopped for a second and squinted at Bearpaw like as if that cowboy was trying to stir him up for a little fun or something.

"But what in Sam Hill are you driving at, anyway?" he asks.

"I'll be glad to tell you," says Bearpaw, "if you'll give me the chance." Then he went on to spread the news why him and the cow-foreman had been called on to the home ranch the last couple of days.

"You boys wont believe me when I tell you," he begins, "but anyway, here's the straight of it: The Y-Bench"

"layout is sold out and has done changed hands."

Here he held on a spell, to sort of let things soak in, and looked around at us to see how that part of the news was taking effect. It was taking effect, all right, but we hadn't got anywheres near to realizing what that really meant to us, nor how it all come about, when old Bearpaw follows on with an uppercut that lays us all out.

"Some lord or duke from somewheres in Europe has bought it, and he's brought his stable valets along to show us how to ride. And what's more," he went on, "this here lord, or something, is dead set against these saddles we use, so he's brought along a carload of nice little flat saddles for us, and so light that even a mosquito could stand up under 'em."

Bearpaw would of most likely went on with a lot more descriptions of this lord and other strange things, but he was interrupted by a loud snort from the old Texan, who had managed to come to, right in the middle of the blow.

"All right," he hollered, "I've heard all I want to hear, far as I'm concerned." He got up, threw his tin cup and plate in the round-up pan with a clatter, and walking away he was heard to say: "I've rode for the Y-Bench for many a year, but I feel it that starting to-morrow I'll be hitting for other countries."

No songs was heard during "cocktail" that evening; no mouth-organ was dug up out of the war-bag; instead we was all busy a-trying to figger out how the Y-Bench changed hands so quick, and without warning, the way it had. Just a few days before, the cow-foreman had remarked that the outfit was figgering on leasing more range and running more stock, and now all of a sudden, and when all seemed to be going well, here comes the news that we had a new owner.

"I bet the reason of the sudden change is due to the big price that was offered," concludes Bearpaw. "I bet the price was so big no sane man would dare refuse it; but what gets me most is how a man such as this lord, what was raised on chopped feed and used to eating out of silver dishes, would want to come out here and get down to tin plates. From all I hear, he's going to run the outfit hisself too."

"Most likely doing it for the sport that's in it," I chips in.

"He'll get plenty of that before he gets through," remarks Bearpaw, "specially if he sticks to them pancake saddles he's brought along."

We done a lot of joking on the subject and kept at it till along about second guard, but the next morning things looked pretty serious. Most of the boys was for quitting without even a look at the new owner and lord, though work was at its heaviest, and riders quitting at that time would sure put things on the kibosh for fair.

The old Texan was the first at the rope corral, and soon as the night-hawk had brought in the *remuda*, he dabbed his line on his private horses, led 'em to his saddle and bed, and kept a-talking to himself as he fastened the rigging, his mumbling keeping up till a shadow on the ground told him somebody was near. A sour look was on his face as he turned to see Bearpaw, who was standing close by and sort of grinning at him a little.

"Now, Straight-up," says Bearpaw ("Straight-up" was the nickname the old feller liked best; he liked to have it remembered that at one time he was the straight-up rider of that country, and on any kind of a horse), "what's the use of you blazing away half-cocked, and quit this outfit cold like this? Why not sort of look forward to a little excitement and fun with this lord on the job? I'm thinking there's going to be lots of that when he comes, and that's what's making me stick around. Besides, you can never tell, and mebbe this lord is a dag-gone good feller."

The old cowboy was plumb against it at first and wouldn't even listen, but as Bearpaw talked on of the possibilities, he got so he'd lend an ear, and soon he was just dubious. Then Bearpaw dug up his hole card and says:

"It sure wont hurt you to stick around just for a few days anyway; and if you do stay, I know I can get the other boys to stay too; besides, I'm thinking you'd miss a lot if you go now."

The Texan thought things over for quite a spell longer and finally he says:

"All right — if you fellers can stick it out, I guess I can too; I'll weather it out with the rest of you."

It was a couple of days later and near sundown when Bearpaw pointed at the sky-line to the east and hollered:

"All you cow-valets look up there on that ridge and see what's a-coming."

We all looked, and right away forgot what Bearpaw had called us as we took in the sight, for showing up plain against the sky-line we could see a loaded wagon coming, and 'longside it a few men on horseback.

"That's him and his outfit," says the old Texan. "It's our lord."

"Gosh-a'mighty," says Bearpaw, "it looks like he even brought a manicure with him, by the size of that escort!"

The outfit came on, and pretty soon two riders started on ahead toward our camp. One of'em was easy to make out; he was our foreman; the other we figgered to be none less than the new owner.

Red-headed and freckle-faced was His Lordship, and as he come close to be introduced to each of us boys, we noticed that his nose was already beginning to peel. His lower lip had started to crack too, but with all his red hair, freckles, peeled nose and cracked lip, there was something about him that was still unruffled and shiny, even if it was a little dusty, and that was his high-class riding-breeches and his flat-heeled riding-boots. The little nickel spurs was still a-hanging onto them boots, too, and set 'em off real stylish.

"Well, boys," we hear our foreman say, "I guess Bearpaw told you how the outfit had changed hands; this gentleman here is the new owner of the Y-Bench. I hope that you'll all be as good men with him as you have been with me, and" — here he winked at us — "if a little storm comes up, don't quit too quick, but weather it out like we've always done and don't leave go of the critter till the critter hollers, 'Enough.'"

The introduction was no more than over when up comes the wagon all loaded down, and by the side of it two men as peeled as His Lordship, wearing the same kind of pants and boots, and setting on the exact same kind of flat saddles. Them we figgered was the two that was to give us some pointers about riding.

"Seems like," Bearpaw says to me, "that all their saddles and boots and pants and all are made alike; I guess they all have the same taste."

A lot of opinions was scattered to the breeze, on guard that night. Every time a rider would pass another while circling the bedded herd, there'd be a short stop, a remark passed, and the next time the riders met again on the opposite side of the herd that remark would be replaced by another.

The next morning came, and not any too early to suit us, because we wanted awful bad to have them stable valets show us how to mount a horse or something. There was quite a few horses we wanted them to use while they was eddicating us that way, and we was real anxious for all the learning they could hand us.

But the dignified silk tents with their air mattresses and folding cots was showing no sign of any life. It was near sun-up too, and Bearpaw, being the straw boss, was near at the point of going to the tent and waking up His Lordship, when the cook stopped him and headed him back.

"You dag-gone fool, don't you know it ain't proper to bust in when nobility's asleep that way, unless you're ordered to?"

Bearpaw was half-peeved when he waved a hand at us boys to saddle up. "Well," he says, "I guess we can get along without him."

Them white silk tents was an awful temptation to all of us as we topped off our ponies and sort of let 'em perambulate around with heads free. A-shining to the sun the way they was, sort of invited initiation, and I think that was the way Bramah Long felt when he sort of hazed his bucking bronc right about dead centre for His Lordship's air mattress. All would of went well maybe, only the cook interfered again, and waving a long yellow slicker over his head, came to the nobility's rescue.

As it was, not a snore was disturbed as we rode on past for the day's first ride; even the old Texan's loop was spoiled by Bearpaw as it started to sail for a holt on one of them peaceful tents.

"Mighty dag-gone nice of you and the cook appointing yourselves as guardians," remarks the old cowboy to Bearpaw. "I thought you told me that we might have a little fun, and here you come along and spoil the best loop I ever spread."

All would of went well maybe, only the cook, waving a long yellow slicker, interfered again.

The morning circle was made as usual and the same as if no new foreman had took holt. So far, nothing had come from him to disturb us in any way, and it looked like Bearpaw had, just natural-like, fell into being a cow-foreman.

Some folks are just lucky that way, and climb up in the world without half trying.

We made our drive, caught fresh horses, and was working the herd we'd brought in, before we seen anything of His Lordship and the valets. We was all busy cutting out when we notices them a-coming like they was riding on the tail-end of a funeral. They was riding the same horses they'd rode in from the home ranch, and to that the old Texan remarked:

"I guess they never change horses, where they come from."

"I don't think it's that, as much as the fact that they're a little leery of what they might draw out of that corral," says a cowboy near him. "Mebbe them thoroughbreds they're riding looks best to 'em, or safest."

His Lordship and his two men came up to within a hundred yards or so of the herd and from there watched the whole goings-on. They sat their horses stiff as statues and gave the feeling that if them horses started right sudden, they'd be left suspended in mid-air and still stiff. Hardly a word or a move of the hand was noticed, and as once in a while one of us would ride by 'em in heading off a bunch-quitting critter, not an eye would seem to notice or recognize any of us.

But them not seeming to see nor recognize us that way wasn't on account of their being stuck-up or such-like; it was that they was so interested in the whole goings-on in general that they were satisfied to just set on their horses and watch. Anyway, that's how we took it, for after the work was through and we all sashayed to the chuck-wagon, His Lordship and valets all seemed mighty sociable, and asked a lot of questions, most of which was sure hard to answer.

It was as we was cutting the meal short as usual and starting to go toward the corral that His Lordship stopped us and asked where we was going.

"On circle," answered Bearpaw.

"What do you mean by circle?"

"Ride."

"Why, you made one ride already," comes back His Lordship. "Besides, if you're going, I would like jolly well to go with you, but I am only half through with my meal."

"Oh, that's all right," says Bearpaw. "You can catch up with us."

We caught our horses and rode on out for the second circle, and it wasn't till we got sight of camp later that afternoon that we seen His Lordship again. Him and his two men showed up as we was working the herd, and the three of 'em watched us cut out, rope and brand, with the same interest that'd been with 'em that forenoon.

"I tried to catch up with you as you told me," says His Lordship, who'd edged up to Bearpaw, "but it seemed like you men disappeared all at once and I couldn't find you anywhere. I'm afraid," he went on after a spell, "that I make a very poor foreman."

"You'll get on to that after a while," says Bearpaw; "it all takes time."

The work that had to be done kind of kept His Lordship from carrying on the conversation as he'd like to, and it wasn't till the evening meal was over, and the night horses caught, that he had a chance to get down to bed-rock with us.

He started with a lot of questions which after they was answered seemed to set His Lordship to doing a lot of figgering. He figgered on for quite a spell, and when he finally spoke again, we already had a hunch of what the subject would be.

"When I bought this ranch," he starts in, "it was with intentions of changing and modernizing the handling of it, to my ideas. Of course, it will take time to do all that, and I might need some advice, but if you men will stay with me while I experiment, I promise that none of you will ever be sorry."

"Sure," interrupts Bearpaw, speaking for us all; "we'll stick — we'll enjoy it."

I don't think His Lordship got the meaning of that last; anyway he didn't seem nowheres disturbed as he went on:

"The first thing I'd like to do," he says, "is to make way with them heavy and awkward-looking saddles you men use in this country." He was looking straight at the camp-fire as he said that, and it's a good thing he was.

"I think your saddles are altogether unnecessary," — the old Texan snorted, at that, — "too cumbersome, and I don't see why they need to be that. We play strenuous games of polo in *our* saddles, jump high fences and do cross-country runs in steeple-chases, and I think that, as a whole, we have a freedom to do things from our saddles that you men can't have in yours.

"I have brought some fine pig-skin saddles with me for the purpose of you men using them, and to-morrow each one of you will be given one to use in the place of what you are now using."

"That's all very plain," says Bearpaw, a-trying hard to keep cool, "and being you're so frank in telling us about our saddles, I can be frank too and tell you, before you start in modernizing things, that them little stickers you brought along would be worse than riding bareback when there's real work and real riding to be done. I see you don't realize what our saddles mean to us; but anyway, I'll tell you what we'll agree to do. You got two men with you what savvies all about setting on them pancake saddles of yours, ain't you?" asks Bearpaw.

"Yes," answers His Lordship.

330

"Well," goes on the cowboy, "to-morrow, we'll all go to work the same as usual. We'll ride our own cumbersome saddles, and you and your two top-notchers can ride your fly-weights. I take it you all have got riding down to a science and it'll be a fair deal. You and your men do what we do, and if, after the day's work is over, you're still with us, we'll agree to use them little saddles of yours and love 'em to death. Is that O. K.?"

"Oh, yes," answers His Lordship, "that will be top-hole."

"And say," hollers the old Texan, "do we get riding-habits with them saddles of yours? It sure wouldn't look right to be riding on one of them things and have to wear chaps."

The break of the new day, and all the excitement that it promised, seemed awful slow coming. A faint streak had no more than showed in the east when us all was up and around. A while later we heard the *remuda* being brought in and corralled by the night-hawk, and we made our way to where the cook had the coffee boiling.

"Say, cook," says Bramah, "better wake up the nobility; it's high time for cowboys to be at work."

But the cook never let on he heard, and there was only one thing for us to do and that was to stick around and wait. There was many a bright remark brought on as the waiting kept up, and all of us was looking forward to the treat we knowed was coming.

The sun was just a-peeping over the ridge, and we should of been ten miles from camp by that time, but it wasn't till then that we begin to hear murmurs coming from the silk tents, and after what seemed an awful long while His Lordship and top hands finally showed themselves.

We'd long ago had our breakfast, so, to rush things a bit, we started out for the corral and begin catching our horses.

"Now, boys," says Bearpaw, "don't all go to catching your worst horses for this event; just catch them that's in turn to be rode; we don't want to make it too hard on His Lordship."

"And it happens that to-day is the day for Skyrocket," says Bramah, grinning.

Even though we took our time and done a lot of kidding while catching our horses, we still had to wait quite a spell for the nobility to join us. We wanted to give 'em a fair start, 'cause we felt they'd sure need it.

"I guess they miss their grapefruit in the mornings and it takes 'em a long time to get over it," remarks a cowboy; but at last, here they come, packing their little pancake saddles.

"Now," says Bearpaw, as His Lordship come near, "according to our agreement of last evening, this contest is to be played on the square. I'm giving you all the best of the deal by letting you pick out your own horses — most of 'em are gentle; and if you pick out a bad one I'll give you the privilege of another pick. Go ahead now and do your picking; I'll rope 'em out for you."

Quite a bit of picking was done before three horses was decided on. The horse His Lordship was to ride was a good-sized bay and one of the best cow-horses in that *remuda*. He only had one little trick, and that was when first getting on him of mornings, he was apt to do anything but stand still; but outside of that, which is never noticed, that horse was plumb gentle.

The two valets drawed pretty fair horses as to size, but neither one of 'em knowed very much. They was just good "circle" horses. One of 'em would buck, but that was very seldom, and he couldn't buck hard —

The horses all caught, we started saddling, and had to wait some more there. It struck us queer how it took so long to put on one of them little bits of saddles.

Bramah got tired of waiting and got aboard his Skyrocket horse just "to top him off," as he put it. There was some more delay about then because His Lordship had got all interested in watching that pony buck and Bramah ride.

Finally, the saddling went on again, and the nobility was making ready to mount. His Lordship grabbed his handful of double reins and stepped back to reach for the stirrup, when his horse whirled and went the other way.

The reins being over his head made a jerk on the bit as he whirled, that caused him to rear up, and the next second His Lordship let go his holt on the reins.

Bearpaw caught the horse and led him back to His Lordship.

"You don't handle your reins right," he says; "besides, you've got enough reins and bits on that bridle for a six-horse team."

His Lordship sort of got red in the face at that, but he had no comeback just then; instead he put his interest in watching Bearpaw, who was showing him how to gather up them reins so he'd have control of his horse while getting on. The style wasn't according to riding-schools mebbe, but it was sure convincing, to both man and horse.

It took quite a little trying before His Lordship could get onto the best way of straddling a horse, and he didn't get onto it very well, but with the coaching of Bearpaw, and after catching the horse a couple of times more, His Lordship finally did get in the saddle, and there he was, setting like a knot on a log and a-hanging onto all the reins with a death-grip.

All the while that was goin' on, the two valets, who knowed all about riding, had stood in their tracks and watched Bearpaw eddicate their master; then came their turn to climb on. A beller came from the old Texan as he watched 'em reach for their stirrups.

"Where did you-all learn to ride — in a merry-go-round?" he asks. "Don't you know you're apt to get your Adam's apple kicked off a-trying to get on a horse that-a-way?"

Here the old feller got off his own horse and showed 'em what he meant. "Never get back of your stirrup to get on," he says, "not with these horses. If you want to stay all together, stick close to their shoulder and get your foot in the stirrup from there."

The old Texan's talk didn't stand for no argument; every word he said was well took in, and acted on according, because it was realized that what he said was for their own good. One man forked his horse without any trouble much, and that left only one more to contend with.

That last one, though, managed to let his horse go out from under him twice. "It's no wonder," says Bramah, who like the rest of us was watching, "with them iron stirrups a-flapping. I guess they're hard to find."

Near an hour was spent in getting the nobility mounted and ready to go; then Bearpaw took the lead out for the day's first circle.

"We're considerable late getting started this morning," says that cowboy to the cook as we all rode by the chuck-wagon, "and don't fix anything to eat till you see us a-coming back."

From there we started on a long lope as usual, and as we was going over a pretty level country, all went well. The nobility kept up in fine shape and seemed to enjoy it to the limit. Only once did they slack up some, and that was when a prairie-dog town was crossed. The big holes them dogs made looked like a natural place for a horse to put his foot into and turn a flip-flop. Bearpaw caught 'em up on that slowing down, soon as they got to speaking distance again.

"You'll never turn nor head off a range critter if you keep a-looking at the ground," he says.

The country kept a-getting rougher and rougher as we rode, and pretty soon we begin to get in some bad-land breaks; it would of been a good goat country, only it was a cow country. A ways further, on reaching a high knoll, we scattered; I drawed one of the valets as a pardner; Bramah drawed the other; and Bearpaw took it onto hisself to initiate His Lordship in chasing the cow.

334

With this valet for a pardner I was hearing considerable about fox-hunting and cross-country runs, as we rode. There was a lot of words that feller said which had me guessing, and far as that goes, his whole talk had me listening mighty close, so I could get the drift, but pretty soon, as the country kept a-getting rougher, I didn't have to listen any more. Sliding down bad-land points seemed to have took the talk out of him.

We rode on till the outside of our territory was reached, and then circled, bringing with us whatever cattle we found. We had upward of sixty head with us and headed for camp in good shape when, spotting another bunch, I left the valet to go get them, telling him to keep the main bunch headed straight for a butte I pointed out.

The cattle had a downhill run and was going at a good clip, and I figgered this valet, being used to chasing wild foxes, sure ought to be able to keep up with spooky range cattle, but as I topped the ridge and got the other bunch and headed 'em down a draw to the main bunch, I was surprised, on looking back, to see that that *hombre* had lost considerable ground. He was just a-trotting along, and in rougher places would even bring his horse down to a slow walk.

It was either lose the valet or the cattle, and being I didn't want to lose the cattle, I fogged in on them and kept 'em headed straight for the cutting-grounds. I figgered the valet would catch up with me soon as we hit level country again, anyway. There was no way of his getting lost, 'cause the cattle and me was sure leaving a good trail and plenty of dust for him to follow.

When I hit level country and looked back, I was surprised how that feller was still so far behind; he was only a little speck in the distance. The cattle had slowed down by then, but even at that, I'd reached the cutting-grounds and camp, turned my horse loose, caught me a fresh one and was back to the herd with the other riders before that feller showed up.

"What," I thought, "would of happened if we'd been running mustangs instead of cows?"

"Well, I see you lost yours too," says Bramah, a-riding up and bringing his horse to a stop alongside of mine. "This valet I had, done pretty well, though," went on Bramah, "and I didn't lose him till his horse started fighting his head on account of all them bits. I guess he was leery that horse might dump him off any minute."

We was a-talking along, when here comes Bearpaw. That cowboy had no cattle with him but instead, and a ways behind, came His Lordship and that other valet which Bramah'd lost.

The noon meal came in the late afternoon that day, and it was over with quick. Fresh horses was caught all around, and leaving a couple of men to hold the morning's drive, the second circle of the day was started off in another direction.

His Lordship and the two valets wasn't in on that second ride; the thirty-mile circle of that morning's seemed enough. They was kinda sore and stiff, and the way they'd rub their shin-bones went to show that the little narrow stirrup-strap on their pancake saddles had developed teeth and dug in from the instep on up. We figgered they'd drawed out of the contest and that they was finding how it was one thing to ride around for sport and when a feller *jolly well* feels like it, and altogether another when that same riding turns out to be *work*.

On account of being delayed that morning, it put us late getting in with our second drive that afternoon, but being we had no nobility to keep track of, we made pretty good time. His Lordship and two men showed up on the cutting-grounds soon as we got there, and, mounted on the same horses they'd rode that morning, watched us cut out and brand. Once in a while one of 'em would try to turn back some critter that'd break out, but most always some cowboy would have to ride up and do that little thing for them. They was having a hard time sticking

As we rode I was hearing considerable fox-hunting and cross-country runs.

to their saddles as the cow-horse would try to outdodge some kinky critter, and they didn't dare let that horse do his work, from which we figgered that the polo game His Lordship described to us as being so strenuous must be kinda tame after all, compared with the side-winding of a cow-horse working on a herd.

A big red steer broke out once and right in the path of His Lordship. Being he was there, His Lordship tried to turn him, but Mr. Steer was on the warpath and wouldn't turn worth a nickel. The light that was in that critter's eyes hadn't been at all noticed by that person, but the good old cow-horse he was riding noticed it, and that's how come that when that pony dodged out of the way, His Lordship didn't dodge with him. Instead, he found hisself near straddling that red steer, as he headed for hard ground.

"Dag-gone queer," says one of the boys, who alongside of me was watching His Lordship shake the dust off hisself, "how a man that's had so much teaching in horsemanship, as they call it, can fall off a horse the way he's done, without that horse even bucking."

"Maybe it's them saddles," I says.

"That has a little to do with it, but he'd a-fell off one of our saddles just the same."

Two grinning riders closest to the bunch-quitting steer started out a-swinging their ropes, with intentions of turning that steer over a few times and to behaving, but Bearpaw, who'd been cutting out, came out of the herd about then and told 'em to put their ropes up and let the steer go.

The boys didn't know what to make of that till Bearpaw explained so everybody could hear.

"We don't want to forget," he says, "that we can't rope and throw a big steer off of them pancake saddles which His Lordship wants us to use, and being we might have to ride on them things later on, we

He found hisself near straddling that red steer as he headed for the hard ground.

better begin to realize it now, and gradual, so as the shock wont be so sudden."

So the steer was let go, and every other critter which couldn't be turned without the help of the convincing rope. Then that night, while every rider, His Lordship and all, was gathered around the fire, Bearpaw got up in the middle of the conversation and gave us boys another blow.

"I've cut out two cows and a steer," says that feller, "and they're in the main herd. The cows have their noses full of porcupine quills, and the steer has a horn growing in his eye. To-morrow, Bill," (pointing at me), "you can start out with 'em, take 'em to the home ranch, run 'em through the chute and squeezer, saw the bum horn off that steer and pull the quills out of them cows' noses. You ought to get over there and back in three days. Of course," he adds on, "we could stretch 'em out and do that little job right here, but we'd have to rope 'em, and that's plumb past the usefulness of a pancake saddle. We'd just as well start getting used to that now."

Things went on that way for a few days, and in all that time no hint was passed that the contest had come to an end. It was plain to see who all was the losers, but so far, there was no giving in from the nobility. If anything, His Lordship seemed harder-headed about it than ever, and even though the little flat saddles was getting abused something terrible, and stirrup-straps and cinch-straps kept a-breaking and being patched up with bailing-wire, there was no sign that they'd ever be set aside.

Then one day Bearpaw got peeved. The wagon had made camp close to a town which was on the skirts of the Y-Bench range, and Bearpaw had rode in and come out with a brand new saddle which he'd had made to order, before he ever dreamed that pancake saddles would ever come into his life.

Bearpaw rode into camp and straight on to where His Lordship was rubbing some greasy stuff over his burned face and cracked lip.

"See this new saddle?" he begins, and without waiting for an answer went on: "well, I aim to use it; if not on this range, it'll be on some other. I've given you the best of the deal and tried to show you how worthless your pancake saddles are out here, and you don't seem convinced. So, to-morrow, if you want to go on with the contest, you'll have to ride the average of the horses *we* do, not the gentlest, and I'll bet that before you get through you'll notice the difference between riding out here and riding out in the parks where you come from."

His Lordship listened to all Bearpaw had to say, but not a word came out of him as the cowboy rode away. We was a-wondering if by sun-up the next morning we wouldn't be all paid off and hitting for new ranges.

It was near dark, and some time after Bearpaw had left His Lordship, that we noticed him a-talking to his two men, and after a while seen 'em all going to where three horses was picketed. We noticed 'em saddle up and ride away, and at that we wondered some more.

We didn't see 'em come back that night, but we noticed the next morning that they'd got back all right, because in the dim light of daybreak we could make out the shape of their horses picketed in the same place as the night before.

Bearpaw was still het up on wanting to teach the nobility a thing or two and he drank his black coffee like he had a grudge against it, but not a word came out of him as he made biscuits and fried beef disappear, until Bramah, who was the last man up that morning, came close to the fire and started reaching for a cup and coffee.

"Did you fellers see what I just seen?" he asks as he filled his cup.

Receiving nothing but blank looks from all around, Bramah laid down his cup and says:

341

"Come on, waddies — I'll show you."

He took the lead, and we followed him to where His Lordship's three horses was picketed, and then a grin begin to spread on each face, even on Bearpaw's, for on each one of them horses was a honest-to-God stock saddle, and on His Lordship's horse we all recognized the old saddle Bearpaw had left at the saddle-shop in part payment for his new one.

"And look up there," says Bramah, pointing at His Lordship's tent.

We looked, and the grins spread, for floating in the morning breeze from top of each tent was a white flag.

So long — See you again.

We encourage you to patronize your local bookstore. Most stores will order any title that they do not stock. You may also order directly from Mountain Press using the order form provided below or by calling our toll-free number and using your MasterCard or VISA. We will gladly send you a complete catalog upon request.

Other fine Will James Titles:

_____ Cowboys North and South	14.00/paper	25.00/cloth
_____ The Drifting Cowboy	16.00/paper	
_____ Smoky, the Cowhorse	16.00/paper	36.00/cloth
_____ Cow Country	14.00/paper	
_____ Sand	16.00/paper	30.00/cloth
_____ Lone Cowboy	16.00/paper	30.00/cloth
_____ Sun Up	18.00/paper	
_____ Big-Eough	16.00/paper	
_____ Uncle Bill	14.00/paper	26.00/cloth
_____ All in the Day's Riding	16.00/paper	
_____ The Three Mustangeers	15.00/paper	30.00/cloth
_____ Home Ranch	16.00/paper	30.00/cloth
_____ Young Cowboy		15.00/cloth
_____ In the Saddle with Uncle Bill	14.00/paper	26.00/cloth
_____ Scorpion, A Good Bad Horse	15.00/paper	30.00/cloth
_____ Cowboy in the Making		15.00/cloth
_____ Flint Spears, Cowboy Rodeo Contestant	15.00/paper	30.00/cloth
_____ Look-See with Uncle Bill	14.00/paper	26.00/cloth
_____ The Will James Cowboy Book		18.00/cloth
_____ The Dark Horse	18.00/paper	35.00/cloth
_____ Horses I've Known	20.00/paper	
_____ My First Horse		16.00/cloth
_____ The American Cowboy	18.00/paper	
_____ Will James' Book of Cowboy Stories		30.00/cloth

Please include $3.00 per order to cover postage and handling.

Please send the books marked above. I have enclosed $ _____

Name_____

Address _____

City/State/Zip _____

☐ Payment enclosed (check or money order in U.S. funds)

Bill my: ☐ VISA ☐ MasterCard Expiration Date: _____

Card No _____

Signature_____

MOUNTAIN PRESS PUBLISHING COMPANY
P. O. Box 2399 • Missoula, Montana 59806
Order Toll-Free **1-800-234-5308** • _Have your MasterCard or VISA ready_
e-mail: info@mtnpress.com • website: www.mountain-press.com